is not about to land herself in prison.

In South Carolina, Tory Conway
is not about to commit fraud.

For both women, there's only one solution.

A marriage—
In name only.

Till Death Us Do Part
From Rebecca York's 43 Light Street

and

Unlawfully Wedded
From Kelsey Roberts's The Rose Tattoo

Rebecca York is the pseudonym of Ruth Glick and Eileen Buckholtz, who started Harlequin Intrigue's popular 43 Light Street series together. Recently, Ruth has been writing the series on her own as Rebecca York. Her book, *Shattered Vows,* was honored as Intrigue's 500th book. *Nowhere Man* was honored by *Romantic Times* as the Best Intrigue of 1998, and by *Affaire de Coeur* as Best Contemporary novel. Please watch for her next 43 Light Street release, *Never Too Late.* Eileen Buckholtz is a master computer scientist and Internet consultant. Taking a break from writing fiction, she fulfilled a lifelong dream to work on Capitol Hill, published a bestselling business e-book and developed several popular worldwide community service web sites.

Kelsey Roberts's first novel, *Legal Tender,* was published by Harlequin Intrigue in October 1993. Since then, she has published sixteen novels and garnered numerous award nominations for her talents in writing romantic suspense. Before turning to writing as a full-time career, Kelsey worked as a paralegal, a profession that has provided wonderful fodder as well as technical expertise for the type of stories she loves to write. Kelsey makes her home outside Annapolis, Maryland, with her college professor husband.

SECRET VOWS

REBECCA YORK

KELSEY ROBERTS

TORONTO • NEW YORK • LONDON
AMSTERDAM • PARIS • SYDNEY • HAMBURG
STOCKHOLM • ATHENS • TOKYO • MILAN • MADRID
PRAGUE • WARSAW • BUDAPEST • AUCKLAND

HARLEQUIN BOOKS

by Request—SECRET VOWS

ISBN 0-373-21702-1

This edition published by arrangement with Harlequin Books S.A.

Visit us at www.romance.net

Printed in U.S.A.

CONTENTS

Till Death Us Do Part

Rebecca York

Chapter One

It required effort to keep the smile on his face.

With his thoughts in sudden turmoil and his fingers tightening dangerously around a tumbler of planter's punch, Jed Prentiss stared across the crowded room at the woman with the upswept golden curls. Was that Marissa? Here to screw things up for him—*again.*

The minister of economic development asked him a question, and he replied automatically in Spanish. At the same time he shifted slightly to the right to catch another look at the blonde through the crowd.

She turned with a graceful motion to put a champagne flute down on a passing waiter's tray, and he got a glimpse of her face. He was right. It was Marissa Devereaux. He'd recognize that silky hair anywhere. It crowned a heart-shaped face with innocent-looking blue eyes, a petite nose and a mouth that could twist facts and half truths together so adroitly you didn't know you'd been had until the middle of the next week.

In fact, she was almost as good at undercover work as he was. Except that she took foolish chances. As if she had nothing to lose.

Damn! She was the last person he wanted to see. What the hell was she doing in San Marcos—much less at a party being held at Miguel Sanchez's town house? What possible reason would San Marcos's army commander in chief have for inviting her? Jed couldn't think of one.

After promising that he'd talk with the minister about mining loans later in the week, he excused himself and made his way across the room. The nearer he got to Marissa, the more burningly aware of her he became. He couldn't possibly be close enough to smell her perfume, yet he imagined the scent of gardenia drifting toward him. She was wearing a little black dress that she probably didn't think of as sexy. But it emphasized her narrow waist and sassy little hips. He hadn't seen the front, but he knew it would be clinging to her high, firm breasts.

He scowled. He'd better keep his mind on business.

He could see she was finishing a conversation with Thomas Leandro, the outspoken university professor who'd made his reputation with pie-in-the-sky blueprints for turning the Central American republic into a socialist paradise. The professor was on Jed's list, too. But he could wait.

When Leandro went off toward the buffet table, Jed stepped into Marissa's path. Her cheeks took on a hint of heightened color, and her blue eyes widened and darkened: but the momentary lapse was her only betrayal of surprise—or anything else.

No matter how many times they met, he was never prepared for her reaction to him. As if she were suppressing strong emotions she didn't want him to read—or couldn't acknowledge. Whenever he'd tried to find out what was going on below the surface of those beautiful blue eyes, they had iced over. The rebuffs had hurt his ego. He'd vowed never to let it happen again.

"Jed. How nice to see you. Are you here on behalf of the Global Bank?"

Smooth, he thought. As if they were nothing more than

friendly colleagues who traveled in the same business circles.

"Yes," he replied, matching her coolness.

They studied each other carefully.

What was she planning for the evening, he wondered. Did she already know he'd be prowling the same turf? Or was she as unpleasantly surprised as he had been? Only one of them was going to leave the capital city with the evidence he'd come to steal. He was going to make damn sure of that.

"You're a long way from Baltimore," he remarked.

She hesitated before replying. "Yes."

"So what brings you to San Marcos?"

"Oh, you know. My usual. I'm scouting out off-the-beaten-track vacation locations for Adventures in Travel."

"Latch onto anything exciting?"

"I should be able to set up a jungle trip to some partially excavated Mayan ruins. And there are excellent snorkeling and diving opportunities along the coral reef. I think I can guide visitors to a stingray feeding location."

"Sounds dangerous."

"Not when you know what you're doing."

"Be careful."

"Oh, I will."

"I didn't realize you knew Miguel Sanchez."

"I don't. Ted Bailey at the embassy was kind enough to get me on the guest list."

"Then you're on assignment for the State Department?"

"No."

It was a good bet she was lying. He knew she often mixed undercover work for Victor Kirkland at State with travel agency research. He was about to probe a little further when one of the uniformed staff approached them.

"Señorita Devereaux?"

"Sí."

"Teléfono para usted."

She gave Jed an apologetic look. "I'll see you later."

"Expecting an important call?"

For a split second she looked as if she weren't sure how to reply. Then she shrugged and followed the man who had delivered the message.

As Jed watched the servant lead her toward a back hall, he wondered if there was some way he could listen in on the phone conversation.

He'd memorized the floor plan of the house. There was another access to the hall, from a door off the enclosed patio.

As if he had nothing more important to do than get a breath of fresh air, he wandered casually toward the French doors.

When he stepped onto the stone terrace, the tropical night, rich with the scent of flowers, enveloped him. It took several moments for his eyes to adjust to the darkness. As they did, he went very still. Marissa had come out the side door he'd been heading for and was walking rapidly toward the far wing of the house where the office complex was located. The office complex that was strictly off-limits to everyone except Sanchez and his handpicked staff. Jed had heard stories of summary executions of suspected spies caught there.

Didn't Marissa know the risk she was taking? For that matter, didn't she know there was a guard? Jed's gaze probed the darkness.

There was *supposed* to be a guard. He didn't seem to be in sight. Had Marissa taken care of him? Jed cursed under his breath. This was just the kind of audacious maneuver she was so good at pulling off.

He was about to follow her; then, before he could, he saw a figure ooze out of the shadows like a night creature crawling out from under a rock. Without making a sound, the man padded after her.

The hair on the back of Jed's neck stood on end as if a cold breeze had blown across the patio. Marissa was in deep banana oil. Unless he could stop her before she reached the office wing.

ABOVE THE SOUND of the mariachi band playing at the party, Marissa thought she heard a voice nearby. Her whole body went rigid while she waited for a large hand to clamp down on her shoulder. When the blow didn't fall, she sprinted the rest of the way to the office wing. The heavy door was unlocked. That had been part of the deal. Jerking it open, she threw herself inside and stood with her shoulders pressed against the carved mahogany.

The door at her back gave her only a partial feeling of security. Now that she was here, she wished she'd come up with some other plan to get the information Victor wanted. Even for her, this was taking a hefty chance.

But it should work out all right.

She'd paid enough bribes to supplement the San Marcos military budget for six months.

Still, as she struggled to bring her breathing into normal range she peered down the hallway searching for signs of life. The place was as silent as a tomb. The only illumination came from a pair of ornate sconces that looked as if they held fifteen-watt bulbs. Since the electricity in San Marcos was likely to be off for half of any twenty-four-hour period, the low wattage made sense. Probably Sanchez was using his own generating plant and needed the bulk of his power supply tonight for the party.

Her high heels sounded like a flamenco dancer as she started down the polished tile passageway. Slipping off her pumps, she looked nervously over her shoulder, half expecting to see Jed Prentiss behind her striding down the hall to catch up. If anyone bollixed up things tonight, it would be him!

All she'd needed a half hour ago, as she was psyching herself for this raid, was to glance up and discover him stalking his way toward her like a jaguar about to pounce on a tethered goat.

Her hands clamped down so tightly on her evening bag that her fingernails dug into the expensive fabric. When she realized what she was doing, she loosened her grip. She'd come here to do a job. And she would finish it and reappear at the party before anyone noticed she was missing.

As she began to tiptoe down the hall again, shoes in hand, she cursed herself for not knowing more about Jed's recent activities. Then again, she hadn't had time to brush up on every agent who'd worked in Latin America before she'd come to San Marcos. She'd better stop obsessing about him before she made some kind of fatal mistake.

With a quick glance at her watch, she saw that three minutes had elapsed since she'd ducked out of the party. That left only a little more than fifteen to get in and out of here with the goods Victor was paying her to bring home.

At least Sanchez's office was on the ground floor, she thought as she turned the corner and started for the end of the hall. She felt less exposed as soon as she'd stepped into the anteroom and quietly shut the door behind her.

The room was spartan, with a secretary's desk, a few wooden chairs and some filing cabinets. Marissa gave them only a quick glance. The good stuff was in Sanchez's private office under lock and key.

Victor had briefed her on the likely places to look, so she went straight to his desk and knelt behind it. His most confidential files were in the two bottom drawers. Willing steadiness into her hands, she extracted a small case from her evening bag. What appeared to be a manicure set was really a set of lock-picking tools. A quick look through the contents of the first drawer told her that she'd struck out. And she only had ten minutes left.

Teeth clenched, she worked the other lock. Then she came across a stack of coded papers neatly filed in manila folders. She couldn't read the text. But this was what Victor had told her to look for.

Adrenaline pumped through her veins as she placed the first one in the center of the desk blotter and got out the small camera disguised as a lipstick. Methodically she began snapping pictures of the incriminating letters and other documents.

She was almost finished when a noise in the hall made the hair on her scalp bristle.

Someone was coming!

Sweeping the papers into the folder, she had them back in place and the drawer locked again in fifteen seconds.

Now all she had to do was get out of here. And quickly. A desperate glance at the barred window told her she wasn't going to escape in that direction. With camera and evening bag clutched in her hand, she bolted for the only other possibility—the general's private bathroom.

"*¿Eres tu?*"

Jed stopped dead on the path, just managing to avoid crashing into a young Hispanic woman who had stepped out of the darkness to block his progress.

"Let me by," he answered in Spanish, only half hearing her words as he tried to push past her to get to Marissa.

Her fingers clamped onto the sleeve of his dinner jacket. "Jed. It's really you. I thought at first I'd made you up."

She stopped abruptly, looking furtively from side to

side as if she were terrified of being overheard. The urgency of her touch arrested him, and he peered at her more closely. There was something familiar about her face. But on the darkened patio he couldn't place her.

"I must—"

"It's Clarita," she interrupted. "Don't you know me? I'm so glad you came back to see us."

The features resolved themselves into familiar lines. Clarita. Miguel Sanchez's daughter. She was more mature now. A girl on the verge of womanhood. She'd been eleven when Jed had been here six years ago helping the general train his troops. He'd recognized her as the neglected child of a rich man who had more important things to do than worry about his offspring's happiness. When he'd come home from the training camp with Miguel on the weekends, he'd tried to make a small difference in the little girl's life.

"I heard them talking about you, so I took a peek at the guest list for the party," she told him. "I knew you would be here. Like old times. When everything was simple." Her tone was high and wistful, as if she longed for the past.

"Clarita, I can't stay here and talk to you now."

She continued as if she hadn't heard. "It's all right. Do you remember how you taught my parrot to say 'no sweat'?" she asked eagerly. "He still remembers. Come see."

While she prattled on about the fun they'd had together, time was ticking by for Marissa. She had disappeared minutes ago—along with the man who was following her.

He forced a false heartiness into his response. "It's great to see you again, but I have important business to take care of. We'll talk later. Okay?" Gently but firmly he disengaged Clarita's fingers from his sleeve and started toward the offices at a rapid clip, praying he wasn't too late.

She stayed right behind him. "No!"

The strangled rasp was like fingernails scraping across a blackboard.

"I'll come right back, *niña,*" he promised, using the old endearment.

"I'm not a little girl anymore! And you must not go into the office wing. I know the rules. It's not allowed. They'll shoot you if they catch you."

"It's okay. The general knows," he lied. Anything to set her mind at ease.

"I don't think so." She looked almost frenzied as she reached to grab hold of him again. "Jed, I can't let you do it."

He peered into her eyes and knew instinctively that if he tried to wrench himself away she'd start to scream. Then every guard in the place would come charging onto the patio to find out what he was doing to her. And when Marissa came back out, they'd be here waiting for her.

He began talking in a low, soothing voice, telling Clarita it was all right. Telling her that nothing was going to happen to him. That he'd come back to her in a few minutes.

But all the time he was talking, he had the sick feeling that he was already too late.

MARISSA'S GAZE DARTED around the little room as she locked the door behind her.

There was a small window. But it was also barred.

Someone rattled the knob and began to pound on the door.

"Come out of there!" a voice commanded in Spanish.

"Just a minute," she answered in the same language, expecting a large fist to splinter the wood.

Sink. Toilet. Medicine cabinet. Tile floor.

Marissa looked down at the camera still clutched in her hand. If she didn't want to get caught with the incriminating evidence, she'd have to flush it down the toilet. If it would go down the toilet. Or maybe she could just flush the film.

"Come out or I'll shoot through the door," the angry voice demanded.

Desperate now, she thrust her hand into her purse to check for the empty film wrapper. Her fingers closed around the small zip-lock container in which she'd stowed the pills that were supposed to keep you from getting Montezuma's revenge.

It was big enough to hold the camera. Did she dare?

Ignoring the pounding on the door, she emptied the pills into the toilet bowl. Then she slipped her camera and film wrapper into the bag, squeezed out the air and sealed the strip across the top. Working as quietly as she could, she lifted the lid on the tank and thrust the plastic bag inside, hardly able to breathe as she watched it sink to the bottom.

The whole operation seemed to take hours. She knew only seconds had passed as she flushed the pills away and rustled her clothing as if she were putting herself back together after using the facilities.

"You have ten seconds, or I'll shoot."

"No. Please." Marissa didn't have to fake the panic rising in her voice as she tried to unlock the door. The mechanism stuck, and her fingers stung as she twisted the lever.

As soon as she'd snapped the lock open, the doorknob flew out of her hand. Wide-eyed, she backed away, staring at the man who stood with a gun trained on her chest. He wasn't wearing a uniform, but he had the look of a policeman.

"I said come out of there." With his free hand he

grabbed her wrist and yanked her roughly out of the bathroom. "What were you doing in El Jefe's office?" he snapped.

"What a question. You can see what I was doing. The ladies' room was occupied." Even as she did her best to look embarrassed, she was evaluating the odds of getting away from an armed man. Not good. "I had to find another quickly. It was an emergency."

"No one is allowed in this wing of the house."

"I'm truly sorry. I didn't know."

"How did you get in?"

She gestured vaguely. "I—I just walked through the door."

"It was locked!"

"No." She shook her head as if she were a bewildered tourist caught trying to snap a forbidden picture of the treasures in the cathedral. But her heart was pounding so hard that she could hardly catch her breath.

He kept the gun pointed at her while he picked up the phone, dialed a number and spoke into the receiver.

His voice was low, his Spanish rapid. But she caught enough to know that her goose was cooked. He was calling for reinforcements.

When he returned his full attention to her, his eyes were hard.

Marissa tried to swallow, but her mouth was too dry.

Pointedly he looked down at her stocking feet and then at the shoes she'd set down on the desk. "You're going to give me some straight answers, *señorita,* or you *are* going to be truly sorry."

Chapter Two

Jed heard several pairs of feet hammer against the paving stones. He whirled and cursed as four khaki-clad soldiers moving in tight formation came dashing along the path from the direction of the guard station. They all carried machine guns, and they looked as if they were on their way to the offices to foil an assassination attempt.

"Holy mother!" Clarita whispered a more ladylike version of Jed's muttered exclamation. Her eyes grew large, and the blood drained from her face. "I told you," she whispered. "It's dangerous to go there."

"They're not after you." Jed reached out to put a reassuring hand on her shoulder. She ducked away from his grasp and ran toward the bedroom wing of the house.

She had the right idea, Jed thought as he watched her disappear into the safety of the interior. He should probably blast out of here, too, while the blasting was good. He knew how Miguel Sanchez treated spies and how his twisted logic could quickly turn a friend into an enemy.

He glanced toward the lighted windows of the reception hall, wondering if anyone else had heard the guards. The guests were all drinking and eating and talking as before. Apparently the mariachi music had drowned out the sounds from the patio. Or perhaps no one chose to acknowledge the disturbance.

He was on his own. And so was Marissa.

His chest tightened as he strode rapidly after the soldiers.

One of them was standing at attention in front of the door of the office wing. Too bad it wasn't a man he'd helped train.

"*¿Qué pasa?*" he asked.

"This area is off-limits, *señor.*"

"I'm Jed Prentiss, a good friend of General Sanchez."

The guard shifted the machine gun in his grasp, as if he were unsure about aiming the gun at a good friend of *El Jefe.* Yet he obviously had his orders. "You'd better go back to the party."

Jed stood his ground.

The sentry, who'd probably never had his authority questioned before, looked uncomfortable.

The stalemate lasted less than a minute—until the rest of the armed contingent returned. The soldiers were escorting a man in civilian clothes who had a firm hold on a woman's arm.

It was Marissa.

Until Jed actually saw her being frog-marched down the hall, he realized he'd been hoping against hope that some other crisis had prompted the summoning of the guards.

Her face was paper white. It went a shade paler when she spotted him with the sentry, and he knew in that instant that she was thinking he was the one who'd turned her in.

"What's he doing here?" the civilian snapped.

"He says he's a good friend of *El Jefe,* sir."

"Go back where you belong," the man in charge said in clipped tones.

All at once the perfumed air of the tropical night was suffocating. This wasn't the good old U.S. of A. where you were presumed innocent until proven guilty. This was the sovereign republic of San Marcos where a two-bit official could slap you in jail and throw away the key on the word of an underworld informant.

Hands resting easily at his sides, Jed summoned up his most guiltless look. "My name's Jed Prentiss. I helped the general set up his training program at *Conquista Fuerte.*"

"So you say."

"You can check it out easily enough." Jed risked shifting his gaze from the man to Marissa. Her body was rigid, her breath shallow. He suspected that if she unstiffened her knees, she'd topple to the ground. His green eyes locked with her blue ones, and he saw how hard she was struggling not to fall apart. He could feel her terror. It cut through his vital organs like a machete blade. And he knew that until a few moments ago she hadn't dreamed how much trouble she could get into in the nominally democratic republic of San Marcos.

He wanted to tell her she'd been a damn fool to raid the office of a general who wielded power with the zeal of a medieval king. At the same time he wanted to wrest her from her captor, fold her into his arms and spirit her out of danger like the hero of an action-adventure film. It was an exceedingly fleeting fantasy. Even with the element of surprise, all he'd get for the grand gesture was a bullet in the back.

"If she's a spy, I'm a Saudi Arabian sheikh," he said. "I was talking to her a few minutes ago at the party. She's a scared-stiff travel agent who wandered into the wrong part of the house."

"Perhaps." The undercover man didn't sound as if he gave the explanation much credence.

"Please. I didn't do anything. Please let me go," Marissa implored.

Jed's mind scrambled for any sort of leverage he could use. If he claimed Marissa was a friend of his, he'd probably get himself detained for questioning. But maybe he still had enough influence with Sanchez to save her. "Let me speak to the general."

"He's in a meeting."

"I'll wait."

"No. You will stop poking your nose in where it doesn't belong."

"The general will want—"

"*I* will arrest you along with this female spy if you're not out of here in five seconds."

Marissa's eyes were bleak. "You'd better leave," she murmured to Jed.

"*¡Silencio!* You will not speak to each other."

Jed hated to abandon her like this. But he'd run out of options. The only thing he could do was offer her a word of comfort. "Everything will be all right. I'll tell the American embassy what's happened."

She acknowledged the help with the barest of nods, but her expression was starting to glaze over.

The man holding her arm jerked her sharply. She winced as he led her toward a door on the far side of the patio. The last view of her he had was of her rigid back and the blond curls he'd first spotted across the crowded reception.

AS THE GUARDS TROTTED Marissa away, one of the guests from the party pressed back into the foliage of the bird of paradise tree where he was standing. Eyes narrowed, he'd been watching the scene on the patio with acute interest.

He'd seen Prentiss slip out of the reception room minutes after Devereaux had also disappeared. And he'd made a silent bet with himself that the two events were no coincidence. It was gratifying to confirm that he was right. Also a bit unsettling.

Devereaux had told everybody who would listen that she was a travel agent. Prentiss was supposed to be on a fact-finding mission for the Global Bank. But it appeared the two of them had more compelling reasons to be in San Marcos. Also, it seemed they knew each other, although neither one had admitted as much. Probably they were working together. And it looked as if Devereaux had gotten caught with her hand in the cookie jar, so to speak.

His lips thinned. Had she discovered anything incriminating before they'd bagged her? He'd have to find out quickly. And make sure she didn't get a chance to talk.

For several seconds he enjoyed watching Prentiss stand with his hands clenched at his sides. At least he had the satisfaction of knowing the bastard was sweating. But the man in the bushes didn't let the pleasure show on his face.

Deep in thought, he left his hiding place and strode toward the mansion. He'd never met Prentiss, although he'd heard of him. He was a once-top agent who was now washed up in the intelligence business. The rumor was he'd lost his nerve. But he'd toughed it out just fine with Sanchez's man.

Too bad. Prentiss and Devereaux were another problem he'd have to solve before he made any final decisions about Sanchez. But right now he'd better get in touch with his man in Junipero Province to make sure nothing out of the ordinary was happening out there.

JED STUDIED CASSANDRA Devereaux, noting the strain etched into her profile. She looked so much like Marissa—so much that it was painful.

"Would you tell the others what you told me?" she asked in a strangled voice.

It had been three days since Marissa was taken away

by Sanchez's guards. Jed had arrived at Cassie's renovated East Baltimore row house at five in the afternoon, given her a summary of her sister's predicament and collapsed into bed for a few hours of badly needed sleep. While he'd been conked out, she'd made half a dozen phone calls, and he was damn impressed with the group of people she'd so quickly assembled.

He looked around the living room at the circle of faces.

He knew Jason Zacharias, of course. They'd worked together on a number of undercover assignments, including the time he'd come to rescue Jason and his wife Noel from a Scottish megalomaniac—and Jason had ended up saving him. The other women of 43 Light Street and their husbands were strangers. But he knew they were Marissa's friends. He'd always thought of her as so cold. But he could see from the faces around him that they were all deeply concerned about the turn of events in San Marcos. And they'd do anything they could to get her out of this mess.

He was especially struck by the couple sitting close together on the couch. She was Jo O'Malley, who'd been introduced as a private detective. He was Cameron Randolph, an electronics genius. Jo was expecting their first child, and it was obvious how happy they were about the pregnancy. Still, Jo had cancelled a prenatal appointment to attend this meeting.

"Start at the party," Cassie requested.

Jed did, skipping over his personal reactions to Marissa and sticking with the facts, "I went straight from Sanchez's to the American embassy, but they couldn't do anything until nine the next morning. By then it was already too late to complain that an American citizen named Marissa Devereaux was being held incommunicado by General Miguel Sanchez." He shifted in his chair.

"Too bad the embassy didn't get right on it. I checked

with the San Marcos Department of Immigration the next day and found out that no one named Marissa Devereaux had entered the country in the past three weeks—the legal limit for a renewable tourist visa."

Jo's eyes narrowed. "Somebody must have been working overtime searching for her entry visa. But it paid off. If she's not legally in the country, there's no way to lodge any kind of official complaint."

"You've got it," Jed agreed.

"I've been burning up the phone lines to the State Department," Cassie added. "Marci was on an undercover assignment for our old boss—Victor Kirkland. He was willing to speak off the record because I've still got my security clearance. He says he's sorry, but he can't do anything to help her because State can't acknowledge her mission.

"Can the U.S. State Department really operate that way?" The question came from a woman sitting in the corner. Small and delicate, she had curly brown hair and big brown eyes that seemed to stare right through Cassie. Her name was Jenny Larkin, and she was blind. Jed had wondered at first what she was doing at the meeting, since it was obvious that she had less experience than the others with the unofficial workings of government—or with detective work. But he'd quickly discovered that her analytic mind and phenomenal memory were an asset to the group.

"I'm afaid they can do whatever they want to, as long as they don't get caught," Cassie explained. "But I'm not going to let Victor get away with stonewalling me."

Jed admired her defiant posture, but he didn't hold out much hope from that quarter. He knew the rules. And so did Marissa. She'd taken a job where it was understood she was on her own if there was trouble.

Until now, Abby Franklin had been silent. "What else have you got for us?" she asked him.

"After the scam at Immigration, I didn't expect to find a record of a Marissa Devereaux checking in to a hotel. But I put it around that I'd be at the Café Primo and that I was willing to pay for information about a blond *gringa* travel agent who might have been in Santa Isabella within the past few days.

"I got lucky with a *portero* from El Grande who remembered commenting on Marissa's snorkeling equipment. He took her to room 345."

"So you let yourself in and had a look around the premises," Jo guessed. Jed was pretty sure she'd have done exactly the same thing. Before her pregnancy, anyway.

"Right. The room had been ragged out. But the maid had forgotten to replace the notepad by the phone. The top sheet looked clean. But I could make out the impression of the previous message, which was the name of a taxi company and Miguel Sanchez's address."

"I couldn't go into court with that," Dan Cassidy muttered. As an assistant state's attorney, he knew the rules of evidence.

Cassie slammed her fist against the arm of her chair. "I've been begging Marci for years not to keep taking these assignments. I told her this one was too dangerous. Damn her. What's wrong with her? Does she *want* to get herself killed?" She shot Abby a pleading look.

The woman shifted uncomfortably in her chair. "There are reasons why she takes risks other people would consider unacceptable."

Startled, Jed stared at the attractive brunette. She'd been introduced as a psychologist. And, like most headshrinkers, she'd shut up and let everyone else do the talking. It sounded as if she'd been seeing Marissa professionally. Remembering the way Marissa had always struggled to hide her emotions from him, he was seized with sudden regret that he'd never tried to understand her; he'd only reacted to what he perceived as her cold arrogance.

"Is that all you're going to say?" Cassie persisted, her voice fierce. "Won't anybody stick their neck out for Marci?"

"It's not a matter of sticking my neck out," Abby said gently. "You know it would be a breach of professional ethics to talk about the things Marissa and I have discussed at her therapy sessions."

Cassie looked down at her hands.

"You think someone betrayed Marissa?" Jenny asked Jed.

"I know she wouldn't have crossed the patio unless she'd been assured it would be empty. There could have been a backup security system only Sanchez knows about. Even a silent alarm," Jed observed. "Or someone at the party could have spotted her heading for forbidden territory and alerted security."

"Who?" Cassie snapped.

"Any of over a hundred guests. She was talking to Thomas Leandro just before she left. But there were a lot of other people there. One of them might have jumped at the chance to do the general a favor. Or it could be someone with his own ax to grind. Pedro Harara, the president of the Banco Nacional, doesn't much like American women."

"Why not?" Cassie asked.

"He married one who caught him in bed with his secretary and took him for several million dollars when she moved back North again."

The laughter around the room cut some of the tension.

Jed answered more questions, gave more opinions and assessments, all the while trying to keep certain pictures out of his mind—pictures of what could be happening to Marissa. He couldn't allow emotion to cloud his judgment. And he dared not let his private fears show on his face because that might panic the group.

Jason had been silent through most of the discussions, letting the others ask questions. Then he began to formulate a plan.

"Too harebrained," Jed snapped when the security expert had finished.

"Do you have a better idea?"

"Give me a little time to think."

MARISSA SHIFTED uncomfortably on the narrow bunk. It was made of wooden planks and topped with a straw tick that prickled where it touched her skin. Not very comfortable, but at least the mattress wasn't resting directly on the unwashed stone floor.

She shuddered. She'd been in this tiny cell for three days, and she knew she was in danger of coming unglued. After the scene on the patio, two women had strip-searched her before she'd been locked up.

It had been humiliating, but thank God they hadn't found anything incriminating. Now she was praying that her hasty addition to Sanchez's toilet tank didn't gum up the works.

At first she'd huddled on the bunk, expecting the general to interrogate her as soon as possible. But minutes of waiting had turned into hours. Was he researching her background before he called her upstairs—to give himself an advantage?

That theory had gone out the window as hours dragged into days. She still hadn't seen the general. Or anyone else, since the guards were shoving her meager meals of rice and beans through a slot in the door.

Some of her clothes and her bag of toiletries preceded the food on her second afternoon. Wondering if anyone was watching on a hidden camera, she changed out of her rumpled black dress into cotton slacks and a T-shirt. The knowledge that someone had been in her hotel room wasn't comforting. Nor was the lack of response to any of the pleas and questions she'd shouted through the door.

What kind of mind game was Sanchez playing, anyway?

It was hard not to feel completely abandoned, but she didn't allow herself to lose hope. Still aware that someone might be spying on her, she furtively took some of the items from her cosmetic kit and slipped them into her pocket. If she was very lucky, she'd get a chance to use them.

Then, for as long as she could keep moving, she did what exercises she could manage without getting down on the squalid floor in her tiny cell. After fatigue claimed her, there was nothing to do but lie on the bunk and think.

First she tried to figure out how she'd gotten caught. Most likely the dirty rat who'd taken her money to unlock the door to the office complex and disappear for twenty minutes had turned her in. Or he could have gotten nailed himself. Or someone else at the party besides Jed might have figured out what she was doing.

Thomas Leandro? The balding professor who spouted Marxist doctrine and combed what hair he had in a swirl around his glossy dome. In a strong wind, he looked like a bird's nest that had blown out of a tree.

Pedro Harara? The five-foot-three banker who dressed like a character in a thirties gangster movie and wore a girdle to hide his paunch. He'd almost put her to sleep standing up with his scintillating discussion of international fund transfers.

Louis Rinaldo? The tough-looking minister of development who'd worked his way up from street gang member to cabinet officer. He wore three gold rings on his fingers to prove he'd made it.

Or what about the man who called himself William Johnson, the one with the horse face and the drawl that stretched all the way to Texas? She had no idea who he was or what he was doing at the party, but she'd had him on her list to check out. Too bad she'd never gotten a chance.

The only guest she was sure hadn't given her up to *El Jefe* was President Juan Palmeriz. San Marcos's elected leader hated Sanchez and was praying for an excuse to get him out of power. But his fear of a coup was so great that he didn't go to sleep at night without first looking under the bed.

After hours of fruitless speculation, Marissa felt as if she'd go insane if she didn't have someone to talk to. Maybe that was what Sanchez wanted. And she wasn't going to give him the satisfaction of breaking her. So she began to make up long silent conversations with various friends and enemies.

She mentally discussed with Abby the character defects that had gotten her into this mess. Abby kept saying it wasn't her fault; she wished she could be as sure.

She railed at Victor Kirkland for sending her on a mission that, in retrospect, had been foolhardy.

She tried to rehearse plausible answers to the questions Sanchez was eventually going to ask her. If he wasn't simply planning to let her rot here.

But when she felt most alone and terrified, she talked to Jed Prentiss. Particularly at night when it was dark and he couldn't see her face.

She knew that was a silly contrivance. He wasn't even in the cell with her. She wasn't sure she could trust him. She didn't even know whether he was still in San Marcos. Yet it was somehow very comforting to lie in bed and mentally whisper to him in the dark, as if they were lovers instead of uneasy rivals.

Somebody turned me in. Was it you? She posed the question to him in her mind for the dozenth time, holding her breath as if she really were waiting for his answer.

I wouldn't do that, honey bee.

She wanted to believe him with all her heart. For the time being, she gave him the benefit of the doubt.

You're the only one who knows what's happened to me.

Yeah.

Are you doing anything to get me out of here?

She waited in the blackness, her mind forming the answer she wanted to hear: he was moving heaven and earth to spring her from this cell. But it was hard to have much faith in wishful thinking. Or anything else.

She closed her eyes and allowed herself to imagine that he had shifted to his side, that he had put his muscular arms around her so that they lay on the bunk spoon fashion. She sighed and scooted a little closer, almost swearing she could smell the spicy after-shave he wore, feel the hard wall of his chest against the back of her head. She pictured his broad shoulders and the sun-streaked hair that always made him look as if he'd climbed out of a lifeguard's chair. It was so good to delegate some of the fear and uncertainty to him. To let him give her his protection.

She longed to ask more of him. Gently she touched her finger to her lips, stroking back and forth with a featherlight touch, imagining what it might be like to kiss him. A little shiver went through her. She'd wanted to taste his mouth. A couple of years ago she'd finally admitted that to herself. Almost every time they met, she looked at his lips. But there was no such thing as sharing a chaste kiss with a man like Jed. He would want more.

Vivid images invaded her mind, and she could feel her body trembling. In the darkness she struggled for control—for the calm center of her soul where she was in charge of her life. It took longer than usual. Her emotions were in too much turmoil, her nerves too raw. But finally her will prevailed the way it always did.

Years ago she'd figured out what was necessary for her survival. Like the way she'd acted to keep Jed at arm's length. She knew he'd been puzzled at first. The perplexity had changed to a mixture of anger and hurt. That had made her ache inside. She'd wanted so badly to erase the wounded look from his eyes.

But he frightened her too much. He was too male. Too assertive. Too much a creature of the tough, aggressive habits he'd developed during long years as an undercover agent.

He was too dangerous for her. The wrong kind of man entirely. If she was going to dare a relationship with anyone, it should be with a mild, unthreatening guy who wouldn't make demands. Who'd let her set the pace. Yet fate kept throwing her into Jed's path in various Latin American countries where they were both doing undercover work. And every time they met, she felt like a moth being drawn to a flame.

But it was different now. Here, in this cell, where she was so defenseless and alone, she was too weak to give up the small amount of comfort she gained by pretending he was lying in back of her, his body shielding hers, ready to overpower the guards when they finally opened the door. With a soft sigh she closed her eyes and hugged her arms around her shoulders.

JED LEANED BACK in the comfortable wing chair in Abby Franklin's office at 43 Light Street. The setting was tastefully soothing, and he tried to fit in by crossing his legs easily at the ankles and sipping at the mug of coffee she'd offered him. Probably he wasn't fooling Dr. Franklin. This crack-of-dawn meeting was his last stop in Baltimore before he decided whether or not to risk his life on a mission that had about a fifty-percent chance of succeeding.

"I appreciate your getting together with me so early," he said, setting down the mug.

"*I* appreciate your volunteering to get Marissa out of San Marcos."

"I'm not exactly working for free."

Abby ignored the clarification. "Now that we know for sure that the State Department won't do a damn thing, you may be her only chance."

"You might have to come up with another alternative. I haven't decided whether I'm going to take the job."

"Jason thinks you're the one who can do it."

He ignored the vote of confidence and sprang a question on her. "Is Marissa just a danger to herself? Or to others, as well?"

"She's not a danger to herself," Abby retorted.

"You told Cassandra her sister takes crazy chances."

"That's a loose interpretation of what I said."

"You have to tell me what's going on in Marissa's head before I make a commitment."

Abby looked regretful. "Jed, she trusts me not to talk about our sessions. I can't betray her confidences to you."

"Not even to save her life?"

Abby paused before replying. "Let me put it this way. If you go back to San Marcos knowing certain things about her that she hasn't chosen to reveal to you, she'll sense it—and react negatively. And she'll never trust either one of us again."

"Let *me* put it *this* way," he countered. "Your group of conspirators has hatched a very flaky plan. And when I get to San Marcos, I'm not going to be able to clue in Marissa. She'll have to take my opening moves on blind faith. Then the two of us are going to have to pull off a performance worthy of the stars in a Gilbert and Sullivan operetta. Is she up to that? Or will she get both of us killed?''

Abby knit her fingers together in her lap. ''Jed, I can't tell you very much. But perhaps you've sensed that she has strong feelings for you.''

''Yeah. She hates me.''

''Hardly.''

''Then what?''

''You have to work that out for yourself.''

''I may not get the chance. From the way she looked at me when the guards took her into custody, I'd be willing to bet she thinks I'm the one who turned her in to Sanchez.''

''You're describing a situation in which she was under a great deal of stress. She's had some time to think things through.'' Abby leaned forward. ''Jed, some very rough things have happened to Marci in her life. Things she hasn't even been able to discuss with her sister. She's done what she had to do to survive, and she's come a long way. I've thought for several months that you might be able to help her.''

''She's discussed *me* with *you?* What the hell did she say?''

''I'm sorry. I shouldn't have let that slip out.'' Abby flushed. ''I'm not going to answer any more questions about my patient. What else did you come here to talk about?''

Jed shifted in his chair, looking from the tasteful prints on the wall to his hands and then toward the window. Everywhere but at Abby's face. He could get up and leave on cue. Or he could make a grab for the brass ring. ''You're too perceptive.''

''That's what they pay me for. But this session is free of charge.''

He forced a laugh. It sounded strained and nervous.

"You mentioned that everything that's said here is strictly confidential."

"Yes."

"So if I wanted to discuss something about myself and I wanted to keep it quiet, it wouldn't go any further."

"That's right."

He almost cut and ran. Then he figured he didn't have anything to lose. If he didn't want to, he never had to see Abby Franklin again. "There's a reason why I might be putting Marissa in danger by taking this assignment. I mean, something in *my* background that might make me a risky choice."

When Abby's expression remained neutral, he continued. "Did Marissa tell you I used to be hooked up with a supersecret spy organization?"

"Yes. She didn't tell me the name," she added.

"She probably doesn't know I was asked to resign." He heard his voice turn gritty as he struggled to keep his face from betraying the depths of his humiliation.

"That was rough on you," Abby murmured.

"Yeah," he whispered.

"So did you really come here to tell me you're no good at your job?"

"I am good at it!"

"But you're the wrong man for the rescue mission?" Abby persisted.

"Maybe."

"I'm willing to give you my professional judgment."

"I found out seven years ago."

"Found out what?"

He clenched his hands on the arms of the chair so he wouldn't bolt from the room. With his emotions under equally rigid restraint, he told Abby Franklin the secret that had been eating him alive.

ROUGH HANDS shook Marissa awake, and she couldn't hold back a startled scream.

"Let's go," a gruff voice ordered in Spanish.

"Wh—what's going on?" she answered in the same language.

"*El Jefe* has sent for you."

Marissa's heart began to pound. With no warning, she was going to be interrogated by the man whose office she'd been caught burglarizing. Had he found the camera in the toilet tank? Was that why he was finally sending for her? She ran a nervous hand through her hair. "Would you let me have a minute alone?"

He shrugged and stepped outside the door, giving her some privacy.

Quickly she used the toilet in the corner of the cell and washed her hands and face, wondering how unkempt she looked after three days in a cell. She expected to be escorted upstairs to the general's office, and braced herself accordingly. Her eyes widened as she was led outside to a gray Chevy van parked by the delivery entrance. Two guards hustled her inside. Yanking her foot to the right, they cuffed her ankle to a ring that had been welded to the floor. Hardly standard equipment from Chevrolet.

"You said *El Jefe*—"

"*¡Silencio!*"

She pressed her lips together as the man slid onto the bench seat beside her. He kept a machine gun cocked under his arm. His companion climbed into the driver's seat and started the engine. After ten minutes it was clear they were heading out of the city. Going west, according to a road sign.

Marissa knew that Sanchez had a *finca* in Colorado Province. Calling it a farm was an understatement, since it occupied more than twenty thousand acres. Despite the heat and humidity, she shivered. In the capital *El Jefe* was a powerful man but not entirely above the law. At his outlying estate he was the lord of the manor. He could do anything with her that he wanted, and no one would ever dig up the facts.

A cold sweat broke out on her skin. Involuntarily, her foot jerked against the cuff.

"Sit still," the man with the gun muttered.

She went rigid.

The scenery changed from overcrowded urban to jungle in almost the blink of an eye. However, she knew from her extensive research on Sanchez and the local area that the two-lane road they took was one of the best paved in San Marcos, undoubtedly for the general's benefit. Marissa had come this way a few days ago on the trip she'd told Jed about—to visit some newly discovered Mayan ruins being excavated by a team from the University of New Mexico.

What would Jed do if he were in a spot like this, she wondered. Somehow, on all the dangerous missions she'd undertaken for the State Department, she'd never pictured herself getting captured. Shot, maybe; put out of her misery with one clean bullet. But not abducted. She shuddered, admitting for the first time that she should have known better.

Every ten or fifteen miles the jungle gave way to a village of thatch-roofed, bamboo huts strung out along the road. More than once a stray cow or goat wandered onto the pavement, and the driver honked furiously. Each time Marissa tensed as she entertained the guilty hope that the speeding van might collide with one of the animals. If the vehicle was forced to stop, she might have a chance to escape.

There were no such fortunate incidents with the livestock. But Marissa's lucky break came about a mile and a half past one of the villages when the van blew a tire.

Cursing, the driver had to wrestle the vehicle to the far right side of the blacktop, since there was no real shoulder. When he opened the back door, he discovered there was no jack. He cursed again.

The two men—who turned out to be named Jose and Jorge—argued in rapid Spanish, each accusing the other of being responsible for getting them into this fix. Jorge, the one who'd sat with her in the back seat, lost the shouting match and ended up trotting back to the village. Jose climbed out and ambled into the shade of a kapok tree. Nearby several goats grazed.

It was only about eight in the morning, but the temperature in the disabled van was already rising to steambath proportions.

"You're not going to leave me in here, are you?" Marissa called through the open window.

"He's got the key." Jose pointed in the direction of his retreating companion before pulling his cap over his face and settling down for a nap.

Thank God they'd been too confident to search her, Marissa thought as she slipped her hand into her pocket and extracted one of the items she'd hidden—her spare manicure set. And thank God she knew a lot about the terrain, both from several previous jungle expeditions and extensive reading.

Working quietly and stealthily, she began to probe at the lock on the cuff that secured her ankle to the floor of the van. Every so often she glanced up at Jose. He looked as if he were asleep.

Her hands were shaking so badly that it took several tries to open the lock. Finally it yielded.

Her breath slowed as she looked through the window of the van. Was this whole thing a setup? An excuse to shoot the prisoner attempting to escape?

She didn't know. But she'd made her decision. Considering what could be waiting for her at Sanchez's estate, she had to try to get away while the getting was good.

After one last furtive glance at the guard, she ducked low and slipped out the open door.

The moment her feet hit the pavement she was crouching and running toward the safety of the trees.

Chapter Three

Marissa muffled her sob of relief as she reached the concealing foliage on the other side of the road. Quickly she slipped farther into the shadows.

She'd gotten free. But that was only the first step. Not a living soul in this part of San Marcos was going to risk Sanchez's wrath by helping her. Her only hope was to reach the American archaeologists at the Mayan ruins, explain what had happened and hope they had the resources to get her out of the country.

That meant she'd have to get far enough away from the van to risk crossing the road, then head north. Going back seemed like a bad idea, since she might run into Jorge. So she continued toward Sanchez's estate and tried to stay more or less parallel to the blacktop.

However, she soon found it was impossible to travel in a straight line without a machete to slash her way through the dense foliage. In addition, she had to move carefully, since she was trying hard not to leave a trail the guards could follow.

The jungle was alive with other dangers, too. The archaeologists had told her about killing a coral snake near the ruins. Since there was no antidote for their venom, a bite meant death within minutes. All she could do was break a dead branch from a small tree to use as a defensive weapon.

Her clothing was soaked with perspiration, but she kept moving at a steady pace, detouring around tarantula holes and the huge hills of the leaf-cutter ants, who could make mincemeat of human flesh as easily as they denuded trees.

When she judged she was half a mile from the van, she sprinted across the road. Then she headed north, using the position of the sun as a guide. Every time she heard a noise in the underbrush, she expected Jorge or Jose to lunge from behind a palm tree. But so far so good.

Marissa pushed herself as hard as she could through the bugs and heat and plants that seemed to grab at her clothing as if they had an agreement with the soldiers to slow her progress. Eventually she had to stop and rest. Wishing that she had a hat and some insect repellent, she reached out a hand to steady herself against a slender tree trunk.

It was an unfortunate move. The bark was covered with thorns. She yelped in pain, and high above her in the trees a colony of howler monkeys reacted. Mortally offended by what they considered the invasion of their territory, they began to protest loudly. She might as well have been standing next to an air raid siren.

She started off again at the fastest pace she could manage. But she was a whole lot less optimistic than she'd been a few minutes ago. She'd been counting on her pursuers not knowing where to look for her. The monkeys had given them a road map.

JED TRIED TO RELAX in the airline seat. At least he was flying to San Marcos first class this time, so there was enough room to stretch his legs.

Of course, there would be plenty of space to stretch out if he and Marissa came home in wooden boxes.

He grimaced. Abby Franklin could pay the funeral expenses, since she'd listened to his story and then made him believe he'd be okay if he took certain precautions. He'd left her office feeling better about himself than he had in years. After a little reflection, he realized how good she was at her job. What she'd really done was the equivalent of patching up a combat soldier and sending him back into battle. But he'd understood her motives. She was convinced that he was the only person with the right set of qualifications to extract Marissa from Sanchez's clutches.

The flight attendant came by and asked him if he wanted a drink. He ordered a bourbon and water. Maybe the liquor would help him sleep—like the rest of the passengers on the red-eye flight to Santa Isabella. Most of them looked as if they were going to San Marcos to visit relatives or relax in an unspoiled tropical paradise. *He* was flying into one of the trickiest assignments of his undercover career.

And he might have to change the rules as he went along if things didn't work out the way Marci's friends thought they would.

Marci. Ever since he'd heard her sister use the nickname, he'd started to think of her like that. It was part of his changing image of her, as if he were dealing with two different women. Marissa was cold and aloof, tough and sophisticated. She'd taken plenty of undercover jobs, and she knew the risks.

Marci was another matter entirely. His face softened as he considered her. She was fragile and vulnerable, shy and a bit naive. She pretended she knew all the rules. In fact, she'd conned *him* pretty well over the past few years, and he was a damn good judge of people. But all along she'd been hiding behind Marissa's tough exterior, hoping no one would notice her.

He pressed his knuckles against his teeth. Now that

Abby and Cassie had given him the right clues, he couldn't understand why he hadn't recognized the symptoms. She was like him, hiding some shameful secret she didn't want anyone to know. Something so bad that it made her reckless—even a little foolhardy—*as if she didn't believe her life was worth much.*

Too bad for her Abby had slipped and revealed more than she should. Or had she? His eyes narrowed as he went back over the scene in the psychologist's office, examining the nuances. Abby had told him she thought he'd be good for Marci. Had that been a calculated maneuver? Part of her plan to get him on her side?

He sighed. Whatever it was, it had worked. It had even starting him wondering if he and Marci could help each other, since neither of them felt there was much to lose.

Of course, Marci was one thing. Marissa was quite another. Getting close to *her* could be a disaster. He'd always known that Marissa Devereaux and Jed Prentiss would be an explosive combination. Either it would be damn good or they'd end up tearing each other apart.

Still, he felt a sense of tingling anticipation that made it difficult to sit still in the airplane seat. One of the reasons he was going back to San Marcos was to find out once and for all what would happen if he let her know he was attracted to her. This time Marissa wasn't going to be able to duck away from him or give him that cold look he now realized was a protective mechanism. Not if she was going to follow the script that the Light Street group had written for her. No, if she wanted to save her hide she was going to have to work with him—up close and very personal.

MARISSA KEPT PUTTING one foot in front of the other even though she'd long since reached the point of exhaustion. Yet she knew she had to put as much distance as she could between herself and the spot where she'd stirred up the howler monkeys.

So far Sanchez's goons hadn't shown. But she wasn't going to breathe easy until she reached the relative safety of the archaeological dig.

She hoped she could get there before nightfall. The jungle during the day was dangerous enough. When the sun went down, it would be pitch-dark and twice as perilous. She'd have to find a tree she could climb and wait for morning before she could risk moving around again. And that wouldn't save her from poisonous tree frogs or snakes. Or the predators that would smell her fear or hear her shivering. Aside from the dangers, when the temperature dropped, her perspiration-soaked clothing was going to feel like a cold compress.

But that was hours away. Her immediate problems were heat and thirst. She'd had nothing to drink but a few gulps of water in her cell that morning. And even with the high humidity, she was getting dehydrated from the jungle heat.

She hadn't crossed any streams, and she knew they would be a risky proposition out here, where she could pick up some nasty parasite while slaking her thirst. But there were hollow vines that were full of water. When she found one, she slashed it off with her penknife and gratefully tipped the cup end to her lips.

She'd taken several swallows when the sound of a branch snapping behind her made her whole body go rigid. Dropping the vine, she made a dash for a nearby thicket. But she didn't get more than a few feet before a muscular arm hooked itself around her neck.

Before her scream had died away she felt the point of a machete pressed against the small of her back.

"Be still, and you won't get hurt," a harsh voice she

didn't recognize instructed in Spanish. She'd been caught, but not by Jorge or Jose.

He was in back of her, so she couldn't see his face or gauge his resolve. As she breathed in the acrid scent of his sweat, she struggled to keep a lid on her fear. It helped a little to remind herself of her martial arts training. He wouldn't be expecting any fancy maneuvers on her part. And the first thing to do was make him think she was completely at his mercy. "What are you going to do to me?" she croaked.

Instead of answering, he called out loudly, "I've found the woman they're looking for."

Moments later he was joined by a friend dressed in the faded cotton trousers and shirts that San Marcos's peasants wore. He, too, was carrying a machete.

"I'm nothing to you. Please, let me go," she begged.

The one who held her began to march her toward the road.

"I just want to get back—home." The last part came out as a choked cry.

"The soldiers want you," he said, as if that settled the matter. "*Vámonos.*"

"I'll pay you," she tried in desperation.

"We don't want your money," the second one answered. "They will be angry with the village if I don't bring you in. They might burn us out or kill our animals."

She understood then that there was no use pleading with these men or trying to bribe them. If they didn't obey the wishes of the soldiers, they would be inviting the wrath of *El Jefe*.

Her captors gave her no opportunity for escape.

In minutes they emerged from the shade of the jungle onto the hot surface of the road. The van from which she'd escaped was parked a hundred yards or so farther on, and she saw immediately that the soldiers had repaired the flat tire. Jose and Jorge were lounging against the vehicle, one on either side. It did nothing to lift her spirits to find out she'd been slogging through rough terrain half the morning, and they'd been riding along in comfort.

When the villagers delivered her up to Jorge, he gave her a look that was equal parts relief and anger.

"*Puta,*" he growled, his hands balled into fists. "What the hell do you think you're doing causing so much trouble? You're going to be sorry."

She braced herself for a blow, but none came. Maybe he didn't want to have to explain how the prisoner had gotten injured. Pivoting away, he honked the horn several times in rapid succession.

When he turned back to her, his anger was under better control. Methodically he began to search her, his hands lingering on her body in a way that made her want to throw up. When he found her knife and the other tools, he gave her a thunderous look.

"This will make the general very angry."

She raised her chin. "You wouldn't be stupid enough to tell him your prisoner got away, would you?"

"Why not?" The question was from Jose, who had come around the van to stand behind her.

"Because he won't be angry only at me. He's going to wonder why you were careless enough to let a woman in a leg iron slip out of your hands."

The two men exchanged a quick, whispered conversation. At least Marissa had the satisfaction of knowing she'd rattled them badly. And maybe her ploy would keep them from talking about the morning's misadventure.

Jorge cuffed her wrists behind her back before he shoved her into the van. The vehicle lurched away in a cloud of exhaust that enveloped the villagers who were standing several yards away watching the spectacle.

AS JED pressed his foot down on the old Land Rover's accelerator he was thinking about the two best features of the road to *El Jefe*'s *finca.* There were no potholes. And there weren't any cops on motorcycles who were going to stop him for speeding. Which was a damn good thing, because he was driving as if the devil was in pursuit.

He slowed marginally as he approached a village, alert for cows with a death wish. But at this time of day they were all lazing in the shade while the egrets picked the bugs from their hides.

As soon as he'd cleared the populated area, Jed accelerated again. He'd shown up at Sanchez's offices in Santa Isabella that morning pretending that he wanted to get together with his old buddy, since they hadn't connected at the party the other night. He'd been told that the general was at his country estate.

Determining the whereabouts of the female prisoner being held incommunicado had been a little trickier. But he'd been lucky enough to run into one of the men he'd trained six years ago. The fellow had made lieutenant, and he attributed much of his military success to Jed's guidance.

As they talked about old times and present duties, Jed asked if the general was loading them up with special assignments. He found out that two guards had taken a good-looking blond woman out to the hacienda the previous morning.

With his heart pounding, he'd gotten out of the conversation as quickly as possible. Five minutes later he had hit the road to Sanchez's estate, trying like hell not to think about what he might find. But he couldn't stop some pretty vivid pictures from jumping into his mind. He'd once walked into a session when *El Jefe* had been demonstrating interrogation techniques on prisoners captured from the revolutionary army.

As he sped west the sky turned to navy blue, and the wind began to blow. A tropical storm was rolling in. He hoped it held off until after he arrived at the *finca*, or the driving rain might slow him to a crawl.

Two miles from the main gate he was stopped at a checkpoint. Again he was damn lucky. It still wasn't raining, and another of his old comrades was on duty. He was passed through on the assumption that Sanchez knew about the visit. He hoped he didn't get the guard in too much trouble.

If things were the same as they'd been six years ago, an electrified fence and another guard station were ahead. Jed's hands tightened on the wheel. Even if they were best buddies, it was doubtful that the sentry up ahead would allow him to pass without authorization from *El Jefe*.

But what if the general was interrogating his prisoner? If he was busy with Marissa, he'd probably left strict orders not to be disturbed because he wouldn't want to break the rhythm of the session.

A sick feeling rose in Jed's throat. Too bad this Land Rover wasn't armor plated so he could steamroll the guardhouse and hope that Sanchez would come out to investigate the disturbance.

As it turned out, the sentry's attention wasn't focused on the road but on the nearby field that *El Jefe* used for disciplinary action. The trees at the edge of the parade ground bent and swayed. The wind tore at the shirts and trousers of soldiers in the field marching in formation as if preparing for a formal drill. Not likely in a gale condition. No, this was no practice session. He recognized the configuration. It was a firing squad.

His blood turned to ice when he spotted the prisoner being marched to a stake facing the troops. It was Marissa.

Chapter Four

Jed gunned the engine of the Land Rover and barreled through the checkpoint. The wooden arm on the barrier snapped like a fence rail in a hurricane. Behind him he heard the sentry bellowing in surprise, then anger.

"*¡Basta!* Or I'll shoot."

Jed didn't stop. Half expecting a volley of machine gun bullets to plow into the vehicle, he kept his foot pressed on the gas. A few seconds later he decided the guard was no fool. *El Jefe* himself was in an open car on the field. Any shots would endanger the general's life.

However, Jed was taking no chances. As quickly as he could, he put the troops between himself and the sentry. When the vehicle zoomed onto the grass, their precise formation dissolved into disarray. Some men stopped in their tracks, a few kept marching. Most broke into a run as if they'd been scattered by the rising wind. It would have been comical if Jed had been watching it on a movie screen. But this wasn't make-believe. It was Marissa's life.

The only soldiers who weren't aware of the disturbance were the ones escorting her toward the wooden stake about fifty yards away. Marissa walked between the uniformed men with her head held high and the breeze blowing the hair back from her face. She made it look as if she was the one in charge, not they. What was it costing her to march to her death with such composure?

As he watched, he felt a hard knot of anxiety inside his chest burst into sharp pieces, sending pain stabbing through his lungs. Lord, what if he'd been a few minutes later?

Behind him he could hear Sanchez snapping out angry orders. Then a troop of running feet hammered toward the Land Rover. Jed didn't wait for the squad to reach him. Screeching to a stop, he jumped out of the vehicle. Marissa wasn't out of danger yet. Neither was he. But he proceeded with what he hoped looked like unswerving confidence.

"Change of plans," he barked in Spanish.

At the sound of his voice, the men holding Marissa dropped her arms and whirled.

She was thrown off balance. Swaying in the gale, she turned on shaky legs and stared around uncomprehendingly as if she'd suddenly awakened from a nightmare and wasn't sure she was really conscious or where she was.

He saw her eyes snap into focus and zero in on him. He wasn't surprised as they widened the way they always did when the two of them first met. Yet this time he knew there was more behind the look than usual. He saw panic, relief and disbelief all warring with each other.

"Jed?" His name was a mere wisp of sound on her trembling lips.

"Come to get you out of this mess, honey bee." He was surprised to be struggling with the rough quality of his own voice. Momentarily, he was as shaken as she.

Tottering on shaky legs, she took a step toward him. At the same time she made a tiny, muted sound that was half sob, half exclamation.

Chaos swirled around the two of them. But it seemed to fade into the background. Marissa was the sole focus of his attention. And she was looking at him with the same intensity.

Closing the distance between them in a few sure strides, he caught her in his embrace and held her tightly, achingly aware of how small and fragile she felt. Like a fluttering bird he'd freed from a trap.

She slumped against him. He wasn't sure when she took hold of his shoulders, but he felt her fingers digging into his flesh so hard that he knew he would see the marks when he got undressed that night. Then her whole body began to tremble.

He bent his head and spoke low and urgently in her ear, glad that the wind gave them a measure of privacy. "It's all right. I'm here. I'm not going to let anything happen to you," he told her, his hands stroking through her hair and up the icy flesh of her arms as he tried to warm her with his touch, tried to project a sense of absolute confidence that he wished he could feel. He'd pictured a dozen harrowing scenarios. But not *this.* "I've got a way to protect you, honey."

His name sighed out of her once more, drawing his attention to her mouth. It looked so soft, so vulnerable, so exposed that he had to kiss her. Seeing his intent, she stiffened and made a startled exclamation. Afraid she was going to push him away, he tried to hold on to her with his gaze. This was the moment of greatest danger, the moment she could give away the whole shooting match.

"Marci, no."

She stared up into his eyes, hers so large and questioning that he could have gotten lost in their blue depths. Perhaps he was as dazed as she, because something strange happened. He knew where he was—on the parade ground, surrounded by uniformed soldiers. But the men and their surroundings had faded into the background so that he was conscious only of Marci. He sought something vital from her as his lips moved against her. At the same time he felt his own vulnerability rise to the surface as if he were the one in need of aid and comfort.

In that instant everything changed. The stiffness left her spine, and she went soft and pliant in his arms. In reaction, his emotions changed from protective to hungry. He drank in her sweetness even as she swayed against him, clinging to him like a lost kitten trying to grasp something solid. But he was as lost as she.

Later he realized that it all must have happened in mere seconds. On the field it felt as if they had stepped out of time into a private space of their own. As they clung together, nothing existed for him besides Marissa and the contact of his mouth against hers. His body against hers. The urgent movement of her hands up and down his back.

Her lips opened under his, and he took advantage of the surrender. He tasted passion, heard a low murmur in her throat that made the blood in his veins run hot.

Then in the space of a heartbeat he sensed her change, as he felt her remember who she was and who he was and that there was a reason—whatever it was—that she had never allowed him this close before.

He longed to bring her back to him. Longed to use every lover's trick he'd ever learned to recapture her heady response, but he realized with a start that they weren't alone and that a harsh voice had intruded into their reality.

The voice rose above the wind. "Arrest this man."

Jed's attention snapped instantly back to the here and now. Marissa went taut in his arms.

Soldiers with guns moved into position around them, cutting off any avenue of escape. But then, Jed had never thought this rescue was going to be easy. Ignoring the troops, he turned and focused on the man who had given the order.

Miguel Sanchez had the grace to look astonished. "Jed?"

"Sé, mi amigo."

Some of the squad had recognized him, and he heard his name whispered in the circle of startled faces as he shifted Marissa to his side.

"What is the meaning of this?" *El Jefe* demanded. "What are you doing here interfering in my private business?"

"I apologize for arriving unannounced. But I can't allow you to execute an innocent woman. Particularly when she's my fiancée."

"Your *what?*" Sanchez bellowed, any pretense of calm vanishing.

Marissa's reaction was no less violent. Her body jerked in Jed's arms. Raising her head, she searched his face, her eyes wide and startled. And so tantalizingly beautiful that he was almost undone. But he managed to remember why he was here and why it was so important to hang on to his wits.

"My fiancée. The woman I'm going to marry." He repeated the words very slowly and very evenly, and not only for Sanchez's benefit. Marissa needed time to take in the information.

"That's impossible. She's a spy!" the general growled. "She escaped into the jungle, and my men had to recapture her."

"Oh, yeah?"

"Do you know who sent her?"

"Nobody sent her. There's obviously been some kind of mistake," Jed countered. He'd been acting on pure instinct when he'd driven headlong in front of the troops. Now he looked at the stake that had been waiting for Marissa and was unable to keep from shuddering. "This is no place for a civilized discussion. Why don't we go back to the hacienda and talk about it before we all get drenched.''

Sanchez nodded—a single, curt movement of his head—and began striding toward his jeep. Jed started to lead Marissa to the Land Rover, but the general's voice stopped him. ''No.'' *El Jefe* spoke over the wind, his voice raised so the assembled troops could hear. ''I insist you ride with me, *amigo.* One of my men will bring your vehicle and put it in the garage.''

Jed didn't bother to argue. His life and Marissa's depended on their getting a chance to communicate. But defying Sanchez at this moment was an even surer ticket to destruction.

Marissa still looked dazed as he helped her into the jeep's back seat. At first she nestled against him like an injured animal. But he felt her coming back to life as *El Jefe* barked orders to the squad. He sensed her struggling to pull herself together, but there was only so much he could do to help without giving away the story line to their attentive audience. When the jeep lurched forward she sat up straighter and squirmed in the seat, trying to put some distance between them. Jed suspected that his leg pressed to hers was making it difficult for her to think. But he held her firmly, aware that Sanchez kept shifting his gaze from the road to glance with interest in the rearview mirror at the engaged couple in the back seat.

''I was worried about you, honey,'' Jed murmured, keeping Marissa close to him and stroking his lips against her temple.

The caress made her shiver, and he wondered if the melting moment in his arms had been a figment of his imagination. No, for a few incredible seconds she'd kissed him like a lover. But he could put that down to disorientation—and a spontaneous reaction to the man who'd snatched her from the jaws of death.

He ached to find out if her surge of emotions had come from more than fear and gratitude. But that discovery would have to wait for another time and place. "I hope you're feeling more like yourself," he murmured, knowing the statement was only partly true. Lord, what he wouldn't give for a few hours with the woman who had come alive in his arms.

She swallowed. "Yes."

"Good girl." He patted her knee, anticipating her response to the intimate gesture. She jumped, and he knew he had gotten her full attention. As much for Miguel's benefit as hers, he began to speak in a half amused, half worried voice. "So I leave you alone for a couple of hours and you get yourself in a real mess again. Cassie and Abby and Sabrina and everybody else are going to be worried sick when they hear about this. Or maybe we shouldn't even tell them."

Her head whipped toward him. "How do you know—?"

His hand tightened on hers, and he clamped down on her sentence before she could give anything away. "How did I know you were here, honey bee? A combination of detective work and luck." He raised his voice and addressed Sanchez. "You weren't really going to shoot my lady love, were you, you old devil?"

"I was still weighing the pros and cons."

"Oh, yeah?"

"There was always the chance that a last-minute reprieve might loosen her tongue."

Marissa made a strangled sound.

They were approaching the stretch of jungle that separated the hacienda from the military complex. Miguel turned onto a hard-packed dirt road that wound past banana trees, tall ferns and countless jungle plants Jed couldn't name. They were all swaying wildly, raining leaves down on the jeep. And the sky was black as midnight. Jed expected the rain to begin pelting them any second.

When Sanchez leaned forward and picked up a portable phone, Jed pressed his fingers tightly over Marissa's.

She looked at him and nodded. And he knew she was functioning on a higher level. She understood that while the other man's attention was focused on giving orders for their reception, they had partial privacy. Still, Jed took the precaution of keeping his tone light and garrulous. "Don't let him fool you into thinking he's harmless."

She glanced toward the front seat. "I won't."

In the dim light he turned her face toward him. "Did he hurt you?" he whispered.

"Not physically."

He let out the breath he'd been holding. "You were in the prison complex in Santa Isabella?"

"Yes. In solitary confinement. I didn't see a living soul until two men brought me here yesterday."

Jed glanced up to see that Miguel was staring at them intently in the mirror again. Probably he'd only used the phone call to see what they would do when they thought his attention was elsewhere.

Just then they emerged from the forest. The wind suddenly died and the sun came out again. A good omen, Jed told himself, wishing he believed in omens.

They headed for a high adobe wall softened with festoons of blooming purple and orange bougainvillea. But the metal gate was all business. Jed watched as Sanchez pressed a remote control that slid the barrier open, interested to find that security had become more automated since his time. The modernization could be helpful if they had to make an unexpected getaway. Electronic devices could be disabled.

However, when they passed the dog kennel, his hopeful

thoughts turned gloomy. Electronics were one thing. The pack of Dobermans that patrolled the grounds at night was another thing altogether.

The barking of the Dobermans stabbed through the last of the fog shrouding Marissa's brain. She gave Jed a quick sideways glance, marveling that he could appear so calm. Trying to follow his example, she sat up straighter and looked around, aware of her surroundings with a sudden aching clarity. The sun had come out from behind the clouds, and the whitewashed walls of the hacienda were bathed in the warm afternoon light. The wind had died to a gentle whisper. And she wasn't dead.

When she shuddered, Jed's arm tightened around her, and she had the uncanny sensation that he understood what she was feeling.

She looked down, hoping he wasn't reading *everything* in her mind. For her own equanimity she struggled to rationalize what had happened between them out there on the field—or more specifically what had happened to her. *His* part was easy enough to grasp. He was a normal man. She'd tumbled into his embrace, and he'd taken advantage of the situation.

But she'd behaved in a manner that was so totally alien that she could only explain it one way: she'd been living in a nightmare that would end with her own death, and just when she'd lost all hope, Jed had come charging to her rescue. She'd been so off balance that she'd let herself feel things she'd been afraid of for years. Particularly with him. Convulsively, she knit her hands together. Perhaps holding tight to her own flesh could bring back the perfect control she'd relied on for so long.

"It's okay," he whispered, and she wondered if he was still following her thoughts.

"Umm." With Jed's thigh pressed against hers and his grip firmly on her shoulder, it was impossible to think clearly, but she clamped down hard on her instinctive urge to pull away. She knew Sanchez was watching, and they had to keep playing by the script Jed had tossed her.

He'd told the general that they were engaged! How were they ever going to pull it off? How could they possibly act as if they were madly in love? As if they were lovers? Contemplating that led to memories of his kiss, which made her heart lurch inside her chest. Perhaps the most disturbing thing of all was that she still felt a tingle of awareness between them like a humming electric current. It had started when he'd kissed her, and she wanted to pretend it wasn't there. But she was coming to realize she couldn't wish it away.

Jed's arm was around her shoulder, but he was leaning forward responding to a question from the general. As she switched her focus to the conversation flowing so easily in Spanish, she realized for the first time how close the two men must have been.

"So why didn't you come to me when Marissa was first apprehended?" Sanchez asked.

"I tried. Ask that undercover man who took her into custody on the patio. He wasn't letting anyone through to you."

"He had his orders. But you should have let me know she was your woman."

Jed laughed. "I remember how you close ranks when you think you've been crossed. For all I know, you were going to assume *I* was part of a plot against you. Then you would have arrested me as well as her. And we'd both be up the creek without a paddle."

"You've got a point," *El Jefe* conceded.

The give-and-take between the men continued. Marissa missed a number of allusions that must have referred to events they both remembered well. She didn't much like being excluded, but she had enough sense to keep her mouth shut and let Jed remind the general of their old bond. She'd rather have the State Department on the job. But Victor Kirkland wasn't the one who had shown up to win her freedom. It seemed that Victor had tossed her to the wolves, and Jed had stepped in. Perhaps his friendship with the general might be the only thing that would get her out of here.

Or was that what was really going on, she wondered with a sudden little jolt. Jed had appeared out of nowhere like a knight in shining armor. But the rescue could have been staged, too. And he could be counting heavily on her vulnerability.

She swallowed painfully. Were Jed and Sanchez putting on a performance for *her?* Was this all part of some diabolical plan to get her to talk about what she'd found in the general's office? Did they think that if she wouldn't tell Sanchez anything, she'd spill the beans to Jed?

But if he was here to trick her, what about the familiar way he'd mentioned Cassie and Abby and Sabrina? He'd met her sister when they'd all been on an assignment together in Colombia. But he'd never met any of the other women from 43 Light Street. He'd made it sound as if they were all working together to get her out of here. Yet that could be faked, as well—when there was no way to get in touch with anyone whose name he'd mentioned so casually.

She had sense enough to know she was too off balance to make any coherent judgments. Her head swam with plots and counterplots as the jeep pulled up in front of the hacienda, where two guards in dress uniforms snapped to attention. She saw the curtains move at one of the windows and wondered who was watching. Jed helped her out of the jeep and kept his arm around her, guiding her toward the house.

Before they reached the front door, it opened. A teenage girl with long dark hair and liquid brown eyes came hurrying out. She had Miguel's features, and Marissa remembered that his dossier had mentioned a daughter and a long-dead wife. But there had been hardly any information about either one.

The girl stopped a few feet from the group.

"Clarita, you're not supposed to be out here," Sanchez said in a voice that raised the hairs on the back of Marissa's neck. If he could speak that way to his daughter, what might he do to a female prisoner?

The girl merely shrugged, clearly accustomed to his intimidating manner. "I'm not one of your soldiers. I don't have to follow orders."

"Everyone in this house follows my orders."

"Yes. And unfortunately everyone in San Marcos, too."

It was a dangerous response, Marissa thought as she waited to see what *El Jefe* would do. She couldn't imagine he was enjoying this little scene. His face contorted. "We'll discuss it later."

The girl looked as if she were about to say something more. At the last moment she turned toward Jed, her expression softening. "You came back to us. I knew you would after I saw you the other night."

"I have business with your father."

As the girl's gaze swung from Jed to Marissa and back again, she went through another rapid change of mood. This time her eyes held a mixture of bewilderment and hurt. "I'm sorry I ran away from you on the patio. I thought you came to see me, and we'd have fun together again. Like in the old days."

Jed seemed perplexed, no more equipped for this scene than Sanchez. "I do want to see you."

"Then why do you have your arm around the woman prisoner? Why are you protecting her from my father?"

"Marissa is my fiancée."

The girl's expression went from questioning to fury in the space of a heartbeat. "She can't be."

"I fell in love with her. And I came here to bring her home."

"Oh." Several seconds of silence ticked by before Clarita tipped her head toward Marissa. "Are you good in bed? Is that what he likes about you?"

"That's enough," Sanchez roared. "Go to your room this instant before you embarrass yourself further."

Marissa stood with her cheeks burning while the girl turned and flounced away. Before she reached the house she pulled a hibiscus blossom off a nearby bush, crushed it in her hand and tossed it onto the pavement.

"I'm sorry," the general muttered as he watched his daughter disappear. "I'm having some trouble with her. But you can be sure she will be punished for that outburst."

Despite her own embarrassment, Marissa murmured, "I think she needs your love, not your anger."

"What do you know about it?" Sanchez snapped.

"I know what it's like to be raised by an army officer who doesn't have much time for his family."

"Well, you know nothing about *this* family, *señorita!*"

Marissa was instantly sorry she hadn't thought before she'd spoken.

"Come inside," *El Jefe* commanded. "We have more important business to discuss than my daughter."

When the general turned his back, Jed gave Marissa a warning look. She nodded tightly, acknowledging her mistake. But despite Clarita's angry words, Marissa's heart had gone out to her. She knew what it was like to feel trapped in a home where love was the last consideration. Bowing her head, she climbed the stairs. Inside, the wide front hall of the hacienda was cool and spacious and furnished like the grand entrance to a museum of colonial art.

The general was limping slightly as he escorted his visitors to the back of the house.

Marissa wondered what was wrong with his foot. He was obviously making an effort not to let his pain slow him down as he escorted them into an office. Glancing around her, she noticed the effort made to blend splendor and practicality. The desk and cabinets looked like valuable antiques, the chairs and sofas were of soft leather. French doors led to a large courtyard, alive with flowering plants.

El Jefe sighed as he took a seat behind a wide desk under the window. The desk rested on a slightly raised platform, giving the effect of a judge's bench towering over a courtroom.

With the option of putting some blessed space between herself and the general, Marissa remained standing near the door. Jed sprawled on one of the sofas as if he'd spent many relaxed evenings in the room. "Your gout acting up?" he asked.

Sanchez nodded tightly.

"Sorry."

"You're one of the few people who knows about it. If the press got hold of the story, they'd say it came from rich food and decadent living."

"Well, *I* know it's inherited from your grandfather. The secret's safe with me."

Marissa expected Sanchez to look relieved. Instead, *El Jefe*'s eyes narrowed dangerously as he studied Jed. "Is it? I trusted you once. But this business with the woman has given me some strong doubts. You claim she's your fiancée. But I've had news of you from time to time, and this is the first I've heard you were engaged. So what are you up to? Is this all some trick to get me to let her go? Or should I have you both arrested and thrown into the cells downstairs while I find out what's really going on?'

Chapter Five

Marissa's knees buckled. Before she toppled over, she clamped a steadying hand against the back of a chair.

Jed didn't move except to look directly at Sanchez. For an endless moment there was only silence in the room. Then Jed laughed deep in his throat. "You know better than to try shock tactics on me."

"Do I? Well, how about this scenario? What if you're both spies—hired by our esteemed president Palmeriz to bring me down," Sanchez answered, his voice icy.

"Palmeriz! He doesn't have the guts to go against the commander in chief of the army. You could flood the capital with your troops and capture him before he gets out of the presidential palace."

Sanchez shrugged. "Perhaps, but I have other enemies. Men who would love to benefit from the power I've worked hard to consolidate."

"And they all know I'm not loco enough to try and put something over on you," Jed answered.

"For enough money, you might take the gamble."

"Money's no good to me in the grave. You know I never risk my hide taking foolish chances."

Sanchez relaxed a degree. "I also know you don't stay in one place for long. You expect me to believe you intend to settle down with Señorita Devereaux?"

"Hardly."

The general raised a questioning eyebrow.

"Settling down wasn't what I had in mind," Jed continued easily. "I'm sure you've researched Marci's background. She's a travel agent who specializes in setting up trips to adventure locales. She's a very exciting woman." He chuckled. "In fact, she's very talented in a variety of delightful ways."

Marissa's hands tightened on the back of the chair. She knew the remark was intended to get the general's mind off spying and onto more intimate aspects of her relationship with Jed. Unable to meet *El Jefe*'s speculative gaze, she turned toward her temporary fiancé, who was also looking at her. She felt her face grow hot and her pulse accelerate.

She couldn't penetrate Jed's deadpan expression. But when he held out his hand, she recognized her cue. What's more, she'd just been given a very pointed lesson that her life might depend on acting the part Sanchez was expecting. Crossing the rug, she curled herself onto the sofa beside Jed as if snuggling up to him was the most natural thing in the world, as if it didn't make her heart beat so fast that she was in danger of passing out.

She drew in a deep breath and plunged into her assigned part, mustering what she hoped was an intimate look. "I wish we had some time alone. I'd like to tell you how glad I was to see you come driving up in that Land Rover." Her voice was pitched low, but not low enough for the general to miss.

Jed reached up to stroke a wayward strand of her hair back into place. "Honey bee, I was real glad I got there when I did."

The rough quality of his voice made the sentiment sound real. So real that she longed to drag him from the room and start asking questions. Personal questions.

Then, over his shoulder, she saw Sanchez watching them, and it suddenly came home to her how well matched the two men were. Superficially they weren't much alike. The general had dark hair, dark eyes and a dark complexion set off by a thin mustache. Jed's hair was sun streaked, his eyes green, his complexion golden from the sun. Yet the two of them had a lot in common. They were both dangerous and ruthless and accustomed to doing what needed to be done. She had to hope that Jed played by civilized rules. The general was different. Here at his *finca* he held absolute power. And as Lord Acton had so aptly put it, absolute power corrupts absolutely.

One of Jed's hands stroked her shoulder possessively, sending little shivers along her nerve endings. With the other he gestured toward Sanchez. "You haven't exactly been treating my fiancée like an honored guest."

"Until a little while ago, I didn't know she belonged to you."

Marissa pressed her lips together to keep from snapping back a retort that the concept of women as property had gone out with the Middle Ages. Except maybe in San Marcos. Then Jed plucked a twig out of her hair, and she was suddenly aware of how she must look. She was still wearing the rumpled slacks and shirt from her jungle adventure. And she hadn't even washed or brushed her hair in days. Automatically she tried to move away from Jed. He kept her firmly in his grasp, his hand continuing to move over her shoulder.

When he forced her closer, she willed her body not to stiffen in his embrace. She hoped she was making it seem natural as she closed her eyes and leaned her head against his chest. She hoped she looked like a woman who was letting her man take charge. So much of this charade rested on his shoulders, and over the past few minutes it had begun to sink in that he had put himself in a great deal of danger for her. "I'm sorry I got myself into this mess. I'm sorry I got *you* into it, dear heart." She swallowed, wondering where the endearment had come from. It had simply seemed like the right thing to say.

Jed gave her a crooked little smile, no doubt congratulating her on the improvisation. "I think it's going to work out."

When he grazed his thumb across her palm, she winced.

He was instantly alert, turning her hand over. They both stared down at the raised red circle in the center.

"I don't like the looks of that. What did you do?" Jed demanded.

She flushed. "Forgot the first rule of jungle survival. Never sit on anything, touch anything or lean on anything before you have a good look at it. I closed my hand around some thorns."

Jed lifted her palm, inspecting the welt and probing at it with his thumbnail.

Marissa struggled not to grimace again. "I tried to get it out, but it broke off."

"Well, I'm not going to take a chance on an infection, honey." He looked toward Sanchez. "Let me have your first aid kit."

The general didn't move for several seconds. Then, to Marissa's surprise, he opened one of his lower desk drawers and pulled out a small metal box.

Jed got up to retrieve it. "Thanks."

The smell of antiseptic filled Marissa's nostrils as he sterilized a needle and then her palm before cradling her hand in his left one. "It may hurt."

"It's okay."

She clamped her teeth together, but as Jed began to probe, she drew in several sharp breaths.

He raised the needle from her flesh. "Sorry."

"It's the only way to get it out. Just do it as fast as you can." She held on to the edge of the sofa with her free hand, focusing on Jed as she tried to shut out the pain.

"You're doing great," he murmured, working carefully. But the thorn was deep, and he couldn't get under it without stabbing into her.

She kept her eyes fixed on his face, watching the way his features contorted in concentration—and concern.

"I don't like hurting you," he muttered.

"I know."

She breathed out a long sigh when he finally freed the thorn and swabbed the wound with more antiseptic. This time the liquid stung.

When it was all over, he stroked his hand across her damp forehead. "Good girl."

She nodded wordlessly. She'd never imagined that Jed Prentiss could be this caring, this gentle. But then, a lot of things had changed in the past few days. And not just her perceptions of Jed. Too much had happened too quickly for her to ever be the same again.

For several heartbeats the room was completely silent. Then Jed cleared his throat, and she reminded herself that she was in no state to be making any sweeping pronouncements.

He addressed himself to Sanchez. "Marci's already paid heavily for her innocent mistake. And I don't mean only this wound. She's had three days in one of your filthy cells. Now I'd like to take her home and do my damnedest to wipe this nightmare out of her head." He sounded sincere, but she'd better keep remembering that this was as much a performance on her part as anything else.

The general's features tightened. "If she made an *innocent* mistake, why did she run away the first chance she got?"

"I was scared," Marissa replied instantly. "I know prisoners brought here have 'disappeared'—as they refer to it in Santa Isabella."

El Jefe didn't deny the accusation. "So you've researched me. You're quite thorough for a *travel agent.*"

"I always collect a great deal of information on a country before I decide it's safe for American tourists."

Sanchez let the answer hang in the air.

"Marci is a resourceful woman. I wouldn't expect her to pass up a chance to get herself out of a sticky situation. She'd been held for days, after all, and it looked like no one was doing anything. However, I can see your point of view, too, Miguel. I understand why you have some doubts about her. But I hope you'll make an exception in her case. Out of friendship for me."

"I have to consider San Marcos before myself."

"I know that. So I've come prepared to offer you something in exchange for Marci. Louis Rinaldo has told me how anxious the government is to develop the copper mining potential in Junipero Province. I'm sure the Global Bank will accept my recommendation of a six million dollar loan for the project."

"Rinaldo wasn't supposed to talk about the copper deposits!" the general snapped.

"No?" Jed sounded genuinely puzzled. "I thought your government was looking for a way to beef up exports."

"We are. But I prefer to keep reports on our natural resources confidential until we're ready to go ahead with a project."

Marissa glanced from Jed to Sanchez. The general's objection didn't make sense. How could you get a loan if you weren't willing to let your banker know how you planned to spend the money?

A buzzer sounded, and Marissa jumped.

Sanchez picked up the phone. After listening for several seconds he spoke in low, rapid Spanish into the mouthpiece. Then, replacing the receiver, he stood. "You'll have to excuse me. I'm needed elsewhere."

Jed also rose, bringing Marissa with him. With his free hand casually in his pocket, he stood facing the general.

"We'll talk about this later," Sanchez said, halfway out the door before he had finished the sentence.

"Convenient," Jed muttered under his breath.

When two armed guards entered, she felt Jed's fingers close around her hand. Were they here to take her back to the basement cells after all? And would Jed try to stop them?

The men walked toward Marissa, and she felt Jed's tension increase. At the last minute the one with a lieutenant's insignia spoke to Jed.

"The general is having rooms prepared for you."

"Upstairs?" Jed demanded.

"*Sí.* But you're to wait here for a few minutes until the maids can get things ready."

Marissa's relief was like a physical weight being lifted off her shoulders. Thank God she wasn't going back into the dark, dark detention center. For now, anyway.

The guards stepped back into the hall, and she heard them take up positions on either side of the door. For the first time since Jed had appeared in the Land Rover, she was alone with him.

He started to cough, turning away and raising his hand to shield his mouth.

"Are you all right?" she asked.

He cleared his throat. "Yeah. I swallowed wrong or something. Guess...I'm...more nervous than I thought."

The coughing stopped in a few seconds, but Jed's face was flushed. She looked at him anxiously. "You're sure you're okay?"

He nodded.

She grasped his arm, aware that this might be their only chance to exchange vital information. When she started to ask what he had planned, he shook his head quickly. "Now that he's out of the room, there's probably a whole bunch of private comments you want to make about how Miguel's been treating you, but you can bet it will all be recorded."

She drew in a shaky breath. "I wasn't thinking."

"You've had a pretty rough time, honey bee."

The endearment and the gentleness of his voice almost undid her. Her lower lip quivered, and she was suddenly afraid that the tears she'd been struggling to suppress were going to get the better of her.

Jed took her by the shoulders, folding her close. She closed her eyes and rested her head against his chest, struggling to get herself back under control. It wouldn't do either of them any good if she let herself start weeping.

"Better?" he finally asked.

"I—yes."

He pivoted them both so that his back was to the desk. "Stay right here with me."

At first she thought he was telling her not to go to pieces again. He squeezed her elbows, and she looked up. His green eyes bored down into hers as if he were trying to communicate some vital message.

"I'm with you," she tried, hoping the dialogue would lead to something constructive.

He gave her an odd half smile, directing her attention to his mouth. Then his lips drew back slightly so that she could see his teeth. She blinked when she realized he was holding something between them. It was flesh-colored plastic and looked like a large medicine capsule. However, the contents did not appear to be cold medication.

Through the translucent sides she could see tiny black printing.

After several seconds, during which he held her gaze, the capsule disappeared back into his mouth. "I've been wanting to give you a real kiss," he said.

Her mouth went dry as she realized exactly what he had in mind. A few moments ago she'd been convinced that some basic part of her had changed. As Jed's grip on her tightened, old fears came zinging back to her. She was alone in this room with a man. He was holding her much too tightly. He could do anything to her he wanted. And she was terrified.

Panicked, she looked toward the door, half wondering what the guards would do if she came charging through. At the same time her hands went up to push against Jed's chest. But she realized he'd been prepared for her reaction. He didn't give her a chance to get away.

"I've got to kiss you, honey. Even if he's getting a kick out of watching."

Her eyes locked with his. He was telling her they were being videotaped as well as recorded. Maybe the general had even arranged this opportunity to see what they'd do the first chance they were alone.

She felt blood roaring in her ears as Jed's mouth slowly lowered to hers. *He'll do it quickly. He won't do anything threatening.*

Even as her conscious mind supplied the reassurance, her body trembled as his lips touched hers. She'd been afraid to let her defenses down with this man for a long, long time. Afraid of intimacy. But the fear hadn't kept her from secretly dreaming about him.

Overwhelmed, she went very still in his arms. Her only salvation was to let herself imagine what it would be like if he really were her fiancée. The fantasy was so compelling that she grasped it like a lifeline. Then she realized she'd made a mistake—that she'd opened herself to the sensual feelings that had been buzzing between them the whole time they'd been together.

Jed must have sensed the change. "Ah, Marci," he whispered, his mouth brushing seductively back and forth against hers.

Her knees weakened, and her hands slid upward to clutch at the broad shelf of his shoulders. It was either hold on to him or topple over.

"That's right. Open up for me, honey," he whispered, his voice husky.

Every conditioned reflex urged her to wrench herself away. Instead, her lips parted. Because she had no choice. She had to go along with his plan or risk the consequences.

She waited tensely, expecting to feel him push the capsule into her mouth. Instead, his tongue boldly traced the edge of her teeth.

Her first reaction was rigid shock. But he didn't allow her to escape the erotic assault. And like a coin flipping in a game of chance, shock turned to pleasure.

When she sighed involuntarily, he gathered her more firmly in his arms. His tongue breached the barrier of her teeth and began to explore the softness beyond with little teasing strokes. A woman with more experience might have reacted less explosively. But after the strain of staying in control of so many emotions, she was suddenly helpless to repress her response. The gliding of his tongue against her sensitive flesh brought a wave of heat crashing through her body like a tidal wave.

The sensations pooled somewhere in her middle, and Marissa moaned deep in her throat. When she swayed against Jed, he growled something low and unintelligible and cupped her bottom, lifting her on her toes so that her body was more perfectly aligned with his.

The pressure of his erection should have been a threat. Instead, she swayed against him. Even the stubble of his beard rasping against her cheek added to the feeling of intimacy—of need.

She hadn't known it would be like this. So hot. So overwhelming. So empowering. Deep inside herself she sensed that he was as much her captive as she was his.

Breathless, she forgot where they were and what was at stake. The only thing real was Jed and the magic he was working on her senses.

Then she felt something pressing against her teeth. It was too rigid for his tongue.

Her eyes snapped open in confusion. His burning gaze helped guide her back to the known universe.

Events of the past few days flashed through her mind like scenes from a spy movie. The party. The patio. The firing squad. Jed coming to get her out of Sanchez's clutches. Jed had important information for her. It was stuffed into a little carrying case he'd put in his mouth. And he was ready to give it to her.

Marissa nodded fractionally, even as she felt his hands in her hair, steadying her head. When he pushed the capsule forward, she felt it slide between her lips, vividly aware of the intimacy of transferring something from his mouth to hers.

Afraid that she might swallow the container, she tucked it down beside her lower teeth, the way she'd concealed chewing gun in school when she'd been a kid.

Still confused and shaken, she looked up into Jed's eyes. She expected to see triumph or perhaps even mockery at the way she'd come undone in his arms. She was surprised to encounter emotions that seemed to mirror her own. Or maybe she was only kidding herself.

She wasn't sure how long they stood that way, as if

they were caught in a stop-motion picture on a TV monitor.

The spell was broken when the door opened.

"We're to take you upstairs now," the lieutenant said.

It was a relief to break away from Jed, from the intensity of what had transpired between them.

When she saw the guard staring at her flushed cheeks, they grew even hotter. Mercifully, he didn't prolong her embarrassment.

Her legs felt as if they wouldn't hold her up, but somehow she followed the man into the hall. Aware of Jed right behind her, she focused on her feet as she climbed the stairs. The little plastic container in her mouth felt as if it had ballooned to the size of a grapefruit. It was all she could do to keep from probing it with her tongue the way she might worry a broken tooth.

The guard halted before a closed door. She was paying so little attention to her surroundings that she stopped mere inches before crashing into him.

"*El Jefe* will see you at dinner."

Her questioning gaze shot to Jed. "It's okay," he said.

Marissa couldn't manage more than a nod before she stepped into the room. The door was shut and then locked behind her. Eyes closed, she leaned against the thick wood, half fearful and half thankful that she was alone at last.

Her body felt hot and achy in ways it never had before. Her pulse was still racing, her palms were wet. Slowly she rubbed them on the sides of her slacks, barely noticing the pain where the thorn had been.

But she was all too aware of the other unwanted physical sensations. What was she going to do? When she and Jed had been with Sanchez, she'd been playing a part thrust upon her. To save her life. And Jed's. But then the general had left, and Jed had kissed her, and everything had rocketed out of control.

Weak and shaking, she squeezed her eyes closed even tighter. The feelings that kiss had aroused were too threatening for her to examine.

It was easier to focus on Jed's behavior. He could have passed the capsule to her and been done with it quickly. Instead, he'd used the opportunity to kiss her senseless.

Her hands clenched at her sides. She was lucky she hadn't swallowed the damn container. What had been so important that he had to give it to her right then? Was he telling her the escape plan he'd worked out in case *El Jefe* wouldn't release her?

Or were his motives what they seemed? Her emotions did a flip-flop again as she scrambled to recall every scrap of information she had on Jed Prentiss. A few years ago he'd been a crack agent for the Peregrine Connection, that supersecret organization nobody ever talked about. She knew he wasn't with them anymore, and from the little she'd heard she gathered that the separation hadn't been exactly amicable. Had the breakup made him bitter? Did he care whose money he took? A little while ago he'd been talking as if he were working for the Global Bank. But he could be getting double pay for all she knew.

She sighed. She was in one hell of a mess. And she was way too off-balance to decide whom she could trust.

But she did know one thing. It was more important than ever to read the message Jed had passed to her with such relish. She raised her hand to her lips and then thought better of it. If there had been a camera in the general's office, there could well be one in here. Maybe Sanchez was still watching to see what she would do.

For the first time since the door had closed, Marissa took an interest in her surroundings. The furnishings were simple but comfortable, the bed covered in a brightly colored spread that looked as if it had been woven by village women.

Beside the bed was a box of tissues. Faking a sneeze that she hoped was as good as Jed's phony coughing fit, Marissa crossed the room and reached for a tissue. She brought it to her mouth and sneezed the capsule inside. At the same moment she heard the door behind her open. Did Sanchez have a zoom lens on his camera? Had he seen what she'd done and come to collect the evidence?

Chapter Six

Marissa went very still.

"I'm here to help you, *señorita,*" a woman said in Spanish.

Help me escape? Not likely. Marissa thrust the tissue-wrapped capsule into her pocket and turned. The servant she confronted was a plump young woman with the dark hair and large brown eyes of a San Marcos native. She was carrying an armload of clothing.

"My name is Anna. I've brought some things for you to wear. The best we have in the village." She laid her bundle on the bed and picked up one of the dresses. A simple design, it was made of delicately woven local fabric set off by stunning embroidery of birds and flowers.

It was the kind of outfit that would draw envious comments at a Washington garden party. However, Marissa knew that wearing such a dress would put her at a disadvantage with the general. If she was clothed like the local women—who had very little status compared to the men—it would be easier to treat her as an inferior.

"Where are my own things?" she asked.

Anna returned to the hall and brought in the suitcase that had arrived in the jail cell days ago. As Marissa poked through the mess inside, her heart sank. The contents looked as if they had been hastily searched, and only some of the items had been put back. In fact, most of her toilet articles and clothes were missing. If she appeared at dinner wearing any of this stuff, she'd look like a refugee from a Florida hurricane.

"I'll put everything away while you're bathing and washing your hair," the woman said.

"*Gracias.*" Marissa gave her a friendly smile, considering and then discarding the idea of pumping her for information. Probably she didn't know much. And she'd likely be questioned about their conversation. "Do I have time for a siesta?"

"*Sí.*"

"Then why don't you turn down the covers when you finish?"

Marissa took a nightgown off the bed and stepped into the bathroom. Unfortunately, she couldn't be sure she wasn't being observed even here. After a quick glance at the door, she left the tissue with the capsule in her pocket and began to get undressed.

Taking a shower and washing her hair should have felt wonderful after her ordeals in the detention cell and the jungle. But the pleasure was spoiled by her raw nerves. She needed to know Jed's plans. Or what line of bull he was feeding her.

JED TURNED HIS HEAD to stare at the wall to his right, wishing Marci was on the other side and that he could punch his fist through the plaster and make a hole big enough to pull her through. He couldn't stop picturing the dazed look on her face when their kiss had ended. Lord, what a sight. Her lips red and glistening. Her eyes bright. Her cheeks flushed.

Who would have thought Marissa Devereaux was capable of such passion? But when he'd demanded a response, she'd come alive in his arms like a woman suddenly let out into the sunshine after years of confinement in a prison cell.

Of course, she *had* been in a cell. Maybe she'd given up hope of ever getting out of here alive. That could explain it. She was grateful to him for showing up in the nick of time, and she'd given him the down payment on a suitable reward.

Except that it had seemed like more than that. It had seemed as if she'd been responding to him woman to man. And he'd reacted with the same intensity.

He touched his hand to his lips, thinking about the little capsule he'd had so much fun transferring from his mouth to hers. He could have gotten the job done a lot more efficiently. But all the cuddling they'd been doing on Miguel's couch had turned him on. And he hadn't been able to resist the knowledge that Marci had to play along with him or risk getting shot as a spy. Then right in the middle of the kiss he'd realized that he'd lost control of the situation and he'd better call a halt before he forgot what he was doing and swallowed the damn thing.

Striding to the bathroom, he turned on the cold water in the shower and stepped inside. He needed to stop thinking with his hormones. The needle spray cleared his head, and his mind switched gears as he began to lather his chest. He was in as much danger of getting shot for a spy as Marci if Sanchez caught on to their charade. What's more, he couldn't blame the general for being cautious. He *did* have enemies, including the president of the country, who would like nothing better than to strip him of his power.

Jed sighed. He and Sanchez had met when he'd been assigned by the Defense Department to help train the civil guard on the weapons San Marcos had purchased from U.S. suppliers. He'd known *El Jefe* was ruthless, but he'd followed orders and cozied up to him. Later he'd learned things about the man that had made his blood run cold.

Miguel Sanchez could act like your best buddy one moment and turn into your executioner the next. Sometimes it was a result of his need to demonstrate his power. Sometimes it was simply a political expedient. But whatever was going on now, Sanchez hadn't jumped at the loan offer. Was he having it checked out with Rinaldo before he agreed to anything? Or was there something bigger at stake? He needed to find out from Marci whether she really had discovered anything incriminating in Sanchez's office. But first he had to figure out how to get her alone.

AS MARISSA stepped out of the shower, her gaze went to her slacks. They were where she'd left them. After pulling on the nightgown, she casually pulled the tissue with the capsule from the pocket and returned to the room. To her relief, the maid was gone. Slipping into bed, she made an elaborate show of snuggling down under the covers so that the sheet was over her forehead. Then she unwrapped the capsule. It was difficult to open the darn thing without crushing the paper inside.

Long ago when she'd been a school kid defying her father's rules, Marci had read with a flashlight under the covers. She felt like that now as she burrowed more deeply under the sheet and doggedly worked to get the two halves of the capsule apart.

After several frustrating minutes she was able to extract a tightly rolled sheet of ultra-thin paper. It was hard to read the tiny print in the dim light of the little tent she'd created. When she finally got the sense of the message, it was all she could do not to start cursing aloud. Was this some kind of joke?

She scanned the material, her mind automatically lengthening abbreviations.

Jed Prentiss. Born December 17, 1956, Palo Alto, California. Roosevelt High School. University of California at Santa Cruz. Major—political science/Spanish. 5 feet 11 inches; 165 lb. On a dare from Dave Springer, college roommate, had boar's head tattooed on right buttock. Sleeps in the buff.

Marissa made a small choking sound. She didn't give a damn about Jed Prentiss's hidden tattoos or what he wore to bed. Yet she was smart enough to know why he'd supplied her with this material. As his fiancée, she'd be expected to have seen his bare butt—and to know what he wore to bed. Those and all the other details on this list.

Her eyes scanned down the sheet.

Drinks coffee—with milk and sugar. Favorite dessert—none. Would rather have espresso or Irish coffee. Hates eggplant. Favorite singer, Bob Seager.

There was more. Like his brand of toothpaste. His mother's maiden name—Sarah Fielding. His preference in football and baseball teams—the 49ers and the Giants.

It was a minicourse on the life of Jed Prentiss—something she'd never considered studying. Yet she made an attempt to memorize the list.

Somewhere between San Francisco sourdough bread—he loved it—and 157 Wintergreen Street in Laurel, Maryland—where his house was located—she nodded off.

Sometime later, a knock on the door jerked her awake. For a terrified moment she didn't know where she was. Then she heard the maid's voice asking if she was all right.

"Un momento," she called out as she began to scrabble through the bed covers searching for the list. Locating it under the pillow, she breathed a little prayer of thanks and squeezed the thin paper into a ball in her fist.

"Señorita?"

The door opened just as Marissa belatedly remembered she hadn't collected all of the incriminating evidence. There was still the capsule. Cursing herself for letting go of the darn thing, she pretended to straighten the bedding as she searched for the halves of the small plastic container. When she jerked on the spread, one rounded piece leaped up at her like a Mexican jumping bean. As it hit the bed again, she captured it in her free hand.

Anna hurried forward. "You don't have to do that. Let me help you."

"Is it time for dinner already?" she asked in a sleepy voice, scanning the floor beside the bed. No capsule half. If Anna found it, maybe she'd think it had something to do with drugs. Marissa grimaced. Her life was in a sorry state when her choices were being taken for a druggie or a spy.

"Sí."

She worked at putting some enthusiasm in her voice. "Pick out a dress you think the general will like while I wash my face."

Praying the woman would leave the bed alone, Marissa made for the bathroom. Behind the closed door she briefly debated hiding the ball of paper in one of the dressing table drawers so she could study it later. But that was taking too much of a chance. Hoping she would remember most of the information, she flushed the list and the half container down the toilet.

The thought of seeing Sanchez and Jed again made her hand shake as she washed her face and dabbed on a little of the eye shadow that was still in her cosmetic bag. Most of her tortoiseshell pins and combs were missing, so she brushed her hair back from her face and left it to fall loosely down her back.

The men would probably like the effect. For her the flowing hair was simply a visible sign of her loss of control.

So was the dress Anna had selected. As she had feared, it made her look like a village girl on her way to the big city. And the lack of a slip was unfortunate, she decided as she inspected her image in the full-length mirror. She could see her legs much too clearly through the gauzy fabric of the skirt.

With a grimace she rummaged through the closet. But there was nothing else that would do any better. She glanced at Anna again, wishing she was alone so she could look for the other capsule half. But that was impossible. When a guard knocked on the door, she squared her shoulders and ignored his scrutiny as she preceded him down the hall to the first floor.

El Jefe was waiting for her in a small sitting room that was almost as expensively furnished as his office. "You look quite refreshed," he remarked, sweeping his eyes up and down her body as if he could see it perfectly through the thin fabric of the dress.

Hands at her sides, Marissa kept herself from tugging at the shoulders to raise the neckline.

The general was wearing a formal uniform, the rows of medals on his chest another token of his elevated status compared to hers.

Anticipating Jed's imminent arrival, she glanced toward the door.

"I expect you're looking for your fiancé." Sanchez smiled as he spoke, yet there was an edge in his voice that made Marissa's nerve endings come to attention.

"Yes."

"He'll be along later. You and I got off on the wrong foot, so I invited you down a little early to make amends," he said, playing the part of the gracious host.

I'll bet, Marissa thought, studying him covertly as she took a seat on the couch. "I understand why you have to be suspicious of me," she remarked graciously as her mind flashed on the camera and the film she'd hidden in his toilet tank.

"Please, we won't let any past misunderstandings spoil the evening. What can I get you to drink? Sherry? White zinfandel?"

"Sherry." She kept her gaze trained on his back as he turned to the drink trolley in the corner. Even the way he poured from the cut glass decanter conveyed a posture of command. Yet he wasn't entirely at ease. Why? All sorts of disturbing speculations leaped to mind. Did he know something? Or was this a fishing expedition?

To regain her equilibrium, she tried to focus on the details of the room—like the bust of George Washington in the corner. Was Sanchez arrogant enough to see himself as an equally important military man?

Looking down at the beautifully inlaid table in front of her, she fixed her gaze on a small statue of the Mayan rain god. Too bad it wasn't the god of fools who get themselves into impossible situations. She could have offered up a prayer.

"Tell me, how did you and Jed meet?" Sanchez asked in a conversational tone as he offered her the drink.

So that was his game. He had her alone, and he was going to try to trap her. She took a small sip of sherry, aware that she had to keep her wits about her. "It's nice of you to take an interest in us."

"Jed and I are old friends. But we've lost touch. I'm counting on you to fill me in."

"We were both with the American embassy in Colombia."

"So you're into undercover work," he remarked too casually.

"Oh, no, nothing so glamorous," she answered with a little laugh. "Most State Department employees have enough to do without worrying about undercover assignments."

"Well, Jed's managed. How long ago were you in Colombia?"

"Five years."

"And the two of you have been close all that time?"

In response to the general's line of attack, Marissa felt her stomach tighten. Had he already asked her "fiancé" the same things so that he could compare their answers? Or would that come later? All at once she was glad of the information on the sheet in the capsule. At least she had a fund of personal details she hadn't known a few hours earlier.

She called up a little smile. "We didn't like each other at first," she answered, sticking with a sanitized version of the truth and playing for time. The longer she could stay with vague generalities, the better.

"Oh?"

"We were both too ambitious, I think. And then it was hard for a man like Jed to accept a woman as an equal."

Sanchez nodded, his full attention on her. It was all she could do to keep from wiping her sweaty palms on her skirt.

"But our work kept throwing us together. And gradually we realized we had a lot in common. We became engaged this year."

Sanchez shook his head. "I can't get over Jed's—how do you Americans put it—making a commitment. Even to someone as lovely as you."

"I like to think I've changed him." Mouthing that line made her stomach knot even tighter, but she kept her voice level.

"Some men do behave themselves when they're engaged. Did he ever tell you about the time we judged a wet T-shirt contest in Cozumel?"

Marissa's hand tightened on the glass of sherry. Sanchez was playing a version of "The Newlywed Game." Only the losing couple wasn't going to get a year's supply of dishwashing detergent as a consolation prize. They were going to be taken out and shot. She sighed and smiled. "I don't know every rowdy incident from his past, but it's no secret that he's enjoyed his bachelorhood."

"And what do you think of that hilarious tattoo on his thigh?"

Her cheeks warmed. "General, really! If you know about his tattoo, you know it isn't on his thigh." She gestured helplessly with her hands. "But I'm the last person you should be talking to about his wild past. What's important to me is that I've got him now, and I've decided it's better not to pry into the things he did before our engagement." The speech sounded convincing to her. She marveled that she hadn't choked on the last word.

Prolonging her agony, Sanchez studied her for silent moments, a smile flickering about his lips. "I apologize for tormenting you, my dear."

"Then let's change the subject."

"Of course. If you'll just satisfy a little more of my curiosity. When did he first kiss you?"

In front of the firing squad. Marissa felt light-headed as she frantically thought of and discarded answers.

"Our first kiss is a little too personal to talk about, don't you think, Miguel?" Jed answered from the doorway. He noted the frustrated look that flashed across *El Jefe*'s face before he managed to conceal the reaction. But

Jed knew how to read the signs. The situation was deteriorating.

He opened his arms to Marissa. Rising from the couch, she crossed to him.

"I'm glad you're here, dear heart," she whispered.

"So am I."

He folded her close, feeling the fine tremor of her body as she pressed her cheek against the starched front of his tuxedo shirt. At that moment he wished he'd worn something softer.

"Are they treating you all right? Did you get some rest, honey bee?"

"Yes. And yes."

"Good." He brushed his nose along her hairline, breathing in her clean, fresh scent, realizing such familiar gestures were becoming second nature.

"Mmm. I like what you do for Miguel's shampoo. But ask the maid to bring you some of that gardenia perfume I like."

He saw her swallow, but she didn't pull away. He couldn't stop himself from taking more liberties, nibbling his lips along her cheek and murmuring a low endearment. He knew Sanchez was watching. He might have argued that cuddling like this was an important part of their act. Except that he was rapidly forgetting about the audience. What he wanted was to draw Marci into a dark corner of the hacienda where they could be alone.

"How long were you standing there?" the general asked, reminding him that they were playing a deadly serious game. But that didn't mean he had to turn his fiancée loose.

"Long enough."

He'd been lurking in the doorway for several minutes listening to Miguel give Marci the third degree, and his admiration for her had grown as he'd noted her confident rejoinders. She'd made up some of her answers out of whole cloth. Others had come from the sheets of paper in the capsule. Lord, she was good under pressure. He'd been half tempted to find out what she would say about their first kiss. But he'd been angry at Sanchez for going too far.

He looked down at Marci and grinned. "Miguel loves to brag about that wet T-shirt contest. It's one of the highlights of his international travels."

Sanchez made a dismissive sound.

"He's a man of dramatic contrasts," Jed continued, knowing he was upping the ante by baiting *El Jefe,* but he needed to let off some steam. "It's all right for the guys from San Marcos to sow their wild oats when they're away from home. But out here on his *finca,* he's not letting an engaged couple sleep in the same bedroom."

Marissa made a little choking noise.

"I know things are quite a bit more liberal in the States," Sanchez said. "But in my country, engaged is one thing. Married is quite another."

"Married?" Marissa croaked.

Jed couldn't repress a little grin. "That's one solution to the problem. But I know your sister and the rest of the Light Street gang would never forgive me if I scuttled the big wedding they've been planning."

Marissa stared up at him with a slightly dazed look as if she'd just realized that an engagement was usually a prelude to a wedding ceremony. He pressed his fingers over her wrist, feeling her pulse leap.

Would marrying me be so bad? he wanted to ask. But he couldn't do it in front of Sanchez. Wasn't there anywhere they could risk having a personal conversation?

Even if they found some privacy, minor considerations like her reaction to him would have to take a back seat to the more important issue of how they were going to get out of San Marcos alive.

Still, he was in a reckless mood. "Just think how great making love is going to be when we finally get back together," he whispered, his fingers playing with a strand of hair at her temple.

Marissa swallowed hard.

"See, I'm actually doing you a favor," Sanchez said with a show of good humor.

"Thanks a lot, *amigo*."

The general slapped him on the back. "Now that I've whetted your appetite, why don't we go in to dinner."

Marissa's face was rigid as she turned and stepped rapidly into the hall. Jed wanted to tell her that bantering about women was a good way to distract Miguel, but he had no chance.

The dining room was large, with a table that seated sixteen. Only three places in the center were set with crisp white linen, fine china and gleaming silver.

Sanchez sat across one long end from his guests where he could watch both of them as he kept up the flow of questions through the avocados vinaigrette and the spicy seafood soup. The meal was a strange mixture of the native foods the general liked and the continental cuisine he felt obligated to serve.

The conversation was a mine field, full of traps for the unwary. Marissa was sitting with her left hand clenched in her lap. When Jed reached unobtrusively across to press his fingers over hers, he felt how cold her skin was.

The main course of stewed chicken with black beans was served. Miguel tore into the food, and Jed hoped he was going to concentrate on eating. But after several bites he was at the interrogation again like a dog with a succulent bone. "So your travel agency is located in Baltimore?" he asked Marissa.

"Yes."

"And Jed's still got his apartment in D.C.?"

"No. He moved to Laurel. To be closer to me."

"I've got half my stuff in her apartment, anyway," Jed added. "We'll get a bigger place after we're married. Maybe something like her sister's town house where we can each have our own bathroom, and I won't have to deal with panty hose drying over the shower rod."

Marci's face contorted as she wondered why he was going into so much intimate detail. Then it dawned on her that he was cutting into Sanchez's interrogation time.

They continued to answer questions, each letting the other take the ones that would sound most natural, and Marissa had the exhilarating feeling that she and Jed were working very well as a team. Perhaps they should have tried it before.

"How do you like his gun collection?" the general asked her, raising his voice above the barking of the dogs that had started outside.

Involuntarily, Jed's fingers dug into hers. Gun collecting had never been one of his hobbies.

"He must have it in storage. I haven't seen it," Marissa answered carefully.

Good for you. He gave her a little grin.

"And what—"

The general stopped in midquestion, interrupted by a slamming door. The noise was followed by a loud voice speaking urgently in Spanish. After several seconds the general got up. *"Un momento, por favor."*

"Certainly," Jed said.

"Stay here."

When the door closed behind him, he and Marissa were alone for the first time in hours.

Marissa could barely repress a scream of frustration. "I can't take much more of this," she blurted.

"I know, honey bee." Jed drew her out of her seat, away from the table and into his arms. She wanted to shout out that he was as much of the problem as Sanchez. She knew she had to keep up the role she'd been assigned, even when it looked as if the audience had disappeared. But if the strain continued like this, she was going to crack.

The noise level in the hall rose.

"Something's going on," Marissa whispered.

"Let's find out what."

"Maybe that's not such a good idea. He told us to stay here."

"I'm as tired as you of playing games." Jed strode to the door and pulled it open.

Peering around Jed, Marissa saw that a group of men had entered the front hall. Thomas Leandro, the socialist university professor, was gesticulating wildly to Sanchez. Behind him stood Pedro Harara, president of the Banco Nacional, and Louis Rinaldo, the minister of development.

The cliché *Latin temperament* leaped into Marissa's mind as she looked at the group that had apparently arrived unannounced. They were some of the leading citizens of San Marcos, and they were all wearing business suits as if they'd gotten up from their desks on short notice and driven directly to the general's *finca*. Yet they looked like an angry lynch mob.

"Where is the woman—Marissa Devereaux—you spirited away?" Leandro demanded. "I hope she's in good health."

"How do you know about that?" *El Jefe* asked, his own voice rising.

"Did you think you could keep it secret? Someone's been asking questions all over Santa Isabella."

Marissa stood transfixed as the front door was thrown open and William Johnson, the mysterious Texan who'd also been at the fateful party, marched into the hall. She didn't know how he fit into all this. But one thing was clear. He felt sure enough of himself with Sanchez to crash the party.

"Well, well. It looks like I've got you by the short and curlies this time. If you think—" He stopped in midsentence when he spotted Jed. "What's this got to do with *him?*" he snapped.

Sanchez turned, finding a focus for his anger in Jed.

There was shocked silence from the group in the hall as they followed his gaze.

"I told you to stay in the dining room," *El Jefe* snapped.

"And I told *you* I'm going to make sure nothing happens to Marissa."

"On that we're in agreement, since I had her brought here for her own protection. It's the only place in San Marcos I could be sure she'd be safe."

Marissa blinked. Had her sense of hearing suddenly failed? Brought here for her own protection? Directly from her prison cell. And then marched out in front of a firing squad. Who did the general think he was kidding?

Sanchez looked as if he were making a considerable effort to control himself as he continued to address Jed. "I'm sorry to cut short our dinner party, but my advisers and I have some internal problems to discuss. You will have to excuse us for the rest of the evening." He made a motion to the guards at the end of the hall and they stepped forward. "Escort my guests to their rooms."

Marissa tried to imagine the expression on Sanchez's face as he turned once again to the men in the hall. Whatever it was, he was back in charge of the situation. Nobody spoke. Nobody moved as the guards ushered her and Jed to the stairs.

Above them in the upper hall, Marissa thought she spotted something white and brown fluttering. She looked up in time to see Clarita sprinting in the opposite direction, her hair streaming out behind her. It was obvious she'd been up there listening to the commotion.

"Please, can you give me a moment with my fiancé?" Marissa asked the guard when he stopped in front of her room.

"No." Opening the door, he ushered her inside, and she was cut off from communication again.

The lock clicked behind her, and she wanted to kick the door in frustration. Instead she acted as if she had nothing better to do than get ready for bed. In the bathroom she changed into a nightgown and washed her face.

Outside on the grounds she could hear the dogs barking. Were more uninvited guests arriving? Or were the Dobermans after some poor animal?

Marissa tried to hang on to her anger. That had worked for her in the past to stave off fear. But tonight her anxiety was too high. She tried another tack. At the dressing table, she began to brush her hair with long, slow strokes the way her mother had taught her so many years ago.

One, two, three. Her concentration was broken at thirty when she heard several sets of heavy footsteps moving back and forth in the hall.

She tensed, listening. It looked as if Leandro, Harara, Rinaldo and Johnson had all come to the hacienda because they knew she was there. Did they want to rescue her? Or were they simply angry that Sanchez had acted on his own? Who on earth was William Johnson that he'd turn up in the middle of such a scene? And how would Jed's presence figure in?

Marissa set the hairbrush back on the counter, feeling the small amount of dinner she'd managed to eat churning in her stomach. As she returned to the bedroom she acknowledged that she would never get to sleep in this condition. But she didn't want whoever was manning the video cameras to see her pacing back and forth all night, either.

While she'd been in the bathroom, the little maid or someone else had come in and straightened the bed. Chagrined at her lack of awareness, Marissa flashed again on the capsule that was lost somewhere in the covers. She'd better find it before it tripped her up. But how? Maybe she could pretend she didn't like the way the bed had been made.

Crossing the room, she grabbed the covers and flipped them down to the bottom of the bed.

A bloodcurdling scream rose in her throat and burst out as she stared in horror at the black, wicked-looking thing she'd uncovered.

Chapter Seven

The black shape skittered across the taut sheet, the fine hairs covering its body shimmering in the light from the bedside lamp. It was a tarantula about six inches in diameter. It was alive. And its natural habitat was not her bed.

Blood roaring in her ears, Marissa backed away, watching the eight-legged creature move cautiously in the other direction. Probably it was as unhappy to see her as she was to find it under the covers. But that didn't make her feel any safer.

The spider had reached the bottom of the bed when the door burst open and one of the soldiers came dashing in.

"*Señorita.* What is it?" His posture was defensive and his rifle was at the ready.

With a shudder Marissa pointed to the spider.

"Stay back." Moving swiftly across the room to the bed, the guard swung the butt of his rifle against the sheet, coming down on the intruder with a mighty blow.

Sick to her stomach, Marissa looked away, imagining that she could hear the hairy black body exploding under the impact of the assault. From down the hall she could also hear Jed pounding on his door, alternately demanding to be let out of his room and to be told what had happened to her.

A splintering sound made her whirl.

Seconds later Jed careened past the guard, a chair leg held in front of him like a club. A wild and dangerous look was on his face as he glanced around the room and located Marissa. Making directly for her, he took her by the shoulders. "Honey, are you all right? What in the name of holy hell is going on?"

"A—a tarantula." Marissa gestured toward the bed.

He spun and raised the club. When he spotted the spattered blob near the footboard, he cursed. "You were in bed with it? It didn't bite you, did it?" He tossed away the chair leg. It clattered against the wall as he went down on one knee in front of her. Lifting her gown, he ran his hands along her legs, searching for bites.

She braced herself against his shoulders. "I—I was fixing the covers when I found it. Otherwise, I...would have—" The sentence choked off in a little sob.

"Marci. It's all right, Marci." His arms went around her, gathering her close so that his head was pressed to her middle.

Every defense she'd learned over the past few years urged her to pull away, and for the first few seconds she pushed against him. Then as she became aware of his warm breath on her navel and the scratchy feel of his beard against her stomach, rational thought deserted her. In that moment she couldn't remember why he had come into her room in the first place. Her eyelids drifted closed, and her hands tunneled through his hair, gathering him closer against her.

This time when he said her name, she felt the vibration of his lips. Transfixed, she forgot to breathe. For several heartbeats neither of them seemed capable of breaking apart.

Finally he stirred. As his warmth deserted her, she reached for him, but he climbed to his feet and stood in front of her shaking his head as if he were having the same problems as she. But when he anchored her with his gaze, he was all business. "Take your time, but tell me what happened."

Her bottom lip trembled. Too much was happening too fast, she thought for the second time that day. With Jed. With the danger closing in around them.

"Honey, stay with me."

He used the phrase from when he'd been about to show her the capsule. He must have known it would get her attention.

She nodded, struggling for coherence. "Somebody sneaked in here and left that in my bed...."

Jed murmured reassuring words as she stroked his hands across her shoulders. "The bite hurts, but it wouldn't have killed you."

"I know. But the idea of getting in bed with it makes me cringe." Eyes closed again, she pressed her face against his chest. It was then she realized for the first time that he was naked to the waist, and she was in her nightgown. As she stared at the well-developed muscles in his arm, her heart started to pound again.

But she knew she didn't want to untangle herself from the sense of safety his powerful body gave her. She closed her eyes and moved her cheek against his bare chest, feeling the springy hair against her flesh and breathing in the clean scent of his body, wishing with an ache in her heart that everything could be simple and uncomplicated between them. But nothing was simple. Not their personal relationship. Not the perils of Sanchez's *finca.*

Jed continued to gentle her, as if the two of them really did mean something to each other. For a moment she let that fantasy tantalize her again. She hadn't known one person could draw such comfort from the physical presence of another. When she felt his lips brush her hair, she sighed and snuggled closer to him.

"Let's get out of here."

She nodded, longing for him to take her away from this place of fear and confusion.

"You're not supposed to be together." The guard broke through the cocoon Jed had woven around them. "How did you get out of your room?"

"The doors aren't all that solid." He gestured toward the chair leg he'd dropped on the floor.

The man looked incredulous.

Marissa's gaze swung from Jed to the massive wood door of her own chamber. If he'd battered his way through one like that, he must be as strong as a stallion. Or desperate.

"Get the general up here." Without waiting for an answer, Jed crossed to the closet and began to shuffle through the clothes. Pulling a robe off the hanger, he came back and draped it over her shoulders.

"Thanks." She slipped her arms through the sleeves and pulled the belt tight.

"El Jefe. Pronto," Jed prompted, addressing the guard again.

The man shifted from one foot to the other as if he wished someone else had drawn this duty. "*El Jefe* is not supposed to be disturbed."

"Get him. Or I will."

The threat proved to be unnecessary. Sanchez himself appeared in the doorway, his expression dark as he looked from Jed to Marissa and back. She imagined he'd already seen the ruined door. "What's the meaning of this? You're supposed to be in separate rooms while you stay in this house."

"We were until I heard Marissa screaming."

"I demand to know what is going on."

Jed gestured toward the ruined bed. "Look. Somebody has it in for her. By now she could have been curling up to a tarantula. Luckily she stopped to fix the covers."

Sanchez appeared genuinely shocked, but he could have been faking the reaction. "The bite isn't fatal."

"Let's put one on your leg and see how you like it!" Jed growled. Then, making an effort to recover his composure, he spoke in a cooler tone. "Then you don't know anything about this?"

"Certainly not," Sanchez snapped.

"In the barracks sometimes we find tarantulas—and other wildlife," the soldier offered.

"Under the bed covers?" Jed inquired.

He shook his head.

"So who do you suppose put it there?" Jed asked his host. "One of your staff? Or one of your fire-breathing advisers? I suppose they all came up to inspect their own rooms."

"That's right. But none of them would dare try such a trick. Maybe it's just an unfortunate accident."

"Don't tell me you've started believing in coincidences?"

"We will discuss this in the morning."

"I can't sleep in that bed," Marissa choked out. "Not now."

El Jefe looked from her to the ruined sheet, considering. "You can move to another room."

"I'm staying with her," Jed growled.

"I don't think so."

Eyes narrowed, shoulders tense, the two men stood facing each other like gunfighters in old Dodge City. But in this case, only Sanchez had a gun in a holster on his belt.

Marissa saw the fingers of his right hand open and close, and she knew she had to defuse the tension between the two men. "Jed, it's okay," she managed to say. "The rules are different down here. We'll follow them while we're General Sanchez's guests. I don't want to have any more trouble tonight.''

Jed nodded tightly. Breaking away from the general, he came back to her and looked down into her eyes. "Are you going to be okay?''

"Yes.''

His gaze bored into hers, and she lowered her lashes. It was a futile gesture. She probably wasn't fooling him about her state of mind. She was a nervous wreck, and she wouldn't be okay until she was home. Maybe not then. But she had sense enough to keep her own counsel.

More soldiers were stationed in the hall, several of them excitedly inspecting the ruined door halfway down the corridor. Their buzz of conversation stopped abruptly and they snapped to attention when Sanchez appeared. He had a hurried consultation with a lieutenant before gesturing toward another wing of the house. "There are only two more rooms that are ready for visitors. Jaime will take you.'' Without further delay he hurried back down the steps.

Marissa spotted two shadowy figures standing in the lower hall craning their necks toward the action like spectators in the cheap seats at a boxing match.

From her vantage point she recognized Leandro's balding head and Harara's squat carriage. The professor caught her inquiring stare and looked guiltily away. Both men disappeared down the hall when they heard Sanchez's footsteps.

Had one of them slipped into her room while she'd been in the bathroom and put the spider in her bed? Not Leandro, certainly. He had been very friendly at the party. And he was reputed to be a pacifist. Of course, Harara was another matter. She'd sensed when they'd first been introduced that he didn't like her. But would he carry his dislike that far? And what about the other men who had arrived tonight? Johnson and Rinaldo. Maybe the perpetrator was deliberately staying out of sight.

She glanced at Jed, wondering if he'd also seen the spectators below. But he was walking with his head bowed. Moments ago his whole body had radiated tension as if he'd been plugged in to a light socket. Now he looked so tired he could hardly put one foot in front of the other.

"Are you all right?" she whispered.

"Yes."

She didn't like the automatic way he answered or the way he turned his face to the side so she couldn't see his eyes. But before they could say any more, she reached her new quarters. The lieutenant stepped between her and Jed, cutting off further communication.

When he opened her door she looked under his arm and saw Jed's guards stop in front of the next doorway. He halted, too, bracing his hand against the wall.

Her chest tightened. She wanted to go to him and find out what was wrong. But when she didn't immediately step into her room, the lieutenant took her by the shoulders and thrust her none too gently through the door.

"Wait."

Ignoring her plea, he shut it behind her with an ominous click. Then she was alone in a pitch-black room. She whirled on thick carpet. There wasn't even a sliver of light coming in from under the door.

"No. Let me out." Raising her fists, Marissa pounded against the rigid barrier. But no one answered, and she stopped after a few moments.

Closing her eyes to shut out the darkness, Marissa pressed her cheek against the smooth wood. Convulsively, her hand fumbled for the knob and twisted one way and then the other. It was a useless exercise. The door was locked. She was trapped in utter blackness. And it had been ten years since she'd felt anything but mindless fear in a dark room.

She understood the symptoms. Abby had explained to her about panic disorder. She knew exactly why this was happening to her. Yet she couldn't stop a fine sheen of perspiration from blooming on her skin. She couldn't stop herself from gasping air into her lungs like a half-drowned swimmer pulled from the bottom of a murky lake. And she couldn't stop the uncontrollable shaking of her body as her ears strained for the sound of someone approaching. Someone who was going to leap on her and—

She gritted her teeth and chopped off the thought. Not now. She wouldn't let this happen.

She *would not* let the old horror take over her mind and soul and make it impossible for her to function like a rational human being. The air around her felt thick and smothering. She wanted to sink to the floor and cover her head protectively with her hands. Instead she focused on taking shallow breaths. Knees locked so she wouldn't topple over, she reached out both hands and began to search along the wall for a light switch or table that might hold a lamp. Perhaps it was only seconds, but it felt like hours before her fingers brushed a switch plate.

Flipping the toggle, Marissa whimpered in relief as blessed light flooded down from a small chandelier. Leaning against the wall, she waited while her heartbeat returned to normal and the fine tremors stopped racing over her skin.

As she came back to normal, she began to look around the room. It was enough of a surprise that she shook her head in disbelief. While her previous quarters had been comfortable, these accommodations looked like the presidential suite in a five-star hotel. She was standing in a large seating area furnished with velvet-covered couches,

Oriental rugs and antique chest and tables. Through a doorway to the right was an even larger bedroom and through that she could see a balcony that looked out over the courtyard.

With a cynical twist of her mouth that only partly hid the fear in her eyes, she considered her surroundings. This room might be more opulent than the last one, but the door was still locked from the outside. That meant Sanchez could come in any time he wanted. Except that it wasn't only the general she had to worry about anymore. An angry group of his advisers had arrived at the hacienda. And someone had tried to…to what? Frighten her out of her mind? Put her out of commission and make it look like an unfortunate accident?

Marissa's skin felt clammy as she considered the possibilities. What was she going to do the next time a plate of food was in front of her? Surely it would be as easy to slip poison into her soup as it had been to slip a tarantula into her bed.

Sinking into one of the chairs, she cradled her head in her hands. She knew she was in danger of losing it—that she was overreacting to the darkness and to the peril all around her. But she simply couldn't help herself. She needed to feel that someone in this place was on her side. No, not just someone. She needed Jed.

As she pictured him, her hand stroked back and forth over the nubby fabric of the bedspread, and she realized she was remembering the feel of Jed's beard against her flesh. She whispered his name aloud as she thought about the way he'd acted at dinner—as if he was as unnerved as she by the questions designed to trip them up. And the way he'd battered down the door at the sound of her scream. It was pretty convincing evidence that he cared about what happened to her. Unless…

She bit back the rest of the thought. She had to hang

on to *something* or lose her mind. And whether Jed liked it or not, he was elected.

JED STOOD NEAR THE DOOR holding on to the wall, sucking in air and expelling it too rapidly. He knew he was hyperventilating. It made him light-headed. Yet he was pretty sure that wasn't the only reason he felt as if he were about to topple over.

Fear of what was happening to him clawed at his insides. He tried to find some reserve of physical and mental strength that would pull him out of the torpor into which he was rapidly sinking. But he was too bone weary.

He'd learned his limitations. He knew what could happen to him when he was running on empty. He'd even told Abby Franklin about it. And he knew he never should have gone berserk and battered that door down. Not in the kind of shape he was already in. But a wild panic had seized him when he'd heard Marci scream. He'd imagined one of Miguel's men stealing into her room to have some fun with her. Or worse—to plunge a knife into her heart. He'd had to save her, whatever the cost. So he'd demolished the barrier between them like a bull elephant trying to get to his mate. And now he was in serious trouble.

Unbidden, his gaze flicked to the bed. He'd been trying to pretend it wasn't there. All at once it was impossible not to stare at the wide, inviting surface. The thing he craved most in the world was to crawl under the covers, close his eyes and give in to blessed sleep. That was all he needed. Just a few hours in the sack and he'd be fine, he told himself. He took an unsteady step toward the bed, then another.

Before he reached it he made a strangled sound deep in his throat and bit down hard on his lower lip. The pain and the coppery taste of blood in his mouth brought back a little of his reasoning ability.

A hollow laugh rumbled in his chest. Who the hell did he think he was kidding? Only himself. It was happening again. The creeping sickness circulating in his bloodstream was taking over his body. And if he lay down it wouldn't be for a mere few hours. It would be more like a day and a half—if he was lucky.

He had to stay awake. Long enough for the terrible craving for sleep to pass. Then he'd be okay. He'd be okay because there was no alternative.

MARISSA SWALLOWED around the lump that had risen in her throat. Since the door had closed behind her, she'd been so focused on her own fears that she'd hardly been thinking about Jed except as her savior. Now that she was a little calmer, she started to consider the way he'd looked just before her view of him had been cut off. He'd gone from violently aggressive to pale and quiet in a matter of minutes.

Her mind made a terrifying leap. My God, had someone been after both of them tonight? Had she gotten the tarantula while Jed had been fed the poison? She might have dismissed the speculation as paranoia. But not in this house where new dangers seemed to spring up around every turn.

Fear clawing at her insides, she shouted Jed's name and pounded on the wall. There was no answer. Either he didn't hear or he couldn't answer. Her pulse was thumping wildly as she looked toward the sliding glass door. Could she get to Jed's room from the balcony?

Midway to the exit she stopped short, wondering if her mind had stopped functioning altogether. The moment she'd walked into her previous quarters she'd assumed she was being watched by a surveillance system.

Brow wrinkled, she tried to think it through, forcing herself to use precious seconds. Sanchez hadn't planned to put her and Jed in these rooms. Unless every bedroom in the whole hacienda was equipped with a video camera, this one could be safe. Still, as she stepped into the tropical night she pulled the drapes closed behind her.

The moon was half full, but it wasn't the only source of illumination. The stars shone down with a brightness that was startling to anyone who lived in a populated area where the ambient light drowned out the natural display. Here in the jungle it was difficult to recognize even the most familiar constellations because there were so many more stars than expected.

Marissa gazed across at the opposite wing of the house. Maybe there was no video camera inside her room, but if she tried to contact Jed, would someone be watching from one of the darkened windows? Would they come sweeping into the room and drag her down to the prison cells? She shuddered, but she didn't return to her room.

Cautiously she made her way to the railing. By leaning far out and peering to the right, she could see into the next room—the one that ought to be Jed's. A lamp was lit, and a surge of relief rose in her chest as she saw him.

Hope leaped in her breast. He was there! On his feet.

But her feeling of relief died almost as soon as it was born. Jed was shuffling slowly across the carpet like a man whose feet were encased in cement boots. As she watched, he flopped into a chair by the window, threw his head back and closed his eyes.

In the next moment his head jerked up again and his lids snapped open. He seemed to be looking in her direction. Mouthing his name, she waved her arms in a wide arc. He didn't respond, but perhaps with the light on beside him, he couldn't see her through the glass. Charging back into her room, she looked around for something suitable to throw at the window—something that wouldn't break but that would still be heavy enough to attract attention. The only thing that came to hand was a small metal vase sitting on one of the tables. Bringing it out to the balcony, she judged the distance to Jed's window as she weighed the missile in her palm. Then she pitched it in an underhand throw that landed it against the bottom of the glass.

Her swing was a little too vigorous. But she was lucky the glass hadn't broken. The loud clanging noise of the vase colliding with the glass made her glance around anxiously for a squad of soldiers or a pack of barking dogs. But no one came running to investigate.

Looking back at the window, she expected to see Jed standing with his hands cupped against the glass trying to figure out what was going on. But he was still sitting in the same position in the chair, staring vacantly as if he were oblivious to his surroundings.

The hair on the top of her scalp prickled. If he hadn't heard that clatter, something was seriously wrong.

Marissa stared at the seven feet of dead space that separated her balcony from Jed's. Hitching up her gown, she climbed outside her railing, held on with her left hand and stretched as far as she could with her right foot. But she couldn't touch the other side.

Looking down, she grimaced in frustration. It was only one story to the ground. But the patio below her was cement. If she fell, she could break a bone—or knock herself unconscious. Then the dogs would be on her.

She turned her gaze to Jed again. He was sitting in exactly the same position, apparently unaware of what was happening even though he was staring in her direction. Her throat constricted with apprehension. He needed her. She felt it in her bones. And that knowledge had a curiously steadying effect on her roiling emotions. Since she'd been thrown into one of Sanchez's cells, she'd lost control of her fate. When Jed had appeared out of nowhere she'd been in danger of surrendering to his strength. That role had made her uneasy. Now there was something *she* had to do for *him,* and she wasn't going to let him down.

Turning back toward the house, she inspected the vines growing on the wall. She would have liked a more secure ladder, but they were her only option.

After tying her gown and robe around her hips so her legs would be free, she climbed up on the railing and grabbed a handful of ropelike lengths. Yanking hard, she tested them as best she could, hoping they would support her weight.

Fingers mentally crossed, she transferred her grip to the vine. It still seemed to hold, so she stepped off the railing. Hanging twelve feet in the air, she began to inch cautiously toward the far balcony, feeling her handholds and footholds in the foliage.

When she was halfway across the chasm there was a terrible ripping sound, and then the awful sensation of falling as the vine gave way.

Chapter Eight

Acting purely on instinct, Marissa threw herself to the left, bouncing painfully against the far railing as pieces of vine rained onto her head and shoulders. Luckily her reflexes were good. Somehow in the tangled confusion of greenery she managed to hook her fingers over the metal balustrade to keep from plummeting to the concrete below.

Eyes closed against the debris, she held on for dear life until the sky stopped falling around her. When she was certain it was safe to move, she pulled herself over the railing, then lay sprawled on the balcony surface, breathing hard, surrounded by broken stems and torn leaves. Cautiously she sat up and assessed the damage. Her shoulder throbbed, but moving it didn't cause any additional pain. So it was probably only bruised. In fact, she seemed to be in remarkably good shape, she decided as she brushed plant debris from her clothing. Apparently no one had heard the commotion. On the other hand, anyone walking below who happened to glance up would realize something drastic had happened. But if she was lucky, that wouldn't be a problem until morning.

Never mind how she'd get back to her own room.

Pulling herself up, she brushed the leaves from her robe and readjusted the front, half expecting Jed to come charging outside to investigate the commotion.

He didn't. As she retied her belt, she peered through the window. He still appeared to be looking in her direction, yet he was sitting in the chair, unmoving, as if he was watching a television screen instead of a death-defying performance on his balcony.

Fear hastening her movements, she yanked open the sliding glass door and stepped inside. "Jed?"

No response.

In half a second she was across the room. Sinking to her knees in front of him, she grasped his large hands in her smaller ones. They were so cold that she sucked in a startled breath. God, he felt as if he'd been in a morgue.

Panic threatened to swamp her, but she forced it down as she studied him more closely, intent on grasping every detail of the situation. He was dressed almost as she'd encountered him last, in the tuxedo pants from this evening. But he'd kicked off his shoes as he'd crossed the room. From the corner of her eye she saw one near the bed. The other was closer to the chair.

His skin was the color of oatmeal. His eyes were still open, but they were unblinking, and they had turned the hue of ice frozen for centuries in an arctic wasteland. Even more alarming, his breathing was so shallow that she wasn't sure she could detect it. Frantically she pressed her hand against his naked chest, burying her palm in the springy hair, feeling for the beat of his heart. She felt no sign of life. That was when gut-wrenching fear really slammed into her. Gasping, she probed harder, her fingers digging into his flesh. The breath left her lungs in a rush when she found a slow but steady beat.

Marissa eased the pressure when she realized that her fingernails were gouging him, although he gave absolutely no sign that he felt the pain. For that matter, he didn't seem aware that she was even in the room.

What in the name of all that was holy could have happened to him so quickly? A half hour ago he'd been ready to duke it out with Sanchez. But something had changed radically. And the only hypothesis that made sense was that her wildest suspicions had been confirmed.

He'd been poisoned. Maybe at dinner. Maybe from food or water in his room. Was Sanchez responsible? Or someone else?

She bit back a frightened sob. Jed's life might depend on getting him to a doctor quickly. But she didn't even know if there was a physician out here in the country—or if he'd be willing to risk getting involved with a patient Sanchez was holding in a locked room.

She hardly knew she was mumbling aloud—half pleas to Jed to come back to her, half pleas to the almighty to bring him back. Opening his knees, she moved between them so that she could get closer as she continued to chafe his cold hands, stroke his bare arms and winnow her fingers through the hair on his chest. Unconsciously she was trying to bring him back to life with her touch. At the same time, some part of her mind realized dimly that she needed the physical contact as much as he.

"I'll get help," she murmured, her lips moving against his cold cheek, her hand cupping possessively around his head. "You'll be okay. You have to be." She started to scramble to her feet when a whisper of sound from his lips made her go very still. Her attention snapped back to his face.

Somehow in her frenzy of touching him and talking to him, a tiny part of the glazed look had lifted from his eyes. He was staring at her, and this time she was sure that he was really seeing her, that he knew who she was. His lips moved, and he seemed to be making a tremendous effort to communicate. What finally came out was a strangled version of her name.

"Mar...ci."

"Oh, Jed, I'm here. Just hang on. I'm going to get a doctor."

The muscles around his mouth contorted into a grimace. "N...o."

She hadn't expected an answer—or an argument from a man in this condition. "I think you've been poisoned," she blurted and then immediately wished she hadn't said so much. She didn't need to add fear to his problems.

He shook his head, the barest movement. She might have missed the gesture if she hadn't been focused on him with every ounce of her concentration.

"I'll be right back."

"Stay...." He gasped in air and expelled it in a series of disjointed syllables. "Happ...ens...to...me." It sounded as if he were dredging up each word from the depths of his soul, letter by painful letter, and she had the feeling he was determined to make the explanation or die.

She clenched her hands in frustration. It was hard to understand his slurred speech—and equally hard to judge if he really knew what he was saying or if he was hallucinating.

Torn between going for help and listening to what he was trying to say, she angled her head so she could get a closer look at him. As she searched his face, she saw that his eyes were piercing, almost pleading for her aid.

"What are you talking about?" she whispered.

"Happ...ened...before...." His tongue flicked against his lips. "Wat...er."

Marci glanced toward the door and back to Jed again.

His hands tightened on hers, the pressure weak but urgent. "Help...."

Torn in two, she tried to decide what to do. She was taking a terrible risk, but his wishes were so strong that she couldn't ignore them. Rising, she sprinted to the bathroom. When she returned with a glass of water, he still hadn't moved, but she could see that his eyes were tracking her, and her heart surged as she realized the improvement in only a few minutes. If he'd been poisoned, wouldn't he be getting worse—not better?

She knelt beside him again, supporting his head with one arm and lifting the glass to his lips with the other. He spilled a little as he drank thirstily, and she wiped her hand against his chin, vividly conscious of the intimacy of helping him with something so basic.

When half the water was gone, he closed his eyes and sighed deeply. She brushed the damp hair back from his forehead. His color was pinker, his breathing more regular. Pressing her hand against his chest, she decided that even his skin temperature seemed closer to normal. Silently she offered a little prayer of thanks.

He was watching her closely. All at once she didn't feel comfortable with her hand plastered against his naked chest. Not when he was staring at her with such intensity. Trying to look matter-of-fact, she lifted her palm away and took his wrist, probing the pulse point. It took a few seconds to feel anything, because the beat was still alarmingly slow. "Are you feeling better?"

"Pain."

She was immediately alert. "What hurts?"

"Noth...ing." She saw his Adam's apple bob. "Need...hit...me."

"What?" She gasped, tipping her head to the side, wondering if she'd heard right and, if she had, whether his mind was coming up with nonsense.

"Need...stimu...la...tion...wake...up...." In his present condition, saying more still seemed to be too much effort.

"Jed, I can't hit you."

"Have...to...."

The urgency in his voice tore at her heart. She felt as

if she had stumbled into a world where black and white had somehow gotten reversed and she was being asked the unthinkable.

"Pain."

The desperation in Jed's voice made her pull back her arm and drive her fist against his shoulder. It wasn't much of a blow. She simply couldn't make herself hit him with much force.

"Harder."

"I'm sorry. I can't."

His eyes searched hers. "Then...other..."

She leaned forward, her ear turned toward his lips to catch his whispered words.

"Other ... stim ... u ... la ... tion ... wake ... me ...up...."

There was a long, pregnant silence in the room.

"What should I do?" Even as she asked, she saw the way his gaze had focused on her lips. He didn't have to spell out what kind of stimulation could affect him as strongly as pain. She could figure that out for herself. When she'd first come into the room and knelt beside him, he'd been cold as ice and barely breathing. Instinctively she'd started to stroke and touch him. The physical contact had made a tremendous difference. He'd come back to life enough to communicate with her. Now she had to bring him all the way back. If she couldn't hurt him, she'd have to please him. With intimacy. Touching.

She couldn't meet his eyes. Feeling as if a giant knot were twisting in her middle, she raised her eyes to his. Even a few days ago she might have suspected that he'd somehow rigged this performance to see how far she would go. Tonight she sensed how much he needed her.

And the realization was like a power trip.

Moving around to the front of the chair, she came up

on her knees so that her mouth was level with his. She felt his breath, felt his tension as he waited for her kiss.

Like Sleeping Beauty, she thought. Only in reverse.

Could she heal him? And perhaps herself? With something so simple yet so profound as a kiss? For one dizzying moment she felt as paralyzed as he. Then she leaned forward and brushed her lips against his as if sealing her fate—and his.

Marissa wasn't sure what she had anticipated. In the back of her mind she half expected that his arms would suddenly snap up and trap her so that any choice she had was taken away. But his large hands remained where they were, palms turned downward, fingers slightly curled, lying on the arms of the chair.

She was testing the waters as she turned one of his hands over, stroking his fingertips gently and then pressing her palm flat against his. When she felt a slight answering pressure, she let out the breath she'd been holding.

"Don't...stop...please."

It gave her an unaccustomed feeling of potency to know that she could bring him back to life. With a sense of awe, she touched his cheek with her fingertips, dragging them up and down, enjoying the way the scratchy endings of his beard moved under her touch—astonished at how much pleasure the simple contact gave her.

He didn't move, but his total attention was focused on her. She kept her gaze on him as she swept her hair over her shoulders and out of the way. She thought she could see the green of his irises deepen when she reached to stroke the arches of his brows, brushing the hairs in the wrong direction and then smoothing them back into place.

He made a sound deep in his throat, a sound that urged her lips back to his.

The first touch made her sigh. She was quickly caught

up in the delight of rubbing her lips back and forth against his once more, teasing him—and herself. She'd never thought she'd have the nerve to play with a man this way. Certainly not *this* man. Part of her was overwhelmed. Part was honest enough to admit how much she was enjoying the heady sensation of power and pleasure.

She cupped Jed's face in her hands; then, with her tongue, she traced the curve of his lips, feeling his shivering reaction all the way to her toes.

"Do you like that?" she asked in wonder, marveling that she could make him tremble.

His answer was a rough growl. For the first time since the contact had begun, he moved, opening his mouth silently, asking her to deepen the kiss.

"Jed." She spoke his name against his lips, nibbling, tasting, testing as she felt something hot and sensuous unfurl within her. He wasn't the only one coming alive. Sensual feelings spiraled through her, making her cry out.

The desire for more was a force she was powerless to resist. Her tongue stroked the insides of his lips and along the edges of his teeth, and she marvelled at the contrast of textures—velvety soft, hard and rigid. The exploration brought her to a new level of sensuality. But it wasn't enough. Caught up in the heady sensations, she wanted—needed—more. She heard herself make a strangled little sound as she sealed her mouth to his, swaying forward so that the upper half of her body was pressed against him.

Marissa wasn't sure when Jed's tongue began to move against hers, wasn't sure when his hands came up to stroke across her back and then tangle in her hair. She was so totally caught up in the encounter that she didn't even know which of them had pulled the robe off her shoulders so that only the thin barrier of her gown separated his heated flesh from hers. But one of them must have dispatched the garment because she was suddenly vividly aware of her breasts moving against his naked chest, her nipples tingling with pleasure at the contact with his thatch of springy blond hair.

Tiny shudders of sensation racked her body, making her inner muscles clench. She hadn't known desire could be this overwhelming, this frantic, this insistent. Had she really denied herself this pleasure for so long?

She was still kneeling on the floor in front of him.

"Marci. Honey." He gathered her up in his arms, pulling her half onto his lap. She sprawled across him, her middle pressed to his. He murmured endearments as his lips nibbled a trail down her neck, then to the V between her breasts.

His hot tongue against her sensitized flesh made her gasp. With his face he nudged aside the top of her gown, his mouth moving back and forth, tantalizing first one breast and then the other. When his mouth found one hardened nipple, she cried out and arched against him, dazed by the pleasure of it. And shocked to the core.

Somewhere along the line the rules had changed. She was no longer the one in charge. She was still hot and wanting. But now a voice inside her head was talking to her, warning her about the monster she'd unleashed.

She thrust it aside, choosing to remain captive in the web of sensuality that bound her to Jed. She wanted him. Wanted him to take her where she'd been afraid to venture. If she could only go ahead and let that happen, it would work out all right. She'd come this far. She could go the rest of the way because it was Jed who was kissing her and touching her, and making her feel so needy. But she didn't have to be frightened; she was safe with him. Then he moved, holding her as he lowered her backward. All at once he was coming down heavily on top of her on the rug. She was trapped. And the fear she'd been so sure she had overcome came surging back in full force.

When she began to struggle, his hands held her so that she couldn't move. With a panicked sob she pushed against him.

"Jed. No. Please."

He was still weak. And she was infused with the strength of near hysteria. Desperately she wiggled away. When he reached for her again, she managed to keep several inches of heated space separating her body and his.

Her breath came in jagged little gasps. So did his.

He looked confused. "Marci, I thought you wanted this."

With shaking hands she pulled her bodice back into place. Then she found her robe where it had fallen on the floor, hauled it over her shoulders and drew the front closed. Pretending that the fabric could protect her from what she was feeling. Mortification. Sexual frustration.

She wanted to curl into a ball and hide her face from him. She wanted to run from the room. Somehow she managed to stay there, facing him.

"What's wrong?"

"We can't. You can't..." She heard the turmoil in her own voice and struggled for calm. Her emotions were too raw for her to explain her panic attack.

"Wrong."

"Jed...a little while ago I thought you were dying. That's how this started. You asked me to—to—"

His face hardened. "I see. You were on a mission of mercy, and it got out of hand."

"No. I mean—" She ran a trembling hand through her hair, wondering what to say.

He leaned back against the bottom of the armchair, drawing in large drafts of air, and she knew he wasn't going to force himself on her.

Half guilty, half relieved, she continued. "I was so

frightened when I came in and found you like that. What happened to you?''

''You don't need to know.''

She pinned him with her gaze, thankful for the change of subject. ''Don't I? Jed, how do you think I got into your room?''

''I—'' He stopped and looked toward the window as if he were dredging up a distant memory. ''You came across from your balcony to mine,'' he said slowly. ''The vines broke, and you fell. You could have killed yourself.

''You mean you saw me? But you were just sitting there like a statue.''

His face was grim. ''I remember it—sort of like a dream. I couldn't move.'' As if in denial he flexed his arms.

''I thought you were in a coma or something. I thought that you'd been poisoned.''

''I was.'' His voice was low and raspy. His eyes told her that he wished he hadn't shared the information.

She felt goose bumps rise on her arms. ''By Sanchez? Tonight?''

''No. Years ago. On an assignment in Royal Verde.'' His voice sounded like ground glass.

''What...what happened?''

''I'll tell you about it when we have more time. All you need to know is that you can't count on me in an emergency because I'm likely to go tharn on you,'' he said bitterly. ''You know what that means?''

''Yes.'' He'd used a word Richard Adams had made up in *Watership Down.* It referred to the way his rabbit characters froze in place when faced with danger.

She scooted across the rug and took his hand. ''You're not like that.''

He grimaced. ''Oh, yeah? I thought I just gave you a graphic demonstration. I was sitting in the chair watching you almost kill yourself, and there wasn't a damn thing I could do about it. The stuff that does it to me is still in my system,'' he snapped. ''It always will be.''

''I don't understand. You were fine until tonight.''

''Usually I'm normal. But when I'm overtired and under a lot of stress, my body reacts by shutting down,'' he said harshly, as if he were revealing that he'd let himself become addicted to drugs.

She tried to get through to him with the steady pressure of her hand over his, wishing he would turn his palm up. But he seemed to be simply enduring her touch. ''It's not your fault.''

''But it's my *problem.* It limits my ability to do my job.''

''Is this thing why you had to quit the Peregrine Connection?'' she blurted.

He snatched his hand away. ''How do you know about that?''

''You hear things.''

''That's just great! What else is grist for the rumor mill?''

''Nothing,'' Marissa managed.

Still, anger simmered in Jed's eyes as he looked away, and she wished she hadn't asked the question. Or maybe she'd done it on purpose, to punish him because he'd made her lose control. Only she knew the accusation was a lie. Losing control had been *her* problem.

''Jed, I'm sorry,'' she whispered. ''I know—''

''How I feel?'' he cut in. ''Were you really going to use that line? Somehow I seriously doubt that you know how I feel.'' Pushing himself up, he swayed on unsteady legs.

She scrambled off the rug and reached a steadying arm toward him, but the mortification in his eyes made her hand drop back to her side.

"I'll be okay in a minute." After taking several deep breaths he made his way to the window where he stood looking out into the night.

Marissa stared at his rigid shoulders, sharing more of his pain than he could imagine. With all her heart she wanted to go to him, comfort him. And make amends for pushing him away when her passion had led him to believe she wanted him. She especially wanted to make amends for that. She *had* wanted him. Only she hadn't had the guts to go through with it. Because she was still fighting her own demons.

Would it make him feel better if he found out how closely she could identify with him? How much they were alike? All at once she wanted to tell him about the unspeakable thing that had happened to *her*. For the first time in years she was willing—no, anxious—to talk about her own worst nightmare. No matter what the personal risks.

Scrambling up, she crossed the space between them. "Jed, I—"

He turned, and she saw that he looked amazingly like his old self. "I'm feeling a lot better."

"I see that." She also saw that a mask had dropped over his face. He'd hated admitting weakness to her, and he was dealing with it the only way he could.

"Thank you for helping me." He might have been thanking her for helping him fix a flat tire for all the emotion he put into the acknowledgment.

"I was frightened for you. I wanted—"

"To wake me up."

"It was a lot more than that." She gulped. Unless she explained what had happened to her, she'd lost him.

However, he continued as if she hadn't spoken. "I guess I should have told you about my little infirmity before I asked you to marry me, honey bee," he said tightly, his gaze sweeping the room before boring into hers.

"Oh." She realized with a start that she'd been so focused on herself and Jed that she hadn't remembered the house rules. There was always the possibility that the room was bugged, and someone might be listening very avidly to what they were saying. She and Jed were supposed to know each other intimately. In fact, their lives might depend on maintaining that fiction.

She was pretty sure he hadn't been thinking about their deception a few moments ago. But as he'd regained his strength, his mind had snapped back into focus.

Her own thoughts raced over the minutes they'd just spent together, trying to examine what they'd said from the point of view of someone glued to a microphone. It might sound as if they weren't communicating too well. But at least neither of them had talked about anything incriminating—with regard to the two big issues at stake, her search of Sanchez's office and their bogus engagement.

And what about the way they'd abruptly broken off lovemaking? She flushed, but her thought processes churned on. It was logical that she might have stopped things because she was worried about Jed's health. Logical, too, that he might not have shared every unpleasant episode from his past.

From his point of view, the worst part of the exchange was that he'd told her an important secret about himself—something that threatened his masculine ego. Something he wouldn't want the general or anyone else to know. In return she'd nearly made a confession that would have handed *El Jefe* the key he needed to break her. Thank God Jed had stopped her.

"What are we going to do?" she whispered.

He fixed her with a wry look. "For starters, unwind in a nice hot shower together."

"What?" Marissa's voice cracked on the syllable. Had she heard that right?

"Now that I finally have you where I want you," he added, then slowly and distinctly mouthed, "Where we can talk." He watched her intently to make sure she'd understood.

Reluctantly she nodded. He was right. The only way they were going to be sure they couldn't be overheard was if some heavy background noise drowned out the sound of their voices. But did it have to be a shower? In desperation she looked around the room. If there had been a radio or a television set, she would have turned it on full blast. But neither device had been provided.

Jed started toward the bathroom, his steps a good bit surer than they had been a few minutes ago. Marissa stared at the broad expanse of his naked back, profoundly relieved that he was feeling better, yet at the same time nervous. He was taking charge again whether she liked it or not.

On legs that felt like someone else's limbs she followed, wondering where she'd find the nerve to go through with what he was suggesting.

The bathroom was large and luxurious, but when Jed closed the door it seemed to shrink to a tiny cell.

Jed turned on the taps full force. His next step would be to disrobe. It was a sure bet that he wouldn't get in the shower with his pants on.

Marissa clenched her hands at her sides and somehow kept herself from backing out of the room. If she'd only been smart enough not to get caught in Sanchez's office in the first place. But here they were in enemy territory with very few options—and it was her fault. Without giving herself time to think about what she was doing, she snatched off her robe and let it drop to the floor.

Jed pivoted back, towering over her, his eyes darkening as they swept over her translucent gown. When they lingered on her bodice, she felt her nipples contract.

She swayed toward him, the flame ignited by their passion still glowing inside her. Then she stopped herself with a hand on the edge of the sink.

He gave her a half smile, slightly mocking, a little sad, mostly reassuring. "We both know there's unfinished business between us."

She moistened dry lips. "Jed, I'm having trouble handling this."

He pitched his voice well below the sound of the pounding water. "You want me."

"We have to talk about us."

He sighed. "When we get out of here. Right now, you don't have to go any further with this shower deal if you don't want to."

"What?"

He stepped closer and lifted her palm to his lips. Transfixed, she felt his gentle kiss. Somehow it steadied her nerves. She hadn't thought he'd be capable of gentleness after what had happened. But he was full of surprises. She knew she had only begun to learn what made Jed Prentiss tick, and she wanted to find out more.

Taking her by the shoulder, he dipped his mouth near her ear. "My educated guess is that our friend doesn't have a video camera in here. Just audio, if that. It ought to be as safe to talk like this as it is under the running water. For a few minutes, anyway."

She swallowed hard, thankful that he was letting her off the hook. "Thank you."

His next words made her head snap up.

"The first thing I have to know is if you trust me."

It was an honest question. She gave him an honest answer. "I wasn't sure at first. I thought you and Sanchez might have cooked up some kind of deal to get me to talk."

"And now?"

"I know you're on my side." When they got out of San Marcos there was a lot more she planned to say. But it would have to wait.

"That's something, anyway. Because we've got to rely on each other to get out of here."

"Yes."

They stripped the conversation to its bare essentials, a hurried exchange of information in staccato bursts of speech.

"Was it your idea to pretend that we were engaged?" she asked.

"Jason came up with the basic plan. Abby refined it," he replied.

"She would. What happens now?"

"I was hoping Miguel would buy the distraught-fiancé act. Now I'm not so sure. Maybe Harara will help us."

"He hates American women."

"He owes me a favor."

"What if he's afraid of Sanchez?"

Jed looked frustrated.

"Maybe there's something we can use. Or maybe it's too dangerous. When I was in his office, I found something."

"Good." His hands gripped her shoulders.

"It's hidden—" Marissa stopped abruptly when she heard a noise in the bedroom.

Jed cursed under his breath. With instant awareness and lightning speed he reached for Marissa and pulled her into his arms. Lowering his mouth to hers, he gave her a hard kiss that she knew would leave her lips reddened.

Seconds later the door burst open, exposing them to hostile eyes.

Chapter Nine

Marissa clung to Jed for stability, gasping as his lips moved over hers like a passionate lover with nothing more urgent on his mind than making the most of a clandestine tryst. However, there was no way she could respond to him as her ears strained to catch the first words from whoever had burst into the room. She could only stand where she was, holding on to Jed, and let him take charge of the performance.

"That's enough," a harsh voice commanded.

Taking his time, Jed slowly lifted his head and turned toward the intruder in the doorway.

Miguel Sanchez glared at them, his gaze flicking to Marissa's reddened lips and then insinuatingly down the length of her gown. "You know this is against the rules."

"Miguel, don't you think this moral mania of yours has gone far enough?" Jed asked mildly. "Since when do you come barging in to your guests' bedrooms?"

The general's eyes glittered dangerously as he regarded them. It had to be after two in the morning, but he was still wearing the dress uniform he'd donned for dinner. Now it was rumpled, and patches of sweat showed under his arms. "Bedrooms. Separate bedrooms."

"See, I told you they were together." The high-pitched female voice in back of him stabbed through Marissa.

Craning her neck, she drew in a startled breath as she caught sight of Clarita. She blinked. The teenager was dolled up as if she were on her way to a nightclub. Heavy shadow set off her dark eyes, her lips were a red slash and her dress was a low-cut gown that showed off too much of her creamy breasts. Her heavy perfume hung in the air, while she stood rubbing her hands as if she were lathering them with soap.

"I said you couldn't trust the woman to follow your orders. I said she was out to make trouble. But you never listen to me. You're one of the ones against me. Like her." There were more accusations. Clarita's words came out in a torrent like a fountain under sudden pressure.

Marissa expected Sanchez to stop her quickly. Instead he looked angry and frustrated.

Marissa stared at Clarita, trying to take the whole thing in, trying to reconcile the various impressions she'd formed of the girl. Her behavior was erratic, hostile, unbalanced, Marissa realized. For a long moment Clarita stared back, her eyes glittering with a hysterical light. As quickly as the storm of words had risen, it subsided, and quite suddenly she shrank against the wall, looking down at her feet.

Jed had angled his body so that Marissa was slightly behind him. When he spoke, it was to Clarita. "Little one, we mean you no harm. Why are you spying on us?"

She shook her dark hair so that it fell in soft waves over her shoulders. "To prove I was right. And don't call me by baby names. I'm hardly a child anymore."

"I see that," he muttered, as if he were having trouble relating this person to the girl he used to know. "But that doesn't mean we have to stop being friends."

"I thought we were," she snapped. "Until I found out you were against me."

"Now what in the name of the blessed virgin is going

on?" The question came from the hallway. They all turned toward the bedroom as Pedro Harara, clad in a red silk robe, strode through the door. Moments later he was joined by the other three men who had arrived unexpectedly that evening. Johnson looked as if he'd hastily pulled on his pants and shirt. Leandro and Rinaldo were in nightclothes. But only Leandro looked as if he'd actually been asleep.

There were several seconds of dead silence while the professor nervously finger-combed his hair over his bald spot.

Then Sanchez laughed and held out his arm dismissively as if he'd been interrupted scolding two naughty children. "You know how it is when visitors from a more permissive society come here. They have trouble conforming to our quaint, old-fashioned ways. I've explained the rules to Jed and Marissa more than once. In this house we set an example for the youth of San Marcos. Engaged couples must sleep in their own rooms. But these two keep finding ingenious ways to get together."

"I know what you mean. I had the same problem with my daughter," Rinaldo said. "I was afraid she was going to disgrace the family name with a tell-tale bulge at the front of her wedding dress."

"How did you handle it?"

He gave a little cough. "Expediently. I moved up the wedding date."

"Ah." Sanchez's face took on a contemplative look. "Now there's a good idea," he murmured, his manner becoming expansive as the idea took hold. "If these lovebirds can wait one more night, we'll hold a wedding ceremony here tomorrow. Then I can stop playing *dueña* and get back to more important business."

Marissa's mouth dropped open. Had she heard him right? "A...wedding?" she croaked.

"Yes. It's short notice, but my people will love the excuse for a fiesta." Sanchez grew more animated as he got down to the particulars. "First thing in the morning I'll contact the village priest and the woman who sees to the bride's instruction. We have our own traditions here that go back centuries. You'll find they add to the sense of ceremony."

The more details he added, the more Marissa felt her throat constrict. This wasn't happening. This man wasn't planning her wedding and intending to carry out the plans tomorrow. Yet he was. Somehow she dredged up a coherent objection. "We can't get married in San Marcos. My...my sister has everything planned at home."

"I know Jed mentioned your friends back in Baltimore. If they're disappointed, you can have a second ceremony when you get back." Sanchez grinned conspiratorially. "You can even keep this one secret, if you like."

Perhaps the general had more to say. But Marissa heard nothing besides the roaring in her ears. Married to Jed. Impossible. If she'd thought she'd be forced into this position, she would have— What? She had no answer. And she'd never felt less in control of her destiny.

She wanted to bolt from the room. Perhaps Jed had read her mind because he kept a hand on her shoulder. His grip wasn't tight, but somehow it held her in place. She felt as if she was going to pass out. Miraculously, she stayed on her feet.

For the second time that evening Jed must have helped her on with her robe, because she found herself wearing it. Dazed, she followed the general back to her room, and moments later she was alone. Without regard to who might be looking, she sank onto the bed, cupped her face in her hands and rocked back and forth, feeling sick and terrified. And desperate.

"WHAT THE HELL ARE YOU trying to pull?" Jed growled as he strode into Sanchez's office. He'd stopped to put on a shirt and shoes that didn't go with the tuxedo pants he was still wearing. At least his bedroom door hadn't been locked, undoubtedly because Miguel was trying to make it look as if he and Marci were guests instead of prisoners. Thank God for small favors.

"I'm convinced you care for Señorita Devereaux. As much as rascals like you or I can care for a woman," *El Jefe* answered.

"I don't need you to run my love life."

"It's a bit more than that, *amigo.*"

Jed took a deep breath. He was angry with himself and angry with Sanchez. But he'd better stop showing it. This was the first private conversation he'd had with the general since he'd charged onto the field and snatched Marci from the firing squad. Since then, Sanchez had had a chance to think things through and decide how he was going to proceed. But he was also under pressure from the contingent who had arrived this evening. "Why don't you fill me in?" he asked, hoping his elevated heart rate didn't filter into his voice.

Sanchez shrugged and spread his hands in a palms-up gesture. "We keep coming back to the basic fact that your fiancée got herself invited to a reception at my house, then slipped out and stole into my office. I have no way of knowing if her story about the door being unlocked is true—or if she broke in. Nor do I know what she might have tampered with before the guard found her."

"She didn't tamper with anything!" Jed retorted, his voice imbued with righteous indignation.

"How can you be sure?" Sanchez drawled. "How do I know you weren't exchanging information instead of kisses a little while ago?"

"You saw what we were doing."

Sanchez gave him a considering look. "I saw what you wanted me to see. I noticed you were running the shower so no one could hear what you were saying."

"Wouldn't you, under the circumstances? But you're determined to put your own interpretation on everything we do."

"On the contrary, I'm doing my utmost to get the two of you out of San Marcos without looking like I'm going soft."

"I'm listening."

"Why do you think Harara and the others came charging out here tonight?"

"I can make some educated guesses about your political advisers. I don't know how Johnson fits into the picture."

"I don't owe you an explanation. But I'll give you the executive summary. Johnson is an arms dealer. What we're negotiating is perfectly legal. However, he's giving me a very special price, and he wants to make certain that the details of the transaction stay private so other clients don't start demanding the same terms."

"All right, I'll buy that," Jed replied. "But I suspect your compatriots have more official motives. They found out you were holding Marci, and they want to make sure you don't do anything that will jeopardize relations with the U.S."

"That's a fair assessment of Rinaldo's position," Sanchez conceded. "He grew up grubbing for money, and he thinks your six million dollars for economic development is a good deal. Leandro is here to monitor the situation for President Palmeriz, although he's pretending he has my best interests at heart. Harara wants me to get rid of Señorita Devereaux to make sure national security hasn't been breached."

"You're lying."

"Of course he'll deny it, if you ask."

"So what do Marci and I have to do, storm your arsenal and shoot our way out of here?"

Smiling, the general shook his head. "Nothing so drastic, old friend. Calm down and think this through like a male chauvinist citizen of San Marcos. Rinaldo gave me the idea. But he's right. Remember how things work down here."

Jed listened intently.

"I wasn't lying when I said this is a country with old-fashioned values. Including our attitude toward the fair sex. Women here don't have equal status. Very few dress up in suits and high heels and go to the office. A good wife stays home and obeys her husband. And if he orders her to keep her mouth shut about confidential government information she might have seen, she does what he says."

Jed's eyes narrowed as he spoke slowly. "You're saying our getting married will satisfy your requirements? That once Marci and I tie the knot, she's safe. And we can go home."

"Yes," Sanchez replied. "You can leave the day after the ceremony, when I know you've consummated the marriage."

"It's that simple?"

"There's one other stipulation."

"Which is?" Jed asked cautiously.

Sanchez paused a moment, and the intensity of his dark, speculative gaze made Jed want to lower his eyes. Ingrained training and long years of experience kept him from moving, but it couldn't keep sweat from forming in the palms of his hands.

"We were friends once," Sanchez began. His tone, full of warmth and sentiment, made Jed even more nervous. What did the old devil want? "Maybe we're not exactly *simpático* anymore," the general continued. "But I still know you're a man of honor. So I want you to give me your word that my private business stays private. In other words, you guarantee that if your wife did see something she shouldn't that she'll keep it between the two of you."

"You trust me to do that?" At least Miguel hadn't asked for proof that it was going to be a real wedding night. Jed didn't honestly know if he could insure that.

The general's gaze was steady. "It's either trust you or kill you."

"I appreciate the frankness—and the vote of confidence."

"I must have your word of honor."

Jed had come downstairs ready to promise the moon if that was what it would take to get Marci out of here. Yet he executed a quick mental tap dance before he answered. If Sanchez were an honorable man, he'd have to deal with him honorably. But he knew of too many occasions when the general had broken his solemn oath. Still, Jed would do his best to keep Marci quiet—unless she'd found something that was too monstrous to suppress. "I give you my word that your private business remains private," Jed replied.

The general pulled a small knife from his drawer. "Do you remember the solemn blood ceremony we used to use in the old days when the men graduated from boot camp? I think that would be a fitting way to seal our bargain. With a mingling of blood. Give me your hand."

Jed felt a knot twist in his stomach. "I didn't do it then. I can't do it now."

Sanchez looked up sharply. "You can't validate your oath?"

Jed swallowed hard. For a second time tonight he was going to have to reveal the weakness that had made a shambles of his career. "I have a sickness in my blood."

The knife jumped in Sanchez's hand. "*Dios.* You're not HIV positive?"

"Not that. It's something else. A very exotic tropical disease I picked up in the Caribbean," he explained, telling Miguel a small part of the truth. "Apparently there's no cure. The pattern is like malaria. The symptoms come back to me from time to time."

El Jefe looked at him speculatively. "What are they?"

Jed kept his gaze steady. "Worse than gout. But leave me a bit of dignity."

"I'm sorry. It's hard for someone like you or me to admit any weakness."

"I've learned to live with it."

"Is it the reason you started thinking about marriage?"

Jed shrugged. "Maybe I'm tired of being alone—of not having anyone who's there for me." He hadn't been sure what he was going to say, but he realized he'd come pretty close to the truth.

"I think I have a better understanding of your behavior." Sanchez held out his hand. "We'll shake on the deal."

They clasped hands.

"Thank you," Jed said with genuine feeling. "Marci means a lot to me." Again he silently acknowledged how true that was and how much he wished that things were different, that the two of them really could make a life together.

But he couldn't worry about the future now. Although Sanchez had made him an offer he couldn't refuse, he knew the man too well to simply relax and take their bargain at face value. For all he knew, Miguel's current decision to trust him could turn into tomorrow's decision to kill him.

THE BIRDS SINGING in the foliage outside her window woke Marissa. She hadn't planned to sleep. In fact, she'd lain in the dark making wild, impractical plans to escape. At one point she'd wondered if braving the dogs was better than braving her wedding night. But sometime in the early-morning hours fatigue had overcome her, and she'd dozed off. Now it must be about six-thirty, the time when the birds began their raucous chorus, she thought as she threw off the covers with a shaky hand and crossed to the window. The morning was misty, but the haze would burn off. It would be a beautiful day for a wedding.

Oh, God. Once again the sick, trapped feeling threatened to sweep away reason. Crossing to the closet, she yanked out a dress the staff had moved from the other room. As she was pulling down the skirt, there was a knock on the door. Without waiting for an invitation, Anna fluttered in.

"Good, you're already up. I heard they gave you this beautiful room," she gushed, talking a mile a minute as she went about straightening the bed. "Everybody's excited about the wedding and the fiesta. But there's so much to do. It's lucky we were working on a wedding gown for Carmelita. But she's not getting married for two weeks, so we'll have time to finish another one for her."

So it wasn't all a nightmare. It was real.

"And you have to go and see Madre Flora right after breakfast." Anna flushed.

"Mother Flora?"

"*Sí.* We have our own ways here, traditions that go back before the Spanish arrived. Madre Flora is in charge of the women's marriage instruction and the special rituals before the vows." She giggled. "I went to her when I got married last year, and she told me so many things. It made all the difference with Carlo—when he—" She broke off, blushing again. "But I think you already know about... about what to expect on your wedding night."

Marissa sucked in a sharp breath.

Anna was in too much of a dither to notice. "This is so exciting. The last woman from the city who got married here was *El Jefe*'s wife. And I was only a little girl, so I don't remember much. But people still talk about it."

Marissa was only half listening to the excited prattle. "I want to see my fiancé." Jed would get her out of this. He had to!

Anna shook her head. "Don't you women from the city know anything? It's bad luck to see him before the ceremony on your wedding day."

Marissa ducked into the bathroom. She tried to focus on salvation as she washed her face and brushed her teeth. But it was hard to keep from dissolving in a pool of tears.

For ten years she'd made sure she was in control of her life. But in a few short, horrifying days she'd been rendered totally helpless. Totally at the mercy of events that were rushing forward, carrying her along. It was like being on a rudderless ship speeding down a fast-flowing river. And coming from around the next bend, she could hear the roar of a tremendous waterfall. No way to stop the boat from plunging over. Impossible to dispel the growing fear that she would be destroyed by the rocks below.

But she couldn't simply bail out. Not and leave Jed on board. Which was why she urgently needed to talk to him. If she did marry him, he'd have to know—

She chopped off the thought with a bone-deep shudder. As she stepped out into the hall, she looked toward Jed's door. It was closed, and she wondered if he could possibly be sleeping.

"This way," Anna urged.

Marissa resisted for a moment. Then it occurred to her that Jed might already be downstairs, so she hurried after the maid. But when she arrived on the patio she didn't find him.

Her eyes flicked toward the doorway on the other side of the open space. Perhaps she would have bolted if a guard hadn't been standing in the shadows. Resigned, she looked around and spotted two of last night's visitors, Rinaldo and Harara. They were walking toward a lavish buffet set along one wall, but they stopped in midstride and looked at her with undisguised interest. Rinaldo, at least, seemed to be in a good mood, as if he heartily approved of the day's events. Harara couldn't hide his disdain.

The amicable one waved her a greeting. "Did you sleep well?"

Marissa made a tremendous effort to pull herself together. She might be half-sick with worry, but she wasn't going to let them see she was anything more than a nervous bride. She flashed a rueful smile. "It's a little hard to sleep when you're so excited. And the change of plans is a bit unnerving."

"Well, you'll be glad you did it. If a man and a woman are in love, then they should get married. And you've got perfect weather for a wedding," Rinaldo continued, unaware that every word he spoke was making her cringe.

Harara turned to the table and began filling his plate with chunks of melon. "Let's hope you have sense enough to listen to your husband," he muttered.

"What?"

Before he could elaborate, a high-pitched shriek rang out from somewhere above them.

Marissa froze. So did the two other guests on the patio. In contrast, the servants went about their business as if nothing out of the ordinary had occurred.

The wail came again—from somewhere on the second

floor across from Marissa's room. The sound choked off in midcry as if a hand had clamped over an open mouth.

Marissa craned her neck toward the windows, trying to determine the exact location of the sound. "Does someone need help?" she asked the uniformed attendant who was straightening up the buffet.

"The women will take care of it."

"Of what?"

"A man was hurt this morning out in the fields. His wife is one of the maids, and I think she must have learned of the accident," he said.

It struck Marissa that there was something odd about the explanation, as if the servant had memorized it, as if he'd already repeated it many times before. She studied his face, but he didn't meet her eyes.

"I hope we haven't disturbed your wedding-day breakfast," he said, looking genuinely distressed. "Can I help you fill a plate?"

Marissa glanced once more toward the second floor, almost certain that something wasn't right. But in this house she was also sure there was nothing she could do.

Snatching a plate, she pivoted toward the buffet. The men stepped aside as she approached the table, and she stared at the sumptuous spread, wondering what would go down past the lump in her throat. Coffee? Dry toast? Melon? The scrambled eggs and the quesadillas would be impossible, but she took some anyway for appearance's sake.

Once seated, she took small sips of coffee and nibbled on a dry roll, but she did little more than push the rest of her meal around the plate.

It was almost a relief when Anna returned with a middle-aged woman and came directly to her table.

"It's normal to be nervous on your wedding day,"

Anna declared as she eyed Marissa's almost untouched breakfast. "It's time for your appointment."

Marissa could see the men at the nearby table listening and exchanging grins—as if they knew something she didn't.

Anna gave them a sideways look. "There's a lot to do to get ready. Rosita and I will take you."

"Oh." Marissa pushed back her chair and tried to look confident.

As they exited, Rosita walked in front of Marissa. Anna was directly in the back so that they formed a little parade. She felt as if she was a prisoner again and that all the men, guests and staff alike, were watching the procession with interest.

The soldiers were a bit more subtle in their scrutiny, but she felt them following her down the hall with their eyes. After she and the two women passed one group of sentries, Marissa thought she heard a low-pitched exchange of suggestive remarks. She felt the back of her neck heat, but she kept her eyes forward. No one stopped her and her escorts when they left through a door in the rear of the hacienda.

As they moved away from the buildings that made up the compound, Marissa felt her nerves jump. She was being led off into an isolated area of the jungle. For all she knew this could be a plot of Sanchez's that Jed knew nothing about. She slowed her steps. "Where are we going?"

Rosita turned and gave her a look that was half stern, half compassionate. "You come from far away, but you must honor our customs while you are here. Anna told you about the wedding instructions all of our women receive. This is a solemn occasion. Do not speak again. You should approach Madre Flora with reverence. And she will decide whether the wedding will proceed."

"You mean—"

"Silence."

Marissa nodded tightly. It sounded as if this was some kind of test. Maybe, if she flunked, she could get out of marrying Jed. Her heart started to race. Was it really that simple? Did the wise woman of the village have the power to decide that the match wasn't suitable?

The escorts kept walking at a brisk pace. Soon they were in the cool shade of towering trees and giant ferns where shafts of light filtered through the leaves. Above her, parrots called out, and a family of spider monkeys chattered as if they resented the human intrusion. The trail was narrow but well-worn, and it seemed to lead Marissa into another, more primitive world. She knew instinctively that hundreds of women before her had taken this same path on their wedding days. This journey might be new to her, but it was steeped in tradition.

Torn between nervousness and awe, she wanted to ask more questions. But she was sure she wouldn't get any answers from her guides.

They crossed over a fast-running stream on a wooden bridge with carved female statues like sentries on the front posts. Marissa wanted to stop and have a better look, but the women urged her on, past mahogany trees and Spanish cedars, the group's progress heralded by the drumming of a red-crested woodpecker.

Beyond the bridge the trail widened. After what seemed like at least a half-mile tramp through the forest, Rosita stopped by a giant kapok tree whose massive gray green trunk and branches were decorated with bromeliads and trailing pink orchids. Breaking off one of the orchids, she turned to Marissa and tucked it into the hair over her ear. "There. Madre Flora likes it when a bride approaches her with a flower in her hair. Since you don't know the custom, I've done it for you."

"Umm," was all Marissa could manage through suddenly parched lips.

The woman took her arm and led her around a curve in the trail where she found herself facing an ancient-looking wall made of massive stones covered with green moss. There was a doorway to one side, its shape that of the flattened corbel arch the Mayans had used.

She hadn't had any idea there were Mayan ruins on Sanchez's *finca.* But she was sure he wouldn't advertise the fact, since he wouldn't want archaeologists mucking about on his property and getting in the way of his military exercises. On the other hand, as she looked at the wall, she decided that ruin wasn't exactly the right word. This construction was in better shape than the site the American team was excavating down the road.

A macaw screeched in a nearby tree and took flight. The woman gestured toward the archway. "You must go in alone."

With her mouth so dry she felt she might never swallow again, Marissa shuffled forward. Caught and held by a sense of unreality, she hardly dared to imagine what was on the other side of the wall. When she stepped through the doorway, she had to stop and give her eyes time to adjust from the filtered light of the jungle to blazing sun. She was in a large paved courtyard bounded on one side by a truncated pyramid, its steps climbing to a flat platform just below the tops of the tallest trees. Around the other sides of the courtyard were low buildings made of the same stone as the wall and topped with thatched roofs.

Carefully tended beds of flowers and shrubs bordered the walls, and Marissa had the strange fantasy that if she closed her eyes and opened them again she might find the place bustling with dozens of women in ancient Mayan costume.

The plaza was completely silent. Yet she sensed that

she wasn't alone. A thatched, open-air structure on her far right gave protection from the tropical sun. As she peered into the shadows she saw that someone was sitting on a low stone bench cushioned with colorful native rugs.

The figure raised a hand, beckoning her to come forward. She wanted to turn and run. Instead a greater force drew her farther into the plaza, as if a string were attached to the middle of her chest, pulling her forward. When she stepped under the canopy she found herself facing a tiny woman who she guessed had to be the fabled Madre Flora. At first glance the old woman hardly looked impressive. Her shoulders were hunched, and the hands clasped in her lap resembled dry sticks. Her white hair was braided and piled on her head, and the brown skin of her face was as wrinkled and cracked as a dry creek bed.

She gestured to a pillow at her feet. "Sit with me, *hija.* We will get to know each other a little."

Marissa sat, feeling the scratchy fabric against her legs. Pulling her skirt close, she clasped her hands over her knees to keep them from trembling. For what seemed like minutes, she and the old woman regarded each other. Marissa saw wisdom and contentment in her black eyes and years of hard living in her face. She swallowed painfully, wondering what her own countenance revealed. Amazingly, she felt her panic subsiding under the old woman's steady gaze. Simply sitting with Madre Flora was having a calming effect on her, almost as if those black eyes had put her under a spell.

"Thank you for honoring me with this visit," the *madre* finally said in Spanish.

"I don't think I had a choice," Marissa answered in the same language.

"There are always choices in this life, *hija.*"

"Not when *El Jefe* holds power over you," Marissa

answered with a little shake of her head. Immediately she wondered if it was wise to say something so revealing.

The old woman peered at her, the look in her eyes becoming almost amused. "You are worried someone might be listening."

"Yes."

"None would dare. Not even *El Jefe.* What passes between us will stay private. As for choices, you made the decision that brought you to his *finca.*"

Marissa shrugged and looked toward one of the flower beds. What was the use of trying to explain about working for the U.S. State Department to an Indian woman who had lived all her life in this place?"

"Why did you ask me here?"

"To help you discover the truth. Do you love this man you are to take as *sposo*—as a husband?" Madre Flora asked suddenly.

Caught completely off guard, Marissa blurted, "I truly don't know. I wish..." She wasn't able to finish the sentence. *Did* she wish she loved Jed? Could she admit that to herself? Or did she wish he had made some kind of unspoken commitment to her? Would that make her feel safe with him tonight?

"The women say you have already been intimate with him."

"That's a lie!"

"Ay. But you know something of his lovemaking."

"I know that when he kisses me and touches me, it feels...wonderful. I didn't know being with a man could be...like that," she admitted with awe in her voice. She felt heat spread across her cheeks as she realized how much she'd revealed. She hadn't thought the interview would start like this. She hadn't dreamed she'd feel compelled—driven—to confront the very issues she'd been avoiding for so long.

The old woman's face was unreadable. Marissa wanted to look away, to hide her raw emotions. But she couldn't; she was held captive by the *madre*'s wise, assessing gaze.

"Slowly we are getting at the truth," Madre Flora said.

"Are we?"

"Mmm. I sense your fear, *hija.* You are afraid of allowing him to be close to you."

Marissa swallowed.

"You're not sure you want to marry this man. But you've learned that you are drawn to him—sexually. You have admitted that much to yourself."

Marissa gave the barest nod.

"A man and a woman giving each other pleasure in their marriage bed is one of the great joys of this life," the old woman continued. "Things go more smoothly when the bride knows what to expect on her wedding night. Do I need to tell you how it is done—the joining of the flesh?"

Marissa flushed more deeply and shook her head.

There were several moments of silence. "Making love is an important part of marriage, but there is much more to linking your destiny with a man's. Each of you has obligations to the other. What are the qualities that make Jed Prentiss a good husband in your eyes?"

Marissa thought about Jed and smiled. "He goes after what he wants—and usually gets it. He's intimidating. Very strong." She swallowed and went on. "But down deep he's a good man. He has a code of honor. He's shown me he cares about me. He's trusted me with knowing his secret weakness. And I don't think he would hurt me," she added. She hadn't realized she knew so much about Jed. But it was all true.

"Those are good things. But will he provide a good living for you and the children you have together? Will he make a good father?"

Marissa had barely thought beyond tonight. But she didn't have to struggle for an answer to the question. "I can provide my own living. I've done that for years."

"A good father is important to a child's success in life."

"That's not essential," Marissa argued. "If the child is strong she can overcome her home life."

"You are more independent than the women from the village. That is good and bad for you."

Marissa hesitated, then admitted, "I've had to be independent. I've learned to take care of myself."

"I can see that. And more. You have been hurt in the past."

Marissa's head jerked up.

"By two men, I think. Your father and another."

"How...how do you know that?"

"By what you told me about your home," Madre Flora said, her voice gentle. "By your fear of intimacy—and of strong men."

Silence settled over the sunlit courtyard. Marissa struggled to draw in a steady breath. Her father...and Lowell Dougan. She'd avoided even thinking his name for years. He was just a shadow. The man in her past who had hurt her. But in Madre Flora's presence, hiding anything, even from oneself, she was learning, was impossible. "I didn't tell you any of that." Marissa spoke defensively.

The old woman smiled kindly. "When a woman comes to me for this talk, she gives away a great deal by the way she answers my questions. And even more—by the things she chooses not to say. You have come a long way by yourself in this life. You have proven you have great strength. But I think you are ready to take the risk of giving your love and your trust to Jed Prentiss."

Marissa realized her hands were clasped in a death grip.

"I want to," she whispered, hearing the truth in her own voice. "But I don't know if I can."

The old woman laid a gnarled hand on Marissa's shoulder. "Have faith in yourself and in Jed Prentiss. He is very different from the other one."

"I know that," Marissa answered. "But it's so hard to let myself be...vulnerable."

Madre Flora nodded. "The gods have been kind to you in this. They have sent him to you at the right time. You are ready for him—for love—if you let yourself be."

More than anything, Marissa wanted to believe the old sage. She'd thought that submitting to this outlandish interview might be a way of getting out of the marriage ceremony, that Madre Flora would issue a fiat even Sanchez couldn't ignore. But things had changed as they'd sat here talking. Her hopes and fears had crystallized. And she knew she was stronger than she imagined. What if somehow it could actually work out with Jed? What if theirs could be a real marriage? She'd been attracted to him for years, but she'd never dared to imagine anything as awesome—or as final—as marriage. Yet what if Madre Flora was right?

Suddenly, almost mystically, as if conjured by the *madre* from whatever magic lingered here in this ancient hallowed place, a spark of hope flowed to life in her heart.

Hope. It was a feeling she hadn't experienced in a long, long time.

Chapter Ten

As Jed automatically lifted his coffee cup and took a sip, his thoughts were entirely of Marissa. She'd looked so damn frightened last night. Was playing at marriage with him for a couple of days really such an awful prospect?

He'd planned to find out if she was still so upset this morning. But the servant Miguel had assigned to him had kept him in his room inspecting the clothes he was going to wear at the ceremony, and he'd finally realized he was being delayed on purpose. Probably so that the bride and groom wouldn't meet at breakfast, he decided.

When he'd come out onto the patio she was nowhere about. But Thomas Leandro and William Johnson had been deep in conversation, the arms dealer's Texas twang contrasting strangely with the professor's cultured Latin American accent. He'd thought about trying to start a casual conversation designed to shake them down for information. Then Pedro Harara had pulled up a chair, and Jed's anger had soared. That little pip-squeak was the one who wanted Marci out of the way. Jed had wanted to drag the bastard out of the room, shove his shoulders against a wall and make him understand the flaws in his logic. But strong-arm tactics weren't exactly appropriate behavior for a man on his wedding day. And there was always the possibility that Sanchez had lied about the man's motives. So Jed had clamped his hands around his cup and eavesdropped with distaste as Harara had started expounding on his favorite topic—international finance, a subject he could stick with for hours. Amusement and relief had broken through Jed's anger as he'd watched the listeners' eyes glaze over. Harara might have his opinions, but as far as political influence went, he was lower than the spots on a snake's ass, thank God.

Shifting his chair so he had a little privacy, Jed tried to swallow some breakfast while he thought about the strange turn events had taken since he'd arrived at the hacienda.

Was Miguel going to produce a marriage license before the ceremony? Were he and Marci really going to be saying their vows in front of a crowd of people? And then what? It wasn't forever, of course. They might be marrying in haste, but they'd have plenty of leisure to undo the damage when they got home.

Yet that still left their wedding night. Maybe he should tell his bride that Miguel wasn't going to let her off the estate unless he was sure they'd consummated the marriage.

He smiled, enjoying the prospect. It wasn't as if they were starting from scratch. They'd gotten to know each other quite well last night. She'd revived him pretty quickly with her comforting little kisses and her hands stroking his body. After that it had taken all his willpower to sit quietly in that chair and let her turn up the heat. When he'd finally gone from passive enjoyment to active participation, he'd felt her passion rise. It was only after he'd gone into overdrive and pushed her down on the rug that she'd frozen up on him.

He thought about that. And about the way she'd been responding to him—up to a certain point. Then, in his mind's eye, he saw the mask of fear that had shrouded her face when he'd started to lose control and get aggressive.

As he remembered the haunted look in her eyes and the way she'd struggled from his grasp, his fingers clenched the fork he was holding. Damn. Why hadn't he figured it out before? The signs were there for anyone with half a brain to read. Anyone sensitive enough to understand what was going on. Some creep had gotten rough with her in the past. He'd bet his life on it. Now she was afraid of letting herself be defenseless again. That's why she'd kept herself so aloof. Not because she was cold. But because she was scared.

How scared, he wondered. How rough had the nameless bastard been with her? Jed grimaced, unwilling to follow that line of reasoning to its logical conclusion. He'd rather think about the kind of approach that would make her feel comfortable. They might not be making lifetime vows to each other at the ceremony, but he cared about her. And she was attracted to him. Hell, it was more than that. She cared, too. Or she wouldn't have come swinging across from her balcony to his, like Tarzan's mate, when she thought he needed help. Then she would have done a better job of socking him instead of choosing the other alternative. But she was the one who'd made the decision to fight ice with fire.

He swallowed a frustrated sigh. Too bad they weren't going to get off to a very promising start this evening. If he remembered his backwoods San Marcos customs, the two of them were going to be teased unmercifully by a drunken crowd and locked in a bedroom together. He'd done it to other guys when he'd been training Miguel's troops, never dreaming it would happen to him. The prospect was a little daunting. On the other hand, it did have its upside, he admitted as he stretched out his legs under the table. Marci would be clinging to him for protection.

Comfort would naturally lead to mutual enjoyment. And they'd both end up having a wonderful time while he showed her how rewarding making love could be.

From the corner of his eye he saw Johnson slide him a glance and then fiddle with his Stetson and look away when he saw he'd been caught.

Funny, he'd have thought Leandro—the San Marcos native—would be the one with the anticipatory glint in his eye. But maybe over their eggs and quesadillas the professor had filled in the arms merchant on the local customs.

Brisk footsteps made him look to see who had entered the patio. It was Sanchez.

He looked pleased with himself as he approached the table. "You've got a beautiful day for a wedding."

"The ancient gods must be smiling on me. By the way, what time is the ceremony?"

"At six. Followed by what you'll doubtless think is an endless wedding supper. Then you're spending the night at that little cottage I use for guests when the main house is full. Nice and private."

"Yeah."

El Jefe grinned and pitched his voice low so that the other guests couldn't hear. "Come with me. I want to show you something."

"What?"

"You'll love it. But I can't explain until we're alone."

Jed followed, wondering if Sanchez was going to let him test the springs on the wedding bed. Or maybe he had a two-hundred-dollar bottle of champagne he'd been saving for a special occasion?

"What's the big mystery?" he asked as they walked through the hall toward the back of the hacienda.

"Something quite special." *El Jefe* paused by the guardhouse and picked up a machete. "You know how women are. They think they can keep secrets from their lords and masters. But we've got the drop on them." He led Jed out the back door of the main house and down a path that disappeared into the jungle.

"According to my sentries, the women came and got the bride about an hour and a half ago. I figure it ought to be about time for the good part," *El Jefe* said in a raspy whisper. "Come on. But keep your voice down."

Before they reached the trees, Miguel angled off to the right. Several hundred yards farther on he paused for a moment and then selected an entrance into the underbrush, where he hacked away at several branches that were partially blocking the path. Jed followed and found himself on a narrow, barely discernible trail. He cocked his head to one side and looked inquiringly at *El Jefe.* "Are you going to come clean with me?"

"Come clean. That's good! The local customs here go back before the Spanish conquest—to ancient times when the Indians worshiped pagan gods. The women have some very interesting rituals to get the bride ready for the groom."

"Oh?"

"You can have a nice view of the proceedings. It's one of the special pleasures of getting married out here in the boonies. But if you're too much of a prude, you can skip the fun and have a siesta."

Jed's mouth was suddenly dry. "Suppose I take you up on the offer?"

His friend slapped him on the shoulder and handed over the machete. "I thought you'd be interested. With a little hacking you'll be able to follow this trail. In about half a mile you'll come to the wall of an ancient Mayan temple. Go around it to the side where there's a steep hill. It's actually the back of a pyramid. If you climb it and go into the enclosed platform on top, you can see down into the ritual baths."

THREE WOMEN CLAD in short halter dresses and heavy gold necklaces and earrings came out of the building at the back of the courtyard. Marissa had never seen any of them before. In fact, she had the strange sensation that they could have stepped directly from an illustration carved into the temple wall.

"Come," one of them said.

"But—"

"There is nothing to fear. Here we serve the ancient ways. We must prepare you for your bridegroom in the manner handed down from mother to daughter through the centuries. The rituals will fill you with joy and anticipation for your marriage."

Before Marissa could protest further, they surrounded her and led her toward the building. The doorway looked dark and forbidding, and she would have held back if she could. But they pressed her relentlessly forward. When she stepped inside, she found it was pleasantly illuminated by shafts of bright light slanting at intervals through the thatched roof. She was aware of Madre Flora somewhere in back of her, silent, watching.

"Oh!" As her eyes adjusted to the light she saw that the walls were painted with vibrant murals. Some were jungle scenes. Others depicted the interiors of stone buildings richly decorated with plush draperies, soft mats and comfortable pillows.

Marissa flushed when she realized that among the greenery and opulent cushions were naked men and women kissing, touching, making love.

"What is this place?"

"The temple of the women," one of them murmured as if that explained everything.

A heavy, perfumed scent hung in the air, and Marissa saw smoke wafting from a metal burner at the side of the room. The women led her toward it.

"No, wait!" No one answered. Instead they pressed on her shoulders, gently forcing her to kneel with her face in the choking smoke.

Panic seized Marissa. She held her breath as long as she could, trying to struggle away from the hands that clamped her in place. But she couldn't get away. Finally she was forced to take a breath.

She heard someone chanting words in a language she couldn't understand and the tones of strange musical instruments coming from another group of costumed women in the corner of the room. The ones at her side kept her kneeling before the burner, and it was impossible not to draw more and more of the heavy incense into her lungs.

Gradually her senses merged with the music and the chanted words swirling around her. She felt transported to another time, another place, where all the civilized conventions of her world had not yet been invented, and ancient gods held sway. Her eyes would no longer keep their focus, and she rocked back on her knees.

"Good. You are ready to go on," Madre Flora pronounced.

The other women helped her up, supporting her languid body.

"What are you doing to me?" She'd thought she'd shouted the question. Yet no one acted as if they'd heard her.

Hands were on her clothing, lifting her dress over her head. Then her underwear was efficiently stripped from her body so that she stood before them naked as the day she was born.

JED MADE HIS WAY along the trail, stopping every few feet to hack at some plant that had grown up in his path. One thing about the jungle, the greenery grew so fast it required constant effort to keep a trail open. He kept his ears tuned to his surroundings and his eyes on the underbrush, alert for hidden dangers from men or wildlife.

On the face of it, this was a pretty crazy thing to be doing. Yet Miguel had intrigued him with his allusions to ancient traditions. What were the women doing? Practicing fertility rituals? Anointing the bride with aphrodisiac herbs?

As he hacked his way past another ironwood seedling, guilt nagged at the back of his mind. Whatever was going on this morning, he shouldn't be spying on Marci. But the invitation was simply too tempting to resist—and a lot more appealing than sitting around the hacienda biting his nails until the ceremony. Besides, hadn't Miguel told him that all the grooms did it? Why should he deny himself the privilege just because he was a visitor?

However, he was beginning to wonder if his host was playing a practical joke on him when he finally saw the wall of the temple Miguel had spoken about. Hands on hips, he surveyed the massive barrier. He'd been to the *finca* dozens of times when he was training troops, and he hadn't known this place existed. If you hadn't heard about ruins buried in the jungle, you certainly wouldn't realize you were looking at a pyramid, he decided as he looked up at the hill rising at a steep angle from the jungle floor. It was covered with everything from vines and ferns to small trees.

The place reminded him of Tikal, the ancient Mayan site he'd visited in Guatemala where a highly sophisticated civilization had flourished while Europe was in the Dark Ages. Abandoned and swallowed completely by the fast-growing tropical vegetation, the city wasn't rediscovered until the mid-eighteen hundreds. Archaeologists had uncovered a number of the temples, but sometimes they restored only the front or the top, leaving the rest as they'd found it. Like this one, Jed thought, where all he could see was the covered platform at the crown.

He reached for a convenient root and pulled himself up, bracing his foot as he stretched for the next handhold. It was a hard climb. He hoped Miguel wasn't putting him on, and that it was going to be worth the effort. Finally he reached the stone platform beneath the treetops and he stopped for a few minutes to catch his breath.

In front of him was a small building about eight feet square, overshadowed by the tops of the trees. Stepping inside, he shaded his eyes from the sun. Probably the structure had once been topped by a roof, but it had long since disappeared.

Narrow windows slashed through the wall opposite the door. Making his way across, he peered downward. To the left and right, the view was obscured by trees. Directly in front of him was a cleared area with what looked like a wide circular well in the center. What he saw about thirty feet below him made the air whoosh out of his lungs.

"YOU ARE VERY BEAUTIFUL. You will please your husband with your body," one of the women murmured in Spanish as she spread Marissa's hair like a curtain of gold around her shoulders.

Marissa wasn't capable of framing an answer. The smoke had taken the edge off her panic and pulled her into the rhythm of the pagan ceremony. She'd lost all will to resist. When her three attendants led her up a flight of steps in the back of the building, she followed.

They were all chanting softly and rhythmically in a language she didn't understand, their voices rising and falling with the music that followed them into a sunlit courtyard slightly smaller than the one where she'd talked with Madre Flora.

They helped her over a low, circular stone wall, and she gasped as she stepped into the cold water up to her knees. It raised goose bumps on her arms and made her nipples tighten to hard pebbles.

Still singing the primitive melody, the women scooped the water up in clay pitchers decorated with more pictures of men and women together and began to pour the water over her shoulders. She closed her eyes as she felt it cascade over her breasts and hips and belly. It was easy to imagine Jed's fingers on her body in place of the water—caressing her in all the places that longed for his attentions. Dimly in the corner of her mind that was still in touch with her modern sensibilities she wondered if the heat of her body was raising the temperature of the water.

FOR LONG MOMENTS at a time Jed forgot how to breathe as he watched Marci standing in the tub, naked and beautiful and regal as any Mayan princess who'd ever lived. She was like those royal women of centuries past who had stood in the sacred pool below, the sun cascading down over her, drenching her body in gold.

He'd never dreamed he'd see such a gorgeous sight. He looked at the hair falling around her shoulders like spun gold and longed to run his greedy fingers through the riches. Her eyes were shut. Her face radiated a strange, almost mystical expression that held him for long moments. Then his enraptured gaze moved a few inches lower to her beautifully rounded breasts, their erect nipples an enchanting deep coral color.

His fingers flexed as he thought about what it would be like to cup her softness and then stroke those hardened tips until she moaned with pleasure. He could almost feel her twisting against him, begging for his mouth to take the place of his hands. In his most private fantasies he had never imagined anything so erotic—Marci standing there in all her glory, eyes closed, skin glowing pink as water sluiced down her body.

His own body tightened painfully, and his fingers clamped onto the window ledge in a death grip. If he didn't look away, he was in danger of going off like a rocket. Still, he was powerless to resist the sight of his bride—and at that moment he reveled in thinking of her in those terms—as she was prepared for their wedding. Prepared for *him*. His chest rose and fell rapidly in unconscious rhythm with hers as he took in every precious detail, following the rivulets of water downward, watching them trace the indentation of her waist and slide lower, weaving through the curly triangle of hair at the top of her legs and then down her rounded thighs.

The women chanted as they worked, and Marissa swayed slightly to the sound, making him ache to come crashing down there and snatch her away. One of the attendants began to wash her long golden hair, and she threw her head back so that her breasts thrust upward, toward him, as if she were offering herself to his hands.

He stifled a groan. At that moment another one of the peasant women looked up, her gaze focusing unerringly on the narrow windows where he hid. Instinctively he jumped back, wondering if he'd made a noise that could be heard in the courtyard. But he knew he'd swallowed the groan and that it was unlikely the women would hear anything besides their own chanting.

When he cautiously looked again, the curious one had switched her attention back to Marci. But the woman had known he was there; Jed was certain of it. Suddenly, in the sort of intuitive flash that had often saved his life, he saw the truth. This whole thing was a setup. And he'd better figure out why he was there.

He wrenched himself away from the seductive view, feeling as if he were going against an elemental force that tugged at every cell in his body. Drawing in a shuddering breath, he struggled to pull his mind back to sanity.

He commanded his brain to work. Commanded himself to think the situation through. Okay, so what did it mean that the women knew he had come to watch this erotic little ceremony? Maybe they always knew they were putting on a performance for the men, and it gave them a secret sense of power. He could understand that—particularly in a society where the women made very few of the rules. But how did that apply to *him*, personally? Since he and Marci were both outsiders.

He felt the hair at the back of his neck prickle. What if Sanchez was taking advantage of a tantalizing local custom to make sure the bridegroom was fully occupied for a couple of hours? While the general— While he what?

Jed's thoughts spun back to the previous evening's conversation. Last night Sanchez had said he had to either trust him or kill him. And he'd jumped at the offer of *El Jefe*'s help. He'd wanted to believe that the general was going to come through for him. Perhaps because they'd once been friends.

He'd like to argue himself into sticking with that comforting scenario. But now he realized he'd let himself be lulled into a dangerous assumption.

If only for his own peace of mind, he'd better find out what was happening back at the ranch. More to the point, from this moment on, he'd better start acting as if he were a moving target. Ducking low, he retraced his steps across the enclosure and descended as quickly as he could.

When he got to the bottom he paused to survey the

immediate area, wishing he was armed with a gun instead of a machete. Then he started up the overgrown trail at a cautious trot, his eyes still scanning the underbrush while his mind raced.

He tried to recall everything he'd learned about Miguel Sanchez's tactics when he was on the attack. Basically, the general had two modes of operation. When he was sure he could get away with it, he was quick and ruthless. A prime example was the way he'd marched Marci in front of the firing squad. On the other hand, if too many witnesses were present, he reverted to elegantly subtle plans that placed the blame squarely on someone else—like opposition terrorists. He never put himself in unnecessary danger. Which meant he wasn't going to send an assassination team with machine guns into the wedding chapel or the reception area.

So where would the smart money place their bets, Jed wondered. It didn't take long to figure out.

His face hardened. The honeymoon cottage Miguel had mentioned. It was perfect. He and Marci would be alone. No one else would be around to get hurt—or to witness the murders. Afterward, there would be a thorough investigation. A suspect would be identified and probably shot as he was being arrested.

The more he thought about it the more certain he was. Because another key facet of Miguel's twisted personality shone through clearly in the plan. *El Jefe* was going to give his friend a last glorious night with his bride before he blew him away.

Jed made it to the edge of the trees in fifteen minutes and stood staring at the expanse of sunlit field ahead. Every nerve in his body screamed for him to cross the open space at a dead run. But he knew a casual stroll would look a lot less as though he'd cottoned on to Miguel's plans.

He used the enforced five-minute walk to mentally review what he knew about the layout of the *finca.* The barracks for the soldiers, garages for their vehicles and armory were separated from the general's house, although there was a small ready room where the troops assigned to the complex could relax. On the way to the ruins he'd noticed, not far from the hacienda, some newer structures that had gone up since he'd been here last. Sanchez wouldn't store ammunition so close to his living quarters. But what did he consider important enough to keep within sight of his office?

Sneaking a look would be a good idea, Jed decided. But it wasn't his top priority. First on his list was a visit to the ready room. Switching directions, he headed for the small facility.

As he sauntered inside, he saw four bored guards slouched in front of an oscillating fan waiting for their turn at the sentry stations. When they saw him, they snapped into models of military posture.

"At ease," he said in Spanish.

They looked doubtful, and he gestured toward the chairs. "Sit back down. Please. I came to ask some advice—man to man."

The corporal raised an inquiring eyebrow. He'd been at the *finca* when Jed had visited before, and they knew each other slightly.

"About a suitable gesture of respect for the troops and the villagers on my wedding day."

That got their attention.

He leaned comfortably against the cabinet near the door. Extra side arms were stored inside—unless Miguel had made some changes. "I'd like to buy drinks for everyone. As much as they want."

All four faces grinned back at him. "You'd earn our eternal gratitude, Señor Prentiss," one of the men said.

"So what's the beverage of choice?" He knew that both potent dark rum and beer were produced in the province. "Come on, help me out. I'm serious. I want your advice. This is the only wedding I'm ever going to have, and I'd like to do things right."

"Beer would be fine," a corporal answered. "But—"

"But we'd rather have rum," a young recruit allowed.

"Sure thing," Jed agreed. "Get some of both. Is there somewhere on the *finca* where I can swing the deal?"

"We'd be glad to take care of it for you," the corporal offered.

"I'd be grateful." He got out his wallet and peeled off the equivalent of three hundred dollars—about twenty bills—knowing that would buy a heck of a lot of joy juice. In fact, there would be enough cash left over to split among these guys, and no one could accuse Señor Prentiss of giving them a bribe.

He laid the money on the edge of the desk, then cursed as the breeze from the fan picked it up and scattered it like dry leaves in a hurricane. While the men scrambled to retrieve the flying bills, he reached into the gun cabinet and wrapped his fingers around the handle of a service revolver. It was under his shirt and in the waistband of his trousers before they had finished picking up the loot.

He shook his head in disgust. "Sorry, this wedding thing has got me pulling all kinds of dumb stunts."

The corporal shoved the cash into a pants pocket. "No problem, Señor Prentiss. I understand how it is when you tie the knot."

Jed took a step farther into the room, cleared his throat and lowered his voice. "Look, like I said I'm, uh, a little nervous about tonight, you know. I don't want to screw up, if you get my drift."

"*Sí,*" the corporal answered.

The others nodded knowingly, some struggling to repress grins.

"I've been to weddings down here, so I realize there's going to be a lot of rowdy stuff going on until we're alone. Maybe even afterward."

The grins widened.

"My bride's never seen anything like it. I think it's going to make her pretty nervous. So once we're alone together, I'd like to keep it that way. Could you do me a favor and make sure no one comes around to rattle the windows or set off a firecracker once we're in bed?"

"You've got it."

"Thanks. Just until midnight. Things ought to calm down by then."

Jed left, then looked up in surprise as the corporal followed him out and accompanied him down the path. Damn. This was a hell of a time to pick up an escort.

They were about twenty-five yards from the guardhouse when the corporal glanced around and cleared his throat. "Perhaps I should keep my mouth shut, but I like you, and you were generous with us."

Jed felt a stab of guilt. He'd been expedient.

"There's something else you should know. If you want a piece of advice."

Jed swung toward him. "Shoot."

The man looked uncomfortable. "Clarita could make trouble for you tonight."

The warning didn't come as a complete surprise. In fact, it fit right in with the girl's recent hostility toward him and Marci. "When she was younger, we used to be friends," Jed said cautiously. "Now she's doing all kinds of crazy stuff. It looks like she's jealous of Marci."

"Crazy stuff. *Sí.* She's not playing with a full deck. And *El Jefe* doesn't want to believe anything's wrong with her. So he just lets it continue, and everybody has to pretend nothing strange is going on. Like that screaming fit of hers this morning when one of the women was helping her pick out a dress for the ceremony. You heard it?''

Jed nodded. He'd used the word *crazy* because he hadn't known how else to put it. The corporal was telling him that the girl was mentally unbalanced—and everyone on the *finca* talked about it behind her father's back. The revelation explained a lot, he realized as he thought back over the girl's behavior. It also saddened him.

''It's been going on for about a year,'' the corporal continued. ''She seemed to change overnight. She can be dangerous if she takes a dislike to you. Like last night when that tarantula turned up in your fiancée's bed. Everybody's betting it was her.''

Jed swore under his breath. ''I appreciate your clueing me in.''

''Don't tell *El Jefe* you heard anything from me.''

''Of course not. But she needs help.''

''It's safer not to get involved.'' The man finished and quickly returned the way he'd come.

Jed mulled over the new information. Clarita was a loose cannon. But she wasn't his most pressing problem. When he was well out of sight of prying eyes, he ducked under the branches of a date palm and checked his weapon. Well, now he knew he had six bullets.

For an unguarded moment he thought about slipping into Miguel's office, pulling the piece and taking *El Jefe* hostage. The plan had a lot of macho appeal. But there were too many unknowns to try anything so brazen. Including his own ability to stay on his feet for the hours required to get them off the *finca* and onto an airplane out of this damned country. He grimaced. Suppose in the middle of the hostage scene he had an attack and conked out the way he had yesterday evening? So much for macho appeal.

Marci was another problem. His insides clenched when he pictured her standing in that tub. She'd looked sexy as hell, but she'd also looked pretty spacey. Chances were good she'd been given some native drug. Which made sense, because he couldn't imagine her holding still for that little bathing ceremony otherwise. He'd have to wait until she was back in commission and at his side before he risked any power plays.

Once more he affected a casual stroll as he crossed the grounds in back of the hacienda. The closer he got to the guest bungalow, the more convinced he was that he'd guessed right about Miguel's plans. The place was isolated. And it was also away from the main flow of activity. Perfect for a honeymoon couple who wanted to be alone. And with a wild party in full swing at the big house, nobody would discover that the newlyweds had been knocked off by invading terrorists until the next day when they didn't appear for lunch.

He was about to pull open the door of the cottage when a noise from inside warned him to retreat. He wasn't a moment too soon. As he slid around the side of the building, the door opened and a man stepped into the sunlight.

"Son of a bitch," Jed muttered under his breath.

Chapter Eleven

William Johnson stood on the brick steps, a satisfied smirk on his long face and what looked like a small toolbox swinging from his right hand. He glanced around to see if anyone had noted his departure from the cottage. Satisfied that he was alone, he tipped his Stetson to a jaunty angle and headed off at a brisk walk toward the hacienda.

As the Texan departed, Jed followed the toolbox with narrowed eyes. Somehow he doubted that the man had been fixing a leaky toilet. His first impulse was to jab his recently acquired pistol into the middle of Johnson's back and make him talk. But then he might not get the straight dope on what he and Miguel were up to. Instead he stayed where he was until he was satisfied that the man wasn't coming back. His face was impassive, but his heart was slamming against the inside of his chest when he finally slipped through the front door and stood waiting for his eyes to adjust to the interior light.

The two-room bungalow was as plush as the quarters where he'd slept last night, with a few additional lavish touches, like an executive-size hot tub in an orchid-filled greenhouse off the bathroom, and a fully stocked bar in the sitting area. Just perfect for a quiet honeymoon. So what little marital aid had the arms dealer added to the premises?

MARISSA NESTLED more comfortably into the soft environment surrounding her. It was warm and billowy. The most luxurious spot she'd ever slept in, and her unconscious mind translated it into another place. In preparation for her wedding, she'd been bathed and perfumed and dressed in a loose-fitting robe. Now she was with Jed in a wonderfully plush, wide bed. They were snuggled together kissing, touching—making each other happy, with the perfect freedom she'd craved for so long.

What had she been so afraid of? Making love with Jed was everything she'd longed for it to be. Sweet and sensual and thrilling. Except that outside someone was operating mining equipment, and the low buzz of machinery kept intruding on her sense of privacy.

She tried to press her ears into the pillows to blot out the annoying intrusion. But the sound wouldn't go away. As she woke up and the dream let go of her mind, she realized that what she was hearing was the low murmur of women's voices. Had they followed her and Jed to the bedroom?

Marissa stirred restlessly. No. She was still in the temple where they'd brought her right after breakfast. Making love with Jed was only a dream.

Disappointment surged through her. Dreaming of Jed was warm and satisfying—and safe. Reality was still frightening.

Her eyelids fluttered, but she didn't fully open them. Her mind was still fuzzy from the drug they'd made her breathe. Knowing she was slow on the uptake, she gave herself a few moments to orient herself. Then suddenly something the women said caught her attention.

They were speaking in low, idiomatic Spanish that was almost too quick for her to understand in her present muzzy state. But she marshaled her attention to grasp the flow of words. They'd mentioned a name, but she'd missed it, and she sensed it was important. Lying very still, she strained to figure out who they were discussing so avidly. It had to be a man.

"Come on, how do you know so much about him, Bonita?"

"Can you keep a secret?"

"I swear it."

"Well, *El Jefe* sent me to his bed the last time he was here."

The other woman sucked in a sharp breath. "I had heard of such things at the hacienda. My husband would never allow that."

So much for the general's moral code, Marissa thought. It sounded as if he only invoked it for his convenience.

Bonita made a clicking sound with her tongue. "My husband thinks *El Jefe* will give him a soft job if he lends out his wife to important visitors."

"How was it?" The question was asked with a mixture of envy and distaste. "Are the gringos good lovers?"

"Well, Carmen, the truth is, he was too fast."

Carmen laughed.

"That's one secret he'd want me to keep. The other is that he's not a gringo."

"*Un momento.* I thought he was from Texas."

Marissa's half-functioning mind scrambled to process that revelation. *Texas.* It took a minute for her fogged brain to figure out that they were talking about William Johnson.

"That's just a story he tells, like the one about supplying guns for the troops," Bonita explained airily. "So nobody knows he came to bring the special mining equipment."

Marissa strained her ears. She'd had no idea what Johnson did. Guns? Mining equipment? They must have mentioned it earlier in the conversation. That's why she'd put mining equipment into her dream.

And it fit in with something that had happened earlier—Sanchez's odd reaction when Jed had offered to arrange a government loan to develop the copper mines in Junipero Province. Did he already have Johnson for a private backer? More to the point, did they have some kind of illegal deal to keep the proceeds out of the government coffers?

"That fake Texan is a powerful man. Sometimes I think *El Jefe* is worried about what he's going to do."

"*El Jefe* has power! Everyone is afraid of him," Carmen protested.

"Here on the *finca,* yes. And in Santa Isabella."

Marissa sat up as she strained to hear the conversation better.

The women turned to her. They were part of the trio who had bathed her. The third was no longer there. "We didn't know you were awake."

Marissa stretched and shook her head. The cobwebs were clearing. "What was that smoke you made me breathe?"

"It comes from a special plant we use for sacred ceremonies. It helps you relax. Don't you feel wonderful now?"

She nodded a fraction. She wouldn't have taken the drug if she'd been offered a choice, and she felt the edge of anger at being forced. But she kept it in check.

"Who were you talking about just now?" she asked.

Bonita looked like a schoolgirl who'd been caught smoking in the bathroom by one of the nuns. "Oh, that's not important."

"It's Señor Johnson, isn't it?"

Bonita flushed.

"He's a mining engineer?"

"I'm sorry we woke you up. We shouldn't have been talking," Carmen said quickly.

"I won't tell anyone if you give me a little information."

Carmen shot Bonita an angry look. "See, you've gotten us in trouble with your big mouth."

"You were the one asking all the questions!"

"I—"

"It's all right," Marissa interjected. "I promise I won't get you in trouble. But my...fiancé has been working as a mining engineer since he left the military," she improvised. "He was hoping to work with *El Jefe* on a project in Junipero Province."

"That's where Señor Johnson goes when he comes here," Carmen answered. "I know because my brother is one of the pilots who flies him."

"So perhaps it would be better for my fiancé if he developed a project elsewhere in San Marcos," Marissa murmured.

"You'll be his wife soon," Bonita answered. "Really, it's time to start getting ready for the wedding ceremony."

Marissa felt her stomach knot. She'd been happy to think about something besides the wedding. "I didn't know it was so late."

"Madre Flora said to let you sleep until four. But now we have to hurry and do up your hair so you can get dressed."

Marissa swung her legs over the side of the low bed. She expected to be light-headed when she stood. In fact, she felt so wonderfully refreshed that it was hard to focus on any of the things that should be worrying her.

The woman went behind a screen in the corner of the room and brought out a lacy white gown with a high waist, a modest neckline and a flowing skirt.

Marissa unconsciously touched her tongue to her dry

lips as her fingers stroked the beautiful fabric. Her wedding dress. It was really going to happen. If she'd said the right things this morning, she could have convinced Madre Flora that the ceremony should be canceled. But deep in her heart, Marissa admitted, she wanted to go ahead with it. Conviction, however, did not entirely prevent her insides from quaking.

As she stepped into the sunlight, Marissa clasped her bouquet of pink-tinged orchids in a death grip. It was the only way she could keep her hands from trembling. Blood pounded in her ears so that she could hardly hear what was going on around her. The sound of an organ playing the "Wedding March" seemed to come from far away. Masses of flowers decorated the patio. A sea of faces turned expectantly toward her. They seemed to swim in her vision. But she saw the pairs of armed sentries well enough, standing at attention at each entrance. An honor guard? Or insurance against the bride escaping?

Swaying on unsteady legs, she scanned the crowd for the one man who mattered.

Jed. She needed to see him waiting for her at the altar.

Then she caught a glimpse of him and felt some of the terrible knot inside her loosen. He was standing next to Sanchez, in front of the priest, looking devastatingly handsome in a white dinner jacket. Behind them were the high-ranking officers from the *finca,* the men who had arrived yesterday, Rinaldo, Leandro, Harara and Johnson, and at least fifty other dignitaries. Leandro smiled at her, and Rinaldo nodded. Harara looked as if he were trying to put the best face possible on a bad situation. Clarita was over to one side, her expression blank.

Marissa viewed the scene like someone trembling at the edge of a fantasy. How else could she explain the gauntlet stretching in front of her? It might be made of flowers and people dressed in party clothes, but it had been created to test her courage. She swallowed hard and took a step forward and then another, slowly closing the distance between her and Jed—trying to focus on him and only him.

The expression on his face, as she drew near enough to see him clearly, made her heart skip a beat, then begin to pound so hard it felt as though it would break through the wall of her chest. He was looking at her as if she were the center of his universe. Never, in her wildest imaginings, had she pictured a man ever looking at her like that.

Her chest tightened painfully as she came down the aisle toward him. She wished with all her heart that this was real—a real wedding that marked the beginning of a real marriage. Wished that he'd *chosen* to take her for his wife, not that he'd been coerced into it.

Yet even as Marissa acknowledged that heartfelt longing, she knew a wedding between her and Jed would have been impossible under normal circumstances. They were here only because she'd been caught in Sanchez's office. And Jed had volunteered to rescue her by pretending to be her fiancé.

Did he truly care what happened to her? Or was she simply an assignment?

Her heart lurched inside her chest. Then she thought about the way he'd been with her since he'd arrived. He'd kissed her like a man who cared. He'd broken down a door to get to her when he thought she was in trouble. He *had to* feel something stronger than duty.

What would happen tonight? Their wedding night. Did she have the guts to make it into something real? A moment in time she could cherish long after this sham of a marriage had ended.

Marissa felt light-headed by the time she reached Jed's side. He gave her a confidential smile. She managed the ghost of a smile in return, and suddenly things came a little better into focus.

Someone lifted the bouquet from her hands. Someone folded back her veil. Then she felt Jed's strong fingers close around hers.

"You look beautiful," he whispered huskily.

"So do you."

His soft laugh zinged along her nerve endings. "Nobody ever said that to me before."

She didn't dare look at him again. She simply stood clutching his hand and listening to the priest's words of welcome to the wedding guests, then his little speech about the solemn obligations and responsibilities of marriage.

As she listened, another emotion bubbled up inside her. Oh, God, could she really go through with a religious ceremony? Until this moment she hadn't considered the idea of exchanging holy vows of love and commitment—on making sacred promises that were supposed to last "until death do you part."

For a panicked moment Marissa wanted to turn and run. She kept herself standing in front of the crowd of onlookers by pressing her shoulder to Jed's arm. Somehow she made the right responses. Thank heaven she managed to kneel and stand again without getting her legs tangled in her dress. And when Anna produced a ring at the right moment and pressed it into her hand, she didn't drop it.

The priest's voice and Jed's reassuring presence beside her carried her along. But she was so dazed that she didn't realize the ceremony was over until Jed turned her gently toward him and covered her lips with his.

The kiss was as sweet and sentimental as a lacy valentine.

"Mrs. Prentiss. At last," he murmured as he lifted his head and looked down at her.

His eyes were a clear sea green. And she knew that whatever happened later, she would remember the look in them until her dying day.

"Congratulations to both of you," Sanchez said.

Jed turned, and Marissa saw tension knot the muscles in his shoulders. Then he grinned and stuck out his hand. The two men shook.

She and Jed moved to the other end of the patio and stood under a canopy made by one of the balconies. A line formed, and well-wishers came to them, smiling and offering congratulations. Marissa knew very few of them, which added to her sense of unreality.

It was a relief to greet Professor Leandro. "See, it's all for the best," he said as he kissed her soundly on the cheek. Stepping back, he brushed several strands of wispy hair out of his face. "You get a wonderful wedding reception at the general's expense."

Next in line was William Johnson. The man who was supposed to be from Texas kissed her, holding her too tightly and sliding his lips from her cheek to her mouth. She pushed away, remembering the things she now knew about him that she needed to tell Jed. But this was hardly the moment.

Her new husband gave the man an angry look. "Don't take liberties with the bride."

"Just a friendly buss, old son." Johnson strolled away.

For a moment Jed's eyes drilled into his shoulder blades. Then he pulled his attention back to the next well-wisher.

A band began to play a lively folk tune. Marissa saw waiters circulating around the patio with trays of champagne flutes. It was twilight, and colored lanterns were switched on overhead, casting a magical glow over the patio.

Back to fantasyland again, Marissa thought. This was

a wedding reception. Her wedding reception! She had to keep reminding herself of that.

The band leader doffed his sombrero and urged Señor and Señora Prentiss to honor them with the first dance. As if he'd done it a hundred times before, Jed took her in his arms and began to lead her around the area that had been cleared for a dance floor.

They'd taken only a few steps when the sound of multiple explosions made her go rigid. Seconds later she tried to drag Jed off the patio and into the protection of the building.

"Easy." He held his ground and grasped her forearms.

"Somebody's shooting. Get down," she gasped, even as she wondered why the crowd around them was laughing instead of running for cover.

"No. It's just some of the villagers setting off firecrackers. They love an excuse to let off steam. Let's hope they keep the pyrotechnics outside."

She nodded and made an effort to relax. He knew the customs here. She didn't. But then, she'd been at a disadvantage from the start.

Somewhere off to her left she heard a high-pitched, uncontrollable spasm of giggles. Without looking she knew who it was. Clarita.

Out of the corner of her eye she watched Sanchez advance swiftly on his daughter. Taking her by the arm, he ushered her off the patio and into the house.

Jed watched them leave with a sad expression on his face. Then he pulled Marissa back into his arms and settled his cheek against her hair. "You're doing great," he murmured.

She moved her mouth next to his ear. "I found out some things this afternoon."

He turned his face, as if kissing her cheek. "Me, too."

She caught a mingled anger and frustration in his voice.

Then he gave a little shrug, telling her that there was nothing they could do right now besides go with the flow. When he pulled her closer, she sighed and closed her eyes. He was right—they were stuck in this crowd until custom dictated they could escape.

She held on to him, letting him guide her around the floor in a slow dance, his legs brushing hers sensually with every step. She knew scores of eyes were avidly watching the bride and groom take their first dance as man and wife. And it was best to look as if they were totally wrapped up in each other, she rationalized as she let the enjoyment of being close to Jed blot out her uncertainties and then the people around them.

The moment she stopped trying to keep tight control over her mind, the dreamlike thoughts she'd had in the bath came back to her. Jed's hands moving erotically over her naked skin, heating her from the outside in. Was the drug she'd breathed still lingering in her system, affecting her? Feeling light-headed, she pressed her face into his shoulder. He pulled her closer, the heat of his body enveloping her, his hands moving up and down her back, playing with the column of tiny buttons that held her dress closed. She knew he was turned on, too. His lips brushed the hair at her temple. He murmured something low and sexy that made her wish the wedding guests would all vanish.

She didn't realize the music had stopped until a chorus of wolf whistles brought her back to reality.

The general was grinning as he moved to the center of the floor. "I hate to interrupt you lovebirds, but it's time for dinner."

Everyone except her and Jed laughed uproariously.

Blushing hotly, Marissa and Jed followed Sanchez into a ballroom filled with beautifully set tables. Huge arrangements of tropical flowers formed the centerpieces. Around the walls, trellises of bougainvillea turned the room into an outdoor bower. For the first time it occurred to her that this reception must be costing the general a fortune.

"This is lovely. But how did you arrange it on such short notice?" she marveled.

"I'd move heaven and earth for you, my dear. You know that. I've had my people working all night," he answered with a grand gesture, as if the sentiment were real and the expense were nothing to him. Maybe it was, if he had an illegal source of income, Marissa mused.

She and Jed were seated in the center of a long table near the wall, with the honored guests on either side of them. But not Clarita. Apparently Sanchez had banished his daughter from the festivities.

It was strange to sit there watching people eating and drinking and enjoying themselves, Marissa reflected several hours later. Her own stomach was so tied in knots that she could do little more than politely taste the food.

She was married to Jed. All during dinner he'd kept touching her and drawing her close, and she'd felt the erotic surge building between them like a power plant on overload. Later that night they were going to be alone in a room together. And, as her husband, he'd have the right to do anything he wanted to her body.

She stole a glance at him where he stood, laughing and joking at the bar with several of the guards. He seemed to be having a much better time than she was. Whenever someone asked her to dance, he went over to have a drink with the men.

He came back to her walking unsteadily with a glazed look in his eyes. She shuddered as the realization hit her that he was getting drunk. She'd planned that when they got to the honeymoon cottage they could sit down quietly and talk. That she could tell him why she was afraid of intimacy and why she needed him to take things slowly with her. But what if he was too out of control to listen? Would he just go ahead—

Marissa's skin turned cold as Jed sat down and draped his arm around her.

"You'd think things would start to wind down soon," he muttered.

"Jed, please don't drink any more."

"Aw, honey bee, don't spoil my fun."

"Please—"

William Johnson approached the table, and Jed's smile faded. The Texan had also been imbibing steadily throughout the evening. His face was flushed, and his lips quirked into a leer as he saw the groom check his watch, something he'd been doing all evening.

"It's getting late. Already one o'clock. I guess you're anxious to spirit the bride to your honeymoon cottage."

Marissa sensed Jed's sudden tension. Johnson had made him angry in the receiving line. Now he was rubbing him the wrong way again. Under the table she latched onto her husband's hand and squeezed it hard, hoping she could have some effect on his behavior. The last thing she wanted was a scene.

Just then the clock in the hall began to strike—twelve bongs in all.

"I guess you're wrong about the time," she said lightly.

The Texan appeared puzzled, then he cursed under his breath. "I forgot it's an hour later in Santa Isabella."

That was true, Marissa recalled for the first time since she'd arrived at the *finca.* They were far enough west to be on the other side of a time zone.

She felt Jed's fingers dig into her palm.

Her head swung toward him. "It's okay. The time doesn't matter."

"I'm afraid it's critical," he hissed as the Texan turned away to face the crowd.

"Are you worried that you're getting overtired again?" She stopped abruptly, knowing he wouldn't want her to mention his illness in public. "Didn't you take a nap this afternoon?"

He glared at her, and she knew by the instant clarity and glittering anger in his eyes that he hadn't been drinking as much as she thought—as much as he *wanted* people to think. "Oh, I did all the right stuff," he said, then darted a quick glance at Johnson, who was waving everyone over and shouting for *silencio.*

When people turned in his direction, he pointed to Jed and Marissa. "Let's get to the real fun of the evening. Let's put the bride and groom to bed."

Marissa went cold and stiff. Now what? Ignoring her reaction, Jed slid his arm around her and nibbled his way across her cheek until his mouth reached her ear. He might look like a man anticipating a steamy wedding night, but the message he delivered was harsh and grating. "Let's hope it doesn't take too long. Because if we end up in that honeymoon cottage after one in the morning, we're going to be very dead."

Chapter Twelve

There were enthusiastic shouts around the room. All at once the crowd had only one purpose.

"Bed!"

"Put them to bed!"

As the band struck up a raucous tune, Marissa tried to focus on Jed. Had she heard him correctly? "What?"

"I hope to hell it's not going to be too long before we're finally alone," was all he said by way of clarification, and she realized he couldn't explain anything to her now. But the look in his eyes assured her that he hadn't been playing some kind of practical joke.

"Get the donkeys!" several people called.

"Start the procession!"

"Strip them first," a drunken voice chimed in—adding to the general amusement of the onlookers.

Looking thoroughly pleased with himself, Johnson turned and winked at Marissa. "Don't you just love these quaint local customs?"

Wide-eyed, she sought to disappear behind Jed. He wrapped his arms protectively around her. "Would they really strip us?" she asked above the clamor.

"I saw it happen once. Let's hope we've got diplomatic immunity."

"Oh, God."

A drunk-looking man staggered toward them with a glass of rum in one hand and a machete in the other. Two others grabbed him and pushed him out of the way. He landed on his rump, the liquor sloshing down the front of his shirt.

"Please, can't you just let us go?" Marissa asked a woman standing close by.

She shrugged. "The men want to have their fun."

Several villagers led two donkeys into the hall. Both animals wore sombreros and halters decorated with flowers. Tin cans were tied to their tails, and bands of bells circled their legs. They made a terrible racket as they moved across the tile floor.

Marissa stared at the beasts in astonishment. If they'd been part of a holiday parade, she would have laughed. As it was, she found nothing about the scene amusing.

Fighting panic, she scanned the room for a way out. Before she could take a step, eager hands lifted her into the sidesaddle on the back of one donkey. She'd never ridden in that position; it felt terribly unstable, and she held on for dear life as the onlookers clapped and stamped their feet. Pretending to be a bit unsteady, Jed climbed onto the other beast before anyone could help him.

Laughing and calling boisterously to each other, the wedding guests began to parade the two of them around the room with Marissa in the lead. Merrymakers surged around her, clapping, laughing and making remarks about what the groom was going to do soon and how the bride was going to respond.

Jed had said they didn't have much time. This had to stop. But how?

As they made the first circuit of the room, Marissa racked her brain for some way to end the ordeal. The man guiding her donkey was none too steady on his feet and kept veering toward the flowered trellises that had been set up around the walls.

He was going to knock one down if he didn't watch out, Marissa thought. Then inspiration struck. Hoping Jed was watching what she was doing, she angled a foot outward and hooked the toe of her shoe through a gap in the latticework. As the donkey moved past the flower-covered screen, it wavered dangerously and began to topple toward her.

Marissa screamed as if she were both surprised and terrified, lifting her arms above her head to ward off the blow. Jed slid from his own animal and sprang forward. Just as the trellis was about to strike him on the shoulders, he gave a tremendous push, so that it landed with a crash on the tile floor.

The music stopped. The crowd went utterly silent at the unexpected turn of events.

Jed stared back at the faces that had gone from gleeful to grave in the blink of an eye—his countenance dark and dangerous. "Thank you for a wonderful party. But I think my bride and I have had enough fun for one evening," he said as he helped her down from her donkey. "Please feel free to continue the festivities without us." His tone was even, but his body language telegraphed the message that the teasing was over for tonight.

Nobody said anything.

He inclined his head and waited for several more seconds. Then, taking Marissa's arm, he led her out of the reception room and down the hall toward the back of the hacienda. Some of the crowd followed, but they were more subdued now.

"Good going," he said as they emerged into the darkness.

"I didn't know if it would be enough."

Marissa saw that the path to the honeymoon cottage

had been marked with a line of lanterns. As they reached the door, Jed stopped and spoke to several men who were standing at attention near the door. "Thanks for keeping watch. I don't think we'll be needing you now."

"Don't you want us to make sure nobody comes around?"

"I appreciate your help. But go in and join the party now. Have yourselves a good time."

The door closed behind them. Mercifully, they had escaped from their tormentors. But now what?

Marissa's eyes were large and round as she stared uncertainly at Jed, smoldering sensuality mingling with layers of uncertainty. He'd said they couldn't stay here. She still had no idea what was going on.

"Alone at last." He gave her a sardonic smile, and her heart rose to block her windpipe.

He took her icy hand. "Come see the surprise I've got."

She looked at him questioningly when he led her to the bar. Kneeling, he removed the panel under the sink and pointed inside. Marissa stared in horror. Wedged between the water pipes was a bomb. The clock on the timer said one-thirty.

"When Johnson came over to us, I realized he was mixed up about the time difference. But that's okay, because it got us out of the party early," Jed commented, his careful choice of words telling her that they still couldn't count on a private conversation.

"Johnson?" Marissa repeated, her eyes fixed on the bomb.

Jed nodded.

The clock said the device was going to go off in half an hour—if Johnson hadn't made some other miscalculation. Pieces of the puzzle were starting to fall into place. The man had a mining deal going with Sanchez, and it looked as if he was willing to kill to get rid of the competition. But did Sanchez know?

"He wanted to give us a real send-off," Jed agreed. He rolled his eyes. Marissa looked at him in frustration. Exchanging information was still impossible.

"So now that we're alone, Mrs. Prentiss, why don't you slip into something more comfortable?"

Totally confused by the abrupt change of subject, she frowned. But her confusion became understanding as Jed pulled a pair of men's slacks, a shirt and sandals from behind one of the sofa cushions. It looked like the outfits the villagers wore. Travel clothes, she realized. He had obviously stashed them here earlier in the day.

Jed looked from the bomb to the line of small buttons down her back. "Let me help you off with your dress."

Marissa nodded wordlessly, and he came up behind her, his hands brushing aside the wisps of hair that had escaped from her French twist.

She stood very still, the touch of his fingers on her hair and neck sending little zings along her nerve endings.

A moment ago he'd been all business. When his fingers came in contact with her skin, everything changed. He drew in a shaky breath as he buried his nose in her hair. Then his lips grazed her neck. "Like silk," he murmured.

Transfixed, Marissa moved her head against his face. She'd been dreading this kind of intimacy, yet her responses to this man held her captive.

For several heartbeats Jed seemed to forget what he was supposed to be doing. Finally he began to unfasten the buttons at the back of her dress.

She tried to stand very still as she felt the fabric slowly open, exposing the skin of her back to his view. Little shivers raced along her skin as he touched her—not only with his fingers. He followed the progress of the buttons with his lips, sensually kissing the flesh that he revealed.

When he slipped the dress from her shoulders, he made no move to pick up the peasant outfit she was supposed to put on.

"Jed?"

He bent to capture her earlobe in his teeth, nibbling with controlled pressure that made her dizzy.

"Jed..." His name sighed out again.

"Your skin is so soft. And you smell so good." He drew in a ragged breath as he nuzzled his cheek and nose against her back. His fingers stroked up and down underneath one of her bra straps.

Her own breath was coming in little gasps. In some part of her mind she knew that the seconds were ticking by—each one moving them closer to terrible danger. She knew they had to get out of this room. But she wasn't capable of moving at this moment. He tugged her dress lower. It would have puddled around her feet if there had been an inch of space between her body and his. "Ah, Marci, I've been looking at you all evening, thinking about undressing you like this. This is our wedding night." He pressed her hips back against his, and she knew unmistakably he was ready to make love to her.

"Yes," she breathed as her body responded to his words, to his touch. She had never felt more aroused—perhaps because some part of her still recognized that she was safe. He wasn't going to take her into the bedroom. He couldn't. Or could he?

"I've got to touch you. Just touch you."

He wasn't asking for permission. He simply took what he wanted. His hands came up to clasp her breasts, kneading them gently through the silky fabric of her bra, making her gasp with pleasure. Involuntarily she closed her eyes and arched backward against him. He found her nipples, drawing small circles around them with his fingertips until they hardened to tight peaks of sensation. She pressed into his hands, whimpering deep in her throat.

"You want me."

She had no thought of denying the truth of his statement. "Yes."

His teeth and lips played with her neck and the sensitive curve of her ear. Starved for more direct contact, she tried to twist around so that she could kiss him. But he held her fast. His hands stroked down her front, pushing the dress out of the way. It slid to the floor, and he slipped his fingers under the edges of her panties.

Her body jerked as he touched her intimately, holding her captive. All thought was driven from her mind but the need to get closer still.

Then Jed's muttered curse brought back a measure of sanity. "We're playing with dynamite here."

This time her little whimper was equal parts fear and arousal as her gaze shot to the bomb. She would have toppled backward if he'd stepped away from her. Instead he reached for the shirt on the couch and helped her slip her arms through the sleeves. He left the buttons for her.

Marissa took gasping little breaths as she closed the front, then stepped into the trousers he was holding out. They were too long, and he knelt to roll up the cuffs, making an obvious attempt not to brush her ankles.

While she shoved her feet into the sandals and tucked her hair under the brim of her hat, he quickly shucked off his dinner jacket, dress pants and shirt and donned an outfit similar to hers—only his looked rumpled, as if he'd already been wearing it. Then he bent and lifted up another cushion. Her eyes widened when she saw he was holding a revolver.

"Where did you get that?" she asked, forgetting for a moment that someone might be listening.

"I won't tell if you don't," he answered as he tucked

the weapon into his waistband. Then he slung a knapsack over his shoulder.

When they stepped into the tropical night, she let out a long sigh. It was a relief to be away from the room with the bomb, but she didn't know much about dynamite. How far from the house would they have to go to be safe from the blast?

Jed took her hand. In the light from the myriad stars and the almost full moon, they began to move rapidly away from the cottage. From destruction.

Marissa glanced back at the little cottage. It stood alone, apart from other buildings, which made it the perfect place for Johnson's scheme. The blast would damage nothing else on the *finca*.

As they reached the edge of the plantings that provided privacy, Jed stopped under a date palm to reconnoiter. Marissa could see that when they crossed the open area they'd be completely exposed. But there was no other way to escape.

They stepped onto the grass, heading toward the nearest clump of foliage. Before they'd gotten more than a few yards the sound of footsteps crunching on the gravel path made them both stop abruptly. Jed's fingers clamped down on Marissa's. They were trapped. And running for the nearest clump of trees would only give them away.

Her body went cold all over as she felt his free hand silently pull the gun from his trousers. Then two dark shapes came into view. It looked like a couple of men from the village heading home after the festivities. They were staggering. Please God, let them be too drunk to notice what was around them, Marissa prayed.

"Come on," Jed whispered. "Act like you belong here, and they won't pay any attention."

She'd forgotten she was dressed like a man. That nobody would take her for the bride unless they saw her face. With her heart in her throat she started walking again, putting one foot in front of the other as the pair lurched away at an angle across the clearing.

She half expected them to turn and clamp a hand on her shoulder. Miraculously, she and Jed reached the nearest knot of trees without incident. After that, to her relief, it was possible to zigzag their way across the *finca* without being exposed for more than a few seconds.

Then, in the distance, she could hear the dogs barking, and for a panicked few seconds she imagined a pack of Dobermans looming out of the darkness.

Jed must have had the same thought, because she felt him tense. Then he relaxed. "Don't worry about them. There are too many people on the grounds tonight. And the general won't want his guests getting torn up."

Marissa took what comfort she could in the reassurance as Jed led her toward a low building that looked like a warehouse made of corrugated steel with a long bank of garage doors.

"Wait here," he whispered.

"Why are we stopping?"

"Call it curiosity."

She doubted mere curiosity would delay Jed at a time like this. Stepping into the shadows, she watched him disappear around the side of the building. Several seconds later Marissa heard a groan and felt her heart lurch. Sprinting around the corner, she found an armed sentry lying on the ground by a small door. Jed handed her the man's machine gun and tucked his own pistol back in his waistband.

"Sorry I had to do that," he muttered.

"He'll report it when he wakes up."

"Yeah. But he didn't see me. So he can't tell Sanchez who it was."

Marissa served as lookout while Jed took a small tool

kit from his knapsack and tackled the padlock on the door. He had it open in a matter of moments.

Inside it was pitch-dark. But Jed must have spent the afternoon getting ready for this, because he'd brought along a flashlight. Marissa held it as he tied up the soldier; all the while she felt her tension balloon. She wanted to leave the *finca* as quickly as possible, and she had to remind herself that Jed wouldn't be stopping in this place if it wasn't important.

"Now let's find out what my great and good friend's got under lock and key," he said. Taking the flashlight from Marissa, he began to play the beam over some large pieces of machinery. "Either he's going in for road building and housing projects in a big way or—"

"I vote for mining equipment," she said in a low voice that matched Jed's.

"Oh, yeah?"

"When they thought I was asleep this afternoon, two of the women were talking about Johnson." She felt her cheeks heat as she recalled the circumstances and was glad the flashlight beam wasn't trained on her face. "Apparently he's a mining engineer who comes here all the time. And he's not from Texas."

"Sanchez told me he's an arms dealer."

"Because it's a plausible explanation for their relationship. And one you'd believe," Marissa supplied. "But the women who were discussing him didn't have an ax to grind. Try this scenario. What if Johnson and your friend have some kind of private deal to develop the copper deposits in Junipero Province? They cut the government out and take all the profits."

Jed's eyes narrowed as he considered the theory. "That would explain why he didn't jump at the loan offer to the Ministry of Development."

The beam stopped as it hit a gigantic circular pan that

must have been fifteen or sixteen feet in diameter. "Wait a minute." He stepped closer and whistled. "Well, I'll be damned. Did the women mention copper mining?"

"Not specifically."

"Well, I think there's a better reason why he wants to keep the Ministry of Development out of Junipero Province. He and Johnson aren't mining copper. They're mining diamonds."

Marissa's eyes widened. "Diamonds? What makes you think so?"

"Ninety-five percent of the world's output still comes from South Africa. But diamonds are in Brazil, Venezuela and Guyana. So why not in the unexplored jungle of San Marcos?"

Jed stepped closer to one of the metallic circles and played the light along the edge. "Here's the manufacturer's name. It's a firm in Cape Town. You've heard about miners panning for gold—separating the ore from the gravel in streambeds by washing it in pans. The gold stays on the bottom because it's denser than the gravel. Well, the same principle is used with diamonds. Only the pans are gigantic."

"You're positive this stuff couldn't be for copper?"

"No. I could give you a lot of technical details about copper refining, but all you have to know is that it's an entirely different process."

Marissa nodded.

Jed looked at his watch. "Let's get out of here. The explosion is going to give us the perfect cover to get off the *finca*."

"How much time do we have?"

"A little less than eight minutes."

"Oh!"

They left the guard tied up in the building and retraced part of their route, angling off to the right and ending up at a wire fence that should have been electrified. Apparently Jed had disabled the mechanism, because his hand didn't sizzle when he lifted it up and helped her down into a deep concrete draining ditch about fifty yards from the honeymoon cottage. At this time of year the ditch was bone-dry.

The overhang of a little platform sheltered them from view. It also hid a motorcycle leaning against the wall of the conduit.

"You've been busy," Marissa commented.

"Yeah. I pulled a straw hat down over my face and went native. With all the hoopla of the wedding preparations, nobody was doing their usual jobs."

Jed had picked a perfect place to watch the fireworks. They were out of sight and protected from the explosion, but they had an unobstructed view of the little house.

"Only three minutes now," Jed whispered, slipping his arm around Marissa and drawing her close. She leaned against him in the dark, feeling tension build inside her that was not only from the anticipated explosion. There were still so many things she wanted to talk about with Jed, yet everything would have to wait.

"Two minutes."

Marissa strained to see the cottage through the darkness. Silently she began to count off the seconds. When she'd reached thirty, she saw a figure approaching the back door. It was a woman walking stealthily and carrying a basket. As she paused and looked around to see if anyone was watching her, Marissa felt her breath still. "Good heavens, it's Clarita!"

Jed groaned. "Damn her."

Clarita took several steps closer to the cottage. In a panic, thinking of nothing but the danger to the girl, Marissa pulled herself up to the rim of the ditch and started to scramble forward.

Chapter Thirteen

Jed moved faster than Marissa, clamping his hand over her arm so hard that she gasped.

"Please. I've got to stop her."

"Are you as cracked as she is?"

"What?"

"You can't go out there now. The place is going to blow at any second. I won't let you kill yourself trying—" Jed stopped abruptly and raised his voice. Speaking in Spanish, he shouted, "Halt. Or I'll shoot."

He sounded just like one of the guards. Clarita whirled toward the command.

"Back up, *señorita,*" Jed added.

The girl raised her chin haughtily. "Do you know whom you're addressing? When I tell *El Jefe* of your presumption, he will—"

The end of her sentence was cut off by a blast that sounded like a volcanic eruption and felt like a ten-ton airplane slamming into the earth.

As the ground shook, Jed pulled Marissa down, shielding her body with his. The last thing she saw was the walls and roof of the cottage flying outward. Then debris began to rain down.

Jed didn't wait for the dust to settle. "We're in the clear. Come on."

Marissa stayed where she was, straining her eyes to see through the dust. "We can't leave Clarita. She may be hurt."

"People are coming. They'll take care of her."

Marissa realized Jed was right. After several seconds of stunned silence, guards began shouting and hurrying toward the blast area from all directions. Reluctantly she let Jed lead her away.

Bending low, he grabbed the handlebars of the motorcycle and began to walk it down the ditch.

"Not yet."

He stopped and shrugged. They both listened to the noise and confusion as the soldiers tried to make sense of what had happened.

"*Madre de Dios!* Señor Jed," someone shouted. "Where are you? Are you all right?"

"Nobody could survive that."

"Here's a woman."

"Was she inside?"

"I don't know."

"By all the saints. It's *El Jefe*'s daughter."

"See. They found her," Jed whispered.

"All right." Marissa nodded in the dark and followed Jed.

"What did you mean when you asked if I was as crazy as she?" Marissa asked in a low voice.

"She's having mental problems. Everybody on the *finca* knows it, but Sanchez won't get her any help."

Marissa sighed. "That explains a lot of her strange behavior."

"I hope this changes Sanchez's mind."

As they moved down the ditch, the noise and disarray behind them faded to a distant babble of voices. About a quarter mile from the blast site Jed started the machine and climbed on. Marissa perched on the seat behind him and circled his waist with her arms. She leaned her head on his shoulder as they moved slowly down the pavement, still with the lamp off. But there was enough light from the moon and brilliant canopy of stars to navigate.

She pressed her cheek to his shoulder and hung on to his powerful body, letting the vibrations of the engine lull her. It was hard to believe they were really getting away from Sanchez.

When the motorcycle slowed, her head jerked up. A chain-link fence blocked the ditch.

"Now what?"

"Not to worry. Can you hold this thing for a minute?"

"Yes."

He dismounted and walked to the fence. Grasping the center of the links, he pulled, and they parted like the Red Sea opening for the Israelites.

He grinned back at her. "Superman!"

"You cut it this afternoon."

"Right."

He came back and guided the machine through the opening. As Marissa followed him outside the fence, she felt as if a hundred-pound weight had been lifted from her shoulders.

"Thank you," she breathed.

Jed propped the bike against the fence. They each took a step forward. Then she was in his arms, and he was crushing her to him. Their lips came together in a long, searing kiss that was broken only when they both had to come up for air.

"Oh, Jed, Jed. You got me out of there. You saved my life. I owe you so much."

"You don't owe me anything."

It wasn't exactly the declaration Marissa wanted to hear. But she knew he wasn't a man who articulated his feelings easily. She gestured toward the cut fence and the motorcycle. "You must have been running around all day getting things set up. If you want, I can drive and you can rest."

"You don't have to coddle me. I'm fine!"

She realized she'd said the wrong thing again and hastened to repair the damage. "Jed, it's been pretty hard for me to stand by like a helpless female and let you run the rescue operation."

He nodded. "Yeah, I understand. But I didn't exactly do it by myself. If you hadn't played the part I tossed at you, we never would have made it."

"That's true."

"So you can leave the driving to me. I'm probably a lot more experienced on a motorcycle than you are."

She climbed in back of him again, and they started off once more at a slow speed, still with the lights off.

"I've got a boat waiting for us at a little town called Zapaca. We can be out of San Marcos in another four hours," he told her.

She shook her head. "We can't. We have to go back to Santa Isabella."

"Impossible. When Sanchez doesn't find any bodies in that cottage, he's going to come looking for us."

"You think he gave the instructions to Johnson?"

Jed nodded grimly.

"All the more reason why I want to get the goods on him."

"You know as well as I do that the next time somebody looks, that diamond mining equipment will have disappeared from those warehouses."

"Of course. But there's another way. I assume you know Victor Kirkland at the State Department sent me down here?"

"On a damn fool mission."

"You were here for the same thing," she challenged.

"I didn't get caught with my hand in the cookie jar."

So they were back where they'd started at the cocktail party—wary opponents.

"I would have been okay," Marissa said, "if somebody hadn't given me away."

"It wasn't me!"

"I know," she said softly. She felt the muscles in his shoulders clench. "Maybe Johnson saw me leave the party. Maybe it was Clarita who called the guards. But that's not the important thing now."

"I'm listening. You've got sixty seconds to convince me we should risk our lives by staying in a country where the head of the army can execute a U.S. citizen without a trial."

She began to speak quickly. "Before I got caught, I photographed some documents that were in code. I couldn't read them, but I assumed they were Sanchez's plans for overthrowing President Palmeriz—because he thinks the army is stronger than the democratic government. That's what Victor sent me down here to scope out. Now it looks like Sanchez is going to use the money from the diamond-mining operation to finance a coup. After I breached his security, he probably moved the documents to a safer location. But we can still get the film. I sealed my camera in a plastic bag and stuck it in his toilet tank. If he'd found it, I'd already be dead."

Jed swore. "I suppose it's in the private bathroom off his office."

"Nobody will be expecting us to break in there. They'll expect us to clear out as fast as we can."

He didn't answer one way or the other.

She felt her tension mount. "So where are we going?" she asked after five minutes of silence.

"To the coast."

"I'm not leaving San Marcos. I'll get the film myself."

"Honey bee, you'll only get caught again, and this whole sideshow will have been a waste."

A sideshow. Was that what he called it? Anger surged inside her. But she knew her reaction was reflexive. For once, she swallowed her pride. "You're right. I'm not being rational," she admitted. "I'm angry about what that bastard did to me—to us—and I want to get back at him in spades. But more than that, I want to come home feeling that I accomplished my mission. I don't want to be talked about for the rest of my life as the bumbling idiot who had to be rescued. But I need your help to pull this off."

She'd laid herself bare, and she waited anxiously for his answer. Although he shifted in his seat, he was silent again for several miles.

Afraid he wasn't going to respond, she had no option but to sit behind him, holding on tightly as he swerved around a tree limb that had fallen into the drainage ditch. When he finally began to speak, his voice was gruff. "I understand how you feel."

"I hoped you would."

"But it's not a simple case of my changing plans. Maybe you'd better hear the whole story of what happened to me in Royal Verde."

"You don't owe me any more explanation than you already gave me."

"I want you to know where I'm coming from, as the touchy-feely types put it." She felt him suck in a long draft of air and let it out slowly, a man working up to some sort of shameful confession. "I was on assignment trying to pinpoint the source of a very nasty street drug. I'd zeroed in on a local mental hospital where some strange stuff was going on—like voodoo ceremonies with human sacrifice."

Marissa sucked in a sharp breath. "How did they get away with that?"

"The director of the place would remind you of Sanchez. He was a law unto himself on his own estate. Unfortunately I picked voodoo night to reconnoiter, got shot out of a tree with a blowgun and ended up locked in the asylum's disturbed ward. The director tried to get me to talk—using a variety of interesting methods. When that didn't work, he decided that I, along with a female agent they captured later, were going to be the next sacrificial victims."

"No!"

"They starved me for a few days to make me weak. Then they brought us to the ceremonial ground, made us drink a vile concoction and tied us to stakes."

Marissa pressed her face against his shoulder, not sure she wanted to hear the rest, but he plowed on. Marissa guessed that the concealing darkness, and the fact that his back was to her, made it easier to talk.

"I wouldn't be alive at all," Jed continued, "if the voodoo priestess hadn't decided to double-cross her partner. I found out later that she put some kind of organic compound on the knife she plunged into our chests. Along with the stuff we drank before the ritual, it sent us into a state of suspended animation, so everybody thought we were dead. And the team that had come down to clean up the flap on Royal Verde was able to get us out of there."

"Oh, Jed, it must have been awful."

"Well, when the priestess plunged the knife into my body, I went out like a light."

Marissa winced.

"After they revived us, I thought I was back to normal. I even joked about being a zombie. But it turned out not to be very funny. It wasn't until months later that I discovered there's a virus in my blood. Too much stress and fatigue trigger the sleeping sickness you saw the other night. The doctors tell me there's no medical treatment. I've just got to live with it.'' He swiveled his head partly around. ''So you're pushing your luck if you're counting on me to help you get in and out of Sanchez's office. I may let you down when you need me the most.''

''Don't call yourself a zombie.''

''And what would you call it?'' he asked bitterly as he focused on the pavement ahead of him once more. ''For my next career I can be exhibit A in that voodoo museum in New Orleans.''

Marissa clasped her hands more tightly around his middle and moved her cheek against his neck, longing to talk face-to-face, to make him understand that the confession didn't change the way she felt about him. ''What happened isn't your fault.''

''I shouldn't have gotten caught.''

''Neither should I!''

''That's different.''

''How?''

He was silent for several moments. Then he sighed. ''Okay. I guess I know how you're feeling about this assignment. If you trust me and you want me to take you back to Santa Isabella, I'll do it.''

''Thank you.''

''Hold the thanks until we're in the clear.''

Marissa closed her eyes and clung to him. He'd been achingly honest with her, and she wanted to be the same with him. But unlike Jed, she didn't feel comfortable having a personal discussion straddling a motorbike. She wanted more time and a better place, where she could watch his face as she spoke. Yet the pressure to confess her own deficiency was like a balloon expanding inside her chest. Trying to ignore it, she leaned into him, hoping he'd know by the way she held him that she trusted him completely.

The machine plowed on through the night. When Jed reached the end of the ditch, he consulted the odometer and a map from his knapsack. Turning left, he bumped across a stretch of open field to the road—where he turned on the light and sped up.

They'd gone only a few miles when he cursed and slammed on the brakes.

Marissa tensed.

"We've got company." He gestured down the blacktop.

She expected to confront one of Sanchez's men. Instead she made a little exclamation when she saw orange fur and black spots. A jaguar! It was sprawled on the pavement only a few yards from where Jed had stopped. The big cat lifted its head, regarding them as if they were intruders in its private bedroom.

"They like the heat the road absorbs during the day," Jed explained.

"I know."

He eased the machine gun off the saddle carrier and handed it to Marissa. "They don't attack people unless they're very hungry."

"Right."

"But keep an eye on him."

Hoping the weapon was just a precaution, she trained it on the animal as Jed revved the engine. The cat watched them warily for several more seconds, its body poised to spring.

Marissa held the gun steady. To her relief, the animal leaped up and trotted into the underbrush.

The next few miles passed without incident. When they came to a road that branched off to the right, Jed consulted the map and the odometer again and turned right.

"Where are you going?"

"I didn't know what the situation would be when I came back from Baltimore, so I arranged for several safe houses where we could hole up if we needed to. One isn't far from here. I rented it in the name of the Audubon Society—for some bird-watchers who are supposed to be coming down to San Marcos in a couple of weeks."

"We'll be safe there?"

"I can't give you an ironclad guarantee. But we'll be as safe as anywhere in the country."

For all her bravado, the thought of falling into Sanchez's clutches again made her shudder. She knew Jed was giving her a chance to change her mind about staying. But she clamped her teeth together and didn't voice any more objections.

As Jed sped on, Marissa realized how wrung out she was. She'd been mentally prepared for a long ride, but the reality was taking its toll. Slumping against him, she closed her eyes as the bike bumped down a gravel road. When they jolted to a halt, she realized to her astonishment that she'd actually fallen asleep. Blinking, she saw they were in front of a native dwelling with a thatched roof and walls of bamboo poles. Dismounting, she staggered over to the rows of vertical posts and braced herself with her hand.

"Are you okay?"

"Just stiff." She made an effort to straighten while Jed pulled out a set of keys. After a couple of tries he unlocked the padlock on the door and shone the light around the interior.

"All clear."

Handing Marissa the light, he retrieved the motorbike and brought it inside with them. She played the beam around the small room, revealing a bed, a rickety table and a pile of supplies. It was about as basic as one of *El Jefe*'s cells.

"Not very plush, I'm afraid," Jed admitted. "But I think we're safe."

"I assume the bathroom's out back."

"Yeah. There aren't any three-star hotels out here."

"I wasn't complaining."

He led the way to the minimal facilities. "Ladies first."

She wished he wasn't standing right on the other side of the door, but she knew he wasn't going to leave her alone in this part of the jungle tonight—or any other night.

After they'd returned to the house she watched him move efficiently around the small room, locking the door behind them and lighting an oil lamp.

When she heard the lock snap, she felt her throat go dry.

Stop it! she shouted inside her head. *This is Jed. He's not going to hurt you.*

He broke the seal on a bottle of water. Marissa took several swallows to moisten her dry mouth. It was tempting to draw into herself—to lie down, roll away from him and pretend all she wanted to do was sleep. But she wasn't going to take the coward's way out. She'd psyched herself up to talk to him, and every moment she waited increased the tight feeling in her chest.

She watched Jed set down his pack and stretch, drawing her attention to his powerful muscles. "We've got field rations if you want something."

"I'm not hungry."

There was nowhere to sit besides a double bed with rope springs attached to the wooden frame. Marissa stared at it for several seconds before gingerly lowering her body onto it.

Jed hesitated, then joined her. As the weight shifted on the thin mattress, she struggled to breathe without giving away her nervousness. But she couldn't stop herself from twisting her stiff fingers around a strand of her hair.

"We'll probably both feel better after a good night's sleep," Jed said noncommittally, and she knew she wasn't fooling him.

The pressure inside her chest made her words come out high and shaky. "After we finish the conversation."

"Which conversation?"

Knowing she was stepping into a mine field, she plowed on. "You said you understood how I felt about getting caught by Sanchez. I wanted to tell you I understood about the...the zombie stuff."

He moved away from her, propping his back against the wall and pinning her with his gaze. "I don't need empathy right now. I need sleep."

Marissa ignored the sarcasm in his voice. "You feel like somebody stepped into your life and took away your power to make your own decisions. You feel angry because your choices are limited. You don't feel quite whole. In fact, used and degraded are better descriptions. And you keep cursing yourself for a fool because you've let that one unfortunate incident rule everything you do." She blurted out the phrases that had been running around and around in her head for the past few hours.

Jed's eyes glittered in the lamplight. "What are you trying to do?" he demanded. "Expose every raw nerve in my body just so you can prove a point?"

Her heart was threatening to pound its way up her throat. "I'm trying to show you that I get it—better than almost anyone else would."

He remained silent, a wary but curious look coming over his handsome features.

She gazed down at her hands clasped tightly in her lap. The knuckles were white. She'd deliberately forced this confrontation, and she'd told herself she wanted to look him in the eye. Yet suddenly she couldn't quite meet his gaze. "What you went through," she began, then paused to draw a steadying breath and start again. "What you went through comes pretty close to the experience of being raped."

The devastated look on his face almost undid her.

"No," he whispered. "No."

She nodded, determined to make him understand how it was for her. "For ten years I've known I wanted the same things a normal woman wants. Being alone made me so sad. But the fear was stronger. I couldn't get close to any man—because one of them won my trust and then tore my heart out. So I made myself tough and cold and unapproachable." She swallowed hard. "Then I met someone I liked. Someone who turned me on. Someone I wanted to be...close to. But that scared me so badly I worked overtime to make sure he kept his distance. And if you haven't figured it out, I'm talking about you."

She'd said it. Not the worst, perhaps. But enough. There was complete silence for several seconds, and she cringed inside, hardly able to believe she'd been that honest. Now what would he think of her?

"Marci?" He closed the space between them, taking her by the shoulders—gently, oh, so gently. Slowly, as if he were afraid she'd bolt, he pulled her into his arms. For a moment she held herself rigid. Then she gave up and went limp against him. She'd told him her deep dark secret, and he had taken her in his arms. That was miracle enough. But all at once it seemed possible that the rest of it was going to be okay, too.

As his hands stroked her hair, her back, the knot of tension in her chest began to loosen. "Honey, I figured out some guy must have been rough with you. I didn't know you were raped."

"Oh, Jed, all these years I've worked so hard to fool you. To keep you from thinking of me as a woman."

He uttered a single short laugh. "I thought of you as a woman, all right."

Compulsively, she continued. "You're so masculine. Aggressive. Intimidating. You take what you want. And I was afraid of that. Then you came down here pretending we were engaged, and you stood all my rules on their heads. Jed, when you kissed me that first time, it was like fireworks going off."

"Yes."

"Afterward, I was quaking inside. But I knew that if I let you or Sanchez see how scared I was, I'd get us both killed."

"I kept pushing you," he muttered. "Seeing how far I could get you to go."

"Why?"

"You're not the only one who's been attracted for years. I guess I liked having you in a position where you couldn't back off." He laughed. "That's the macho answer. And it's part of the truth. The other part is that once I kissed you, I could hardly remember my own name."

"Oh, Jed."

He turned her to him and started to kiss her. Then he pulled back as if he'd put his face too close to an open flame.

She felt her world shatter. "I've dumped a lot of heavy stuff on you," she murmured. "I understand if you can't deal with it."

When she started to turn away so he couldn't see the tears in her eyes, he took her fiercely by the arms. "Honey, don't ever make the mistake of thinking I don't want you. Or that I don't care. I'm trying my damnedest to get this right."

"I—"

He touched her quivering lips with his finger. "There are things I need to know. Like, how do you feel now? Are you still afraid of me? And how close do you want me to get? Tonight."

She raised her head and looked at him, feeling as if time were standing still, waiting for her answer. Here it was, at last. Was she going to continue being a coward? Or could she finally, here and now, reclaim her life? "I'm still afraid," she said, her voice shaking as much as her body. "And at the same time, I feel like I'll die if I can't make love with you."

His knuckles grazed her cheek. "Have you made love since…I mean…since it happened?"

"No," she whispered. "But when you kissed me and touched me, it made me so hot and shaky that I felt like I was going to jump out of my skin." She nestled against him, daring to let the warm feeling steal over her once more. It was wonderful to finally be honest with him—with herself. To let him know what she wanted. She could do this. It was going to be all right.

He chuckled. "I understand the feeling."

"But…but…I have to explain something to you first," she said, breaking past shyness. "Remember that night in your room when you tried to…to push me down onto the rug. I…"

"That scared you," he finished.

"Yes. Your weight on top of me. So maybe we can't… I mean…could we…?"

"I think we can work around that. If you're sure it's what you want to do. Or we can, you know, take it slow, get to know each other better."

"I don't want to take it slow. This is…" She hesitated, raising her face to his. "Jed, this is our wedding night."

She'd thought she had everything figured out. She'd thought she could simply have what she wanted, now that she'd bared her soul. In the next moment, to her astonishment, she burst into tears.

Chapter Fourteen

"Marci, honey?"

Marissa tried to answer but found she was incapable of speaking around the sobs that racked her body. All she could do was cling to Jed as she fought to get control of herself.

"It's okay. It's okay," he murmured, along with other soothing words she only half heard.

By slow degrees she managed to subdue the storm of tears. Jed held her, continuing his gentle reassurance until she was calmer. When he brought a tissue out of the knapsack, she blew her nose.

"Honey, we don't have to—"

"Don't you understand? I want you so much I feel like I'm going to burn up from the inside out!" she cut in fiercely. "I thought...I could...we could..."

He waited patiently, not pushing her into difficult explanations.

She gulped in a lungful of air. "I told you, I want to be normal."

"You are!"

"I don't think this is going to work unless I tell you what happened. I need you to understand why tonight is so threatening to me."

"Okay," he said softly.

She held the edge of the mattress in a death grip, her fingers so rigid that she wondered vaguely if she'd ever pry them open again. "Did you ever see that movie *Cape Fear,* where a man who was sent to prison terrorizes his lawyer's family—especially the wife and daughter?"

Jed nodded.

"I've seen it a dozen times. Maybe to convince myself I'm not the only fool who could be taken in by a smooth-talking stranger."

"Don't call yourself a fool," he said harshly.

"Okay. Sure. I was eighteen, in my first year of college at the University of Maryland. There was this guy named Lowell Dougan. He started a conversation with me in the library. I was pretty shy. But I was happy to finally be on my own, away from my father. Lowell was so charming and funny that he got me to go out to dinner with him that night. After that he sort of...swept me off my feet." She sighed, trying once more to come to terms with what had happened. "I was pretty naive. My father had hardly let me date in high school. So I didn't know much about men. Lowell flattered me. Made me feel special. Convinced me we were madly in love with each other and that we should get married. Probably you're thinking I was pretty stupid."

"No. It sounds like you were lonely—and susceptible."

"I was. Lowell kept sidestepping any questions I had about his family or his background. I didn't know he'd been in the army and been court-martialed and spent four years at Leavenworth Penitentiary. I didn't know my father had started the court-martial proceedings because he'd caught Lowell hitting on female GIs. I didn't know he was being so nice to me to get back at Colonel Devereaux."

"Because he deliberately hid all that from you."

"But I should have had more sense than to run off and marry him!" she protested. "On our wed-wedding night I found out that what he really wanted was revenge."

Jed cursed vehemently.

"He kept me captive in a motel room for two days—raping me and...other things. He'd leave me there tied up in the dark for hours, wondering when he was going to come back. Then he'd leap into the room and—and—" She didn't want to tell him any more.

Jed's eyes blazed. He pounded his fist against the wall. "I'll kill the bastard!"

"You can't. He shot himself. At least he didn't make me watch. He left me tied up until the maid found me in the morning."

Jed held her tightly. "Oh, Marci. Oh, Lord."

"My sister Cassie doesn't know because she was away at the University of Virginia. My father told me it was my fault. For years I believed him."

"No!"

"Abby Franklin's been helping me deal with it. She's a psychologist in the building where I work. She's been great."

"I know. Remember, she helped refine the rescue plan." He swallowed. "Before I left, I had a session with Abby. I told her about what happened on Royal Verde and asked her if I was up to this rescue mission. She told me she thought you and I would be good for each other."

Marissa laughed. "I made the mistake of talking to her about you. She's been after me for six months to stop acting like a coward."

"You're not! A coward wouldn't have raided Miguel's office."

"No. It had to be someone with nothing left to lose." Marissa looked down at her hands. She'd thought she was past the hard part. But there was one more confession she felt compelled to make. "I didn't want to tell you about Lowell—about him specifically. I didn't want you to be thinking about what he did to me when we make love," she whispered.

"The only thing I'm going to think about is how much I like being close to you."

"Oh, Jed." Her eyes misted. Blinking back the tears, she moved closer to him quickly and slipped her arms around his neck. When she felt more in control, she whispered, "I've waited a long time for this."

"So have I. But we don't have to rush. Maybe it would be better to hold off until another night. One that's not so...loaded."

"No. I've got a chance to replace that other wedding night with this one. That's the only way I'm going to wipe out the horror of what happened." She stopped as another thought struck her. "I'm sorry. I just realized I'm putting a lot of pressure on you. More than I have any right to. I know it's not a real marriage. But—"

"It's as real as we want to make it."

Her eyes shone as she gazed at him. He gave her a little smile and glanced around the confines of the shack. "I just wish I could check us into the Ritz, instead of this hovel."

"It's not on Sanchez's estate, and that's the only thing that matters."

He looked at her with such tenderness that she dared to let hope bloom. Perhaps that was the moment she knew for sure that she had fallen in love with him. Her heart swelled with gladness. She wanted to tell him how she felt. Yet she didn't want to put any more pressure on him. She couldn't be certain what would happen when they returned to civilization, but she would take whatever he offered tonight.

He gathered her close and covered her lips with his,

kissing her at first with leashed passion. As she made her eager response known, he deepened the kiss, and she realized she was playing in the big leagues.

"Jed, I don't have much experience with this sort of thing," she whispered.

"Then we're both in the same boat."

"Oh, come on!"

He gave her a rueful little grin. "Sure, I've had my share of fun. The difference is, I've never been with anyone who was so sure of herself in every situation except in bed. And I've never been with anyone who turned me on so much that she made my hands shake. But, honey, I want to do this right. I want this to be as perfect for you as I can make it."

His words brought a warm flush to her skin. "I want to please you, too," she whispered. "I want that so much."

"You do."

"What if I can't—"

"We're not setting goals. We're just doing things together that feel good to both of us. The only rule is that if you're uncomfortable with something, you tell me."

He paused to prop up several pillows along the wall so he could sit comfortably against them, his legs stretched out and crossed at the ankles. He looked completely at ease, and when he held out his hand to her, she nestled beside him. He gave her a lazy kiss that started with her mouth and ended with his lips and tongue exploring her neck. It was warm and sweet and very arousing. When he'd finished, she found that he'd angled her body around so that she was facing him, her breasts inches from his chest. "*Now* I've got you where I want you."

Still a little nervous, she hesitatingly returned the smile. This was all so new. But she felt a fierce trust gathering inside her.

He carefully pulled out the last of her tortoiseshell pins and combed her hair around her shoulders, burying his nose in the golden strands and turning his head so that he could nibble on her ear. "You smell so good. But you taste even better."

There were things she'd been wanting to do, too. Tentatively, she touched her tongue to the edge of his jaw. "You're bristly."

"Maybe I should use some of that bottled water to shave."

"Don't. I like you the way you are."

"Then we're on the same wavelength."

He kept the pace slow and light, getting a little more intimate with each kiss. Finally he unbuttoned the top of her shirt and nibbled along her collarbone and down to the tops of her breasts.

She whimpered, amazed that anything could feel so good. So erotic.

"Okay?"

"I'm burning up."

"Well, we're probably both a little overdressed."

Marissa giggled, silently admitting that she was still a bit on edge.

Jed pulled off his shirt and tossed it on the floor, and she knew he was waiting to see if she was comfortable with that. Catching her lower lip between her teeth, she flattened her hand against his chest.

"You have a sexy chest."

"Not as sexy as yours."

"I don't know about that." She traced the contours of his muscles and slid her fingers through his springy hair, enjoying the freedom to touch him. While she did, he slowly unbuttoned her shirt but didn't take it off. Instead, he unsnapped his trousers, worked them over his hips and kicked them out of the way.

Her gaze dropped to his briefs. She swallowed as she zeroed in on the bulge that proclaimed his arousal.

He waited several seconds, then crooked a finger under her chin, forcing her eyes to meet his. "Honey, being with you like this turns me on. I can't hide that. I wouldn't want to. I want you to know what you do to me."

"What if you lose control?" she blurted. "What if—"

"Do you trust me?"

"More than anyone else in the world."

"Well, any time you want me to stop, all you have to do is tell me. And I will. No matter what we're doing. Okay?"

She nodded. This was the moment of truth. The moment she well and truly put herself into his hands. Perhaps because she wanted to prove something to herself, she undid her trousers and skinned them down her legs. It didn't take a lot of exertion, but she was breathing hard and her heart was pounding when she finished.

Jed stroked his hand along her calf. "You've got gorgeous legs." After a long kiss, he pulled her onto his lap facing him, guiding her knees to either side of his hips so she was straddling him.

The pose was so blatantly erotic that Marissa's legs stiffened. Then she gradually relaxed, lowering her body until she was pressed intimately to him, their flesh separated by only a couple of layers of underclothes.

"Mmm. That feels wonderful," he rumbled as he dropped butterfly kisses over her neck and shoulders.

"Yes." The position might have frightened her, except that she was the one on top—with the freedom to bail out if she wanted.

Jed kept his arms at his sides as if he understood that she needed to feel unfettered. He nibbled at her jawline, her neck. Then, using his mouth, he skimmed back her shirt as his fingers played with the fabric at the top of her bra. She held her breath as he dipped inside. Trembled as her skin prickled and her nipples hardened.

More. She wanted more.

Maybe she'd said it aloud. Because he dipped lower with little strokes that were like heat lightning crackling over her nerve endings.

She made small, incoherent noises in her throat, unsure of what to ask for. "Jed, Jed. That's so good."

"Oh, yes."

Somehow her shirt disappeared. Then her bra. She cried out again and again as he caressed her breasts, lifting and squeezing them gently. Every time he came back to the centers, she felt as if tiny explosions were going off inside her body.

"Oh...oh..."The waves of sensation brought incoherent syllables to her lips. An ache started deep inside her. An ache that made her instinctively rock her hips against him.

"That's it, honey," he crooned. "That's it. Do what feels good."

"What?" she gasped.

"Anything you like."

She moved frantically against him, knowing her body needed *something*—that it was reaching desperately for *something*. If she didn't find it, she would go mad.

Then as he sucked one nipple into his mouth and tugged at the other with his thumb and finger, she felt a knot of tension inside her break apart. It was as though a gateway of bliss had opened up. She rocked and pressed against him, crying out as a burst of sensation took her, making her feel as if she were flying, spinning, shattering.

He held her, kissed her, murmured words of praise as she came back to something approaching normal. Only normal had changed. She would never be the same again.

"I—I—is that what it's supposed to be like?" she gasped, little aftershocks of pleasure rippling through her.

"I don't know. We'll have to try it again and make comparisons."

"We." Her cheeks grew rosy. "I think it was just me."

He laughed a little shakily. "How's that for iron control?"

"Jed—"

"All in good time."

"But you—"

"I wanted you to find out what that felt like."

She closed her eyes and moved her cheek against his, still caught up in the miracle of her body's response. "You're making this seem easy. You're making me wonder why I was ever afraid of you."

"Good."

She turned her head and their lips met, caught, sealed with heat. He led her back along the path she'd just taken, and she was astonished at how quickly her passion built again. He caressed her breasts the way he had before, making her whimper with the pleasure of his touch.

"Jed, I want—I need—"

"Yes. Raise up a little, so I can..."

She did, and he helped her off with her panties, his fingers stroking the warm, wet place that she understood was the seat of her sexual sensations. Then his briefs were gone, too. And there were only the two of them—naked on the bed.

His eyes met hers, mistaking her uncertainty for fear. "It's okay. We can stop right here if you want."

"I don't want to stop. I just don't know what to do."

"What do you want to do?"

"I want you inside me." The words came out as a wispy gasp.

Without any hesitation he guided her hips down once

more, watching her face as the tip of his erection touched her.

She had thought she'd be afraid when the ultimate moment came. Instead she felt a terrible urgency to join her body with his. Plunging downward, she gave a little cry as she felt his heat and hardness press into her.

"Are you all right?"

"Yes. Oh, yes."

He let out a long, luxurious sigh.

She kissed his neck, his jaw, his mouth. "Jed, I want this to be...good...for you."

"It's wonderful for me."

She pressed her forehead against his.

"But you're going to have to do most of the work. Except for this part, and this," he whispered as his hands found her breasts again and his lips nibbled at hers.

This time she understood what to do. This time she knew how to move against him. How to court the sensations that were building once again to a peak.

She heard his breath coming in great gasps. Felt his body shake and his hips strain upward against hers as low, sexy words tumbled from his lips. She moved faster and faster, exulting in the pleasure and in the knowledge that she was taking him with her.

"I can't—" He called out her name. His body jerked against hers, inside hers, sending her over the edge once more into that world of pure sensation. Only this time he was with her. She was giving pleasure, not just receiving it. And his gratification multiplied her joy a thousandfold.

SOME TIME LATER she was aware that her cheeks were wet. He kissed the tracks of moisture.

"Oh, Jed, I didn't know it could be like that. Thank you."

"Anytime."

She curled against him, her head on his shoulder.

His fingers combed through her hair, and he stirred. "Marci?"

"Umm?"

"I'm not sure I can sleep like this. Is it okay to lie down?"

She laughed softly. "I think I'm past worrying about that."

He took her down to the surface of the bed, kissing her tenderly, murmuring gentle words. She was exhausted and exalted. Triumphant in the knowledge that she'd conquered the fear that had ravaged her for so long. "We ought to have done this a long time ago."

"We'll just have to make up for lost time. But not now. I don't know about you, but I'm beat."

"Pleasantly fatigued."

He settled them under the covers, and she snuggled against him, feeling safe for the first time in days.

A LOUD CHATTERING in the trees woke Marissa just after dawn. For a moment she was disoriented as she stared at the misty light seeping through the cracks in the bamboo walls. Then she sensed the warmth of Jed's body next to hers, and a feeling of well-being stole over her as she remembered the incredible journey he'd led her on, right in this bed.

"I'd like to take a shot at those damn monkeys," he muttered, burying his face in her neck and pulling her closer.

"The birds will start up soon." She closed her eyes and snuggled against him, marveling at the wonder of waking up next to him. To the man she loved. She longed to make that declaration aloud. But she wasn't going to do it until they were safe and could think about the future.

His lips and teeth played with her ear. "We can't travel

until it's dark again. So we can stay in bed all day if we want to."

She felt a warm glow spread across her skin. "I'd like that. But..."

He raised his head so he could look down at her. "Are you okay?"

"Wonderful," she answered softly. His lips traveled across her cheek to her mouth. "I just need to make a quick trip to the facilities."

He started to get up.

She gently pushed him back. "You relax. I'll be fine by myself."

In the act of pulling back the light covers, she realized she was naked. And that she didn't know where her clothes had landed the night before. And that Jed was lying on his side with a grin playing around his lips—watching her.

Her shirt was hanging off the end of the bed. Quickly she snatched it up and buttoned the front. Feeling a bit more secure, she risked a sideways glance at Jed as she made a search for her pants. They were half under the edge of the covers. "Enjoying yourself?"

"It's a very pretty view. Almost as good as—" He stopped abruptly.

"As what?"

Looking like a schoolboy who'd been caught spying on the girls' locker room, he sat up. "As the bathing ceremony."

She stared at him, her face growing hot. "You saw that?"

"Part of it."

"Oh, God!"

He knit his hands together. "I knew I was going to feel like a sneak until I fessed up. There's a place at the top of the pyramid where the guys watch their brides. Sanchez sent me over there to get me out of the way while Johnson put the bomb in our honeymoon cottage."

Marissa made a strangled exclamation.

"One of the women looked up at me for an instant and clued me in. I started wondering what Sanchez was up to, and I knew I had to get back to the hacienda." He swallowed. "But it wasn't easy tearing my eyes away from you standing there in all your glory."

"You saw—"

"Come here." His voice was rough.

Uncertainly she crossed to the bed and let him draw her down into his embrace.

His lips nuzzled her hairline. "You're embarrassed."

"Wouldn't you be?"

"Sure."

"You didn't hear what I talked about with Madre Flora, did you?"

"No. That must have been before I arrived."

She relaxed a fraction.

"There are lots of ancient customs that modern man dismisses as primitive. But sometimes it's a good idea to go back to our roots."

"Are you quoting Sociology 101?"

He laughed. "No. The way I look at it, you and I were lucky to get a chance to participate."

"Maybe," she allowed, her voice soft as she thought about the soul-searching interview with the wise woman. Madre Flora had helped her sort out her feelings about Jed. But she wasn't ready to talk about that conversation with him yet.

"So do you want me to come help you bathe?"

"No!" She wasn't ready for that, either.

"Then hurry back."

He was still watching her as she found her slacks and shoes and started toward the door.

"Take the revolver. And watch out for wildlife."

Marissa nodded. If she'd been a little more clearheaded, she would have thought of the weapon herself.

"There's a barrel of water in a screened area outside. Soap and towels are in the supply boxes."

"Thanks."

Finally equipped, she stepped out the door and closed it behind her. The early morning was cool and foggy, typical of the jungle. In a few hours the sun would burn off the mist, and the heat would start to build up.

Alert for animals or humans, Marissa followed the short trail they'd taken the night before. After visiting the outhouse, she found the primitive bathing facilities and washed quickly. Despite what she'd told Jed, she wasn't perfectly comfortable out here by herself. Especially with her clothes off.

The spider monkeys set up a loud chatter again. Looking up, she saw them swinging from branch to branch, moving rapidly toward a large kapok tree. Had Jed come out and shooed them away?

Turning, she started back toward the house, her eyes scanning the underbrush. Her gaze collided with the fender of a jeep almost hidden from view.

Had it been there when she and Jed arrived last night? Moving closer, she gingerly touched the hood. It was hot. Not from the sun. From the engine.

Despite the heat radiating from her fingers, goose bumps surfaced up and down her arms. Someone else had found this place. Someone who didn't want them to know.

Her heart in her throat, she tiptoed back to the house, being careful to make as little noise as possible. She arrived in time to see a man standing in the doorway.

In the split second before he disappeared inside, it registered that he wasn't Jed. He was too short. And his hair was black instead of sun-streaked blond.

Chapter Fifteen

Marissa's mouth fell open when she realized who had stepped into the hut. It was Pedro Harara, the banker. He'd exchanged his usual broad-shouldered suit for peasant garb. What in the name of heaven was he doing here? And how had he figured out where they were?

Caution sent her to the side of the building. Screened by a small palm, she peered through one of the chinks in the bamboo wall. She could see Jed on his feet, shirtless and buttoning his pants. Harara was standing just inside the doorway pointing a pistol in his direction.

"Where's the *gringa* bitch?" he demanded in a voice he might have used to tell a delinquent loan holder he'd either have to pay up or go into bankruptcy.

"I don't know anyone who fits that description."

Harara jerked the gun at Jed. "Don't play games with me."

"If you happen to be referring to Marissa, she's not here," Jed said between clenched teeth.

Harara looked around the room, taking in the supplies on the table, the rumpled bed and the clothing on the floor. Being careful to keep the weapon trained on Jed, he reached down and scooped up Marissa's bra from the floor. Dangling it in the air, he fingered the silky fabric. "I presume this isn't yours. Unless you've been hiding some rather kinky proclivities.'' He laughed. ''Is that why you were fired from your undercover job?''

Jed's eyes narrowed, but he didn't bother to answer.

''Did you have a good time in bed with her last night? Your wedding night, actually. You have the right kind of arrangement. Enjoy her while you're here. Then dump her.''

He didn't succeed in provoking Jed, who remained silent.

Marissa wiped her sweaty palm on her pants. Shifting her grip on the revolver, she tried to decide what to do. She could probably maneuver in back of Harara, since his attention was focused elsewhere. But he'd still have a shot at Jed, and she couldn't risk that.

''I've heard she's frigid,'' Harara said conversationally.

Marissa locked her teeth together to keep from giving her presence away.

''Did you spend some time warming her up or just go ahead and take your pleasure with her?''

Jed stood like a stone.

Harara's expression changed. ''If you don't want to brag about your wedding night, that's one thing. But there's still the question of where she is now. Maybe you're planning to tell her sister you couldn't get her out of Sanchez's compound alive. I assume the deal is that you get to keep the money they paid you. Fifty thousand dollars is a nice piece of change.''

Marissa's skin went cold. Jed hadn't said anything about getting paid to rescue her. But now that someone had mentioned a cash payment, it made sense.

A terrible wave of hurt and betrayal swept over her, cutting off her breath. She'd been so grateful to Jed for rescuing her. And all along he'd done it for money. A lot of money.

In some corner of her mind a tiny voice argued that she

wasn't exactly being reasonable. She and Jed hadn't been close before he arrived at the hacienda. Why should he risk his life for a woman who'd gone out of her way to keep him at arm's length?

Yet she simply couldn't make herself deal with her roiling emotions in cool, logical terms. She'd opened her vulnerable heart to Jed. She'd trusted him with her deepest, most damaging secrets. She'd given herself to him, body and soul. Now she felt a terrible choking sensation as she tried to come to grips with what sounded like betrayal.

Please, tell him you love me.

When Jed finally spoke, he made it sound as if she were nothing to him. "Congratulations," he answered in a gritty voice. "You figured it out. She's dead."

She held back a gasp. Jed was putting on an act. An act to fool Harara into dropping his guard. Yet she couldn't shrug off the sick, shaky feeling that had taken her over. It was like the way she'd been in the pitch-dark room before she'd climbed over to Jed's balcony. She was reacting the way she'd been conditioned to react for years.

"Oh?" the banker asked.

"She had an unfortunate accident early this morning."

"Show me the body." Harara stepped aside and motioned with the gun.

Jed walked to the door. "Sure."

"Keep your hands in the air."

Jed glanced at the machine gun in the corner, but he obeyed the curt order. "How do you know about the money?"

"When you've got a solid base of operation in the international financial community, you can find out about *anything* that has to do with money. I've had a team of computer experts digging up every scrap of information I could get on you. You deposited fifty thousand dollars in your bank account before you left Baltimore. And you arranged to rent several properties in San Marcos and have them stocked with supplies. You probably think you covered your tracks by working through third parties. But my computer analysts were able to match withdrawals from your account to local transactions. I checked here first, since this is the hideout closest to Sanchez's *finca.*"

Marissa listened, the sick feeling inside her expanding as the men moved out of her line of sight but not out of her hearing. It was terrible to listen to Jed sounding so convincing.

"You went to a damn lot of trouble to get a fix on me," Jed remarked as Marissa edged along the side of the building.

"Don't flatter yourself. You're just small time. I've been monitoring my good friend Miguel's transactions for years. And now I've got something on him I can use. I know he's buying diamond mining equipment. My plans didn't include the *gringa* blabbing about it."

"So were you the one who turned her in that night at the reception?"

"No. I assume it was Clarita. Miguel told her she couldn't come to the party because she'd made a scene several times before. So she was out on the patio watching the festivities. Luckily for me."

"What happened to her last night? In the explosion."

"Why waste your time worrying about her?"

"I used to like her."

"She's in the hospital. I think she's going to be okay. Physically. Mentally..." He shrugged.

"Since you've studied my deposits and withdrawals, you know I'm for sale to the highest bidder," Jed observed. "And you do owe me a favor for swinging your bank a big loan last year. Let's see what else we can work out now."

"After I'm satisfied your bride is out of the picture."

Marissa saw that Jed had chosen a trail that led away from the place where she was supposed to be. As he made his way through the jungle, he stepped on several fallen sticks, cracking them loudly in half.

The part of her mind still functioning on a rational level knew that he was trying to warn her—and that he assumed the banker was planning to kill him as soon as he saw the body. When Harara found out Jed was stalling for time, the result would be the same.

Struggling to stay calm, she looked around for something to distract Harara. Someone had discarded a pile of giant seed pods near the corner of the house where she was standing. Picking one up, she hefted it in her hand. It was fairly heavy. If she heaved it into the bushes, would Harara turn? If he did, she could take a shot at him.

She was about to step into the open when a noise from the other direction made her freeze. Seconds later, to her astonishment, another figure glided out from behind a screen of trees, Uzi in hand.

It was William Johnson. She stood like a statue, aware that if she'd come out of hiding a split second sooner, he'd have seen her.

"Drop the gun and turn around slowly," he called to Harara. "And, Prentiss, you stay where you are."

Harara didn't follow orders. Instead, he pivoted to face the newcomer and fired off a shot. As Johnson cursed and ducked, the banker dodged into the underbrush, palm fronds hiding him from view almost at once.

Jed threw himself behind the nearest tree as Johnson recovered his presence of mind and squeezed off a burst of shots in the direction of the fleeing figure. Bullets slashed through broad leaves. But Harara didn't slacken his pace. Marissa could hear him crashing headlong through the dense vegetation. Just as she was sure he was going to make his escape, a bloodcurdling scream split the air.

"Dios. No."

Johnson hesitated, looking from the direction of the anguished cry to the place where Jed had disappeared. He went after Jed.

"Help me," Harara wheezed, his voice rising in panic and then choking off in an anguished gurgle.

Was it a trick? Would he come charging out of the bushes as soon as Johnson turned his back?

Marissa didn't know. But she had to act quickly. Praying that her left-handed aim would be accurate, she heaved the seed pod at Johnson. It struck him a glancing blow on the shoulder, enough to make him curse and turn to his left.

She was about to fire when Jed leaped out from behind the tree and brought the other man crashing to the ground. The machine gun flew out of Johnson's reach. Marissa sprinted forward, picked it up and backed away from the fighting men, who were now locked together and rolling across the group.

"Stop!" she shouted.

Neither combatant paid any attention.

Johnson got his arms up and wrapped his hands around Jed's neck.

Jed gasped, and Marissa watched in horror as his face darkened. She was going to have to take a chance and fire. Heart blocking her windpipe, she held the gun extended in both hands and tried to sight a clean shot.

Then Jed managed to jab at the other man with his knee. The mining engineer bellowed and loosened his hold. Jed wrenched away and landed a punch on Johnson's jaw. Stunned, the other man went still for several seconds. Marissa darted in and brought the butt of the gun down on the back of his head. He groaned and collapsed limply on top of Jed.

Coughing, Jed shoved the deadweight away and sat up. For several seconds he could only suck in great gulps of air.

"Are you all right?" Marissa asked. Kneeling beside him, she gently touched the finger marks on his neck. The skin was red. Later it would be bruised.

"I'm okay. What about you?" he wheezed.

"Okay," she whispered, not trusting herself to say more.

He took her in his arms.

She held herself stiffly, wanting to melt against him. But the hurt, frightened part of her spirit wouldn't let her. She'd wakened this morning happier than she'd ever been in her life. Now she felt as if sharp knives had slashed her insides.

"I'm sorry," he rasped.

"For what? You didn't know either one of them was coming."

"You were outside the hut. You heard us talking. I know what you're thinking now."

She couldn't hold back a small sound that started as a sob. She managed to turn it into a snort.

"Marci. I—"

"We've got to find out about Harara. Maybe that scream was just a ruse and he's waiting his chance to come back."

Jed muttered a curse under his breath. "You're right, even if you've got the wrong reason. But as soon as we find out what happened to him, we'll talk."

She nodded again, because she knew that if she spoke, it would be impossible to hold back her tears.

Jed glanced from Harara's untidy trail to the unconscious man on the ground. "I'd hate to have Sleeping

Beauty wake up and come after us.'' As he spoke he reached into Johnson's pocket. ''Thought I felt these!'' he said as he pulled out a pair of handcuffs. Deftly he rolled the man over and secured his hands behind his back.

Marissa stood and stared toward the recently cut path through the foliage. She could see nothing. Hear nothing. But she sensed something bad was out there waiting for them. Either it was Harara or whatever had made him scream. Jed stepped in front of her. ''I'll go first. Give me the Uzi.''

Marissa handed over the machine gun. She wanted to hold on to Jed. She contented herself with clutching the butt of the pistol and following him as he moved cautiously through the trees, scanning the foliage for signs of danger.

Every time a leaf brushed against her face she felt a shiver go down her spine. Half expecting a wild animal to leap out from behind each new tree, she tried to penetrate the dim light. But she could see only a few feet into the tangle of vegetation.

When Jed halted suddenly, she almost bumped into him.

''Over there.''

She looked where he was pointing and saw a pair of legs stretched in front of them.

''Pedro?''

There was no answer.

Jed cautiously approached. Marissa followed.

Before he'd taken two steps he stopped in his tracks and swore, grabbing Marissa's arm to keep her from moving forward.

''What?''

He pointed to what looked like a vivid red-and-pink ribbon almost hidden by one of the pants legs.

Marissa sucked in a sharp breath and took an automatic

step back as she stared at the beautifully colored strand. That was no innocent ribbon! It was a coral snake, its bite an almost immediate death sentence, and Harara must have fled directly into its path.

She shuddered and clutched at Jed's shirt to hold him back. "Stay away from it!"

"Don't worry." Looking around, he found a dead branch hanging from a nearby tree and pulled it down.

Heart pounding, Marissa watched as he lifted up Harara's leg with the end of a stick. When the snake wiggled, he beat it with the improvised weapon. Marissa turned her face away.

The snake had stopped moving when Jed gingerly lifted it away and flung it into the underbrush. Then he turned the banker over. He was already dead, his mouth open in a silent scream, his face swollen.

Marissa shuddered, thinking that it could have been her a few days ago when she'd fled through the jungle.

"It couldn't have happened to a nicer guy. Except maybe Johnson," Jed said harshly. "And speaking of snakes, we'd better see if he's come around."

She nodded tightly.

"You think I did it for the money," he accused, startling her by changing subjects too abruptly.

"Did what?"

"Came back to San Marcos to rescue you."

"Didn't you?" She turned away and started up the trail, running away so he couldn't continue the conversation.

He kept pace with her. "That was part of it. I wasn't going to risk my neck for free, not after the way you'd treated me all these years. But I wouldn't have agreed if I didn't care about you. For that matter, I wouldn't have spent a couple of days in Santa Isabella finding out what had happened to you. And I wouldn't have gone to Baltimore to tell your sister.'' He was breathing hard as he finished the declaration.

''Maybe you needed the job.'' She kept her back to him, afraid that she was going to cry. To fend off the tears, she drew on every defense mechanism she'd ever learned.

''Damn you, stop running away and let me explain.''

''I don't want to hear it!''

''I thought you'd changed,'' he said in a voice that seemed to issue a challenge.

''You were wrong,'' was all she could get out.

They had reached the clearing. Marissa gestured toward Johnson, who was struggling to sit up. ''We've got other problems to deal with.''

When Johnson spotted them he tried to move away but only succeeded in toppling to his side.

Jed righted him and hauled him against the trunk of a tree. ''We're going to have a little chat.''

''I don't think so.''

''You may find you want to cooperate. Unless you'd like to spend the rest of your life rotting in a San Marcos prison.''

''And who's going to put me there?''

''Sanchez.''

''You think he's going to take the blame for trying to cheat his countrymen out of a fortune?'' Marissa entered the conversation, her voice harsh. It felt good to focus her anger on Johnson. She knew exactly how to deal with *him*. ''You're the one who's going to be his scapegoat. He'll have to explain why he was keeping a diamond mining operation secret. And he'll convince everyone you used him. You'll end up in front of a firing squad and there will be no one charging onto the field to sweep you out of the way of the bullets. Unless you turn the tables on him.''

Marissa could see by the panic in his eyes that he'd heard the story of her own eleventh-hour rescue.

"I'm listening."

"All right, this is what we're going to do," she said, noting that she had both Johnson's and Jed's complete attention.

MARISSA'S HEART SLAMMED against her ribs as she followed William Johnson down the dark, silent hall to the room where she'd been arrested the week before. Behind her, a third pair of footsteps clicked on the tile floor. Jed. Even if she couldn't talk to him about their personal relationship, she was reassured that he was covering her back. He was a good man to have on your side. At least she was willing to admit that much.

She squeezed her eyes shut for just a moment while she forced the focus of her thoughts away from anything personal and back onto their present mission. God, she wished Jed or somebody else had told her this plan was demented. But he'd gone along with her proposition and made some astute suggestions that put the icing on the cake. Still, she knew that the two of them could be risking everything if the operation hit an unexpected snag. There had been so little time to think everything through. They'd been forced to act quickly before Sanchez figured out what they were up to.

But at least they'd gotten this far with no problem. The guard at the door hadn't questioned Johnson's authority to get them inside.

They reached *El Jefe*'s office, and Marissa heard the mining engineer suck in a deep breath. He was as nervous as she. Had he figured out some last-minute double cross that would get her and Jed killed? Or was he worried that Sanchez was going to come swooping down on them like a falcon from the clouds—tearing all of them to bits with razor talons?

The door closed behind them, and she felt the walls of Sanchez's private office close in around her. Like the night of the party when she'd been boxed up and delivered to a prison cell. Only this time she'd dragged Jed in with her. If anything went wrong, he'd get captured, too.

They'd almost reached the most dangerous moment of this whole operation, and Jed had insisted on being the one to take the biggest risk.

She glanced up to find him looking at her, and the mixture of pain and determination in his eyes made her heart squeeze. Even now, even when she knew it was all over between them, she wanted to reach for his hand. But she hadn't been able to let herself unbend with him since the scene with Harara at the hut. Emotionally, there was no way she could take that risk.

Jed held her gaze for another long second.

"You shouldn't have expected so much from me," he muttered. Then he turned his back and strode past her toward the little bathroom where she'd hidden the film and the camera. She heard him lifting off the top of the toilet tank.

Her mounting tension made it almost impossible to breathe. Even though she'd been subliminally waiting for it, the sound of the door crashing open made her gasp.

El Jefe stepped into the room, backed up by a contingent of armed guards.

Chapter Sixteen

"Got you," he snarled. "Come out with your hands up. Or my men will shoot your bride," he called to Jed. "And don't bother to hide the film of the incriminating documents. I know she put it in the toilet tank."

Marissa pressed a hand against her mouth.

Jed stepped out of the bathroom, his arms above his head, the plastic bag dangling from one hand like a flag of surrender. Sanchez snatched it out of his grasp and stuffed it in his pocket.

Marissa backed away from him. Being in the same room with *El Jefe* again made her hands tremble, and she pressed them against her sides.

He looked at her and grinned. "You should have left the country while you could. Your security was inadequate. My loyal friend managed to get in touch with me when you left him alone for a few minutes." He gestured toward Johnson.

The mining engineer moved to Sanchez's side, and the general clapped him on the back. "Well done."

Johnson looked uncomfortable.

"He's not your friend. He's your business partner," Marissa corrected, trying to keep her voice steady. "In a scheme to cheat your country out of millions of pesos."

El Jefe's gaze narrowed. "So you're the one who broke

in to the building with my diamond mining equipment? I must say, you had a very unusual wedding night."

"Yes. Too bad we missed your explosive finale," Jed snapped. "If we'd stayed in your guest cottage, we'd have been blown to bits."

"That wasn't my idea."

Johnson reddened.

"But you went along with the plan," Jed clarified.

Sanchez managed to look regretful. "I wanted to trust you, *amigo.* But I couldn't. It's unfortunate you had to fall in love with Señorita Devereaux. I saw it bloom on your face like a hibiscus flower unfurling in the first morning light. You put her life above yours, and that was too dangerous for me."

Marissa went rigid as the general's words sank into her mind, sank into every cell in her body. Had she heard him right? Had he really said that he knew Jed loved her? She drew in a strangled breath and turned toward Jed. He was gazing at her with an intensity that made her heart skip a beat and then start up in double time. When her eyes met his, he looked quickly away—like a man unable to face the destruction of everything he holds dear. She understood in that blinding instant that the general had spoken the truth. And she'd been an utter fool.

Nothing else existed in the room besides Jed. She started toward him. But he was already speaking to Sanchez again. And she realized with sick desperation that she might not get another chance with the man she loved.

"Now that you've got us, at least tell me what documents she found in your files," Jed demanded. "Your agreement with Johnson to develop the diamond mines and steal the profits from San Marcos?"

El Jefe shrugged. "I'll have to read the text to be sure. I have notes about the diamond mining operation, yes. Also my plans for having President Palmeriz declared incompetent so I can use the eighty-sixth amendment to our constitution to legally take over the government. I had the amendment pushed through several years ago. It allows the cabinet to elect an interim successor."

"You?"

"Of course. But you've asked enough questions. It's time to get on with the good part." He grinned at Johnson. "I like your idea of having a crew from the Televisión Nacional film the capture of these two American spies." He opened the door and Marissa saw a cameraman, sound engineer and lighting technician standing in the hall. "We're ready for you now."

All but one of the guards withdrew as the men began setting up their equipment. Sanchez ordered Marissa to Jed's side. She stood rigid, her heart thumping, her mouth so dry she could hardly swallow.

"Jed, I'm sorry," she whispered, pressing her shoulder against his, knowing in her heart that anything she said was inadequate. She was bursting with the need to turn and take him in her arms—to tell him she loved him. To make things right between them if that was still possible. But they were trapped here.

Sanchez came out of the bathroom where he'd been combing his hair in preparation for his performance.

"Let me do a test," the sound engineer said. He pressed a button and the conversation they'd been having about diamond mines and attempted murder began to play back.

"You fool," *El Jefe* bellowed. "Erase that part."

"Too late." A new, authoritative voice answered the general. "It's already been transmitted to the station, ready for broadcast when I give the signal. Thanks to the plans worked out by Señor and Señora Prentiss."

Sanchez whirled toward the door and found himself facing President Palmeriz, who stood with his shoulders back and his eyes glittering. He was flanked by Thomas Leandro, Louis Rinaldo and a contingent of municipal police. One of the officers disarmed the general's guard. The rest surrounded *El Jefe*.

As it dawned on Sanchez that he'd been trapped, his mouth dropped open and his eyes widened, making him look like a bug impaled on a specimen card. His gaze shifted rapidly from Palmeriz to Johnson to Jed and Marissa as if he couldn't believe what he was seeing.

The chief executive permitted himself a small smile as he enjoyed the expression on his rival's face. "In the past you've managed to hide your illegal activities. But this time you've just hanged yourself. We've got the proof on tape. Not just a sound recording, but video from your surveillance camera."

"No!" Sanchez bellowed, completely out of control. As he kicked at the men trying to restrain him, the toe of his boot collided with a chair leg, and he yelped in pain.

"Your gout acting up?" Marissa inquired.

Somehow her cool voice got through to him. He turned and glared at her. If looks could kill. Marissa shivered as the old cliché leaped into her mind. Jed put a protective arm around her shoulders and drew her against his side.

Marissa looked at him, seeing that his face reflected a mixture of anger and regret, and she felt a stab of pain for him. Once he and Miguel Sanchez had been friends. But she knew their wildly different values must have made the relationship an uneasy one for Jed. Then the general's murderous plans had proven he put his own interests before anything as trivial as friendship.

Jed pulled the film from the general's pocket and handed it to Palmeriz. "More evidence."

"Gracias."

Sanchez growled low in his throat like a cornered dog.

"Your stranglehold on the country is over," Palmeriz

said. "But there's one way you can keep from being arrested."

Sanchez straightened his shoulders.

Jed's eyes were cold. "Ask Marissa to give you the details."

She looked at him in astonishment. She and Jed had hashed out the arrangement with the president after he'd agreed to the plan. But she'd assumed Palmeriz would want to do the talking—especially in a country where the men jealously guarded their prerogatives. What kind of private deal had Jed struck with the president to get her such power? The implications were overwhelming.

Her vision blurred, and she struggled to keep from going to pieces.

"You earned it," he told her.

No. She'd made a mess of her assignment. And he'd bailed her out.

The president smiled at her. "After the way General Sanchez treated you, honor demands that you deliver my terms."

"I won't hear it from *her!*" Sanchez growled, his manner switching to his accustomed hauteur.

"Then rot in hell." Jed grabbed Marissa's hand and started toward the door.

They were almost out of the room when the general called them back in a voice that had lost a great deal of its solidity. "Wait."

Marissa turned slowly, aware that all eyes were on her. She should feel jubilant now that she was the one in charge. But she was too numb with her own personal pain. All she wanted was to get this finished so she and Jed could leave. So she could try to make him understand why she'd stopped trusting him.

In a wooden voice she delivered the ultimatum. "You will announce that you have found diamond mines in one of the provinces. And you're such a patriot that you want to turn over the proceeds from the mining operation to the government to alleviate some of the country's pressing social problems."

"But I put in the development money," Sanchez yelped.

"That makes you even more of a benefactor. They'll probably put up a statue in your honor," Jed observed, his voice dripping with sarcasm.

"What about me?" Johnson interjected. "I'm losing a bundle on this, too."

"Your cooperation will be taken into consideration before charges are filed," the president responded. "You may get off with a simple deportation order."

Johnson had no time to argue further. Two policemen escorted him from the room.

With a bit more enthusiasm Marissa took up where she'd left off with Sanchez. This was the part she'd insisted on including because she wanted to help Clarita, even though the girl had treated her like an enemy. And she wanted Sanchez to face up to his family problems. "You're also donating some of your personal fortune to establishing a state-of-the-art mental health facility for needy citizens. You don't have to mention that you're anxious to get your own daughter the care she needs."

The general looked daggers at Marissa. Yet below the surface wrath she thought she detected a modicum of guilt—unless that was simply her own wishful thinking.

There was one more important stipulation. Marissa braced for a verbal onslaught. "You're also stepping down as commander in chief—for health reasons."

He drew himself up straighter and cursed her loudly, heedless that Palmeriz looked shocked and Jed's face reddened with anger. "That's going too far! I'm in perfect health."

Jed took a step closer and brought his foot down on the general's gout-ridden toe. He bellowed in pain.

Jed folded his arms across his chest and stared back evenly. Sanchez looked away first. "This is blackmail."

Jed shrugged.

"Things could be worse," the president interjected. "You don't have to go into retirement at your age. Señor Rinaldo has graciously agreed to allow you to personally head the mining operation for him."

"That would mean I'd be stuck in the middle of nowhere in Junipero Province."

"Which should help keep you out of trouble," Rinaldo muttered.

Palmeriz handed the general a statement to read to the nation in front of the live television cameras. Sanchez ground his teeth. But with the threat of exposure hanging over him, he sat down at the desk and held the paper in his rigid hands.

At least as far as the general was concerned, Marissa felt a profound sense of relief. This scam had been her idea; they'd managed to pull it off, and justice was finally being done. But she was too tense and worried to watch the broadcast. All she wanted now was to be alone with her husband. As the film crew resumed their preparations, she caught Jed's eye, and they slipped out of the room.

He started off down the hall at a rapid clip. She grabbed his hand. "Please. We have to talk."

"All right. I guess it might as well be sooner than later." Grim faced, he led her to a comfortably furnished sitting room with a view of the courtyard. He didn't give her a chance to speak first. Immediately after the door closed behind them, he turned to her and started in, his words coming in staccato bursts. "Let's get this over with. I agreed to stay and help Palmeriz stabilize the government. But you don't have to hang around. There's a ticket waiting for you at the airport on a flight to Miami this evening.''

''Jed, please—''

He plowed on. ''You can be back in Baltimore tomorrow. And that lawyer friend of yours, Laura Roswell, should be able to advise you on whether our marriage is legal and if you need a divorce to get me out of your life.''

Marissa tried to swallow around the baseball-size lump in her throat. ''Is that what you want?''

''What does it matter?'' His tone was bleak.

''Oh, God, Jed.'' She twined her arms around his waist and held him close, trying to ignore his rigid posture. Despite her heroic efforts, the tears she'd been fighting so hard to hold back welled up and ran down her cheeks, and her shoulders began to shake.

''Don't. I didn't mean to make you cry,'' he said with anguish. ''I don't seem to get it right, do I?'' His hand brushed the back of her head, clasped her for a moment and then dropped away.

She struggled to control her sobs, fighting to get out the words she needed to say. She couldn't let him think this mess was his fault or that she had come in here intending to leave him. Or perhaps that was what he really wanted, she thought as sudden cold fear stabbed into her. Every self-defense mechanism urged her to cut and run. But she stood her ground. She had turned away from him this morning. The only way she might get him back was to risk everything. ''Jed...I...love...you.'' Once she'd said it, she realized how much she wanted him to know what was in her heart. Whatever happened next.

He went very still, surprise and hope mingling on his countenance. ''Marci?''

She lifted her tearstained face to his. ''I love you. I don't want a divorce.'' With the back of her hand she swiped at the tracks of moisture running down her face. "Jed, I'm so sorry. When Harara started talking about the money something inside me went cold and stiff." She fumbled for words. "One moment I was so happy. The next I was afraid of getting hurt all over again. I was still reacting like the old Marissa Devereaux. The woman who was afraid to trust you. But I know what kind of risk you were taking to come down here and save me. You could have bailed out any time, but you stuck with me."

"I'd never have left without you."

"You did what nobody else could. You got me out of there *alive.* But you did a lot more than that. You rescued me from the bleak life I carved out for myself. And you made me ache to make our marriage real. I want to stay married to you. If you'll still have me."

"If I what?" Then his mouth came down on hers—hard, possessive, insistent.

She cleaved to him, opened to him, poured her soul into him. And he returned the fervor, measure for measure. When he finally lifted his lips from hers, her head was spinning. But she heard his heartfelt words. "I love you, Marci. I thought I'd messed up. I thought I'd lost you forever."

"No, Jed. No. I'm the one who messed up. I was too afraid to trust my happiness. I was afraid to tell you that I want to be with you—always. Our wedding ceremony was the most important thing that ever happened to me." She gave a wry little laugh. "Well, maybe it's a toss-up between that and our wedding night."

His hands stroked the curve of her back, gently touched her face, her hair as he told her wordlessly that he felt the same way.

Yet his eyes were still shadowed. "Before you make a final decision, don't forget about my big liability. You're sure you're willing to be saddled with a guy who nods off at inconvenient times?''

Her face shone with her love for him. ''If his name is Jed Prentiss.''

The look of wonder on his features made her heart contract.

''Marci. Marci.''

They kissed again with aching passion.

''And don't *you* forget I know how to wake you up,'' she whispered.

''Oh, yeah.'' Jed looked around, located the door and locked it. Then he pulled her close once more, and there was no mistaking his intentions.

Her eyes widened. ''The president's out there,'' she whispered. ''And the camera crew. And all the guards.''

''So? They know better than to bother a couple on their honeymoon!'' He laughed and led her to the couch, and she stopped thinking about anything besides the joy of being with her husband once more.

Unlawfully Wedded
Kelsey Roberts

Chapter One

J. D. Porter. She knew the initials stood for "Jackass Deluxe," and he was sitting at a table in her station!

A frown curved the corners of her mouth as she donned an air of false confidence. Brushing a few strands of hair away from her eyes, Tory Conway pushed through the hinged kitchen doors of the Rose Tattoo, a tray clamped tightly to her chest.

With practiced aloofness, she held her breath as she marched past where he sat hunched over a mound of paperwork. The pleasant smell of his decidedly masculine cologne chased her behind the bar, threatening her resolve.

After placing the tray on the polished wooden surface of the horseshoe-shaped bar, Tory bent down and began collecting the salt and pepper shakers.

Her motion was halted in midstream when she felt long, tapered fingers close around her wrist. She rose slowly, trying not to devote too much thought to the devastating feel of his touch.

Their eyes collided—hers wide from the shock, his a deep, penetrating gray, the same shade as a South Carolina summer sky before a violent storm. She swallowed against the irrational belief that those eyes could see through her clothing. His lopsided, sexy display of even white teeth hovered somewhere very near a leer.

"Good morning, Miss Conway."

Not from where I'm standing, she thought. She didn't speak immediately, mostly because she had a sinking feeling that her words might come out in a squeaky, helium-high voice.

"No greeting?" he taunted, one dark eyebrow arched questioningly. "You wound me."

"No," she returned with a sweet smile. "But I'd be happy to, as soon as I've finished my setup."

"Ouch," he returned easily, placing his free hand over his heart.

Or, she thought, where his heart would be if he actually had one.

Annoyance crept up her spine when he refused her subtle request to be released when she gave his hand a small tug. "I have work to do," she insisted through tight lips.

"So do I," he said in a frustratingly calm voice that was just too smooth, too velvety to have emanated from such a massive man.

"Then why don't you do it?"

The smile widened, accentuating the chiseled perfection of his angled features. "Would you like to do it? I'm game if you are."

Tory groaned and sucked in a breath in exasperation. The man was infuriating. "Not in your lifetime, Sparky."

The sound of his laugh was deep, rich. It caressed her ears and made her skin tingle. "Haven't you heard of sexual harassment?" she managed to say between her clenched teeth.

"Doesn't apply," he returned easily. "You don't work for me."

"Thank God and anyone else responsible," she grumbled. His hold on her wrist was getting on her nerves. She didn't like being touched, especially by the visiting Neanderthal.

"You aren't very friendly for a waitress, Miss Conway."

"Depends on the customer," she retorted.

"No wonder you can't live off what you earn in tips."

She bristled and might have stiffened her spine had it not been for the unfortunate fact that she had not yet fastened the top button of her uniform. The last thing she wanted, or needed, was to give *Mr. Deluxe* an eyeful of cleavage. Especially since he'd no doubt take it as a come-on.

"I live just fine," she promised him. "And thanks for asking. Your concern is touching."

"I'm not concerned, but I'd be happy to touch." The last half of his statement was delivered in a low, sensual pitch that made her want to scream.

"Come on, J.D.," she pleaded after a brief pause. "Can the double entendre and let me get ready for the lunch crowd."

His eyes dropped to where his dark fingers encircled her small wrist. She followed his lead. His tanned, weathered complexion was a stark contrast to her pale skin. The grip loosened until all she was aware of was the featherlight stroke of his fingertip as it traced the pattern of small bones in her hand.

Tory snatched her hand away, feeling her face flush as the sound of his chuckle reached her ears. The man was maddening, she thought, fuming as she slammed various containers on the top of the bar. He was egotistical. He had enough arrogance for ten men, and he was the most attractive man she'd seen in all her twenty-five years.

My hormones are probably suffering from some sort of deprivation reaction, she reasoned as she arranged the half-empty jars and bottles on her tray.

Trying to ignore J.D.'s presence as she worked was like trying to ignore a rocket launch. Her peripheral vision was filled with images of his broad shoulders and that unruly mass of jet black hair he kept raking his fingers through as he quietly studied the piles of documents spread before him on the table. The worn fabric of his denim shirt clung to the definition of well-muscled arms. One booted toe kept time to the Elvis tune playing on the jukebox.

She didn't like him—hadn't from that very first day. J.D. was one of those stuck-up, abrupt sorts. His expression was always cool, aloof, giving her the impression that he somehow felt he was superior to the whole world. She guessed his attitude might have something to do with the truckloads of money he earned as one of Florida's premier architects. Or, she thought glibly, it could just be the result of his being one of the most gorgeous men on the face of the earth.

"Tory!"

She turned in the direction of the familiar female voice, her eyes homing in on her boss's harsh features. Rose Porter leaned against the kitchen door, her heavily jeweled hand patting the stiff mass of blond hair lacquered against her head.

"Yes?"

"There's a guy here for you."

Tory pointedly ignored J.D.'s apparent interest in Rose's announcement. The woman's stiletto heels clicked against the wood-planked floor as she held the door open wide.

Tory smiled as she caught sight of Dr. Mitchell Greyson, dean of student services at Oglethorpe College. Dr. Greyson shuffled in, his small body listing to the side where his hand toted a sizable briefcase. The scent of witch hazel reached her a fraction of a second before the rumpled, balding man. His appearance sent signals of disaster surging through her. Greyson only left his office to deliver bad news. She braced herself against the table....

"Miss Conway," he greeted in his proper southern accent. "I'm sorry to trouble you at your place of employment."

Tory's grin grew wider. She was a waitress, not the CEO of some fancy corporation. Greyson acted as if he'd interrupted important merger negotiations.

"No problem," she told him brightly, tucking a dish towel into the waistband of her apron. Gesturing to one of the chairs, Tory offered him a seat as she glared at J.D. He was leaning back in his chair, watching her as if she were the main feature at the theater.

J.D.'s expression didn't falter when their eyes briefly met. That bothered her.

"I'm afraid I have some rather distressing news," Dr. Greyson began as he sat down and placed his briefcase on the table, then slowly extracted a crisp, white sheet of letterhead, which he handed to her.

Taking the letter, Tory's eyes scanned the neatly typed print. She read it again, sure she had somehow misconstrued its meaning.

"This isn't possible," she managed to say in a strangled voice.

Rose came over then, standing behind her with one hand comfortingly resting on Tory's shoulder.

"What does it mean?" Rose asked.

"I'm dead," Tory answered as the full impact of the news settled over her like a heavy blanket.

"Not necessarily," Dr. Greyson cut in. "I've brought along a directory of college funding," he said, pulling a tattered paperback from his briefcase.

Tory groaned. "I've been all through that. I couldn't find a single one I qualified for."

"Perhaps there are some new listings?" Greyson suggested.

"Maybe," she responded dismally.

"You know," Greyson said as he patted the back of her hand with his pudgy fingers. "You can take a year or so off. Perhaps by then the 'forces that be' will reinstate the program."

"Maybe," Tory repeated.

"I'll keep my ears open," Greyson promised as he scooted his chair back and rose to his modest height. "Perhaps the board of trustees..."

Of course, she knew the board could do nothing on her behalf.

"I'm finished," Tory whispered, expelling an anguished sigh.

"Can we help?" Rose asked, taking the seat Greyson had vacated. "Shelby and I—"

"Are hardly in a position to cough up seventeen thousand dollars," Tory finished. "Shelby has Chad and she's expecting another baby any minute. And I know you have all your cash committed to the rehab of the outbuildings. Until you finish the work on the dependencies, you aren't in any condition to loan me money."

Rose's painted red lips thinned and she adjusted the black leather belt cinching her waist. She reached forward and grabbed the directory that Dr. Greyson had left behind.

"Forget it." Tory shrugged. "I've already maxed out my eligibility for student loans, along with every grant and scholarship known to mankind."

"But you haven't even tried to find alternative funding," Rose argued with a snort.

"Rose," Tory began slowly. "All you'll find in that directory is a bunch of weird stuff. Scholarships for blue-eyed women with Spanish surnames born in the month of

May. Grants for anyone born under the same star as some philanthropist's Maltese.''

She followed the sound of the deep, throaty chuckle. Having J. D. Porter laugh when her whole world was shattering didn't sit well.

''Amused?'' she asked tartly. ''I'm so glad you find my crisis funny.'' She stood and braced her hands on her hips. ''I need some air,'' she told Rose. ''If I don't get away from him, I might just take out my frustrations on your useless son.''

She stormed out of the room, the vision of J.D.'s dancing gray eyes vividly etched in her brain. He had laughed at her! She fumed as she stepped into the early-June humidity. What kind of unfeeling jerk would laugh at a time like this? ''Jackass Deluxe,'' she grumbled as she stalked through the overgrown gardens behind the property.

The tall, damp grass licked at her ankles above her socks, leaving a sheen of moisture on her white aerobic shoes. The air was thick with the scent of the wild vines growing along the brick exterior of the dependency.

The scent inspired memories from the past. Memories of when her family had owned this place. She had been a ten-year-old princess and this had been her kingdom. Her hand reached out to touch the coolness of the weather-beaten stone wall. A small lizard skittered along the surface, then disappeared behind the growth of vegetation threatening to overtake the dilapidated building.

She was thrilled that Rose and Shelby had decided to restore the outbuilding of the Charleston single house. The dependency, which had once served as both kitchen and servants quarters, had been neglected for more than a hundred years. Her only misgiving was the man hired to do the work.

J. D. Porter was an architect known for his dramatic, modern structures. She frowned, imagining what Mr.

Steel-and-Glass Towers might do to this historically significant structure. Cringing, she allowed her fingers to admire the stone. J.D. didn't appreciate or even understand historical preservation. He didn't appreciate Rose, either. He was charging his own mother an hourly rate for the renovation. "That man is a piece of work."

"Thanks."

Tory spun around and her hand flew to her mouth. Wide-eyed, she looked into the relaxed face and instantly felt her cheeks burn. "I didn't...hear you," she stammered.

J.D. shifted so that his large body cast a long shadow over Tory. Deep lines appeared on either side of his eyes as he squinted against the sunlight.

"I take it you're being squeezed out of the world of academe."

Tory felt her shoulders slump forward. "It seems that way."

"What will you do?"

She shrugged and dropped her gaze to the front of his shirt. It was a stupid move, she realized too late. Her eyes lingered at the deep V where he'd neglected to button his shirt. A thick mat of dark hair curled over solid, tanned skin. She swallowed and forced her eyes to the ground.

"I may have to wait a year or so until I can get another grant."

He shifted his weight again as his thumbs looped into the waistband of his jeans. "What about your family? Can't they help with your tuition?"

"Interesting concept, coming from you," she said as she met his eyes. "I don't really have any family." Needing to change the subject, Tory asked, "How can you charge your own mother top dollar?"

His expression grew dark, and something vaguely dangerous flashed in his eyes. "I'm a businessman, Tory. Not a philanthropist."

Heartless creep! her mind screamed. "She's your mother."

"Biologically," he qualified.

"It still counts," Tory told him with a saccharine smile.

Lifting sunglasses from the breast pocket of his shirt, J.D. placed them on the bridge of his slightly crooked nose. Tory was left to view her own reflection in their mirrored lenses.

"Want to give me a hand?"

"What?" she fairly squealed.

Her voice caused an immediate smile to cut the sharp angles of his face. "Assist me?"

"Doing what *exactly?*"

"I'm open for suggestions," he countered with a wolfish grin.

"And I'm outta here," she answered as she took her first step.

"Hey," he said as his large hand closed around her arm. "I was just teasing you. No need to get huffy."

"I don't care for your brand of teasing, J.D. Everything that comes out of your mouth has some sort of sexual meaning behind it."

"I'll behave," he promised, one hand raised in an oath.

"I'll bet," she told him wearily.

"Honest. I just want you to hold the tape while I measure." He produced a shiny metal tape measure in support of his statement. "I need to get the dimensions of the outhouse so I can finish that ream of paperwork the historical society requires."

"It isn't an outhouse. It's called a dependency. And the forms are necessary," she told him with great hauteur in her voice. "We have to maintain the historical fabric of the city."

His mouth thinned in a definite sneer. "Just because something is old, that doesn't make it worth saving."

"I'd save you, Mr. Porter."

"Think I'm old, huh?"

"Not old," she said with an exaggerated bat of her long lashes. "Historically significant."

The skin of her upper arm tingled where his fingers gently held her. It was annoying that she felt herself respond to him, but she silently vowed not to show any reaction. She suspected J.D. would enjoy knowing his touch affected her—and she wasn't about to give him that much power.

"Will you?"

"What?" she answered, wondering if he had psychic powers in his arsenal.

"Help me measure."

"It's almost noon," she hedged. "The lunch crowd cometh."

"So does Susan."

"Susan isn't working this shift."

"She is now," he stated. "Rose thought you might like to take the afternoon off in light of your sudden financial upheaval."

"How is losing a day's tips supposed to make me feel better?"

Nodding his dark head, J.D. used his free hand to stroke the faint growth on his deeply clefted chin. "Good point. Tell you what," he said with a sigh, as if he were about to announce a change in world leaders. "I'll pay you the going rate for helping me measure."

"How generous," she gasped. "Sure you can spare seven-fifty an hour?"

He leaned down, so close that Tory could feel the warmth of his breath against her ear. "For you? Anything."

Her resolve not to react to this man disintegrated when the scent of his cologne lingered in the mere inches separating them. Shrugging away from him, Tory could still feel the imprint of his callused fingers against her skin. A smart person would cut and run. But then, a woman with less than a hundred dollars in the bank didn't always act intelligently.

"Has your mother already called Susan?"

"Yes, Rose called."

She stifled the urge to ask him why he wouldn't call Rose "mom" or "mother." "Then give me the tape."

Reaching behind him, J.D. again produced the tape measure as well as a folded sketch of the dependency's exterior. "Here," he said, handing her the drawing and a mechanical pencil. "We'll start on the south wall. We'll measure it, then you mark the drawing."

"Fine," Tory said. She kept the bent end of the tape between her fingers as he took long strides through the dense foliage. He had a great derriere, she mused. Tight and rounded above those long, muscular legs. Absently, she fanned herself with the sketch, trying to convince herself that the heat she felt in the pit of her stomach was probably nothing more than the effect of having drunk too much coffee.

The strip of metal tape acted like an umbilical cord, connecting her to the large man. Dutifully, she followed his instructions as they spent the better part of an hour documenting the contours of the old building. She attributed her dry throat to the stifling early-summer heat. It couldn't possibly have anything to do with the fact that her eyes had been riveted to his body the entire hour. She wasn't the type to be interested in things like the washboard-like muscles of his flat stomach, or the gentle slope of his back where his broad shoulders tapered at his waist. No—such things were irrelevant to a woman like Tory.

"You look hot."

"I beg your pardon?" she yelped.

His smile was slow and deliberate. "I was referring to the temperature." He swabbed his forehead with the back of his hand. "It must be near ninety."

"Must be," she agreed as she swallowed her guilt.

"Need a break before we tackle the interior?"

"Not me," she told him. She wanted to get this over with—quickly. "The inside is a disaster."

"I know. I took a cursory look when I was putting together the budget for the project."

"I'm sure your estimate was high," she said without looking at him.

"I'm sure it was reasonable."

Ignoring the slight edge to his voice, Tory moved to the near-rotten door and grasped the knob. The door wouldn't budge.

"Let me," J.D. said, coming up behind her so that his thighs brushed her back.

Tory stepped out of his way almost instantly, feeling branded by the outline of his body.

J.D. wrestled with the humidity-swollen door for a short time before finally pulling it free of the frame. Reaching into his back pocket, he produced a small flashlight and directed the beam in front of them.

The air inside the building was stale and musty. "Let's start on the left," J.D. suggested.

The interior was a long, rectangular-shaped space with bowed stone walls and a few rotted timbers piled at the far end. Bars of yellow light filtered in from the boarded windows, imprisoning J.D. as he placed the measure against what was left of the old flooring.

"Sixty-three feet, seven inches," he called.

Tory was about to mark the diagram when she noted the inconsistency. "The tape must be twisted."

She heard his boots scrape as he checked the length of the tape. "Nope."

"Then that back wall is three feet deep," she told him.

J.D. took the sketch from her, his eyebrows drawn together as he looked from the drawing to the room, then back to the paper.

"This doesn't make sense."

"You must have measured incorrectly."

He offered her a baleful stare before walking off to the back of the room. "Hold this," he called, handing her the flashlight as she came up behind him.

Using his pocketknife as well as his fingers, J.D. loosened the stones by scraping away the limestone mortar.

"What are you doing?" Tory asked.

"I'm trying to find the other three feet."

An oddly unpleasant odor accompanied the shower of small rocks as he created a small opening in the wall.

"Give me the light."

J.D. stuck his arm through the opening, then she heard him suck in his breath.

"What?"

His arm came out of the hole and he faced her slowly. His expression was hard, his eyes wide. "We'd better go back to the Tattoo."

"Why? What's behind the wall?" she asked, frustration adding volume to her litany of questions.

"A body."

Chapter Two

"I think he's probably some poor, unfortunate homeless person who wandered into the building to escape the winter chill," Susan was saying. The woman's brown eyes were wide as she excitedly continued expounding her theory. "He must have been sick. And he probably assumed he was suffering from nothing more than a bad cold."

"I think you're letting your imagination run wild," Tory cautioned. The pout the other woman offered was at odds with her athletically lean face. Susan was a runner and it showed in her slender build. She was forever hounding Tory about the lack of physical activity in her life. Thankfully, the discovery of the skeleton had provided a diversion from Susan's usual boring reprimands on the perils of passivity.

"No," Susan insisted, looking to J.D., who gave a small nod of encouragement. "He must have crawled in through the window before succumbing to bacterial pneumonia."

"Bacterial pneumonia?" Tory echoed, feeling her eyebrows draw together.

"Sure," Susan replied. "It's very deadly if not treated. And it kills really fast."

"Well, hell," Tory said as she theatrically slapped her palm against her forehead. "The police are wasting their time investigating. Why don't you run out there and tell them what happened. It'll save the city a whole lot of time and money."

J.D. folded his arms over the back of the chair, his eyes leveled on the redhead. His expression told Tory nothing of his thoughts.

"I think your theory has a few holes in it," J.D. said.

"Really?"

"If the guy was on death's door, how do you suppose he built the wall?"

"What wall?" Susan asked.

Shrugging his shoulders, J.D. tilted his head and looked directly at Tory as he answered. "The stones that covered him aren't the same as the ones used in rest of the building. It's my guess that—"

"You can't be serious," Tory cut in. "You're suggesting that someone entombed that body in the dependency?"

"It's a real probability," he answered slowly.

"I think you've been watching too much television or something." Tory dismissed his speculation with a wave of her hand. The lingering seed of doubt wasn't as easily discharged.

His gaze didn't falter as his eyes roamed over her face. Rubbing her arms against a sudden chill, Tory shook her head, hoping to rid her mind of sudden vivid images of that nameless, faceless person meeting such a gruesome demise.

"I think you're being a bit melodramatic, J.D.," she said with forced lightness.

"Maybe," he agreed as he rose to his full height and went behind the bar.

Tory should have gone home. There was really no point in hanging around the Tattoo since the police had asked them to close down while vanloads of forensic teams scoured the area.

About an hour after the initial discovery, Shelby and Dylan Tanner arrived with their son Chad in tow. A pang of envy tugged at her heart as she watched the couple move toward her. Dylan was tall, dark and handsome; Shelby dark, exotic-looking and hugely pregnant. Dylan almost always had a tender hand on his wife—small, seemingly insignificant touches that proclaimed the extent of their deep emotional commitment to each other.

Chad was a different story. Polite people called him all-boy. He bounded into the room and immediately began pressing the buttons on the jukebox. Shelby's stern warning to stay away from the machine fell on deaf ears. Chad had a mind of his own at the tender age of eighteen months. Tory liked that.

Tory ran over and scooped the squealing child into her arms, planting kisses against his plump tummy.

"How's my favorite little man?" she asked.

"Man, man, man," was his babbled response.

"Terror is more like it," Dylan called as he draped his arm across his wife's shoulders.

"Are you a terror?" Tory asked the small boy.

He shook his head vigorously, then said, "Man."

"See?" Tory said as she shifted Chad in her arms. "He's not a terror."

"Then maybe Auntie Tory would like to take him for the weekend?" Shelby teased, a sarcastic light in her blue eyes.

"Anytime," she said earnestly. "Right, little man?"

"Man," Chad answered, nodding his dark head.

Looping his pudgy arms around her neck, Chad proceeded to give her a "skeeze." The delight in her eyes faded somewhat when she noticed J.D. leaning against the bar, a long-neck bottle of beer balanced between his thumb and forefinger. When he began to move toward them, the word *swagger* flashed across her brain. His expression was sour, distracted. Why did such an unpleasant man have to exude such sensuality? she wondered.

"You must be J.D.," Dylan said as he offered the taller man his hand.

"Guilty," J.D. responded.

"Shelby is really excited about the work you're going to do."

J.D. turned those devastating eyes on Shelby, nodding politely. "I think adding a club will allow you to draw in a younger crowd."

"That's what we're hoping," Shelby answered as she rested her head against her husband's shoulder. "And I know your mother is equally thrilled that you agreed to do the work."

"For a hefty price," Tory grumbled in a stage whisper.

Three sets of eyes turned on her. But it was the simmering hostility in J.D.'s expression that made her instantly regret the barb.

"Miss Conway thinks I'm overpriced and incapable of doing the job," J.D. explained, though his eyes never left hers.

"I'm sure that's not the case," Shelby insisted. "Tory?" she questioned. "Surely you know—"

"She knows that I prefer dramatic buildings," J.D. interrupted. "And she's right."

"Well," Tory said as she captured Chad's hand in hers to prevent his sudden fascination with the buttons of her white blouse. "I don't get a vote, now, do I, Mr. Porter? I'm nothing but a lowly waitress."

Shifting the child on her hip, Tory returned her attention to the baby. It was much easier than having to suffer the intense scrutiny of his eyes. "How about we raid the fridge?'' she asked. When she got no response, she added, ''Ice cream?''

''Get it,'' Chad answered, his fat legs bouncing with excitement.

''Not a lot,'' Shelby warned.

J.D. watched her disappear into the kitchen, a knot of tension forming between his shoulders.

''What was that all about?'' Dylan asked.

J.D. offered a noncommittal shrug. ''Miss Conway believes I'm incapable of rehabbing the building because historical sites aren't exactly part of my résumé.''

''Tory believes in preserving the city,'' Shelby agreed. ''Lord knows, she's been studying it long enough.''

''She won't be studying much longer,'' J.D. said as he frowned. Why did he care if she'd lost her grant? He should be looking upon that bit of information as a gift from above. It could be the answer to his prayers. It was certainly a way to get Tory Conway out of his life.

''Why?'' Shelby asked him.

J.D. had just finished recounting the visit by Dr. Greyson when Rose joined them. He felt the tension in his body grow worse. ''So it looks like her academic career is history.''

''Not if I can help it,'' Rose countered, patting the paperback directory.

J.D. noted a glint in his mother's eyes that instantly had him on red alert.

''That girl's entitled to her education. She's worked damned hard and I'm going to see she finishes,'' Rose huffed, tracing the edge of one line on her zebra-print pants.

Stifling a groan, J.D. sucked in a deep breath, then let it out slowly. ''That might not be such a good idea,'' he suggested. He wondered if any of what he had told his mother in confidence that morning had penetrated the layers of her lacquered curls.

"Leave that to me," she told him. Her hand came out and hovered just above his arm. "I've got a plan."

"Would someone like to clue me in?" Shelby piped up, her hand moving in a circular motion over her large belly.

"Upstairs," Rose instructed.

J.D. was left alone in the dining room with Susan. He wasn't much in the mood for company, he was feeling too restless. He was starting to wonder about this trip. Perhaps it would have been easier just to have ignored Rose's request to come to South Carolina. He could have happily stayed in Florida, doing his kind of work. Rose would have remained nothing more than a name and a vague memory.

"Want me to do your palm?" Susan chirped.

"Excuse me?"

"Your palm," she repeated, glancing at his balled fist. "I sense some really intense discord in your aura."

"My aura?"

"Very telling," Susan said, her brown eyes solemn. "I can usually tell everything about a person from their aura. Yours is red."

"Red, huh?" he asked, faintly amused.

"That's bad," she insisted, genuineness dripping from each syllable. "If you let me have a look at your palm, I might be able to determine the cause of the red in your aura."

"This ought to be a kick," he mumbled as he took a seat across from her and offered his hand, palm up.

Susan bent forward and traced the lines on his hand. Her face was totally serious, as if she was completely absorbed in her examination. Her fingers were long and bony, and not nearly as soft as Tory's.

He frowned, wondering why his mind would recognize such a traitorous thought. But his subconscious wasn't finished, not by a long shot. As he sat there, he noted the many differences between the two waitresses. Susan was lanky and shapeless. Tory could only be described as voluptuous. Though he noted how hard she tried to conceal her attributes, her curvaceous body had not gone unnoticed. His frown deepened.

"I think you're about to make a life-altering decision," Susan predicted.

"Such as?"

"I'm not a fortune-teller," Susan informed him haughtily. "I can only tell you what I see, based on the physical aspects of your palm."

"Sorry." J.D. managed to sound moderately sincere.

"And see here?" She followed one of the long lines on his hand. "This is your love line. It's very long, but there's a definite interruption."

"Meaning?"

"Your love life won't be a smooth one."

Safe answer, he thought.

"But this is what concerns me," she continued, tapping her blunt nail against the edge of his hand. "These lines dissecting your life line indicate that you're in for a great deal of discord in your life. And they're all clustered together, which probably explains your bad aura."

"Come again?"

"Basically, lots of bad things will happen to you at one time. You'll experience one disaster after another."

"I can't wait," he groaned, wondering if this trip to South Carolina would prove to be the catalyst for this "disturbance of his aura."

"But there's hope," Susan said brightly. "Once you get past that stuff, you should be very content with your life."

"Great," he mused aloud. "I'll keep that in mind whenever my life starts going to hell."

Susan's dark eyes met his. "As for your aura, I think you might want to try some deep-breathing exercises. Relaxation techniques are quite effective in achieving a color change. You might even make it all the way to yellow."

"There's a goal," he whispered as he gently pulled his hand away. "Thanks for the insights."

"Anytime," Susan answered. Grabbing her oversize nylon knapsack, the woman slung it over her thin shoulder as she got to her feet. "Practice that breathing," she called out as she left.

He took a long pull on his beer and savored the bitterness as it went down. This was certainly one of the more interesting days in his life. He'd discovered a skeleton and had had his palm and aura analyzed. He began to chuckle.

"Something funny?"

Tory approached him with something akin to trepidation in her eyes.

"Susan just checked out my aura and my palm."

His explanation erased the caution from her expression. Her half smile had a disturbing effect on him.

"Don't let her hear you laugh," he warned. "She takes that stuff seriously. I made that mistake when she warned me of impending doom."

"Really? And what did our little soothsayer tell you?"

His eyes drifted to her shapely backside as she slipped behind the bar and filled a glass with soda.

"She's convinced I'm about to have a life-altering experience. Something about too many intersections in my life line."

J.D. felt his mouth curve in a wide smile. "It would seem that Susan is a one-trick pony," Tory said.

"Why's that?"

"That's basically the same story she handed me."

She stood next to the table, but made no move to join him. She brought the glass to her lips. It was the first time he'd really looked at her mouth. He guessed it would be soft.

"Want to join me?"

"No," she answered quickly.

Too quickly, he thought.

"They were just placing that disgusting thing on a stretcher when I gave Chad back to Shelby."

"He's a cute kid."

His observation was greeted by a surprised look.

"Yes," she agreed. "Chad's adorable."

"So." He paused long enough to take another swallow. "How come you're hanging around?"

"I'm just waiting for the police to finish," she told him. "They've got my car blocked in."

"You could ask them to move it."

"I could, but I don't mind waiting."

"Patience is a virtue."

He could almost hear her spine stiffen.

"Why do you feel the need to mock me?" she asked pointedly.

"I wasn't mocking. Simply making an observation."

"Miss?"

Tory turned in answer to the male voice. One of the detectives marched forward, his badge dangling from the breast pocket of his tan suit jacket.

"Would it be possible for me to get a glass of water?"

"Sure," Tory answered as she slipped behind the bar and filled a glass with ice.

"J. D. Porter," he said, extending his hand to the man.

"Greer," the detective responded, wiping his hand on his slacks before engaging in the handshake. "You're Rose's..."

"Son," J.D. answered without inflection.

The detective regarded him briefly before Tory appeared with the glass. "Thanks," he said. "It's hot as all get-out today."

"Have they taken the body away?" Tory asked.

"What was left of him."

"Then it was a man?" J.D. asked.

"We're pretty sure, based on the size and shape of the pelvic bones."

"Any idea who he was?"

"Not a clue," Greer answered. "But the lab boys think he's been here a while. Some medical mumbo jumbo about the condition and density of the bone."

"How creepy," Tory groaned. "I can't tell you how many times I've been near that building in the five years I've been working here."

"That long?" Greer asked, immediately putting down his glass and feeling for his pad and pen.

"Yes, sir," J.D. heard her answer. "I worked for the previous owner—Mr. Brewster."

"Didn't your family use to own this place before Brewster?" J.D. queried.

Tory shot him a quick glance of annoyance, then turned her attention back to the detective. "My father owned this place until about fifteen years ago."

"Do you know where I can find Brewster?" Greer asked.

"He died," Tory answered.

"How about your father?"

"I'm afraid you won't have any luck there, either."

"He's deceased?" Greer asked.

J.D. watched as she lowered her eyes.

"He left town."

"Do you have an address?"

"I haven't heard from him," she answered in a small voice.

J.D. felt a small stab of compassion for the woman. He knew all too well what it was like to have a parent suddenly disappear from your life. He placed his hand on her shoulder. She shrugged away from his touch.

''My father left us when I was ten. We never heard from him.''

''Sorry,'' Greer mumbled as he flipped the notebook closed. ''I guess there's—''

''Detective?''

An obviously excited man dressed in a wilted uniform rushed into the room. A plastic bag dangled from his dirt-smudged hand.

''What have you got?'' Greer asked as he cupped his hand beneath the item in the evidence bag.

''We found this in the soil after they moved the remains.''

J.D. moved closer, as did Tory. The item caught and reflected the light. ''A ring,'' Greer mumbled.

''Has initials, too,'' the officer chimed excitedly.

''R.C.,'' Greer read.

J.D. watched the horror fill Tory's wide eyes. Her mouth opened for a scream that never materialized. She simply went limp, falling right into his outstretched arms. His handsome features grew faint and fuzzy, until she could no longer hold on to his image.

Chapter Three

His eyes opened reluctantly, followed almost immediately by a telltale stab of pain in his lower back. Using his legs for leverage, J.D. hoisted his stiff frame to a sitting position. Rubbing the stubble on his chin, he squinted against the harsh rays of morning light spilling over a faded set of clashing curtains. Holding his breath, he listened for sound. Nothing.

He found a clock on the kitchen wall. Well, he decided, as he began a burglar-quiet search of the cabinets, it wasn't really much of a kitchen. Hell, he added, feeling the frown on his lips, it wasn't really much of an apartment.

Leaning against the counter, he surveyed the single room, feeling his stomach lurch in protest to the stark surroundings. Tory Conway appeared to be living one step above poverty. For some unknown reason, that rankled.

The single-serving coffeepot gurgled behind him. In the center of the room there was a card table with two mismatched chairs, their seats little more than shredded strips of faded vinyl. The computer sitting on top of the table was antiquated, probably five years removed from the sleek electronic notebook he had so casually brought along from Miami. The first stirrings of guilt did little to improve his mood.

He found a coffee cup on the drain board and actually smiled when he realized it was from the Rose Tattoo. A quick check of the drawers indicated that the utensils and most of the other items were also from his mother's restaurant.

Mother. His grimace returned with a vengeance. What in hell had he gotten himself into? he wondered as he poured the coffee and took a sip. The liquid scalded his mouth. Why had he listened to Wesley? This little exercise in closure had turned into an unmitigated disaster. He wasn't a preservationist. He was an architect. And a damned good one. No matter what the sassy little blonde sleeping in the other room thought.

Stifling the groan that rose in his throat, J.D. returned to the lumpy sofa, which had served as his bed, and grabbed the telephone. Pounding the keypad, he cradled the receiver against his chin as he took another sip of the too strong coffee.

"Hello?"

"Wes, it's me."

"Big brother?" came the groggy reply. "Do you realize what time it is?"

He hadn't realized, but he didn't feel the inclination to apologize. "Early."

"No sh—"

"I've got a problem."

He could hear the rustle of bed covers, and he could easily envision his brother groping on the nightstand for his round, metal-framed glasses. Wesley was one of those people who couldn't hear without his glasses.

"You and mother aren't relating well?"

That I-just-got-my-degree-in-psychiatry, inflection-free voice was enough to make J.D. grit his teeth. He was beginning to think Wes's budding medical career was going to be a stiff pain in his rump.

"We aren't relating at all," he answered flatly. "But that isn't the problem."

"How can that not be a problem?" Wes countered.

"Because I have a more pressing problem with a body."

"Oh." Wesley snickered. "And is this body a blonde, brunette or redhead?"

"I'm serious," J.D. insisted. "It's a dead body. Deceased. Not living."

"She was married and you did something rash?"

"Good Lord, Wes! I thought psychiatrists were supposed to be good listeners. You're not hearing me."

"You're serious?" his brother asked, his tone indicating he had finally grasped the situation.

"Hell, yes," J.D. answered, raking his hand through his hair. "And it looks like the body might be the father of the girl I told you about."

"Woman."

"What?"

He heard his brother expel one of those condescendingly patient breaths. "The person you described was a woman, not a girl. We're talking about Victoria Conway, right?"

"Right."

"The one with pretty blue eyes, an incredible mouth and boobs that—"

"Yes," he growled.

"Hey," Wesley continued. "You're the one who told me you were astounded she didn't fall facedown from the weight of those hooters."

"Thank you," J.D. managed to say tightly. "Forget what I said before. Fact is, the body I found might just turn out to be her father."

He heard a low whistle before Wesley said, "Gonna be

kind of tough to shaft the lady when she's in the midst of burying Daddy, isn't it.''

"No kidding,'' J.D. admitted. "And I wasn't going to shaft her. I was thinking more along the lines of a nice, quiet buyout.''

"Think she'll be interested in doing business with a man who originally judged her by her bra size?''

"Wesley,'' J.D. said from between clenched teeth. "I called for your advice, not a lecture.''

"Then you shouldn't have confided all your observations about the lady's physical attributes.''

"Brothers are supposed to confide things like that. It's part of the male-bonding process.''

Wesley's laugh was low and easy. It served as a vivid reminder to J.D. of their inherent differences.

"Careful, big brother. That sounded dangerously like an introspective moment. Not your usual style.''

"Finding skeletons in walls isn't par for the course, either.''

"I don't know,'' Wesley began arbitrarily. "If you're willing to come to grips with the skeletons in your closet, one more in the wall should be no sweat.''

"You aren't helping.''

"What would you suggest I do?''

"Get your butt up here.''

"In good time,'' Wesley announced. "That was the deal.''

"But things have changed since we struck that bargain,'' J.D. said on a breath.

"And you can roll with the punches,'' Wesley said easily. "I think this may turn out to be a very healthy experience for you.''

"Right,'' J.D. grumbled. His coffee had gone cold and it left a bitter taste in his mouth as he forced himself to swallow. "If you came up here, you could deal with the girl. She needs someone like you."

"That's not what you said the other evening," Wesley countered. "You indicated that one night in your capable arms would have her eating out of your hand."

"I was wrong," J.D. admitted. Hearing his own arrogant words made him squirm uncomfortably in his seat. "She's not what I thought at first."

"Wouldn't let you in her pants, huh?"

"Not a chance."

OPENING HER EYES, Tory blinked against the confusion clouding her lagging brain. Her hand ran over the surface of the rumpled comforter. The movement caused her to feel the coolness of the sheets against her skin. *Too much skin,* she thought as she threw the bedspread toward her feet. "What?" she mumbled as she discovered she was wearing nothing but her bra and panties. The flame red garments stood out against the stark white sheets. With wide eyes, she allowed her gaze to dart around the room as she tried to pry memories from her brain.

Her fingers feathered her bangs as she concentrated. Recall came slowly. Pain, followed by so many emotions that she lost count. Her father was dead. Had been all these years. A small groan escaped her slightly parted lips.

Images from childhood mingled with bits and pieces of the scene she had waged in the Tattoo. Images of her parents, recalled through the eyes of a mere child. Images of being in J.D.'s arms, remembered by a lingering heat on her skin.

Tory stood on wobbly legs. Only then did she recollect Rose forcing several pills down her throat last night. At least she thought it was last night. Everything seemed to be trapped in a haze. Grabbing her short robe off the hook, she tugged it over her shoulders and yanked open the door. Her eyes collided with a set of gray ones.

"What...?" She managed to tear the word from her constricted throat.

"Good morning," he said easily, unfolding himself from the sofa.

Her mouth remained open as she took in the scene. J.D. had a tousled, rugged look that cemented her to the spot. His dark hair was mussed, as if someone had been running their fingers through it. His shirt was open, and the edges pulled farther apart as he rose to his full height of well over six feet. Tory's eyes fell to the thick, black curls and then lower, where they tapered and disappeared beneath the waistband of his jeans.

Realizing too late that such a brazen appraisal might prove dangerous, she lifted her gaze to his. His expression was intense, his eyes narrowed to a glistening silver. Again she realized the error of her ways too late. She could feel his eyes as they took in the lacy edges of her bra, could feel them linger at the valley between her breasts.

Feeling her skin color the same deep red as her lingerie, Tory grabbed the edges of her belt, twisting her exposed body away from the scrutiny of his examination. She'd given him an eyeful, she thought ruefully as she tied the belt so tightly that it actually made each breath painful.

"I made another pot of coffee," he told her, his voice deep and as smooth as smoke.

"Thanks," she said, willing herself into composure. "What are you doing here?" she asked as she padded into the kitchen. The vision of his eyes followed, narrowed with interest and a purely dangerous glint.

"Rose didn't think you should be alone."

"So she left you here with me?"

Tory turned to find that his expression had changed.

His eyes were still narrowed, but she saw flashes of barely leashed anger that stilled her stiff movements.

"Any reason Rose wouldn't trust us together?" he asked, one dark eyebrow arched high.

"We aren't exactly close," she offered, hoping her voice sounded more calm than she actually felt.

"Not because I haven't tried," he returned as a lazy half smile curved one corner of his mouth.

Tory directed a heavy sigh toward her bangs. "Don't start, J.D."

He moved with a quickness and grace that belied his size. Suddenly he was in front of her, his broad, bare chest dominating her vision. "Believe me, doll," he began in a low hum, "when I start on you, you'll know it."

His words burned against her ears and she fought the instinct to raise a hand and slap his arrogant face. But she decided to stand her ground. She would not react. It was, she had learned, her only weapon against this man's blatant maleness. "Well," she said, clearing her throat on the word. "As you can see, I'm fine, so you can just go crawl back under your rock."

She smiled up at him, fighting the constriction in her throat when she looked at him through the thickness of her lashes. J.D. didn't move. Not at all. He simply allowed his body to heat the air between them. Forced her to breathe in the scent of his skin. Power fairly radiated from this man. Power that Tory was only beginning to comprehend. One thing she knew, she realized as she struggled to hold his gaze, J. D. Porter was way out of her league. She surrendered, closing her eyes before lowering her chin fractionally.

"Thank you for staying," she said after a drawn-out silence, punctuated only by the even sound of his breathing. Perhaps graciousness might accomplish her goal of dismissing this disturbing man.

"No problem," he said as he slowly stepped back. The edge to his voice was still there, but it wasn't quite as sharp.

Tory turned back to the sink, thinking how helpful it might be to douse herself with cold water. J.D. somehow managed to ignite small fires in every cell of her body. She reached up into the cabinet in search of a coffee cup. His sharp intake of breath was as thrilling as it was disquieting. It didn't take a rocket scientist to realize that the action, however innocent, had resulted in her flashing the big man a goodly amount of leg. She lowered her arm slowly, snidely hoping to give him a healthy dose of his own medicine.

With a cup of coffee in hand, she finally mustered the nerve to look at him again. The flash of anger was gone, all right, but it had been replaced by something even more devastating. Hunger—raw, passionate and definitely frightening. A small voice of reason chanted that saying about playing with fire as she bolted for the living room.

J.D. followed, his pace slow, but determined. It conjured visions of a predator stalking its prey. Tory wasn't at all sure she could handle being this man's quarry.

"Rose called earlier," he said conversationally.

His calm, businesslike demeanor only made her more aware of her own raging pulse. The man was obviously some sort of machine. She'd seen him do this time and time again during the course of their short acquaintance. J.D. could be in a rage one minute, calm as a gentle breeze the next.

"I should call and apologize," Tory said, tracing the top of her cup with her fingernail.

"For what?"

"Falling apart yesterday."

"Appropriate under the circumstances," he said as he

turned one of her metal chairs and mounted it. His well-developed forearms rested against its back.

Her interest fell to his exposed stomach, wondering absently how those ripples of muscle would feel beneath her fingertips.

"Don't you think?"

"Sorry," Tory mumbled as her attention dropped to study a polyurethaned knot in the wooden floor.

"I said, I thought your actions were appropriate under the circumstances. That must have been quite a shock for you."

"It was," she admitted softly. "I still can't believe he's been there all this time."

"Where did you think he was?"

Sitting at the table and tucking her bare feet under the hem of her short robe, Tory placed the coffee cup on the table. "I just always believed he'd suffered some sort of midlife crisis and bolted."

"Leaving his loving wife and daughter behind?"

Tory peered up at him through her lashes, trying to gauge his sincerity. Unfortunately, J.D. had the perfect face for poker. It revealed absolutely nothing.

Her lids fluttered closed as she felt a swell of emotion grip her chest. "I can't tell you how much I've hated him all these years. How many times I've wished him dead for what he did to my mother."

"You didn't know."

Somehow his words failed to bring absolution.

"Mother," she said, her eyes open and straining against her tight lids. "I've got to go out to Ashley Villas."

"Where?"

"My mother's home," she said by way of explanation.

Tory deposited her coffee cup and turned toward the bedroom in a flurry of activity. It took several seconds for her brain to register the fact that J.D. hadn't moved a blessed muscle.

"I don't mean to be antisocial, Mr. Porter," she said stiffly, "but I've got to go see my mother. Tell her..."

Nodding, J.D. rose and began buttoning his shirt. Tory refused to look, no matter how much she might want to.

"How long will it take you to get ready?"

"How long?" she gasped.

"Minutes? Hours? How long?"

"Why?"

"Because I need to know how soon to pick you up."

"Why would you pick me up?"

"Because your car is still at the Rose Tattoo."

"So," she said, her voice faltering slightly. "I can grab the bus and pick it up."

"No, you can't." J.D. dug into the front pocket of his jeans. Instantly she recognized her key ring as it dangled from his forefinger.

"Give me my keys," she instructed, annoyance stiffening her spine.

"Can't," he drawled with an exaggerated sigh.

"Can't or won't?"

"Can't," he insisted, pretending to be hurt by her insinuation. "The doctor said you weren't to drive for twenty-four hours after taking those pills."

"Then I'll make other arrangements," she told him with a wave of her hand.

"Seems kind of stupid since I'm ready and able."

But for what, exactly? her brain screamed. "I don't think—"

"No thought required," he said as he tossed her keys in the air, captured them in his big palm, then slipped them back into his pocket. "I'll be back in about forty-five minutes."

THE PURPOSE FOR the cold shower was twofold. First, J.D. hoped it might revive his sleep-deprived senses. But, more important, he was trying to cleanse the memory of her voluptuous body from his mind. Closing his eyes against the spray, his mind immediately brought forth the image of her pale skin...and the slope of her full breasts spilling over the lacy top of her bra. He didn't have to touch the garment to know it was silk—like her skin. The vivid red lingerie set against her creamy skin reminded him of a ripe, red berry atop a snowdrift.

"God," he groaned, earning himself a mouthful of cool, chlorine-scented water. He'd been too long without a woman. That was the only explanation for his body's rigid and painful response to Tory.

He stepped from the shower, grabbed a towel and blotted the water from his skin. Droplets of water fell from his hair as he grabbed his razor. He was glad for a task that required his full attention.

J.D. vigorously towel dried his hair as he stepped into the master suite of his condo. Guilt tugged at his conscience as he paused to look at his surroundings. A king-size white rattan bed dominated the large space, with no fewer than three chests of drawers. There was a desk in the corner, his laptop lay open on it, gathering dust. His condo also included a living room, dining area and a kitchen that could have swallowed Tory's entire apartment. His intellect reminded him that he'd had no way of knowing she would be a person of such modest means. But that knowledge didn't seem to stem the surge of guilt as he tossed the towel into a pile of laundry that would be handled by the cleaning woman.

Selecting a fresh pair of jeans and a thin cotton shirt, J.D. tucked his wallet and keys into his pants pockets and took the stairs to the parking lot two at a time. He was greeted by a slap of humid air that barely fazed his well-conditioned body. The air in the red interior of his white Mercedes was stale before he flipped on the air-conditioning. He turned out into the midday traffic and tapped a disk into the CD player as he drove.

Ashley Villas. He repeated her words in his brain. It sounded like one of those golf and tennis communities that lined the southeastern seaboard like smooth shells. He tried to develop a mental image of Tory's mother. The woman would probably be in her fifties and have a strong personality. He guessed she would be small, like her daughter, but more athletic than soft. Her skin would be wrinkled and weathered from too many trips around the back nine and not enough sunscreen. He grimaced, envisioning a brash woman wearing a white golf skirt and those funny little socks with the fuzzy little pastel balls that stuck out the back of her shoes. She was probably fiercely competitive. Tory was a fighter, that much he knew. That attribute was normally learned at home.

He frowned, suddenly realizing his thoughts were more suited to his inquisitive younger brother. Wesley was into analysis, not him.

Her apartment didn't look much better in the light of day. It looked exactly like what it was—a garage converted into barely livable space.

She came through the door before he had an opportunity to kill the engine. Her dress forced a small smile to his lips. It fell far short of flattering, he mused as he watched her move toward him. It basically covered her from her throat to her ankles, a swirl of gauzy beige fabric designed specifically *not* to cling to her in any of the right places. His eyes fell to where her breasts strained against the material. He wondered if beneath that shapeless, colorless dress, she wore those wispy, sexy undergarments. His body responded uncomfortably to his imagination.

"You're punctual," she said as she slid in beside him.

"A regular Boy Scout," he grumbled.

"Boy Scouts aren't surly, as a rule," she told him as she folded her delicate hands in her lap.

"Have much experience with Boy Scouts, do you?"

"Probably as much as you do."

"I'll have you know I almost made it to Eagle Scout," he informed her, his chest puffed out slightly.

"Almost doesn't count."

His chest deflated. "I suppose not," he acknowledged reluctantly. "Which way?"

"Take the Mark Clark." She pointed north.

The expressway was crowded with minivans and trucks sporting business logos. But his attention was on the woman to his right. "You can relax, I won't bite."

"I am relaxed."

"You don't look it."

"How can I not be relaxed? Sitting in this car is like sitting in your living room."

"Not *your* living room, doll," he promised her with a sidelong glance. "I slept on what you've got passing for a couch."

"It serves its purpose," she said with a shrug of her shoulders.

That small movement filled the interior of the car with the distinctive scent of gardenia. His mind immediately demanded to know if it was her soap, her shampoo or her cologne. Would he be able to taste it on her skin? Would he be able to keep his mind on the road long enough to prevent a ten-car pileup?

J.D. decided to concentrate on making polite conversation. "Did you call your mother to let her know you were coming?"

"It isn't necessary."

He sensed a tension in her voice that piqued his interest. "You two that close?"

"I love my mother."

He realized instantly that she hadn't actually answered his question. This from the woman who had not bothered to spare her tongue when it came to his strained relationship with Rose.

"Do you think she saw the newspaper?" he asked, nodding to the folded copy lying on the seat between them.

"No."

"She's not a reader?"

"No."

"How do you think she'll take the news about your father?"

"Calmly."

His only hint that she wasn't quite as composed as her limited answers implied was the sight of her hand as she played with the strands of wheat-colored hair sculpted around her slender throat. The tremor in her fingers was undeniable.

"You tense?"

"Tense?"

"Nervous? Agitated? Upset?"

She didn't answer right away. He glanced over once, only to have his eyes fall on the gentle rise and fall of her chest as she breathed deeply through her slightly parted lips.

"I'm just not sure how Mama will handle the news."

J.D. gripped the wheel a bit more tightly. "Her long-lost husband is dead. If she loved him, I'm sure she'll be devastated."

"What do you mean 'if she loved him'?" Tory fairly shouted at him.

He saw the spark in her ice blue eyes and was glad to see some of the life come back to her.

"Sorry," he mumbled, lifting his hands off the wheel

in a brief gesture of mock surrender. "I just meant that it's been, what? Fifteen years? Love and memories fade."

She turned her head so that he could no longer get a fix on her expression.

"How about you?"

"How about I what?" she answered dully.

"How are you holding up?"

"Are you asking me if I read the newspaper article?" Tory asked, gesturing toward the paper between them.

"Yes." He realized he was holding his breath, not certain why he had suddenly broached this potentially dangerous subject.

"I don't believe everything I read in the papers."

"Smart approach."

"But," she said as she turned, "if the police are correct in their early assessment of the case, my father didn't desert me. He was murdered."

"They weren't clear on that point," J.D. told her.

"One of them stated that there appeared to be a bullet wound in the skull—"

"But that they needed to run tests."

She scooted closer to the door, as if she wanted as much distance between them as possible.

"I must admit, Tory," he began in a deliberately soft, nonthreatening tone, "I'm astounded by your composure. If someone told me my father might have been murdered, I think I'd go ballistic."

"As strange as this may sound, hearing their theory made me feel strangely comforted."

"How so?"

"Because it means he didn't choose to walk out of my life. It means he didn't leave me."

J.D. hated the effect her soft, almost choked, words were having on his gut. Feeling compassion for this woman was dangerous.

"Turn here," she said as they approached an exit.

Silently, J.D. followed her instructions for the next several miles. The landscape was little more than swampy grasses and clusters of evergreens. Hardly an ideal sight for a golf and tennis community.

His eyes fixed on a wooden sign about a hundred yards down the road. It swayed gently on the currents of the passing cars, but he could still make out the bold, black print.

"Ashley Villas Convalescent Center?" he read aloud as he pulled into the lot, threw the car into park and killed the engine.

"None other," she responded, her voice cracking with emotion.

"Your mother lives in a convalescent center?" he asked.

"Yes," she answered as she opened the door and stepped from the car.

Grabbing the folded newspaper, J.D. tucked it under his arm and then jogged to catch up to her. "You could have said something."

"I did," she responded without looking at him. "I told you I would have preferred coming alone."

He inclined his head in respect as he held open one of the center's shining glass doors.

"Tory!" a male voice bellowed down the otherwise silent corridor. Tory smiled wanely at the dark-haired man sauntering toward her. "I should have guessed I'd run into you here today. Tough thing about your dad."

He watched as she accepted the huge hand from the man he guessed to be about fifty, though his physique belied his age. His clothes told J.D. two things—first, the guy definitely had bucks; and second, he dressed for the sole purpose of attracting women.

"Cal Matthews," she said, almost as an afterthought, "This is J.D. Porter."

The two men shook hands.

Tory continued, "Cal used to work for my dad."

"Sorry I can't stay," Cal cut in, making a point of looking at the Rolex on his wrist, "but you know how it is."

Tory nodded. J.D. wanted to question her about the guy, when a plump nurse approached

"Poor child," the large woman with skin the color of chocolate came shuffling forward, her arms held open.

"Hello, Gladys," she answered before being enfolded in the woman's ample bosom.

Gladys gave him a once-over that made J.D. feel as if he were back in Sunday school. He didn't think he'd passed inspection, either—not judging from the wary look on the nurse's round face.

"I read all about what happened in the paper," Gladys said, crooking Tory beneath her arm in a purely protective fashion. Her dark eyes continued to assess J.D. "And who is this young man?"

"J.D. Porter," Tory said. "He's in Charleston visiting Rose."

"You told me about him," Gladys said with a thoughtful nod. "This is the man who's going to ruin the Tattoo?"

"The same," Tory admitted without so much as a trace of apology in her expression. "J.D., this is Gladys Halloday, R.N."

"I prefer to think of my work as improving the property," J.D. corrected as he offered his hand to the rather imposing woman.

"Change can be good," Gladys said with a nod of her graying head.

Arms locked, the two women began to move down the hall. J.D. followed, feeling much like an intruder.

The place reminded him more of a hotel than a nursing home. There was no ammonia smell, no hiss of oxygen tanks. The place had carpeting and wallpaper, comfortable chairs and a bulletin board full of scheduled activities.

"There's Dr. Trimble. He's been waiting for you," he heard Gladys say. "He spent a lot of time with your mama this morning."

J.D. saw a paternalistic look appear in the doctor's eyes when the man spotted them moving down the hall. It was becoming obvious to J.D. that Tory was a frequent and popular visitor here.

The doctor uttered words of condolence and didn't bother giving J.D. a second glance. His face was a palette of concerned lines as he took both of Tory's hands in his.

"I'm afraid I didn't get any reaction when I told her about Robert."

"None?"

He watched as the doctor's expression grew sad. "I'm sorry, Tory. There was nothing."

"I'd like to see her now." Tory glanced over her shoulder but didn't quite meet J.D.'s eyes. "Alone," she added.

Gladys planted herself in the center of the hallway, her expression all but daring him to try to push past her. J.D. wasn't about to take on the nurse. He'd learned a long time ago when to back down from confrontation. And this was definitely one of those times. He watched Tory disappear into the last room on the right.

For the next forty minutes, he sat in a small lounge under the watchful eye of his self-appointed guard. J.D. thumbed through the paper, wondering what Tory and her mother were discussing. *No reaction at all.* The words filtered back through his brain. He finished reading the paper and piled it on the seat next to him. He looked up to find Gladys away from her post.

Feeling restless and a bit intrigued, J.D. got up, telling himself that he was only going to walk far enough to stretch the cramped muscles of his legs.

His walk took him past the lookout station, down to the last door on the right. The door was ajar and he gave a soft push, widening the crack.

He was shocked by what he saw. At first glance, he could have been looking at a child, she was so tiny. Then he saw her face. Tory's mother couldn't have weighed more than eighty pounds. The white sheets nearly swallowed her frail, limp body. But it wasn't her size as much as her face that forced him to suck in a breath. She looked barely older than her daughter. Her pale skin was smooth, nearly devoid of lines. The difference was in the eyes. The woman in bed stared blankly into space, apparently untouched by the things and people around her.

"You would have laughed, Mama." He heard Tory's voice and followed it. She was framed by the light from the window, her back to him. "You remember when I was ten and I started to develop? That nasty David Coultraine paid two of his friends to hold my arms while he peeked down my blouse? And I screamed that I'd hate all boys until my dying day?"

She paused, as if awaiting a response that never came.

"After I stopped crying, you told me one day I'd be swooning over boys. Well, you should have seen me last night. I fell right into a man's waiting arms, just like you said."

J.D. nearly jumped back when she turned and moved to the bed, sitting on, but barely rumpling, the neatly tucked bed coverings. The woman didn't move, he noted. She gave no indication that she was even aware that her beautiful daughter sat at her side. J.D. swallowed the lump of emotion in his throat.

"The doctor said he told you about Daddy," Tory said as she continued her monologue. The pauses, he quickly realized, were the result of a long history of these one-sided conversations.

Tory lifted the woman's limp hand. Something glittered in the light. J.D. moved closer to pull the object into focus. It was a ring, a copy of the one that the cops had found with the skeleton. From its placement on the lifeless hand, he guessed it was her wedding band.

"He didn't leave us, Mama. No matter what else, he didn't run off."

Tory took the hand to her face and forced it along the side of her cheek, simulating a loving, motherly stroke.

"That day after he left," Tory began, her voice dropping to a hard-to-hear whisper, "you told me he wasn't coming back. You sat me on top of the bar and told me that."

J.D. could easily imagine the scene. He felt it in the twisted knot of his stomach.

"Please, Mama," she begged, holding the hand to her heart. "Please tell me you didn't kill him."

Chapter Four

J.D. backed out of the doorway slowly, soundlessly pulling on the door as he made his exit.

Confusion caused deep lines of concentration to tug at the corners of his mouth. Glancing down the corridor, he spotted Dr. Trimble flipping through a chart near the nurse's station. J.D. reached him in three purposeful strides.

"Dr. Trimble?"

The man peered at him over the top of his half glasses. His graying eyebrows thinned above his clear brown eyes.

"I'm J. D. Porter," he said, offering his hand. "I came with Tory."

The doctor nodded, apparently approving on some unspoken level. "Nice of you to come along. I'm sure today has been particularly difficult for her."

"Yes," J.D. agreed quickly.

"Of course, she'd never admit it," Trimble added with a wry smile. "But I'm sure you already know that about her."

"Sir?"

"She has this incredible capacity for only focusing on the positive. Heaven help her if she ever loses that defense mechanism."

J.D. stifled a groan. This guy sounded exactly like his

brother. Why the hell couldn't they just say it in plain English? he wondered.

"About her mother," J.D. began.

The doctor nodded, making him wonder if the gesture was some sort of technique taught in medical school. Wesley nodded a lot, too.

"Mrs. Conway didn't respond when she was informed of her husband's fate," Dr. Trimble said.

"Stroke?"

The doctor's eyebrows drew together and he regarded J.D. with sudden interest. "Tory hasn't explained her mother's illness?"

J.D. shook his head. "You know Tory," he said with a shrug.

His seemingly innocent remark appeared to relax the other man. "I suppose it's still quite difficult for her to verbalize her feelings."

"Very," J.D. agreed.

"I've suggested counseling on several occasions," he said as he placed the chart on the counter and pulled the glasses off the bridge of his nose. "Especially after her grandmother died. I felt, and still feel, that Tory is unwilling to accept the finality of her mother's condition."

"Cancer?" J.D. said.

The doctor smiled sadly. "Nothing quite so socially acceptable, Mr. Porter."

"AIDS?"

The doctor's laugh was even sadder than his smile. "Tory's mother has suffered a complete and total personality break. It is my opinion that she will never recover."

"Personality break?"

"Nervous breakdown times ten," Dr. Trimble explained. "She hasn't moved or spoken for almost fifteen years."

"Sweet Jesus," J.D. uttered between clenched teeth.

"I don't think Jesus will listen if you speak to Him in that tone," a familiar female voice said.

J.D. spun on the heels of his boots, feeling his face burn under the accusation in Tory's eyes.

"I wasn't trying to pry."

"Not much."

"I think it might be good for you to share your confidences with your friend," Dr. Trimble told her.

"I'll keep that in mind the next time I'm in the company of a friend."

J.D. heard the shuffling of paper behind him as the doctor continued. "I know this is probably an awkward time, Tory, but you need to contact the business office on your next visit."

J.D. watched what little color there was drain from her face. Her thick lashes fluttered before her eyes closed tightly. Without making a sound, she sucked in several deep breaths and nodded to the doctor.

"I'm ready to leave," she informed him in a frosty tone.

J.D. followed her from the building, knowing he should apologize, but unable to find the appropriate words. No more grant; no more father; and the next worst thing to no mother. The reality of her life pierced some private part of his heart. He unlocked the car door for her and held it open.

"I forgot my paper," he said just as he slammed the door.

He disappeared into the building and came back ten minutes later with the paper tucked beneath his arm.

"I could have suffocated in here," she told him when he slid behind the wheel. "If I were a dog, you might have thought to leave the window open a crack."

"If you were a dog," he told her as his finger flicked the underside of her chin, "you'd be better trained."

TWO WEEKS AFTER the discovery of the body, Tory was dutifully back waiting tables at the Rose Tattoo. It was Friday, she thought with a resigned sigh. Payday for most folks, which usually meant decent tips for her. The week she'd taken off had cost her dearly. She'd be pulling double shifts for the rest of the month just to meet her bills. Forget luxuries like food.

"Evening, girlie."

"Hi, Grif," she said, smiling at the old man's watery blue eyes. "The usual?"

"And keep 'em coming."

Sliding a napkin in front of him, she tugged the pencil from behind her ear and made a note on her pad. Grif—short for Cliff Griffen—had occupied that particular table every Friday and Saturday night for nearly twenty years. Tory liked him—liked the comfort his continuity brought.

Placing her tray on the side bar, she waited until Josh the bartender sauntered over, towel draped over one shoulder.

She said, "Dewars and water—"

"Easy on the water," they said in unison.

"How is old Grif this evening?"

"Fine," Tory answered just before popping an olive in her mouth.

"You aren't supposed to do that," Josh chided. "They're for paying customers."

Good-naturedly, she stuck out her tongue, careful to hide the gesture as she moved off, drink balanced in the center of her tray.

"Miss?"

"Be right there," she promised the man before depositing the drink in front of Grif.

Quickly, she retraced her steps. "Yes, sir?"

"Our food?" he demanded in a huff.

"I'll go check," she said, offering a smile.

"We have theater tickets," he announced, as if that alone would charbroil the salmon fillets faster.

"I'll see what I can do."

She went directly to the kitchen, hoping the hostility she sensed from "Mr. Theater Tickets" wasn't going to set the tone for the evening.

"My dinners?" she called to the chef.

He looked up from his grill and said, "Almost ready."

Snagging a halved cherry tomato and popping it in her mouth, she got up on her toes and looked out into the dining room. "Theater Tickets" looked restless.

"C'mon, Mickey," she yelled. "Customer's waiting."

Clutching her tray, Tory felt an odd tingling at the base of her spine. She turned slowly and saw him lingering in the doorway.

His dark head was tilted to one side, shrouding his eyes with a disturbing shadow.

"Miss Conway," he drawled as he pushed himself away from the doorjamb.

"Mr. Porter," she returned with false friendliness. She surveyed his clothing and added, "I didn't know they made silk paisley ties in clip-on."

His laughter was deep and the sound circled her like a caress. "Mind that sharp tongue, doll. You might cut yourself."

"Sorry to disappoint you," she said sweetly, "but I've got more important fish to serve."

"I think you mean fry."

For once in her life, her timing was perfect. No sooner had the words left his mouth than Mickey placed the plates of grilled fish up on the serving counter. Placing them on the tray, Tory escaped the heat of the kitchen, trying not to notice the smoldering gray eyes that bore into her back.

Over the next several hours, Tory didn't have time to

think, let alone to wonder where J.D. was hiding. The pockets of her apron began to fill to a comfortable level of tips at about the same time her feet gave out. She was bone-tired and filled with relief when the crowd thinned to just a single couple and Grif, who sat nursing his fourth drink as he watched out the window.

"Need another?" she asked cheerfully as she leaned against his table.

"Not tonight," he said in that raspy voice that spoke of too many cigarettes. "I'm going hunting in the morning. Ever hunt with a hangover?"

"Can't say as I have," Tory answered with a laugh. She patted the back of his callused hand, her fingers brushing the gaudy gold band on his pudgy pinkie. "I'll ring you out." She often wondered why he wore that awful ring when his clothing fairly screamed aging yachtsman.

Susan was perched on one of the bar stools, counting her tips. Tory smiled as she watched the methodical way her mystical friend placed all the bills in the same direction, matching the edges on all four sides. Susan's reverence for all things metaphysical was surpassed only by her reverence for all things monetary.

"Have a good night?" Tory queried as she ran a check through the register.

"I had a walk-out," Susan complained. "They stuck me with two rounds of shooters with beer chasers. I hate frat boys. No class."

"No argument," Tory said with feeling.

She gave Grif and the couple at her other table their checks and waited to collect their money.

Rolling her head around her stiff shoulders, Tory stood on one foot and cleared her throat. The bartender managed to drag himself away from a swaying redhead to strut to her end of the bar. "Could you ring these two before you play your nightly game of roulette?"

"I'm careful, Tory."

"The CDC would probably beg to differ," she countered, some of the teasing gone from her voice. "They would classify you as engaging in dangerous behavior."

"Don't knock it 'til you've tried it," he retorted. "I'll be happy to keep tomorrow night open for you."

"She's busy tomorrow night."

Tory stifled her groan when she recognized that deep voice. She was too tired to spar with J.D.

She turned in a sleek, slow movement, tilting her chin so that she met his gaze straight on. "You're right, J.D.," she purred.

She knew the surprise wouldn't register anywhere other than his eyes, so that's where she kept her attention. She waited until the gray turned dark, almost smoky. "I'm working tomorrow night."

She brushed past him, holding crisp bills in her fist. The bartender tried to hide his laugh behind his hand. Tory felt triumphant as she placed the change in front of Grif.

"What d'ya say to him?" Grif asked, nodding in the direction of J.D.

"I told him no," she replied honestly.

"Good for you," Grif grumbled, peeling off some of the bills before pocketing the rest. "But he don't look too inclined to take no for an answer."

That wasn't her concern, she told herself as she lingered, clearing off the tables. She even checked Susan's tables, delaying her return to the bar until she could find no other alternative.

She noted J.D. quietly watched her from his seat near the jukebox, taking the occasional pull on a long-neck bottle of beer. His scrutiny was wreaking havoc with her nerves. I'm just tired, she insisted to herself as she recounted one stack of crumpled bills for the third time. She soon gave up and settled for an estimate of her earnings, then divided out the appropriate percentage for the bartender.

"Thanks," she called down to him, waving the bills and tucking them beneath an ashtray.

"Are you finished?" J.D. asked.

"Time to go home," she answered without looking at him.

"Not just yet."

"Not now, J.D.," she whined. "I'm too tired to play."

"I wasn't thinking of playing."

There was something disturbingly nonthreatening about his voice. Normally, nearly every syllable he flung at her held some sort of challenge. Grudgingly, she turned and met his hooded gaze. "What were you thinking of?"

He shrugged. "Call upstairs and let Rose know you're done for the night."

"Why?"

"She wants to talk to you."

"About what?"

"Tory." He said her name like an exasperated curse. "Just do it."

She did, though it annoyed her to do so.

He hadn't even bothered to make it sound like a request. It was an order. Nothing less. She wasn't too keen on orders, but Rose *was* her boss. She told herself she was responding to her ingrained respect for authority and not the infuriating finality of his instructions.

"You might want to get yourself a drink," J.D. suggested.

A chill ran along her spine just as the bartender and his conquest du jour sauntered out the door.

"Have you convinced your mother to fire me?" she

asked, her head tilted, her eyes studying his immobile features. "That explains the tie. You've dressed for the occasion."

"I've dressed for the occasion, all right," he grumbled against the bottle he brought to his lips.

Tory watched his Adam's apple bob above the loosened collar of his shirt. He looked good in a white shirt and tie. It was a perfect contrast to his unkempt hair and the faint shadow of a beard he seemed to have no matter what the time of day. Recent days, working in the afternoon sun had turned his skin a deep shade of bronze. She thought it might also have hardened the muscles that sculpted every inch of his solid body.

"I think I'll get that drink now," she said, hoping it might douse the heat churning in the pit of her stomach. Grabbing a glass, she poured a healthy amount of wine and fortified herself with a quick sip before joining him at the table.

He leaned back in his chair with that casual arrogance that both annoyed and intrigued her. Tory wondered when she had developed these self-abusive tendencies. It wasn't her style to be interested in a man like J.D. Quite the contrary, she avoided his type like the plague.

"I can almost hear your mind working," he said finally.

"I'm impressed," she returned, drowning the butterflies in her stomach with a swallow of wine. "I didn't think you'd noticed I had a mind."

She wanted to reach out and grab the words and shove them back down her throat. Unfortunately, that wasn't an option.

J.D. leaned forward, elbow on the table. His eyes held hers briefly before he meaningfully allowed his gaze to drop lower, to where her body strained against the flimsy fabric of her uniform. "I've noticed everything about you, Tory. Your mind—" he paused and drank "—and your other attributes.'' His voice was liquid with promise, his eyes flickered with just a hint of the desire she heard in his words.

Shoving her chair back, she was torn between tossing the rest of her drink in his face and jumping into his lap.

''Sorry it took me so long,'' Rose said as she came upon them.

Tory was half out of her seat—and completely out of her mind.

Rose stood next to the table, her eyes moving between Tory and her stoic companion. As usual, Rose's appearance acted like a shut-off valve where J.D. was concerned. His expression closed and locked. He appeared so cool, aloof and distant, Tory wondered if she might have imagined the scene between them. This robot couldn't possibly be capable of any human emotion, certainly not lust or desire. Not with the flat look he donned every time his mother entered the room.

''I've found a solution to your problem,'' Rose began.

''Sorry,'' Tory said with an exaggerated sigh. ''I think you're about thirty-five years too late to be putting him up for adoption,'' she whispered for J.D.'s benefit alone.

Direct hit, she thought as she watched his eyes narrow for just an instant.

''Victoria!'' Rose said with a snort as she fell into the chair between them. ''I was talking about your problems at school.''

That got her attention. Tearing her eyes away from him, she urged a smile to her lips. ''I'm sorry, Rose. You were saying?''

Rose produced the battered paperback directory of college funding and slipped her perfectly manicured, blood-red nail to a place marked by a plastic stirstick.

''I've been all through this, and I found a grant that will cover your tuition.''

Tory regarded the woman speculatively. She'd been through it too and had found nothing.

"Right here," Rose announced, her lips pursed as she tapped the entry. "This is perfect."

Tory slid the book closer and read the entry. The Charleston Ladies Foundation provided up to twenty thousand dollars to an applicant enrolled in graduate studies in an accredited college or university. The funds were available only to women who were residents of South Carolina; there was no age limit set; and there was no differential for private versus state colleges.

"It's fine," Tory said, trying to keep her frustration in check. "But I'm not eligible," she explained. "Read the last requirement."

"I know," Rose said excitedly, rubbing her hands in front of her face. "This is simply too perfect."

Tory wondered for a brief moment if Rose had been spending too much time with Susan. Her normally down-to-earth boss was almost as out of touch with reality as her spaced-out employee. "I don't qualify," Tory repeated, saying each word slowly. "I'm not married. The grant is for married women only."

"That's where I come in," J.D. spoke up. "I'm going to marry you."

Chapter Five

"This is crazy." Tory managed to strangle the words from her tight, dry throat. "Marry you?"

"It's the perfect solution," Rose insisted.

Tory gaped at her boss. Didn't she see that the suggestion was neither perfect nor a solution?

"What's wrong, Tory?" J.D. asked in a slow, careful tone, as if they were discussing something as benign as the weather. "You said you were willing to do *anything* to finish your degree."

"Anything *sane*," she retorted. "And legal. Pretending to be married to you would amount to committing fraud."

"But we won't be pretending," he countered easily.

Wide-eyed, she regarded him for a long moment. She suddenly found his cool control infuriating. Nothing of what he was thinking was evident from the relaxed way his large body lounged back in the chair. Anger, tinged with just a hint of curiosity, simmered in the pit of her stomach as she took in the bland expression on his handsome face.

"If you're of a mind to help me, why don't you just lend me the money?"

"No collateral," J.D. answered with a sigh.

"I'd be happy to sign a note."

"Which," he said, speaking now in a louder, more

even voice, "wouldn't be worth the paper it was written on."

"But after I get my degree—"

"There's no guarantee you'll find employment."

Digging her nails into her palms, Tory wanted to slap that superior smirk off his face. She had the sinking suspicion that she was being manipulated by a master. She just couldn't figure out why.

"Rose?" J.D.'s eyes never left Tory's face as he addressed his mother. "Would you mind leaving us alone to finish this discussion?"

Tory wasn't too thrilled with the idea of being left alone with J.D., not when he was in one of his steamroller moods. But voicing her fears would only give him another weapon for his already full arsenal.

"This can work," Rose insisted as she gave Tory's hand a squeeze. Leaning over, Rose added in a whisper, "Don't cut your nose off to spite your face. Pride's a cold bedfellow when it costs you your dreams."

Rose's footsteps echoed and died into an uncomfortable silence. Tory's heart was pounding against her ribs. She wondered why she didn't just thank him politely and walk out the door.

"You're about to tell me to take my proposal and stick it in my ear, aren't you?"

Tory felt her cheeks color. "Basically."

"You won't, though. Your education means too much to you."

"Not enough to commit fraud."

"I told you," he explained with exaggerated patience, "it won't be fraud. The marriage will be legal—and real."

"Define real." Tory chewed on her bottom lip.

J.D.'s eyes gleamed. "I think I'll leave that up to you."

"How uncharacteristically chivalrous of you," she

said. Then she watched his eyes darken to a threatening, shimmering silver.

"If you want me to set the boundaries of our marriage, I would be more than willing."

Her stomach clenched as she digested the subtle meaning of his words. "That won't be necessary. We can't possibly get married."

"Why not?"

A short breath of exasperation spilled from her opened mouth. "Because we can't!"

"Why?" he asked quietly.

His calm had her teetering left of center. Trying to regain some semblance of rationality, Tory nervously twisted the hairs at the nape of her neck with trembling fingers. "Because it isn't right."

"Right for whom?"

"For you. Or me, either."

"I'm willing," he assured her with an easy half smile. "So that leaves you."

Her head tilted to one side. "Why are you so willing?"

The half smile widened into a wolfish grin. "The usual reasons."

His words caressed her as her mind brought forth heated images of his large hands on her body. Grasping her wineglass by the stem, she brought it to her lips and averted her eyes. "I'm sure you can find a willing partner without getting married, J.D."

"No doubt," he agreed without any real conceit.

"Then why?"

"Because Rose asked me to."

Peering over the rim of her glass, Tory found his gray eyes unusually cold. "So you're doing this to please your mother?"

"Among other things."

Her chin came up proudly. "If you've finally decided

to be nice to your mother, why not start with something simple? Like treating her to dinner? Or coloring a picture she can hang on the refrigerator?''

The chuckle was little more than a rumble deep in his throat. ''So what's it going to be, Victoria?''

The sound of her name on his lips stilled her breath. ''I've already told you, this whole idea is preposterous.''

''It is a bit...unconventional.''

''Nose rings are unconventional,'' she said. ''Marrying a man I don't know, or particularly li—''

''Like?'' he interrupted. One eyebrow arched in a high taunt.

Tory sighed. ''We don't exactly get along like best buddies.''

''No,'' he agreed. ''But I think you can learn to be nice to me, given time.''

She was incensed. The adolescent urge to throw something at his sneering face was almost overwhelming. ''*Nice?* You think I need to learn to be *nice* to you? That seals it,'' she said through clenched teeth as she rose from her chair. ''Thanks, but no thanks, J.D. I'll find some other, *reasonable* way to finish school.''

His hand shot out and caught her wrist. It was a steely hold, yet it didn't hurt. J.D., as usual, was in full control of his power. She knew that, even before she looked up to briefly meet his stormy gaze.

He loomed above her, his breath washing over her face. The scent of soap and cologne hung in the scant space between her body and his. His other hand hung at his side, his thumb brushing the pads of his fingertips. Tory concentrated on the pattern of his tie.

''Look at me.''

It was an order, and she was not about to submit to his command. She didn't move so much as an eyelash.

The hand on her wrist moved, slowly working its way

up her arm, leaving her skin feeling warm and alive on its path. His fingers glided over her shoulder until he found the underside of her chin. Gently, but with authority, J.D. nudged with enough pressure to force her to meet his eyes.

His thumb worked its way up over her chin, coming to rest just beneath her lower lip. His eyes fixed on her lips and then narrowed as his thumb gently explored the contours of her mouth.

Pressing her lips together, Tory fought a sudden burst of desire-inspired curiosity.

J.D. smiled, apparently all too happy to meet the challenge of her tight-lipped response. She expected his hard mouth to come crashing down on hers. But it didn't happen that way. J.D.'s free hand snaked around her waist, though he didn't pull her against him. His fingers simply rested against her hip. The hand on her mouth moved slowly, deliberately. She was keenly aware of the heat of her skin where his palm rested against her cheek. His thumb continued a slow, thorough assault on her lower lip. Her breath stilled as he gradually increased the pressure as well as the scope of exploration. He ran his thumb roughly across her mouth until her lips parted of their own volition. It was strange and exhilarating to watch the intense expression on his face as he followed the movements of his thumb. The pressure increased, until her lower lip was malleable and hot beneath his expert touch. It was a heady experience—more exciting than any kiss.

"Marry me," he said quietly, drawing his hand away from her face.

"I can't."

"Yes, you can."

Squeezing her eyes shut for a second, Tory composed herself. Did this jerk actually think his touch would render her stupid?

Tory stepped away from him and glared up at him. ''I will not marry you. I am not that desperate.''

''Yes, you are,'' he countered with a sigh as he leaned against the table.

''Earth to J.D. Did you think all you had to do was put your hands on me and I'd abandon all reason?''

He offered a roguish grin. ''I wouldn't have minded.''

''It won't happen. Just as this silly notion of our getting married won't happen.''

''Yes, it will.''

''God,'' she groaned. ''What does it take to get through to you? I appreciate what you're trying to do, but I am not going to marry you.''

His eyebrows drew together as he stood watching her, obviously lost in private thought. ''How about if I sweeten the pot?''

''J.D.,'' she began reasonably, ''you, yourself, acknowledged that school is the most important thing in the world to me. If I won't marry you to finish my education, what could you possibly offer me that could change my mind?''

His expression never faltered when he said, ''Your mother.''

''M-my mother?''

''As long as we're married, I'll see to it that your mother receives the best possible care.''

Tory closed her eyes. The long list of expensive therapies scrolled through her mind. Things Dr. Trimble had said were too expensive and impractical to try, given her limited financial resources.

Opening her eyes slowly, willing all thought from her mind, she said simply, ''Pick a date.''

She'd expected to see a flash of triumph, something to symbolize his victory. She hadn't bargained on the relief she saw on his face. It was almost her undoing.

"I'll drive you home," he suggested.

"That isn't necessary."

"But it is," he assured her as he anchored her elbow in his hand. "We still have some details to hammer out."

TORY LEFT HIM in the small living room and sought refuge behind the safety of her bedroom door. "I should tell him to forget it," she mumbled as she stripped off her uniform. "I'm crazy for even considering this."

Tugging on a pair of faded, denim shorts, Tory pulled an oversize sweatshirt from her closet and slipped it over her head. Absently, she fluffed the top of her hair with her fingers as she searched for her sneakers. She gave up after a few minutes when she realized she was just delaying the inevitable. Straightening, she mustered all her courage and practiced a small speech in her mind.

Sorry, J.D., but I've thought it over and this is nuts. Have a nice night. She moaned audibly. Something told her J.D. wouldn't be so easily dismissed.

She found him lounging on the sofa, the knot of his loosened tie slightly askew in relation to his open collar. His eyes roamed over her entire body as she moved forward. His blatant appraisal did little to fortify her resolve.

"So," he began slowly, "have you decided on which way you're going to tell me to take a hike?"

Her eyes narrowed. She wasn't too thrilled to realize how easily this man could anticipate her thoughts.

"Yes, as a matter of fact, I've decided on a polite kiss-off," she told him with a saccharine smirk.

J.D. smiled then. She noted a small measure of something strangely reminiscent of regret in the action. "Sorry, doll. It's not going to be that easy."

"Something tells me nothing about you is easy."

"See?" he said, crossing one leg and grasping his ankle with both hands. "You're learning."

Tory gave him a stern, reproachful look. "And you're patronizing." She considered his half smile for a long time, then relented and offered one of her own.

"We'll get married at the end of the week," he said.

"So soon?" She hoped her voice revealed none of her shock at hearing his plan.

"That way, you can apply for the grant in plenty of time before the fall quarter starts."

"And you?" she asked. "Why are you *really* doing this, J.D.?"

Rubbing his hand across his chin, J.D.'s expression closed, the easy smile vanished. "I've already explained my reasons, Tory. Now I think we should get down to the nitty-gritty, so to speak."

Lacing her fingers together, Tory found herself interested, in spite of her vacillating thoughts about reneging on the deal. Listening to his proposal held the promise of a real experience, if nothing else.

"We won't tell anyone about our 'reasons' for getting married," he said.

"That might be tough," she countered. "They'll probably figure this isn't a match made in heaven when they realize we have separate addresses."

"But we won't have separate addresses."

"You can't think that I would even consider—"

"Sleeping with me?" he finished, struggling with a twinge of amusement at the corner of his mouth.

"I believe I've already told you where you stand on that issue, J.D."

"Yes." His smile broadened into a satisfied grin. "Well, the rules have changed."

"Not my rules."

"I'm making the rules now, Tory."

"Then I'm not going through with this farce," she told him flat out.

"Yes, you will. And you'll do it on my terms."

"Really?"

"Really. Marrying me will give you all the things you want."

"Such as?"

"School," he said evenly. "And I'll take care of your mother."

"I think I'll pass, just the same," Tory said with a smile.

"No, you won't," J.D. said with a dismissive little shake of his head. "You'll marry me because it's a viable solution to all your problems. You're a smart lady, you'll do the smart thing."

"You're very sure of yourself, aren't you, J.D.?"

"Yep," he said as he rose, stretching his long legs.

"This time you're going to be disappointed."

"Not by you, doll."

HIS CRYPTIC REMARK followed her into a fitful sleep. It was also the first thing she thought of when she woke the next morning. That disturbed her. Why was she having so much trouble putting J.D. and his ridiculous proposal into perspective? "Marry him," she scoffed as she pulled on her robe. "Not flaming likely."

Several sharp raps on her door summoned her from the task of filling the coffeepot. Gripping the edges of her robe, Tory opened the door a crack and peered out.

"Why are you here?" she said with a groan. "I thought we said everything we had to say last night."

"We did," J.D. answered. "Which is why I'm here."

"Haven't you ever heard it's rude to go visiting before 10:00 a.m.?"

"Doesn't apply," he said. He left her to glare at his back as he moved into the kitchen.

His broad shoulders were encased in a soft cotton pull-over in a shade of muted gray that matched his eyes. His jeans were snug, hugging his tapered hips and well-defined thighs. His hair was still damp, and it curled slightly where it brushed the collar of his shirt.

"You're exempt from all the normal social graces?" she queried as she belted her robe.

"Nope," he answered as he opened the cabinet and took down a mug. "But I don't think we have to adhere to antiquated social traditions when we're engaged to be married."

Tory felt a mound of tension pool at the top of her spine. "We aren't getting married."

"Well," he said reasonably, leaning against the counter. "Not today."

"Good," Tory said with mock relief. "Because I have to be at work by eleven-thirty, so we'd be pressed for time."

"No you don't."

"No I don't what?" she asked, dreading his next words.

"You don't have to work today."

Sudden fury narrowed her eyes. "What have you done?"

His shrug pulled the fabric of his shirt taut against the vast expanse of muscle sculpting his broad chest. "I thought we should spend some time together before the wedding. Rose agreed."

"Well, I didn't," she said indignantly. "I need to work, J.D. I need the money, *damn it!*"

"I know that," he told her in that patronizing, low voice. "And I have no objection to your continuing to work after we're married. I just think we need to take a little time out to get to know each other before the end of the week."

"Stop it," she said, balling her fists at her sides as she

tilted her head back to meet his bemused gray eyes. "We are not getting married. I thought I made myself perfectly clear last night."

"You accepted my proposal last night."

"I took it back!" she wailed in frustration.

"Minor detail," he remarked. His thick, inky lashes fluttered above his eyes until his expression became strangely seductive.

His eyes wandered over her face, taking in each feature before roaming boldly down to the front of her robe. Her cheeks burned from his frank appraisal, but not, she discovered dejectedly, from embarrassment. If she closed her eyes, Tory knew she would remember the rough tenderness of his thumb on her mouth. A coil of desire tightened in her stomach.

Moving with the fluid ease that typified all his actions, J.D. pulled her against him, bracing his legs apart so that she was firmly wedged in the valley of his thighs. His hands dipped beneath her arms, his fingers locked behind the slope at the small of her back. Her palms flattened against his chest.

Her emotions were in chaos. The heat and power emanating from this man were a near-lethal combination. He made absolutely no move to kiss her, to touch her more intimately. He seemed content to simply have her in his arms. Her eyes fixed on his mouth, on the rigid set of his jaw. She could feel the even rise and fall of his chest beneath her fingers.

"Tory?"

Why did that single word have to sound so breathy? "Yes."

"There's an item in this morning's paper about your father. The police lab has confirmed it was murder."

"I knew that from the moment you discovered his body."

"It could have been suicide."

"No," she said as she carefully pushed out of his arms. "My father wouldn't have taken his own life."

"You're sure?"

Tory nodded and lowered her head, away from his intense inspection. "Very sure."

"The police will begin an investigation."

"I'm sure they will," she agreed. "But I wonder how much success they'll have, given the fact that almost fifteen years have passed."

"If you marry me, I can protect you."

"Protect me from what?" she asked.

"From whatever the police dig up."

Tory laughed nervously. "I hardly need to be protected, J.D. Nothing the police learn could possibly hurt me."

"Maybe," he returned. "But what about your mother? If you marry me, I won't ever tell them that you think she's the killer."

Chapter Six

An insistent series of sharp knocks split the silence, dividing J.D. and Tory.

"That's probably Detective Greer," he told her. "I want your answer."

It took all his concentration to keep his expression bland as he watched the play of emotion in her big blue eyes. He recognized and understood the defiance and confusion—along with a small speck of desire she tried so hard to conceal. He was not, however, pleased to see fear win out as she regarded him warily, arms crossed just beneath the rounded curved of her breasts.

He waited, trying not to be distracted by the hint of turquoise lace peeking at him from where the folds of her robe met.

The knock sounded again.

"I've got to get that," she hedged, but J.D. planted himself between her and the door.

"I want your answer now, Tory. Will you marry me?"

Her bowlike mouth pulled into a tight line, and her eyes flashed her fury as she flung her reply at him like a gauntlet. One he found himself quite content to accept.

"Yes."

"Then let's not keep the detective waiting."

Her disposition didn't improve with the arrival of yet

another uninvited person. J.D. wondered how long it would be before huge puffs of dark smoke billowed from her ears. If her jerky movements and clipped speech were any indication, she was one angry lady.

After showing Detective Greer into her apartment, Tory regarded both men with blatant hostility. "J.D. can keep you company while I throw on something more appropriate," she said before marching off and closing the door to her bedroom with a wall-shattering slam.

J.D. smiled at the shorter man. "Morning isn't her best time."

Greer shrugged and seated himself on the sofa. J.D. knew Rose disliked this man because of something that had happened to the Tanners' son, Chad. But he was willing to reserve judgment. At least for the time being.

"So Bob Conway's death was definitely murder?"

The police detective regarded him briefly before giving a slight nod of his balding head. "So they tell me." Greer shifted, pulling a small notebook from the inside pocket of his jacket. Wetting one finger, he flipped through the first third of the pages, then he rummaged and finally produced a pen.

"You're Mrs. Porter's son."

It wasn't a question, so J.D. remained stoic as he took a seat across from the man.

"Joseph Porter?"

"I prefer J.D.," he corrected. "It saved me from that wonderful southern tradition of being called Junior or Little Joe."

"Smart move," Greer commiserated. "You visiting Charleston?"

"I'm here working. I'm going to do some renovations for Rose."

Greer's eyes raised inquisitively at his use of his

mother's given name, but J.D. didn't feel the need to explain.

"Where do you live?"

"Miami area."

"But you came all the way up here to hammer a few nails."

J.D. turned at the feminine grunt of disgust Tory made as she rejoined them. She glanced at the chair next to J.D., but apparently opted to stand.

He didn't think much of her outfit, but then he didn't think much of her fashion sense in general. Today she had gone for a safari motif. Baggy shorts and a baggy shirt that hung loosely from her small shoulders. The clothes nearly swallowed her, but he also knew they accomplished her purpose.

"J.D. is an architect, Detective," she said in a slightly amused voice. Sorting through a stack of architectural magazines on the table, she pulled one free and flipped to the center feature. J.D. remembered that project well.

"This is just one example of his work."

Leaning back, he studied her profile, wondering if he should read anything into her knowledge of his professional accomplishments. Probably not, he decided. She'd already made it perfectly clear that she didn't much care for his modern buildings.

"Nice," Greer said.

J.D. brought his hand to his mouth to hide a snicker. The detective's single adjective would have been an insult to the investors who had paid a sizable price for the design and construction.

"Anyway—" Tory tossed the magazine on the floor and feathered her bangs nervously "—what did you want to see me about?"

"I just wanted to let you know what we're doing about your father's murder."

"That isn't necessary."

Her comment earned her the undivided attention of the law enforcement officer. "I should think you would be very interested in our investigation into the murder." The detective leveled his eyes on Tory and added, "He was shot once in the back of the head." He paused, apparently waiting for her reaction. Tory wasn't about to comply.

"Almost execution-style," he added.

Tory blandly asked, "Will your grisly little diatribe bring back my father?"

Excellent comeback, J.D. thought as he mentally placed a tally in her column. He'd bet a year's profit that Tory had no idea what a powerful weapon her honesty was. Too late, he asked himself how she might react to learning of his deception.

"Of course not," Greer answered in a clipped, official-sounding voice. "I just wanted to assure you that my department will investigate this matter fully."

"I'm sure you will," Tory told him without inflection.

"How old were you when your father disappeared?"

"Ten, almost eleven."

"And your mother was...?"

"Still a functioning member of society."

J.D. heard none of the bitterness he might have expected. Only sadness and regret. He didn't like the swell of compassion building in his chest.

"Yes, well," Greer stammered. "Would you mind explaining her illness to me?"

"My mother had a nervous breakdown after my father disappeared. She isn't expected to recover."

"Do you mind if I interview her?"

J.D. intercepted the question. "I think that decision would be best handled by her physician."

"Just what is your interest in all this, Mr. Porter?" Greer asked.

"Tory is my fiancée. We're getting married at the end of the week."

Greer's brown eyes volleyed between him and the rigid woman standing next to him. J.D. reached for her hand and found it clammy.

"I see," Greer said with an unconvinced nod. "I was under the impression that you had just recently come to Charleston."

"What can I say?" J.D. said as he got to his feet. He tugged Tory against him, molding her soft body to his side. She wasn't exactly pliant, but she didn't jerk away, either. He figured it was a start.

"He can't say anything," he heard Tory tell the detective. "Words couldn't begin to describe what's happened between us in such a short time."

J.D. lowered his head until his mouth was next to her ear and his nostrils filled with the subtle floral fragrance of her hair. "Careful, doll," he whispered as he brushed his lips against her exposed earlobe. He smiled as he felt the small shudder in her body.

"I guess you could say J.D. and I have decided we simply can't live without each other," she said as she placed a tentative hand at his waist, apparently trying to add conviction to her statement.

If his expression was any indication, Greer was willing to accept it for the moment, but J.D. wasn't certain that the detective was buying into the love-at-first-sight routine.

Greer wet the end of his pencil with the tip of his serpentlike tongue and turned his focus back on Tory. "What can you tell me about the time your father disappeared?"

Her hand fell away from his waist and he could sense the sudden tension emanating from her small frame. "I was just a little girl back then. All I remember is that my father—whom I loved dearly—stopped coming home."

"What about before his disappearance? Did he seem distracted? Did he fight with anyone? Did he—"

Tory visibly shivered and moved over to the window. "He gave me rides on his back through the bar before it opened. We played hide-and-seek in the dependency. He let me squirt the soda water into the sink whenever my mother wasn't around. No matter how busy the bar was, he always came up at nine-thirty and kissed me good-night."

She spun on the ball of her bare foot, her resentful glare shooting daggers into Greer. "Those are the things I remember, Detective Greer. And I don't think any of those memories will help you find his killer."

Without skipping a beat, Greer asked, "And your mother?"

"Always smelled like the grease from the kitchen." Tory paused just long enough to take in a deep breath, then stared into space as she spoke. "Even though she waited tables until the wee hours of the morning, my mother always got up to make my breakfast. She checked my homework and kissed my boo-boos. In those days, she was always perfectly made-up, and her blond hair was usually in a long braid. She used to let me tie the ribbon at the end of it as a special reward." Rigidly, Tory turned back to the men.

Her eyes moved to Greer's notepad, where the detective hadn't written a word. J.D. felt as if someone had kicked him in the gut. Though her descriptions were vivid and emotional, her expression was completely blank.

"So," Tory continued, "I think you're wasting your time interrogating me. I was too young and too naive to remember anything significant. I was a sheltered, only child. Even if there was some sort of problem, neither of my parents would have breathed a word of it to me."

Greer nodded thoughtfully as he got to his feet. J.D. could see Tory relax as the detective prepared to leave.

She reached for the door and politely held it open for him. Greer stopped suddenly when he had one foot on the threshold. "The place was called the Rusty Nail when your family owned it, right?"

"Yes," she answered.

"Do you remember any of the employees?"

"I wasn't allowed downstairs once the bar opened," Tory told him, clearly becoming annoyed. "You seem to keep forgetting that I was a child at the time."

"So," Greer said as he peered at her over his shoulder, "you weren't aware of the fact that the current owner was a waitress when your folks owned the place?"

"Rose?" Tory said with a gasp.

"Six nights a week," Greer supplied with what seemed like rather perverse satisfaction.

Tory leaned against the door as if her legs had suddenly turned to mush. "She never said anything to me."

"I knew," J.D. said quietly.

Instantly he felt her intense blue eyes questioning him.

"Rose sent letters to us when we were kids. She mentioned where she worked."

"Us?" Greer asked.

"My younger brother, Dr. Wesley Porter."

"How can I reach him?" Greer demanded, quickly gathering the necessary materials from his rumpled jacket.

"He's in Miami now," J.D. answered. "But he'll be here at the end of the week for the wedding."

Tory's eyes grew wide as the detective pursed his thin lips and nodded. "I'll wait until he's here. But please let your brother know that I'll need to speak to him before he leaves Charleston."

"No problem," J.D. said.

Greer moved a fraction of an inch before turning to a

stunned Tory one last time. "Does the name Evan Richards mean anything to you?"

"No," she answered quickly.

Too quickly, J.D. thought. And judging by Greer's slight hesitation, the detective had picked up on it, too.

"I'll be in touch," Greer promised.

When she closed the door, she leaned against it, looking tense and fully exhausted. J.D. allowed his eyes to linger on the hint of skin at the base of her throat near the top button of her shapeless shirt. Just the smallest insinuation of cleavage teased his senses—senses he was certain he had completely lost when he'd agreed to participate in this incredible scheme his mother had cooked up.

"Well?" she asked him on an impatient breath.

"Well what?"

"How did you know to get here one step ahead of Greer?"

"He called Rose," he said with a shrug. "She called me."

The frown marring her pretty mouth appeared to lessen as she digested his explanation. Of course, she had no way of knowing that Rose had told him much more than just the simple matter of Detective Greer's zealous interest in the fifteen-year-old murder.

"May I have something to drink?" he asked in a polite voice that his well-educated stepmother would have applauded.

"Coffee?"

He shook his head. "Something cold. It's mighty hot out there."

"Spoken like a true Floridian," she quipped as she moved into the kitchen.

Her movements were fluid, soft—and they exuded a certain naive femininity that belied her smart mouth and above-average intelligence. Sitting on the lumpy sofa, he listened to the sounds from the kitchen—ice being twisted from the tray, the protesting squeal of the aged refrigerator being opened. He also thought about Tory. She was going to be his wife.

The word alone should have brought perspiration to his forehead, a tremor to his hands and severe nausea to his midsection. Instead, he discovered that he was actually consumed with curiosity.

Okay, he thought as he adjusted himself away from an attack coil in the sofa cushion, the worst-case scenario is we play this charade out for a year. Long enough for Tory to get her degree.

"Hell," he mumbled under his breath, "a person can do anything for a year."

His mind suddenly flashed to an image of Tory and him, tangled in the sheets of his big bed, making mad, passionate love to each other. Now his body did react, though not in the obvious fashion. His palms became clammy, droplets of sweat began to form just above his upper lip and his chest was suddenly tight with a mixture of emotions he wasn't yet ready to acknowledge or define. Of course, if Tory knew the real reason for the marriage, she'd probably use the sheet to hang him from the ceiling.

CARRYING A STEAMING MUG of coffee in one hand and a tall glass of iced tea in the other, Tory had run out of things to delay her in the kitchen. For some unexplained reason, J.D. had the uncanny ability to make her nervous. Luckily, she didn't think it showed as she leaned forward to place his glass on the stack of magazines in front of him on the table.

She settled for a seat at the rickety table across from him, holding her mug in both hands as she brought it to her lips. She watched with complete fascination as his large, nimble fingers squeezed the wedge of lemon into the tea. How, she wondered, could such large hands be capable of such delicate movement? She swallowed without really tasting. J.D.'s appearance of total control made her as tense as it made her curious. The lemon wedge was simply a metaphor for what bothered her most about this attractive man. Instead of gently and precisely squeezing the juice into the glass, he could just as easily have crushed it between his massive thumb and forefinger. Heat found its way to her cheeks when she envisioned what it might be like to have those fingers against her flesh.

"Hot?" J.D. queried.

"What?" she chirped, then "Damn it!" as she sloshed coffee on herself.

J.D. remained expressionless as he watched her futile attempt to blot the stain from the leg of her shorts. "I was just asking if you were warm. You looked flushed there for a minute."

Keeping her eyes downcast, Tory said, "I was just replaying the visit from the detective."

"They discovered a body. The police have to investigate."

"It was a skeleton," she corrected quickly, still unwilling to meet his gaze. "And it was fifteen years ago. I'm sure the Charleston Police Department has more pressing matters to attend to than waste their time on how my father died."

"Don't you mean *why?*"

Her head came up then, her eyes wide as they collided with his intense gray gaze. "Why?"

"The man was murdered. If it were my father, I'd want to know why."

"Well," she retorted hotly, squaring her shoulders, "he wasn't your father, so don't presume to tell me what I should be feeling."

"Is that really the reason?" he asked, his voice soft, soothing and irritatingly kind.

"Of course."

"Are you *that* certain your mother killed him?" J.D. asked after a brief silence.

Tory virtually ran into the kitchen, her heart pounding from the secret pain she'd been feeling ever since they'd discovered her father's remains. Bracing her palms against the damp edge of the sink, she sucked in deep breaths of the odd mixture of freshly cut lemon and coffee grounds.

A new scent was added a few minutes later. A purely masculine scent that told her J.D. had joined her in the kitchen area. The fact that his presence was comforting on some level was almost as strange as the fact that she had agreed to marry this virtual stranger. *Marry.* The word made her swallow the thick lump lodged in her throat.

Soundlessly, he moved behind her until she could feel the hard outline of his body against her back. The feel of him only managed to further scramble her already jumbled thoughts.

"What if you're wrong?"

"I've been telling you that all along," she answered. "While I appreciate the offer, something tells me marrying you will be a colossal mistake."

She felt him stiffen.

"I was referring to your belief that your mother is the killer."

It was her turn to tense. "Gee, J.D., maybe we can run on out to Ashley Villas and ask her. Or better yet," she continued, her voice sharp and slightly angry as it thundered through the small room, "maybe she'll confess to Detective Greer and save us all from endless speculation."

His hands clamped on her shoulders, his grasp tempered as he spun her to face him. "I was only suggesting that maybe you're wrong about your mother."

Tory's whole body felt heavy whenever she thought of her mother's present state. "Do you have any idea how long I've wondered why my mother fell apart after my father disappeared?" she asked with genuine feeling. "Even though I was only a child, I knew instinctively that her breakdown was a reaction to her husband's having up and vanished."

"People react to things differently, Tory," he said as his fingers began a slow massage of her shoulders.

"You sound like my grandmother. She simply chalked up my mother's breakdown to her inherently weak character."

"And you didn't buy that?" he asked, one dark eyebrow arched upward.

"My mother wasn't a weak woman," she explained, feeling herself relax under his touch. "She was a tad on the subservient side when it came to my father, but she didn't get the vapors or anything."

His lopsided grin coaxed a small half smile from Tory.

"She lived to please my father and to care for me. She did everything but iron his underwear. The upstairs of the bar was as neat as a pin, and I always looked like the poster child for the Perfect Parenting Society."

"Then why did you lie to Greer?"

His accusation caused her to suck in a breath.

J.D. brushed his hand up over her throat until his warm, slightly callused palm rested against her cheek. "Maybe you didn't lie, but I had the distinct impression that you omitted some things about your recollections."

Shrugging away from him, Tory tried—futilely—to withdraw from him. Since she couldn't accomplish that, she settled for fixing her gaze on the front of his shirt.

"I don't know what you're talking about."

"Yes, you do."

"I was a child!" she wailed.

"A bright child who knew more than she just told the police."

Expelling her breath slowly, Tory met his eyes. "What do you expect me to do, J.D.? Tell the police that I think my own mother is a murderer?"

His expression softened. "I expect you to keep an open mind."

"Meaning?"

"Apparently, a lot was happening fifteen years ago."

Her head tilted off to one side and she regarded him for a short time. "What would you know about it? You weren't even here fifteen years ago."

"I wasn't," he admitted. "But Rose was."

"Excuse me?" Tory felt her eyes widen as she gaped at him.

"Rose worked for your parents. She did the nine-to-two shift, which is why you probably don't remember her. And she wasn't a child when all this was happening."

"Why hasn't she ever...?" Tory's voice trailed off as her brain assimilated this information.

"You were already working there when she and Shelby bought the place from Brewster. She said that when she found out what had happened to your mother, she was reluctant to bring it up."

"So why are you telling me this."

"Because it's the right thing to do."

"And why is that?"

"Because she has some theories of her own about the murder. And they don't match yours."

Chapter Seven

For the first time since the gruesome discovery of the skeleton, Tory felt a glimmer of hope. "Rose knows who murdered my father?"

"Not exactly," J.D. answered.

Exasperation oozed from every one of her pores as she stared up at the large man. As if sensing her growing frustration with him, J.D. grasped her hand and led her into the living room area.

He sat down, tugging her along with him so that she felt the coarseness of his jeans brush the side of her upper thigh through her shorts.

His eyes scanned her face, then he said, "Rose and Shelby will be here soon."

"For what?" she demanded.

His grin was boyishly shy, bordering on apologetic. "They've kind of appointed themselves your personal shoppers for the wedding on Friday afternoon."

Wedding...Friday...Good Lord, what had she gotten herself into?

"And while we're wasting the morning shopping, is your mother going to tell me who she thinks killed my father?"

She watched his expression. It closed and became as benign as a pair of blinds suddenly snapped shut.

"That's up to her," J.D. hedged. "I don't know how she'll want to handle all this."

"What is *all this?*" Tory practically screamed at him. The annoying feel of his body pressed against the side of hers wasn't helping matters much. That little voice of reason told her she was simply too aware of this man. She'd been attracted to men before, but never with the intensity she felt whenever J.D. was within five miles of her. And it didn't make any sense. He personified everything she disliked in a man. *So why am I going to marry him in a matter of days?* she asked herself with amazement.

"Look," he began patiently. "Rose didn't tell me all that much, and what she did say, she said in confidence." His gray eyes darkened slightly before he added, "And I always keep confidences."

Tory frowned but knew full well that no amount of coaxing or pleading would get him to open up. Not J.D., the King of Control. Sighing loudly, she looked down at the coffee stain on her shorts, then she glanced at the cheap but reliable goldstone watch on her wrist. "Why are your mother and Shelby taking me shopping?"

J.D. rose and began the slow pace of a newly captured animal getting a feel for its cage. "Rose has insisted on a real ceremony."

"What?" Tory yelped.

J.D. didn't look at her, nor did he stop the fluid back-and-forth movements. "She's making arrangements to close the Rose Tattoo on Friday. She's already found a preacher and decided on flowers and—"

"Who the hell told her she could do all this?"

J.D. stopped abruptly and met her shocked gaze straight on. "I did."

This was getting out of hand, Tory thought. "You mean to tell me that we're going through this sham of a marriage with all the frills and trimmings of the real thing? And no one bothered to so much as ask me if it was okay with me?''

''If we do it this way, we'll have pictures and witnesses to show the Charleston Ladies Foundation, should they wish to question the validity of our hasty marriage.''

''A certificate from a justice of the peace would surely be sufficient,'' Tory argued.

Bracing his feet a shoulder-width apart, J.D. looped his thumbs into the waistband of his jeans, his eyes boring into hers. ''Apparently, it is also very important to Rose that we do it this way. I know she and Shelby have helped you out in the past. Will it kill you to do this for her?''

Tory felt her cheeks burn with color. Rose and Shelby *had* been awfully good to her. Lacing her fingers together, she placed them in her lap and said, ''Of course it won't kill me. I just wish one of you would have discussed this idea with me before you set the wheels in motion.''

''I never touched the wheel,'' he returned, a certain edge to his voice. ''I'm pretty sure Rose has an ulterior motive for doing this.''

''Such as?''

''Wesley is flying up on Thursday night to act as best man.''

''Your brother?''

''So Rose gets her wish,'' J.D. began. ''Both her sons in the same room at the same time.''

Tory knew from years of hearing stories just how much the separation of her family hurt Rose. After a slight hesitation, she said, ''Then I'll cooperate.''

J.D.'s dark head tilted slightly to one side, conveying a mixture of surprise and gratification. ''Can I expect you to give in to everything so easily once we're married?'' he asked teasingly, a smile tugging at the corners of his mouth.

Tory grunted before telling him in no uncertain terms, "I'm agreeing to the ceremony for Rose. And we're going to be married in name only, so you needn't concern yourself with how or why I make my decisions."

With eyes as silver as a storm cloud, J.D. simply stared at her, his mouth a hard line.

Tory felt her palms grow damp in the nerve-racking silence that stretched between them. "What I meant to say was that since this isn't like a real marriage—"

"I'm renting a real tux. I'm paying a real photographer."

"J.D.," Tory said with a groan, rising from the sofa but remaining on the safe side of the scratched and scarred coffee table. "I'm trying to discuss the logistics of what will happen *after* this elaborate ceremony *I* just found out about."

"Logistics?" he repeated with a huge grin.

Rolling her eyes, Tory said a silent prayer for patience. "You're intentionally being obtuse."

"Are we talking about your conjugal responsibilities following the ceremony?"

"I won't have any conjugal responsibilities," she told him disdainfully.

J.D.'s grin graduated into a smile that produced phenomenally sexy dimples on either side of his mouth. "We'll see," he told her in an inviting tone.

Tory was about to launch into the many reasons that she would never agree to having any sort of sexual relationship with him, when he raised his hand in anticipation of her response.

"I'm supposed to tell you to be prepared to try on every wedding gown in Charleston." Just a hint of redness appeared against his cheeks. "But I think Rose already has a dress in mind for you."

"Really?" Tory asked cautiously. She could just imagine herself in a replica of the dress Priscilla Presley wore when she married Elvis. Knowing Rose, the consummate Elvis fan, Tory would probably be expected to wear a black wig and inch-long false eyelashes, to boot.

"Have fun," J.D. told her, adding a playful wink. "I'll be meeting you at the Tattoo when you're finished with Rose and Shelby."

"What for?"

"Lunch."

"Lunch?"

"The midday meal. Surely an educated woman like you knows what lunch is."

"I know what it is. I just don't know why we're having it together."

His bronze-colored fingers grasped the worn knob of the door, and he looked back at her over his broad shoulder. "It's usually called a date, Tory. I thought it might be nice for us to have at least one before the wedding."

With that, he was gone, leaving his words behind to taunt her as she went into the small bedroom to change her clothes.

ROSE ARRIVED with Shelby waddling a short distance behind, her balance hindered by the swell of her forthcoming child. Tory smiled at them both, even though what she really felt like doing was demanding an immediate halt to the whole ceremonial charade.

Rose's snug, leopard-print slacks outlined her generous hips, and a bright orange patent-leather belt cinched her small waist. A matching orange tank top and ten pounds of costume jewelry completed the look. It was a typical Rose ensemble, which Tory normally accepted without much notice. Today, she realized, was to be different—drastically so.

Rose stood in the center of the room, her hands

clamped on her hips as she gave Tory a very unflattering once-over. "That gunnysack of a dress will be a pain in the rear every time you have to try on a gown."

"She has a point," Shelby chimed in as she lowered her swollen body into the closest chair. "I think I tried on three dozen dresses before I found my wedding gown."

Tory looked to the attractive, raven-haired woman and asked, "If you wouldn't mind letting me borrow yours, we can forget this whole shopping thing." Ignoring Rose's snort of protest, Tory continued, "You're in no condition to be traipsing all over Charleston in this heat looking for a dress for me."

"I'm not going," Shelby answered. "You and Rose are going to drop me off at the Tattoo on your way." Shelby ran her fingertips over her belly in what appeared to be soothing, circular motions. "And besides," Shelby added with a small smirk, "my dress would only fit you from the waist down. The Good Lord wasn't quite as generous with me when he handed out the breast DNA."

Tory felt herself blush furiously. While Shelby had a lovely figure when she wasn't pregnant, she wasn't anywhere nearly as top-heavy as Tory.

In one respect, Tory was glad she would have an opportunity to spend some time alone with Rose to discuss the murder of her father. On the other hand, it also meant she would be at the mercy of Rose's rather flamboyant, almost garish taste. It reminded her of a Christmas when she was about six. Santa had brought her the toy she'd been begging for for months, only he forgot the batteries. Shopping for a wedding dress alone with Rose was definitely going to be a forgotten-battery experience.

Rose pointed one long fingernail coated in bright orange polish in the direction of the bedroom and said,

"Make sure you have on hose and something that doesn't have to be pulled over your head."

Tory moved on command.

"And don't dally. Dylan and J.D. will kill me if we don't get back to the Tattoo before the lunch crunch," Rose called after her.

Tory ran through the scant offerings in her closet with about as much enthusiasm as a person dressing for a trip to the dentist. "Wedding gown," she grumbled as she yanked a formless, floral-print dress from the closet. "If Rose wants buttons, she'll sure get 'em with this baby."

The dress buttoned at the throat, then at inch-and-a-quarter intervals it buttoned again, all the way down to where it brushed her ankles. The material swirled around her legs as she quickly made up the bed and slipped two gold-plate bracelets onto her wrist.

"Come on, Tory!" she heard Rose call out impatiently.

"Almost done," she called back, struggling to ease the last gold hoop into her ear.

Whatever her expectations when she joined her bosses, it wasn't the frown from Rose and the poorly hidden wince from Shelby. Tory felt instantly hurt and self-conscious. "I can change again," she told them.

"That isn't necessary," Shelby insisted as she got to her feet. The smile she offered was as warm and generous as the woman herself. "But..." Shelby hesitated. "You're going shopping for a wedding gown," she said in a voice softened by kindness. "That shapeless thing you're wearing will make it really hard for the sales people."

"Am I supposed to wear tights and a leotard?" Tory grumbled.

"That wasn't what Shelby was trying to say," Rose insisted. "I know you have this thing about hiding your body, but Friday *is* your wedding day." Rose gave a wicked wink and added, "You don't want J.D. to think he's marrying a sack of potatoes, do you?"

Had Shelby not been in the room, Tory would have told her future mother-in-law exactly what J.D. was marrying—a woman using a desperate measure to finish graduate school. Instead, her head held high, Tory turned on her heels, and headed back into her room.

"Something easy to take on and off," she mimicked as she scraped hangers across the rod. "Something that will show my shape so the salesperson won't have to waste her precious time guessing which dress might be appropriate for me."

She finally settled on a beige blouse and tucked it into a short brown skirt. It took two safety pins to keep the front of the blouse from puckering at the closure near her overly ample breasts. Tory felt uncomfortable, but she was certain Rose would approve.

She was right.

"Good heavens, child!" Rose exclaimed as Tory returned to the living room. "If I had a body like that, I sure as hell wouldn't hide it the way you do."

Tory blushed profusely and crossed her arms in front of her chest.

"Just goes to show," Rose said philosophically as the trio left the dingy apartment, "we definitely aren't all created equal. Do you have any idea how much I pay for those fancy bras that create the illusion of cleavage?"

"I wouldn't have the faintest idea," Tory mumbled. "Could we please talk about something else?" she added, hugging her purse in front of her as she waited to take her seat in Rose's pink Cadillac.

The Elvis Presley air freshener swayed in time with the Elvis tune crooning softly from the cassette deck. Three songs later, Rose dropped Shelby off at the back entrance to the Tattoo.

"I see J.D. has already started the excavation on the dependency," Tory noted as she surveyed the mounds of freshly turned dirt and stone surrounding the building.

"That moron Greer wasn't too thrilled, but J.D. told him he had to get started since he's only staying in Charleston long enough to renovate the building. Of course he wasn't too thrilled that some bozo on his crew started digging before he got here, either."

An odd wave of sadness engulfed her at the thought of J.D. leaving Charleston. Tory shook her head, banishing the foolish thoughts from her brain. *I don't even like him, she reminded herself. I'm only marrying him for practical reasons.*

Rose barreled backward out of the alleyway as if they were being chased by the devil himself. Bracing herself against the dashboard, Tory tried to think of an appropriate way to broach the subject of her father's murder.

"We're going to Faye's," Rose announced as she cut off another driver in order to make a quick left into a parking lot less than three blocks from the Rose Tattoo. "Faye and I go way back. She'll take good care of us."

"Rose," Tory began softly, placing her hand on the other woman's forearm, "you're acting like a real mother of the groom."

Rose's professionally waxed eyebrows rose high on her forehead as she turned her eyes on Tory. Her expression still held that little thrilled look over the upcoming festivities, yet there was a tempering of reality there, as well.

"I know this marriage isn't exactly traditional, but that doesn't mean we have to treat it like a wake." Cutting the engine, Rose continued. "Wesley is coming in on Thursday to be fitted for his tux as best man. Hell," she said as she patted her stiff hair, "even my useless ex and the coed are flying up for the nuptials."

"What?" Tory squealed.

"J.D. was insistent that we treat this like a true love-at-first-sight thing."

"A best man? His father and stepmother?"

"It'll be a kick, don't you think?" Rose gleamed, a purely venomous look in her eyes. "I haven't seen the coed for years." Rose ran her hands along the slender outline of her waist and hips. "I hope she's gained a hundred pounds and lost all her teeth."

Tory regarded her companion for a second. "Are you still in love with J.D.'s father?"

"Hell, no," Rose grunted with a dismissive flick of her bejeweled wrist. "I'm just looking very forward to showing that weasel that I've made a good life for myself in spite of the fact that he walked out on me without so much as a glance backward."

Tory smiled, seeing the sparkle of anticipation in the other woman's expression. It suddenly dawned on her why this farce of a wedding was so important to her flamboyant employer. Tory's only reservation was keeping the reasons for the marriage a secret. She could still see Shelby's excited expression. And J.D.'s adamant proclamation that they tell no one of the circumstances behind the speedy wedding reverberated in her mind as they made their way into the shop.

It was a long, narrow building, with rows of frilly white and ivory dresses hanging on one side. On the opposite side she saw an eclectic collection of dresses meant for attendants and other members of the wedding party. To her utter relief, Tory saw nothing flashy or vulgar hanging on the racks.

A tall woman she guessed to be about Rose's age, and whom she assumed was Rose's friend Faye, appeared from behind a blue curtain at the rear of the shop. Unlike Rose, she wore a tailored ecru suit and tasteful jewelry. She flashed Rose a smile of instant recognition. Faye and

Rose exchanged hugs, their perfumes competing in the process.

Faye turned and offered Tory her hand. "You must be the bride."

Tory only nodded, fighting the urge to yell, "No! I'm the fraud!"

"Do you have the dress?" Rose asked.

Faye nodded then turned her trained eye on Tory. "I'd guess a size six, but we'll probably have to alter an eight in order to accommodate her bosom."

Again with the boobs, Tory groaned inwardly.

"Follow me," Faye instructed. "Rose, help yourself to some tea. There's a table over there complete with lemon and sugar."

Dutifully, Tory followed Faye behind the blue curtain. It was like no other dressing room she'd ever been in. It was oval, with mirrored walls and a platform in the center. Off to the left she spotted several dresses encased in zippered, protective plastic.

"We'll try the six, but I don't think it will work."

Tory was directed into a small stall, with Faye toting the heavy dress. With utmost care, Faye unzipped the plastic and freed the gown from the covering. Tory's breath caught in her throat. Stunning didn't even begin to describe the delicate damask gown. Its off-the-shoulder neckline was trimmed with a tiny row of pearls, the pattern repeated along the edges, which would fall in the vicinity of her upper arms. It even had a train. A train long enough to be elegant without being ostentatious.

"Rose picked this dress?" she gasped.

Faye smiled. "She said your mother wore a similar gown when she married your father. Apparently, you showed her a picture or something." Faye suddenly looked stricken. "How indelicate of me to mention your father in light of recent events."

"No apology necessary."

Tory reached into her handbag and produced a faded black-and-white picture of her parents on their wedding day. While the gown wasn't exactly the same, it was quite close. She handed the photograph to Faye.

"Same style, the fabric doesn't match, but that's only a minor detail," Faye said, her smile growing into a definite leer. "And with your looks, J.D. will probably be oblivious to the difference."

"J.D.?"

Faye's naturally white eyebrows drew together questioningly. "When he left the deposit, he said you were to select whatever you wanted."

"J.D. was here?"

"Yesterday. He and Rose came by to see if I had anything in stock close to your mother's gown. With the wedding just days away, I wouldn't have time for a special order and alterations."

"And J.D. is footing the bill?"

Faye's smile bordered on condescension. "He mentioned that you were rather short on cash at the moment."

"That's an interesting way of putting it," Tory said under her breath.

Faye patted Tory's shoulder. "These days, it isn't at all uncommon for the bride and groom to pay their own expenses."

Tory immediately reached for the price tag and nearly choked when she saw the figure printed in neat dark letters.

Faye ripped the tag from her hand and made a tsking sound with her tongue. "J.D. left strict instructions that you were not to concern yourself with the price."

"That's my J.D.," Tory agreed with a snide smirk.

When Faye left her to try on the garment, Tory found herself considering referring to herself as Mrs. Autocratic after the wedding. J.D.'s propensity for issuing orders grated.

The dress fit perfectly, if she was willing to overlook the fact that the back could not be zipped up.

"How are we doing?" Faye called.

Tory stepped from the changing area and found Rose with Faye. Both women stared in appreciative awe as she stepped up onto the platform, damask swirling around her feet.

Tory's first vision of herself as a bride brought her to the verge of tears. Like most girls, she'd dreamed of this day. In her dreams, her father escorted her down the aisle. Her mother cried and dabbed at her eyes with one of those linen handkerchiefs she used to carry no matter what the occasion.

"We're going to have to go with the eight," Faye said, coming up behind Tory and tugging at the open edges of the bodice.

"Maybe we should try a different style," Tory suggested. The excessive amount of cleavage revealed by the dress was sexy, but she wasn't marrying J.D. for sex.

"Don't be silly," Rose said. "A daughter should follow in the tradition of her mother on her wedding day."

"But—"

"But nothing," Rose interrupted. "You've shown me that picture of your parents at least a hundred times. You're going to marry my son in a dress like the one your mother wore."

"But—"

"Rose is right," Faye said, sighing. "Years from now, you'll look back at your wedding pictures and be glad you held the tradition."

"Years from now—"

"You can't see into the future," Rose interrupted again. "Try on the eight."

Tory, disregarding her reservations, changed into the larger size. In less than a second, a woman with glowing brown skin appeared to pin the dress into a proper fit. The final result was nothing short of picture perfect, especially when Faye produced a silk bouquet for Tory to hold.

"Not up there," Rose moaned, reaching up to lower the flowers so that Tory was no longer able to discreetly cover her chest. "You hold it waist-high," she explained.

"It's a beautiful gown," Tory began, "but I feel so... exposed."

"Count your blessings." Faye chuckled. "Many of the young women who come in here want that particular cut but don't have the shape to carry it off."

"We'll take it," Rose announced. "Susan will be in tomorrow to be fitted for her dress."

"Susan?"

"I simply assumed that you would want her to serve as your maid of honor," Rose said. "If you'd prefer someone else..."

"No," she answered. "Susan is the perfect choice." Since her fellow waitress wasn't exactly the sharpest knife in the drawer, Tory figured the woman wouldn't catch on that the whole thing was a farce.

Tory nodded her way through the selection of flowers and an outfit for Rose. Then, with Faye's guidance, they made arrangements for a final fitting after the alterations and arranged a time for the gown to be picked up prior to the wedding.

"Take these out and start the car for me, would you?" Rose asked, handing Tory an Elvis key ring.

Tory used the ensuing five minutes to try to formulate a discreet way to broach the subject of her father with Rose. By the time Rose slid behind the wheel, Tory was ready.

"I hope all this wasn't too taxing for you," Rose commented. "I know you're just getting over the shock of them finding your daddy, and all."

This is too easy, Tory thought. "Of course I'm sorry to learn of his death, but somehow, and I know this sounds weird, it's easier knowing he's been dead all these years than trying to understand why he abandoned me and my mother."

In her peripheral vision, Tory watched Rose's expression grow hard, almost hateful.

"I'm sorry," she amended quickly. "I forgot about you and J.D.'s father."

"It isn't that," Rose responded quickly.

"J.D. told me that you had a theory about who might have killed my father."

Now Rose's expression did turn hateful. "Apparently, the coed didn't teach my boy when to keep his mouth shut."

Tory shifted and tucked one foot beneath her on the seat. She also reached over and lowered the volume on the perpetually playing Elvis tape. "If you know something, I think you should tell Detective Greer."

Rose grunted with total disgust. "That man couldn't solve a murder if it happened right in front of his beady little eyes."

Tory felt her stomach knot and tried to convince herself her queasiness resulted from the combination of the Elvis air freshener and Rose's perfume. Lacing her fingers in an attempt to keep her hands from shaking, it took Tory a long time to coax the question from her lips. "Do you think my mother shot my father?"

Rose's fingers froze on the steering wheel. Her head spun around quickly so that Tory could see her wide-open green eyes. "Your mama?" she repeated incredulously.

"I don't remember much," Tory admitted, "but I know they used to argue a lot."

"Gloria."

"Excuse me?" Tory asked.

"One of the other waitresses back when the Rose Tattoo was the Rusty Nail."

"You think she killed my father?"

"Who knows," Rose answered in a much softer tone. "I'm pretty sure that's what your parents were arguing about, though. See—" Rose's eyes glazed over with remembered pain "—your daddy was having one hell of a fling with Gloria. One he never bothered to hide from your poor mama."

Chapter Eight

"An affair?" Tory said, the words coming out in a whisper.

She heard Rose's deep intake of breath as her head swirled with vague images of her father.

"Look," Rose said, her voice firm, "just because your father was carrying on with a tramp like Gloria, it doesn't mean he didn't love your mama."

Tory felt her mouth fall open as she gaped at Rose.

The other woman's expression became a mixture of guilt and cynicism. "Your father was nothing like my useless ex-husband, of course. Joe Don left me and the boys. Your father *never* would have left your mama for *that* woman."

"Is that why you think she was the one who killed Daddy?"

Rose's expression suddenly became unreadable. She shrugged and started the engine before she finally answered, "I don't *know* anything. Not for certain, at least."

"But you think it's a possibility?" she pressed.

"It's a possibility that I was the killer," Rose said philosophically. "Or any of the others who worked for your dad. Hell, for all I know, it could have been Grif. They were close fishing buddies."

"Grif and my father were friends? I thought he was just a customer."

"He's been at the restaurant every Friday and Saturday night for nearly twenty years." Rose smiled as she added, "I kinda hoped he'd get lost when Shelby and I turned it in to a fancier place and filled it with ferns."

Tory felt the corners of her lips begin to tug into a grin. "I remember when it was the Rusty Nail. Brewster didn't do much to it while he owned it, but you and Shelby have turned it into a pretty swank place."

"And renovating the dependency will only make things better."

"Only if your son manages to maintain the historical feel of the building. When people dine in the Tattoo, they have the sense that they're dinner guests in a home back in the nineteenth century."

"J.D. knows what we want done," Rose defended.

Tory heard the trace of maternal anger in her employer's voice and decided to shut up.

"And Lord knows the city and the historical society have given him enough grief that he wouldn't dare do anything to jeopardize the project or the zillions of permits, title searches and letters of approval he's been working on for the past few weeks."

They reached the Rose Tattoo before the beginning of lunch service. Tory watched as Chad struggled with the heavy back door. His high-pitched little voice chanted a singsong version of the word *hello.* Since, at his young age, Chad had yet to master consonant sounds, many of his l's came out as w's, making him sound like Elmer Fudd.

"Hi, sweetie," Tory said as she scooped the small boy into her arms to receive a tight hug from his pudgy little arms.

Dylan appeared instantly, his eyes fixed on his son. "You must not try to open the back door," he scolded.

Dylan's stern voice only served to tighten Chad's hold on Tory. He resisted when Dylan reached for him, clutching her as Dylan claimed the wriggling child.

"Noooo!" Chad cried.

"Yes," Dylan insisted. "You'll have to sit in your chair for five minutes for breaking the rules."

"Noooo!" Chad said more emphatically. His small legs began to kick at Dylan's body. "No chair."

Dylan turned and anchored the flailing child on his hip, speaking over his shoulder. "His mother believes in 'time outs.' My mother believed in the back of her hand. I'm beginning to see the wisdom in my mother's method."

Tory swallowed her laughter.

Dylan held the door for them with his foot as Chad changed tactics and began a soft whimper.

The kitchen was a maze of gleaming stainless steel with a full variety of dishes in various stages of preparation. The aroma of freshly chopped herbs competed with the scents of roasting meats and baked goods.

Tory's stomach responded almost instantly, churning and gurgling to remind her that it had been much too long since her last meal. She was about to move toward the setup counter to steal a few olives, when Rose stopped her by placing her hand at the center of her back.

"Come upstairs with me."

Reluctantly, and with a hand flattened against her empty stomach, Tory followed Rose up the narrow staircase that led to the second story.

The upstairs level had been her home, yet with the many changes made, she didn't get that sense of nostalgia that came with homecoming. Bedrooms were now offices, and the windows, although they resembled the originals, were now double-paned and energy-efficient replicas, which completely eliminated the drafts of hot and cold air she had battled as a child.

On hot days like today, the heat would have warmed the worn wooden floor and the air would have been stifling between the infrequent cross breezes. Every door and window would have been opened in a vain attempt to keep the large home cool while the kitchen below added to the heat.

Shelby was behind her desk, her chair pushed back to accommodate her ever-increasing abdomen. She greeted them with a half smile, probably because Chad's pleas for leniency could be heard through the thin wall.

"How did it go?" Shelby asked.

"We found the perfect dresses," Rose answered enthusiastically. "The last cog in the wheel is having Susan get her fanny down to Faye's shop."

Tory, who stood lingering in the doorway of what was once her parents' bedroom, simply listened as Rose continued to ramble.

Rose turned sideways, her eyes finding Tory. The woman's expression indicated that a new detail had entered her head—one that wasn't making her too happy.

"What are we going to do about having you escorted down the aisle?"

"Escorted?" Tory parroted.

Rose's expression moved off to visit her wandering thoughts.

Shelby stood, stretching as she got to her feet. "It won't actually be an aisle, more like the tables arranged so that there's a walkway between the front door and the fireplace."

Tory held up both hands, her head shaking as she tried to digest this sudden turn of events.

"The wedding is going to happen here?" she asked.

"You bet," Rose chimed in. "We're closing down for the whole day and doing it right."

"You're closing the restaurant on a Friday?" Tory asked. "But that's one of our busiest nights and, besides—" she paused to take a deep breath "—J.D. and I can just track down a justice of the pe—"

"Not on your life," Rose interrupted. "Now that Wesley is coming, I want to show off this place. What better way than to host a private affair like a wedding with all the trimmings? We'll decorate the fireplace with candles, flowers and ribbons. It will make a stunning altar."

"Rose." Tory heard caution in Shelby's tone. "I'm getting a sense here that you didn't discuss any of this with Tory. I've just spent the morning canceling all our reservations for Friday and Tory looks like she's about to scream."

"You don't mind, do you?" Rose asked, giving Tory her full attention. "J.D. said it would be fine. He gave me the green light to handle the arrangements. He said anything I decided was okay with him."

"I suppose I just wasn't expecting anything quite this elaborate. Our wedding being so...sudden."

"If I wasn't married and I met a man like J.D...." Shelby smiled wistfully. "Believe me, I know what it's like to fall hard in the first ten minutes. I hadn't known Dylan more than a few seconds before he swept me off my feet."

"She's leaving out the fact that I picked her up because there was glass on the floor and she was barefoot at the time," Dylan commented as he joined them, carrying a red-eyed Chad. Faint stains of frustrated tears still dampened the little boy's cheeks and he was sucking in short, dramatic little breaths.

"Dylan's such a romantic," Shelby grumbled to Tory.

"He needs a nap," Dylan said as he moved next to his wife. "And so do you," he added to Shelby.

Chad thrust himself toward his mother, only to have the move countered easily by Dylan's strong hold. "You can take a nap with Mommy," he soothed his son. "But you're too big for her to carry right now."

"Actually," Shelby said as she placed a kiss on Chad's cheek, "I'm the one who's too big."

Chad giggled and said, "Fat," pointing to his mother's stomach.

"You'll be a real charmer when you grow up," Shelby returned as she slung her tiny purse over her shoulder. "You'd better start having those father-son talks with him, Dylan. You know, a male-bonding opportunity where you explain to him why he should never call a lady fat."

"I'll work on it," Dylan replied.

"Speaking of male activities," Rose chimed up, looking directly at Tory. "We still need to find someone to walk you down the aisle."

"Grif," Tory answered without really thinking it through.

"The lush who's in here every weekend?" came a deep voice from directly behind her.

Tory started at the unexpected appearance of J.D., then offered him a wilting look for sneaking up on her and for his nasty remark about Grif.

"Grif isn't a lush, he's a regular."

"A regular alcoholic," J.D. retorted dryly.

Tory and J.D. stepped out of the way of the Tanner family as soon as all the appropriate goodbyes were said. It wasn't long before she felt J.D.'s eyes on her, his face clearly registering his dismay as he took in the easily discernible outline of her body. The intensity of his perusal made her feel almost naked, and she struggled to repress her sudden urge to cover up.

"All set for lunch?" he asked, his voice slightly hoarse.

"Definitely," she said. Taking in his attire, Tory felt a tad overdressed in her skirt and blouse. If he hadn't already announced that he had rented a tux for the ceremony, she would have sworn the man wore nothing but faded jeans and neatly pressed cotton shirts. The shirt he had selected for their "date" was emerald green and managed to compliment her outfit as if they'd somehow coordinated their efforts. *As if they were a couple,* her traitorous thoughts taunted.

"I need to go by my apartment," she said, unable to meet his eyes.

"For what?"

"To change," she answered in a barely audible voice.

"You don't need to change. You're dressed perfectly for the restaurant I have in mind. And," he added, bending forward so that Rose could not hear his words, "I think you look great dressed as a girl."

Her temper simmered but she kept her mouth clamped shut. Though she knew he was teasing, it didn't keep her from feeling annoyed with his comment. It seemed as if this was the day when her anatomy was going to be the chief topic of every conversation, and there wasn't a damned thing she could do about it.

"Where are you taking her?" Rose asked, her expression gleeful as her palms rubbed together excitedly. Apparently, she already knew about and approved of this date idea.

"WaHoo! Grill and Raw Bar," he told his mother. "Susan told me the local cuisine would be good for my karma."

"I can't believe you took a recommendation from Susan,'' Rose responded. ''The girl isn't capable of using both lobes of her brain on the same day.''

''The food there is really good,'' Tory spoke up. It wasn't so much that she felt Susan needed defending, since Rose's assessment of the other waitress was right on, but that she had a hunch Susan had recommended the place to J.D. because she knew it was one of Tory's favorite spots. All that stuff about karma was just flavoring.

''Well,'' Rose said with a sigh, ''I guess I best get downstairs and make sure everything is ready for the lunch crowd.'' She smoothed her hair and moved toward the door. ''You two enjoy yourselves.''

Tory wanted to tell her boss that she didn't think that was possible. All of a sudden, the mere thought of being on a date with J.D. had every nerve in her body tingling with some sort of undefined anticipation, mixed with a healthy dose of hesitancy.

HE FOLLOWED HER down the staircase, his eyes riveted to the way the brown skirt outlined her shapely figure. His body began to respond in a most embarrassing fashion as he escorted her to his waiting car. When he slipped behind the wheel, he almost moaned from the discomfort and his inability to do anything about it.

''Did you find a dress?''

''Yes.''

''Did Rose pick it out or did you?''

''It was my decision.''

''Did they give you a selection to choose from?''

Tory was apparently growing impatient with his interrogation. He could see her stiff posture and that slight narrowing of her eyes when he gave a quick glance in her direction before starting the car and pulling into traffic.

''I have a damn wedding gown, J.D. And in case you care, it cost more than my first car.''

"Did I ask how much it cost?"

"No."

"Then don't make an issue out of it, doll."

"If you have so much money to spend on this sham of a wedding, why won't you just lend me the money to finish school and we can forget this whole marriage thing?"

"I've already explained that. You have no collateral, and, in case you haven't noticed, this 'sham of a wedding', as you so eloquently put it, is making Rose immensely happy."

"If you're so hell-bent on making her happy, why don't you try calling her Mom instead of Rose?" Tory asked. "Can't you see the pain in her eyes every time you call her by name?"

One hand remained on the wheel while the other balled into a fist and gave the steering wheel a minor punch. "Do us both a favor, Tory. Spare me your well-intentioned insights into my dysfunctional relationship with Rose. I get enough of that crap from Wes."

"It isn't crap," she argued. "We're two intelligent adults about to do something very crazy and very stupid. Even Susan wouldn't be irresponsible enough to marry a complete stranger."

"It's a done deal, doll," he said, expelling a breath.

In the ensuing silence, J.D. didn't know whether to be angry at her for continually insisting that all he had to do was call Rose "Mom" and give her a big kiss, in order for all those years of childhood pain to go away. Or, maybe, he was feeling annoyed because he couldn't kiss Tory. Her mouth had become something of a fixation lately. He imagined the soft, pliant moistness of her lips, anticipated the sweet, almost naive response. He dreamed about it—thought about kissing her when he was supposed to be working. Hell, when he should have been watching the crew begin work around the dependency, he stood watching the kitchen window, hoping to catch an occasional glimpse of her as she worked. It wasn't making any sense, this fierce curiosity he felt for Tory on every level. Physically, it was killing him to keep his hands off her. But there was more to it than that. He just didn't know yet what that "more" was.

"This is *your* favorite place?" he asked in a surprised tone when he was handed a menu and read the eclectic selections, many of which had a distinctive Caribbean flare—conch fritters and chowder, mango salsa. It was almost like being back home. He missed his home, but he was also beginning to wonder how much he would miss Tory when she found out the truth.

"I've never had a bad meal here, and it's a nice change from the traditional southern-fried specialties."

The soft lighting in the room illuminated the shimmering fire in her eyes. It was like looking at a professionally done photograph. Her skin was flawless, shadows appearing on her high cheekbones from her thick, feathery lashes. Her menu was in the defensive position, what he now recognized as her way of making sure no one noticed her ample figure.

"Have you decided?" the waiter asked.

"I'm still thinking," J.D. told him. Of course, his first choice was to drag Tory across the table and kiss her until she couldn't see straight. Unfortunately, she definitely wasn't an entrée.

"I ran a few errands while you were out with Rose," he said as he poured wine into each of their glasses.

"Does this mean I can count on you to go to the dry cleaners and do the shopping after we're married?" she teased.

He grinned. "Don't push it. Anyway, we have full laundry service at the condo. Cleaning service, too."

"The condo? We?"

"You didn't think I would move into your place, did you?"

He watched as she brought the glass to her lips and drained nearly half of the Chablis. "I guess I hadn't really thought about it."

"I think you'll find my place comfortable. It's closer to Oglethorpe College, but a little farther away from your mother."

That veil of sadness fell across her face at the mere mention of her mother.

"But with your reduced work schedule, I'll make sure you see her whenever you want."

"What reduced work schedule?"

"Rose is going to cut back your hours and hire another waitress to pick up the slack."

He found the flash of anger in her eyes almost amusing. "I only suggested it because I was under the impression that you wanted some hands-on experience with renovating the dependency." J.D. leaned back in his chair, taking his wineglass with him. "But if you'd rather wait tables..."

The anger vanished and she became as excited as a child seeing her first new bicycle on Christmas morning. "You really are going to let me work with you?"

"*For* me," he corrected, his expression growing solemn. "I know you have an impressive academic record when it comes to old buildings, but I suspect you haven't been around too much actual construction. I'll expect you to follow my directions, even when you don't agree with them, just like any other employee."

Tory gave him a salute. "Sir, yes sir."

"Cute," he mocked. "But I'm serious. You'll be allowed to work on the project as long as you behave."

J.D. winced as the final word crossed his lips. It was

instantly apparent that Tory hadn't taken well to the use of that particular condescension. Since he could think of no graceful way to back out of his blunder, he opted to summon the waiter, order their food and change the subject.

"I found out who Evan Richards is," he said.

"The guy who Detective Greer mentioned this morning?"

J.D. nodded just as the waiter placed a steaming, fragrant bowl of conch chowder in front of him. "He's a CPA. Has a decent-size office in Summerville."

"What did he have to do with my father?"

"I don't know yet, but I thought you might like to take a drive up there and ask him after lunch."

Chapter Nine

Summerville was a bedroom community far removed from the historic part of the city. It was a maze of lovely developments where swing sets and gas grills were standard issue. It did have a small business district, which is where they found the offices of Evan Richards.

Tory was impressed. Evan's accounting firm occupied both floors of the large, custom-designed building.

"Looks like the guy's doing pretty well for himself," J.D. commented as he held the door for her.

"I bet your offices make this place look like a converted garage," she retorted.

"You'll find out soon enough," he answered as they approached the receptionist's desk.

Yeah, right, Tory thought, though she decided not to call him on it.

A well-groomed woman, who appeared to be about Tory's age, offered a welcoming smile. Actually, Tory amended, she offered J.D. the smile—Tory she barely noticed.

"Can I help you?" she asked from behind a highly polished oval desk.

"We'd like to see Mr. Richards," J.D. answered.

The woman looked down, then up at them, her face

perplexed. "Mr. Richards doesn't have any appointments scheduled for this afternoon."

"We don't have an appointment," J.D. told her.

"I see," she said with a nod. "I'd be happy to let you see his secretary, perhaps she can—"

"Mr. Richards is an old friend of my family's," Tory interjected. "When I saw his name on the sign outside, I just thought it would be nice if I dropped in to say a quick hello."

The excuse appeared to appease the woman, since she grabbed the phone and called some person named Margaret. After repeating Tory's lie, she covered the mouthpiece and asked, "Your name?"

"Victoria Conway."

A flicker of morbid curiosity passed across the woman's face. Apparently, she'd been reading the newspaper accounts of the remains of Bob Conway recently discovered in the dependency. The receptionist passed along the information to Margaret, then waited a few moments before saying to them, "Take the elevator up to the second floor. Mr. Richards's office is at the far end to the left."

As soon as the elevator doors slid closed, J.D. said, "You're a fairly decent little fibber, doll."

"I didn't actually lie," she corrected. "I simply omitted the fact that we drove out here specifically to see him." Crossing her arms in front of her, Tory stood rigidly still as J.D. reached around her to depress the illuminated button marked with the number two. His forearm brushed her side for just a fraction of a second, but it was enough to cause tiny sparks of vivid awareness to start racing through her veins.

His scent filled the small elevator compartment, tantalizing her further. How was she going to handle living in the same house with this man? And why did he have this almost magical ability to make her wonder how it would feel to be locked in his arms? Would his kisses be as demanding as the man himself?

"Are you waiting for some sort of invitation?" J.D. asked as he placed one large hand at the small of her back and nudged her from the elevator.

"I was just lost in thought for a minute," she told him testily, swatting his hand away.

"Do you remember this Richards character?"

Tory shook her head. "Maybe when I see him."

The plush carpeting drowned out the sounds of their footsteps. Unfortunately, it did nothing to quiet the sound of her heart beating in her ears. She had to stop thinking such provocative thoughts about J.D. Her curiosity was becoming far too intense, not to mention the way he'd wormed himself into her dreams. If this marriage thing was going to work, she was definitely going to have to find some way to shut off the flood of raging hormones.

Evan's office was decorated in what she could only call "Early Roadkill." Sundry dead creatures were mounted on every wall, their glass eyes staring down from above. She shivered as she stepped over the spotted rug of some poor creature's hide and introduced herself to the secretary who she assumed was Margaret.

The attractive brunette told them to have a seat, then disappeared behind a door marked Private.

J.D. sprawled on the zebra-striped sofa, while Tory opted for one of the high-backed leather chairs in front of a small coffee table. Actually, it wasn't a coffee table, but a Plexiglas rectangle that housed yet another collection of stuffed and posed critters. She found the display more disgusting than Rose's authentic Elvis Presley toenail.

Leaning forward was a mistake for two reasons. First, the magazine selection dealt only with hunting, fishing, guns and rifles. Second, she was immediately aware that

J.D.'s eyes had wandered over to peek down the front of her blouse. She should have reprimanded him for such a childish action, but for some unexplainable reason, she continued to thumb through the titles. She had always shied away from allowing men to ogle her body, yet a large part of her was thrilled to think that this man found her appealing.

"Victoria!"

She shot out of the chair at the unfamiliar voice calling her name.

"Mr. Richards," she said in an unusually husky voice. A remnant, no doubt, of a J.D. fantasy interrupted.

"Evan, please," he said in a smooth, cultured southern accent. He held out both hands, taking hers as he stood back for a long appraisal of her. "You certainly have changed a good deal since the last time I saw you."

His attention moved back to her face, and she noticed instantly that he wasn't making eye contact. Then she remembered her companion.

She introduced J.D. to the short, lean man. J.D.'s larger hand swallowed Evan's for a quick handshake.

Evan ushered them into his office, where, unfortunately, the dead-animal motif was continued. Separating the various stuffed beasts was a variety of wall plaques, awards and a single photograph. It was the photograph that caught her eye.

Evan was standing next to a large winch from which dangled a huge fish—the same huge fish mounted and hanging behind his mahogany desk. On the opposite side of the fish was another man—Grif. And, she thought as she tried not to be too obvious in her study, the picture was fairly recent.

"Sit, sit," Evan said, waving his arm in the general direction of the comfortable chairs angled toward his clutter-free desktop.

"So," he began, speaking mainly to J.D., "I can't tell you how shocked I was when I read about Bob's body being found at the Rusty Nail."

"Rose Tattoo," Tory corrected. "The new owners have changed the place. You'd probably like it. It's upscale and the food is superb."

Evan seemed taken aback by her endorsement. Blotting small beads of perspiration from his upper lip with what looked to be an expensive linen handkerchief, he forced a smile. "I don't get into town very often."

"Too busy hunting and fishing?" J.D. asked, making absolutely no attempt to keep the contempt from his question.

Evan didn't immediately react to J.D.'s tone. He was too preoccupied in growing more nervous by the second. Faint perspiration stains were beginning to form beneath the armpits of his monogrammed shirt.

"I enjoy sporting," he said slightly defensively. "I take it you aren't a sportsman, Mr. Porter."

"Never got into it myself," J.D. answered easily as he crossed one leg over the other. "I don't see much sport in camouflaging myself in the woods with a high-powered gun at my side. Now, if you tell me you got all these kills by chasing the animal down and hitting it with a rock, then I'll be impressed."

Evan's round face took on the distinctive red hue of barely contained anger. Tory took in a breath and expelled it slowly. She then placed her hand on J.D.'s knee. She felt him start at the contact and saw, out of the corner of her eye, his surprised expression. The surprise multiplied when she stabbed her fingernails into the taut tendons on either side of his knee.

"You'll have to forgive J.D., Evan. I'm sure he didn't mean to preach." Pulling her hand away from J.D. she continued, "He's just one of those people who can't keep their opinions to themselves.'' She gave J.D. a fast reprimand with her eyes before turning back to their host.

Evan appeared to relax a bit. At least he stopped dabbing at his upper lip. But the stains beneath his arms seemed to continue to grow and spread. ''No offense taken,'' he said.

''You have a lovely office,'' Tory managed to say with a straight face. ''And you must have had an excellent architect. The building is so...distinctive.''

Evan beamed. ''Henderson did the design.''

''Greg Henderson?'' J.D. asked.

''Yes. Do you know him?''

''Only professionally. Trade shows, that sort of thing,'' J.D. answered, his tone now civil.

''You're an architect?'' Evan asked, scratching his scalp through perfectly styled brown hair.

''Down in Miami.''

''He's up here to help Rose and Shelby renovate the dependency behind the Tattoo.''

''So that's how they discovered the....''

''Remains,'' Tory supplied, hoping to get the man past his discomfort. ''I was wondering what you did for my father back when he owned the place.''

Evan shrugged. ''I balanced the books,'' he said, a faintly disapproving smile curled his lips. ''Your father wasn't one of my easiest clients. He had a difficult time maintaining good records.''

''You had other clients besides Tory's father?'' J.D. asked.

The redness returned. ''Not a lot,'' he admitted. ''I was just starting out back then. Building my client base.''

''So you only handled the bar?'' J.D. pressed.

Evan nodded. ''Except for tax time. Then I did a little free-lancing.''

She watched as J.D. stroked his chin thoughtfully. ''I

was given to believe that you had been working for one of those franchise tax-return joints before you took on the Rusty Nail."

Evan's redness evolved into a drained paleness and out came the handkerchief again. "I did a lot of things back then, Mr. Porter. Who doesn't when they're fresh out of college?"

"I know what you mean," J.D. agreed. "But I don't understand how you could have afforded to leave the franchise joint to take on a single client who had no business skills. Tough to pay the bills that way."

"I told you," Evan said, his voice increasing in volume. "I supplemented my income by doing 1040s. And who are you to come in here asking about my background?" He turned angry brown eyes on Tory. "You told my receptionist that this was a friendly visit. It feels more like an interrogation."

"I'm sorry, Evan. But surely you can understand that I'm interested in my father's life prior to his murder. This has all been something of a shock for me."

"So you bring along this gorilla to intimidate me?" Evan countered.

"If I were a gorilla, you'd probably be thrilled," J.D. interjected. "Then you could take aim, kill me and have me stuffed and mounted. As it happens, Tory is my fiancée, which should explain my presence."

"Congratulations," Evan muttered. "But I can't be of any help to you. I only worked for Bob Conway for a year or so, and it was a long time ago."

"Can you tell me anything about a woman named Gloria?" Tory asked.

Evan hesitated, then nodded slowly and said, "I believe there was a waitress by that name at the Rusty Nail."

"I was told she was more than just a waitress."

Her bluntness apparently caught him off guard. "There

were rumors,'' he said, obviously choosing his words carefully.

Tory frowned at him. ''Rumors, or a blatant affair?''

Pinching the bridge of his nose, Evan sucked in a gulp of air and nodded. ''They were pretty open about the whole thing. It was really pathetic.''

''How so?'' J.D. asked.

''Tory,'' Evan said in a pleading voice, ''do you think dredging up all this old unpleasantness is really necessary?''

''It won't bring my father back, Evan. But it might tell me who killed him.''

''While we're on the subject,'' J.D. said, uncrossing his legs and leaning forward. ''Did you kill him?''

''J.D.!''

''Of all the nerve,'' Evan bellowed. His cheeks puffed out to match those of the fish mounted behind him. ''I don't—'' The buzz of the intercom cut him off and he picked up the receiver. ''Give me five minutes,'' Evan instructed his secretary, then slammed the receiver back into place.

Pushing himself away from the desk, Evan stood, his posture indicating their dismissal. ''It seems there is a police officer here to interview me, so I believe we'll have to conclude our reunion.''

''I'm really sorry if we upset you, Evan,'' Tory said as she got up. ''Grif will no doubt chew me out when he finds out J.D. and I came here and wasted your time.''

''Yes,'' Evan began, clearing his throat before continuing. ''I'll leave your reprimanding to Grif. He always has been better at that sort of thing. I wish you well in your marriage,'' he added almost as an afterthought.

''I wish you well with Detective Greer,'' J.D. countered. ''For some strange reason, he's hell-bent on solving this case.''

They left Evan panting and pale. Out in the anteroom, Greer's reaction was a different matter. He seemed amazed when he saw them. Then he appeared to get a tad perturbed. "I thought you had no interest in finding your father's killer," he stated.

"She never said she had no interest," J.D. corrected. "She just told you that finding the culprit wouldn't bring back her father."

Greer glared at him. J.D. was beginning to understand why Rose so disliked this guy. He reminded J.D. of one of those small, annoying breeds of dogs—the kind that nipped at your ankles.

"Either help me or don't," the detective told Tory. "But don't get in my way. Or have you already talked to Griffen and Matthews?"

"Cal Matthews?" he heard Tory ask.

J.D. thought he heard something in her voice—recognition, perhaps?

With a grunt of pure annoyance, Greer flipped through his notebook until he found a particular page. "Right, Calvin Matthews. Currently he owns—"

"Cal's Place on Market Street," Tory said. "He used to work for my father. I remember him being there all the time when I was little. He's been visiting my mother on and off over the years."

"Selective memory?" Greer sneered. "Or are you suddenly feeling cooperative?"

J.D. stepped between Tory and the police official, his hands balled in tight fists by his sides. "You seem to have trouble remembering she was just a kid when all this happened. Is *that* selective memory or are you just too lazy to do your own legwork?"

"Stop it," Tory told him at the same time he felt her small fingers wrap around his arm.

It was his undoing. It was a little hard to maintain his

anger at the detective with the feel of her soft, delicate hand touching him. Sidestepping Greer as if the man were a pile of animal excrement, J.D. took hold of Tory's hand and walked her past the detective, straight to the elevator. Thanks to his residual anger, he punched the button with extra force.

"Are you always so confrontational?"

He waited for the elevator doors to close before offering his answer. He still held tightly to her hand. "Did you think I was just going to stand there and let him talk to you like that?"

"Not Greer," she said, jerking her arm, but making no effort to pull away from him. "I was talking about Evan."

"The Great White Sweating Hunter?"

He heard her soft laughter and it had an amazingly calming effect on his system.

"Your old friend Evan is a liar."

"You should be marrying Susan on Friday," she suggested. "Apparently, you two share the gift of psychic communication."

He let her little taunt pass as they made their way to his car. When they reached the passenger side, J.D. turned her gently, his palms resting on her shoulders, his eyes locked on hers. "I'm not marrying anyone but you on Friday, doll. Understand?"

He watched as a faint blush painted her high cheekbones. "It w-was a joke," she stammered.

"Well, I just wanted to make sure you understood that the wedding will take place on Friday. Period."

Her eyes narrowed as her annoyance came to life. "I've already said yes. I have a dress. You have a tux. What part of this wedding *haven't* I cooperated with?"

"This part," he said as his hands moved over the silken skin of her neck, tilting her head back to receive his kiss.

Chapter Ten

"Now, now," she said as she ducked out of his grasp. "Don't you know it's bad luck to kiss the bride before the ceremony?"

J.D. allowed his arms to fall limply to his sides, his nostrils still filled with the scent of her perfume, his memory etched with the silken feel of her skin. Forcing a smile to his lips, he responded, "I believe the tradition is that I'm not supposed to *see* the bride before the ceremony."

"Well, since this isn't exactly a traditional marriage, I thought it would be okay to make up a few things along the way."

Several minutes later, J.D. found himself pulling onto the expressway and wondering why Tory had rebuked his attempt to kiss her. It wasn't a normal rejection, he thought as he melded into the steady stream of late-day traffic. He sensed she was as curious about him as he was about her; yet something was holding her back.

His conclusion was confirmed when he turned to take a quick look at her profile. She looked content, almost happy. Hardly the behavior of a woman disgusted by a man's attempt at an ordinary kiss. *Ordinary* kiss, his brain repeated sarcastically. Something told him kissing Tory would be a lot of things—and ordinary wasn't one of them.

"Where are we going?"

"I thought you might like to see my place since you'll be moving in after Friday." He could almost feel the tension begin to stiffen her small body. Battling to keep his attention on driving, J.D. decided he might as well tell her about all the arrangements. *No,* his conscience piped up. What he should be doing is telling her the truth.

"I've arranged for a moving company to get the stuff out of your apartment next week. They'll take it to a storage place near the airport."

"You did what?" she wailed.

"My condo is furnished," he told her. "And a whole hell of a lot better than your yard-sale decor."

"But those are my personal belongings. What gives you the right to place my things in storage without checking with me first?" she demanded indignantly. "You and your mother are really starting to get on my nerves, J.D. First, I'm railroaded into a marriage. Instead of a simple exchange of lies in front of a justice of the peace, I'm having the wedding of the century. Now, you tell me I'm not even going to have access to my own stuff?"

He let out a slow, calming breath. This woman's temper was the last thing he wanted to deal with. He was having a hard enough time dealing with his own frustrations. "You're welcome to bring anything to the condo you want."

"Gee, thanks," she retorted. "Will I also be given one half of one dresser drawer?"

He laughed aloud, which didn't seem to sit too well with his companion. "There's plenty of room for anything and everything you want to bring with you. Except," he said as he veered off an exit into a tree-lined suburb, "that damned sofa of yours goes into storage. It's more uncomfortable than it is ugly, and that's a phenomenal accomplishment."

"Sorry my furniture doesn't meet with your approval. Perhaps I should call Evan and ask him the name of *his* decorator."

"It would be more productive if you asked him how he managed such a smooth and speedy rise to his present professional status."

"Meaning?"

J.D. whipped the Mercedes into one of the spots reserved for his unit. "Before he had that fancy building built, he rented some pricey office space downtown."

"How do you know?"

"I asked Dylan to check the guy out for me."

"An alcohol, tobacco and firearms agent has nothing better to do than look into the life and times of a harmless accountant?"

Cutting the engine, J.D. turned to take in her innocent expression. "What makes you think he's harmless? The guy's office looks like a sick version of a wax petting zoo. An avid hunter doesn't find it hard to pull a trigger."

He felt a twinge of regret at the harshness of his words when she visibly blanched.

"I see your point." She reached for the door handle and J.D. wished he could do something to erase the pain he'd seen in her eyes. He was already beginning to imagine the pain he would cause when she eventually learned the truth.

SHE COULD HAVE described where he lived even before she stepped foot in the spacious condo overlooking Charleston Harbor. It was one of those sterile-looking places—all open spaces, stark white walls and white furniture. Tory made a mental note to invite Chad over for a chocolate ice-cream cone as soon as she was in residence.

"You don't like it," J.D. said before his lips pulled into a tight line.

"What's not to like?" she answered, moving forward to take in the magnificent view of the water and the Charleston skyline beyond. "It must be beautiful at night," she murmured when she sensed he'd come up behind her. "I can even see Fort Sumter from here," she said with genuine enthusiasm.

"It has a great kitchen," he said, his breath warm where it washed across the exposed skin of her neck.

Tory felt her pulse quicken and knew it was imperative that she put some space between herself and J.D. The temptation to touch him was nearly overwhelming. "Show it to me," she suggested as she sidestepped the big man.

He was right. It was a great kitchen, with every modern convenience, including a built-in grill and a warming oven. "You've got a better setup here than we have at the Tattoo," she teased. "Rose must have been blown away when she saw this."

"She's never been here," he said in a voice devoid of emotion.

Tory met and held his silver eyes. "Inviting your mother over for dinner is a crime in your book?"

His expression hardened. "There just hasn't been an opportunity."

"Yet," Tory said with a satisfied smile. "I'll enjoy inviting my boss to dinner once I'm mistress of this sterile abode."

J.D. matched her expression with a lopsided smirk. He took a step forward so that he loomed above her, mere inches separating them. "Since you used the word mistress, I guess that means I can look forward to coming home to elegantly prepared dishes from my *mistress.*"

The emphasis he placed on the last word made her

blush from the roots of her hair to the tips of her toes. She made a mental note to pay stricter attention to her word choices. "Show me the rest of the place," she stated in an uncharacteristically high-pitched voice.

J.D. led her down the hallway, pointing out a linen closet and powder room along the way. "This is my office," he said as he pushed open the door and flipped a switch on the wall to combat the growing darkness.

"Wow," was all she could manage to say when she moved in to admire the state-of-the-art setup. The drafting table was neatly arranged with the tools of his trade. And the computer station was like something out of a science-fiction novel. "Does it have CAD?" she asked as she walked over to the computer.

"The latest version," he said as he reached over and pushed the "on" button.

In no time at all, she was treated to a full-color version of the computer-aided design program that she had only read about in magazines and journals.

"Wanna see what I've come up with so far?"

"For the dependency?" she asked, her eyes still riveted to the screen as she sat in the padded rolling chair in front of the machine.

J.D. reached around her and Tory felt the hardness of well-defined muscle press against her back. Her body was electrified where it touched his. The soft mat of dark hair on his forearms tickled as his large fingers worked nimbly on the keyboard. He had a scent all his own, heady and masculine—and incredibly distracting.

Tory forced her attention straight ahead to the image filling the screen. She didn't find it nearly as interesting as the gentle brush of his face against her earlobe. The room felt suddenly warm, a stark contrast to the clammy dampness of her palms as she flattened them against the front of her skirt. She remembered Evan's telltale sweat stains and jerked her hands away from her clothing.

In the process, she managed to give J.D. a decent whack in the jaw with the back of her head.

"Sorry," she said as complete humiliation overcame budding desire. "One of those muscle spasms, I guess."

"No harm done," he said, reaching around her and continuing his work.

Tory squirmed in the chair as he showed her the various renovations in different dimensions and scale. Normally, she would have been riveted by the impressive computer program. However, normal didn't seem to apply where J.D. was concerned. Not in the way she was so cognizant of the fluid motions of his body, the deep, soothing tone of his voice.

"This has been great," she said, pushing away from the computer and rolling over his foot in the process. "Oops."

"Now I know why they say most accidents happen in the home," he grunted as he hopped on one leg, rubbing his injured instep.

"I'm not usually this klutzy," she told him, her eyes downcast.

"You're nervous. I understand."

Never had she been the recipient of such kindness. It was in the deep gray of his eyes, in the sexy half smile on his lips. What should have made her feel better only magnified her own awkwardness. Suddenly, Tory was conscious of herself in a whole new way. Somehow, things like posture, her hair, her skirt length—it all seemed to matter. She knew immediately it was time for a change in venue.

"So show me the rest of this place."

"The only room left is the bedroom," he told her, his eyes fixed on hers.

Tory swallowed, then forced a smile to her lips. "This place came with a bedroom? What will they think of next." Her humor seemed to short-circuit the currents flowing between them as she followed him into the adjacent room.

Of course, the electricity came flooding back the instant she caught a glimpse of the huge bed dominating the room. Immediately, she averted her eyes, fixing her gaze on what she could see of the bathroom.

"It comes with a pool, too," she quipped as she walked into the bathroom and moved to run her fingers along the smooth, cool tiles of the first step leading up to a deep, more-than-one-person Jacuzzi. Tilting her head back slightly, she grinned and asked, "What, no diving board?"

"They only come with the three-bedroom models."

Wrapped in the warmth of good humor, Tory and J.D. made their way back to the kitchen. He directed her to one of the bar stools while he moved to the refrigerator.

After rummaging a bit, he appeared from behind the door balancing the ingredients for a salad and two steaks.

"You cook?" she asked with mock exaggeration.

"PBS won't be giving me my own show, but I get by. Before I forget," J.D. said as soon as he had placed the food on top of the center island, "here's a card for you to use, and our flight leaves at eight o'clock Saturday morning."

Accepting the credit card, Tory nearly gasped when she read the name stamped in the plastic—Victoria Porter. "Why do I need a credit card? And what flight? Going where?"

J.D. didn't say anything at first, he rinsed mushrooms instead. "You can charge anything you might need for our..."

"Honeymoon?" Tory suggested, saying the word as if it had just then been invented.

"Yeah," he grumbled as he savagely chopped the poor vegetables into bits and pieces.

"To where?" she asked, dazed. Then amended her question before he answered. "Why are we going on a honeymoon?"

"It would look sort of strange if we didn't."

"It already looks strange," she told him pointedly. "Wasting good money on—"

"It's a gift from my father and stepmother. Their wedding present."

Tory blinked and said, "Your father and stepmother think you're really getting married?"

He turned then, his eyes shimmering with annoyance. "I am really getting married, Tory. In three days. But then, you should know that since you're the woman I'm marrying."

"I didn't mean it like that," she said, forcing calmness into her tone. "I'm just surprised that you haven't told your family the truth about all this."

"I've told my brother," J.D. said before he went back to his task. "Wes won't breathe a word of any of it to Dad and Shelia."

"Why did you tell him?"

"We're close."

Something about the clipped, two-word response didn't ring true.

"TWO DAYS," she said as she surveyed the clutter in her apartment. In her mind's eye, she pictured J.D.'s place and secretly admitted that it would be a nice change. "And dinner was nice," she continued talking as she began to make piles of things to take and things to leave for storage.

"That's because all we talked about was architecture and preservation," she reminded herself. "Safe subjects." Feeling her eyebrows draw together, Tory tried to fit the puzzle of J.D. in her brain. But there seemed to be too many pieces missing. "Like why are we flying to the Bahamas for a honeymoon on his father and stepmother? Why did he tell his brother the truth and not his father and stepmother?" She reached into her purse and extracted her new credit card. "And how come he won't give me a loan, but he's already gotten me an American Express Gold Card, no less. And why am I talking to—"

The shrill ring of the telephone cut off her monologue. Glancing at her watch, Tory figured it was J.D., who had probably forgotten to tell her they were going to file a joint tax return on top of everything else.

"Hello?"

"Stay out of it," the muffled voice mumbled.

"I'm sorry," she said, shivering at the creepy-sounding voice. "You must have the wrong number."

"I've got the right number, Tory."

Fear tiptoed up her spine at the sound of her own name. "Who is this?" she demanded, trying to stay calm. "Josh, if this is you, I swear I'll—"

"I'm not the bartender, Tory. I'm just warning you and that boyfriend of yours. The cops will never solve the murder. It would be a shame if something happened to you."

"Like what?" she managed to ask, her voice betraying none of the anxiety knotting the pit of her stomach.

"Like a bullet in the back of your head. Just like I did with your father."

The line went dead and Tory very nearly expired from the memory of the hoarse, menacing voice. Looking down, she noticed her hand, which still held the receiver, was shaking along with the rest of her body.

Slamming the receiver back on the cradle, Tory hugged herself and said, "It was nothing more than a prank. Some sicko read about the murder in the paper and decided to do something cruel." Still, she made a quick run through the apartment, checking every window and door, and even peeking behind the shower curtain and under the bed. She felt more secure and even debated calling J.D. and telling him of the threat. Instead, Tory took the phone off the hook and spent the next several hours sorting, packing and trying to convince herself that she had somehow blown the whole incident out of proportion.

The next morning, she was still bothered by the call and the lack of restful sleep. Dark circles had formed beneath her bloodshot eyes and no amount of cold water splashed on her face lifted that foggy feeling.

After a shower, her whole body still felt heavy as she pulled on a pair of faded denim shorts and a T-shirt with the expression Bad Hair Day emblazoned across the front. It seemed appropriate since she hadn't bothered to blow-dry her hair or apply makeup. After all, she was simply going to make sure the alterations on her wedding dress were correct. Slinging her purse over her shoulder, she had her hand on the doorknob when a knock sounded from the other side.

Normally, she would have opened the door without a thought. However, the creepy call in the wee hours of the morning was still too fresh in her mind. "Who is it?"

"J.D."

"Of course," she grumbled, knowing she couldn't look worse if she tried. She also knew that short of putting a bag over her head, there wasn't a thing she could do to transform herself in the time it took to open a door.

"Tory?" she heard him yell, impatient as ever.

"All right already," she groaned as she yanked open the door.

It was J.D. all right and she didn't need Susan's psychic abilities to know what he thought of her appearance. But it got better and better. To her utter mortification, Tory realized J.D. had brought guests, as well. Judging from the basic physical resemblance of the two men behind J.D., it didn't take her long to realize the Jackass Deluxe had brought the family by without bothering to call.

A tall, willowy blonde who looked close to J.D.'s age stepped forward with more grace and poise than Tory had ever seen.

Extending her hand along with a warm smile, the woman said, "I'm Shelia." Then with a mildly amused look in her pretty green eyes, she added, "But you probably know me better as 'that coed.'"

Tory could feel herself blush. "Nice to meet you," she managed to say with a polite expression, then turned angry eyes up to J.D. "You could have called first," she said through nearly gritted teeth.

"I've been calling all morning. Either your phone is broken or you're worse than a teenager."

"I took it off the hook," Tory admitted.

J.D.'s expression was one of instant concern. "Why?"

"Prank calls last night," she said, averting her eyes. "I just forgot to put it back on the hook when I got up."

"You don't look like you ever went to bed."

"Thanks," she mumbled.

"My brother isn't exactly known for his tact," the youngest man said as he stepped forward. "Or his manners. I'm Wesley Porter, nice to meet you."

He was good, Tory thought as she shook his hand. He knew this whole thing was a sham, but neither his expression nor his actions gave him away. It made her wonder if all the Porter men could lie with such ease.

"And I'm Joseph," the elder Porter said as he stepped forward. He wrapped Tory in his large frame and gave her a tight squeeze. "I can't tell you how happy I am that one of my sons is finally settling down."

Tory couldn't bring herself to say a word. Wesley and J.D. might be capable of deceiving this kind man, but she wasn't up to it.

"Hope there are lots of grandchildren in the plans," he continued.

That's it! Tory thought as she said a silent prayer for a spaceship to fly overhead and remove her from the planet.

"I think we should concentrate on the wedding first," J.D. told his father.

"Speaking of which, I have a fitting for my dress in less than ten minutes." She surveyed the various pairs of curious eyes fixed on her and could only offer an apologetic smile. "You're welcome to stay here," she suggested. "It won't take me too long."

"I'll stay here," J.D. said. Then he reached into his pocket and tossed his car keys to his brother. "We passed the tux place on the way over here. Drop Shelia and Dad at the Omni to shop while you get fitted."

He really did feel sorry for Tory, he thought once he was finally alone in her apartment, which was in complete chaos. The first thing he did was find the phone and put the receiver back on the hook. He shouldn't have brought the family by without warning, but his father had been his usual insistent self. He could only imagine what his father must think of his bride. Tory was attractive, but this morning hadn't exactly been one of her better days. He wondered if she really was getting her dress fitted or if she was off someplace digging a large hole to crawl into. The thought made him smile. So did the lingering scent of her, which filled the dingy apartment.

J.D. had managed his secret mission in her bedroom when he heard a knock at the front door. Careful to step over what he could only assume was some sort of organization system only Tory understood, he answered the knock.

"You're supposed to be renting a tux," he reminded his younger brother.

"Been there, done that," Wes retorted, tossing the keys in the air for J.D. to catch. "I thought I'd keep you company until your bride returns."

"Don't start on me," J.D. warned.

Wesley held up both hands and said, "You're the one who will have to explain all this to Dad when the time comes." He dropped his arms and sat in one of the folding chairs. "Then Dad can be my first patient. I can provide him with grief therapy when he discovers his favorite son lied to him."

"I'm not his favorite," J.D. insisted. "You just suffer from an inferiority complex. Maybe you should be your own first patient. Heal thyself and all that."

"Cute," Wes said with a snicker. "Shelia seems to be taking this pretty well, don't you think?"

"I hadn't thought about it," J.D. admitted. In fact, he thought of little else besides Tory these days. "Why shouldn't she take it well? Rose invited her to the wedding, not pistols at dawn."

"Still haven't gotten past calling her Rose, huh?"

"Go to hell, Wes."

"Or the hostility, either."

"Why don't you go practice your analysis on someone else?" J.D. suggested, tossing a tattered pillow at his brother.

"Because I have so much to work with right here."

"I'm nothing compared to the collection you'll find at the Rose Tattoo," J.D. said with a deep chuckle. "Rose prays at a shrine she's built to Elvis Presley and even makes an annual pilgrimage to Graceland to pay homage. Then there's the bartender, Josh, who sleeps around as if he's trying to commit suicide. Oh..." J.D. paused and shook his head. "Wait until you get a load of the guy Tory has chosen to walk her down the aisle. Thinks he's some sort of cross between Hemingway and the skipper from Gilligan's Island."

Wesley rubbed his hands together excitedly. "A regular psychiatrist's mecca."

"Then there's the palm-reading, karma-counseling waitress. About the only normal people in this whole setup are Shelby and her husband, Dylan. Nice couple. Cute kid, another one on the way."

"Tory isn't normal?" Wes asked in a tone J.D. found as annoying as the way his brother fiddled with the rims of his glasses whenever he asked a "probing" question.

"Of course she's normal," J.D. defended instantly and loudly.

"But?"

"But nothing. She's just not the easiest person in the world to read."

"Translation," his brother said as he pulled the glasses from the bridge of his nose, "you haven't told her the real reason you're marrying her."

Chapter Eleven

"I feel like a real bride," Tory said when Shelby jabbed her with a bobby pin as she continued to secure the simple veil to Tory's professionally coiffed hair.

The remark earned her a stern look of reprimand from Rose.

"You are a real bride," Shelby said. "And you're holding up the start of the ceremony."

Grif, who was leaning against the credenza in the office, looked uncomfortable in his tux. Tory was uncomfortable as she watched him pour himself a third Scotch.

"Stop that," Rose said, taking the glass from the white-haired man. "You can drink yourself into a stupor after the ceremony."

Grif shrugged his acceptance. "You look a lot like your mother did the day she married your father," he observed.

Tory stilled. Looking at Grif through the netting of her veil, she realized that she had almost forgotten that he had attended her parents' wedding.

"Only, your mother wouldn't have let me walk her down the aisle if I were the last man on earth."

"Why not?" Tory asked.

"She thought I drank too much."

"Wonder where she got that notion," Rose mumbled in a stage whisper.

"Well, I'm glad you agreed to escort me," Tory told him. "I've known you my whole life. You were my first and only choice."

Grif blushed at her compliment. "Then I guess we'd best get this show on the road."

"I'll go down and tell them we're ready," Shelby offered. "By the time I take my seat, you should be at the front door."

"I remember," Grif grumbled at her. "We went over all this last night. I drink, but I don't always forget."

"Just be a good boy," Shelby told him in the same tone she used on her young son. "And you," she said as she gave Tory a hug. "I know you're doing the right thing."

"I wish you'd let me take one last look at your palm," Susan said from where she'd been standing quietly and stiffly in the corner. "I'm telling you, Tory. I had a vivid image last night about today. I think maybe you and—"

"I think you'd better shut up," Rose snapped. "You just worry about your own karma and leave Tory and my son alone. This is a wedding, not a 900-psychic line."

"Jeez," Susan muttered. "I am only trying to help."

"Then get downstairs and wait in the alley for your signal," Rose commanded.

Tory and Susan headed for the stairs. After a few minutes had gone by, Tory was marginally aware of a man watching her from the end of the alley, she lifted the hem of her gown to protect it from the layers of dust and dirt on the ground. She probably did look a bit out of place, dressed in her flowing white gown with her arm laced through Grif's, following the procession of Rose and Susan. A bee came to investigate the bouquet of pale pink roses she was carrying and she stopped long enough to swat it away. When she looked up again, the man was gone, probably no longer intrigued by the bride in the alley.

The soft sounds of organ music greeted her as she crossed the checkered threshold at the entrance of the restaurant. Her short walk through the bright sunlight had rendered her nearly blind, a condition further exacerbated by the netting of her veil.

It wasn't until she and Grif were a third of the way down the aisle that she stopped dead in her carefully practiced, timed step. Her eyes filled with tears when she saw the two women seated in the front row. She probably had no idea that Tory was getting married, but there was something immensely touching about having her mother seated there to witness the wedding. Her nurse, Gladys, sat protectively beside her.

With a gentle nudge from Grif, Tory blinked back her tears and focused forward. If her mother's presence was a shock, seeing J.D., so magnificently gorgeous in his tuxedo, was a close second. His dark, sculpted features were contrasted by the crisp white shirt he wore and complemented by his rich black suit. A single pink rose was pinned to his lapel, a perfect match to the flowers she carried.

But it was more than just his appearance that held Tory enthralled. It was the look of sheer delight on his relaxed face as he watched her approach. There could have been ten thousand guests in the room for all she knew. Right then, at that moment, she saw no one but J.D.

Grif brought her to the appointed spot on the hearth and stood between Tory and her groom. Susan was at her side, stiff and grinning like a poorly snapped photograph.

The minister smiled at her and gave a small nod of his head, which immediately stopped the music. Tory listened as he spoke of the importance of the sanctity of marriage and all the attendant responsibilities of joining her life to J.D.'s. She was growing more nervous by the second.

"Who gives this woman to this man?" the minister asked.

"Her mother does," Grif answered. Apparently, he had known. He turned on his heels and left her to stand next to J.D.

After she relinquished her bouquet to Susan with visibly trembling hands, Tory turned and tilted her head back to meet his eyes. His expression was solemn.

The minister had them repeat their vows. Tory was glad when her "I do" came out in the same clear, assured fashion as his had just moments earlier.

"May I have the ring?" The minister directed the question to Wesley.

Tory's stomach dropped when Wesley produced a sparkling band of diamonds and sapphires. Her stomach positively lurched when J.D. slipped it onto her finger and it fit perfectly.

She heard the minister mumble something as J.D. reached for the edge of her veil and lifted it away from her tear-stained face. One of his arms went around her, pulling her against the solidness of his body. In the process, she was forced to arch her back to accommodate his superior height. She had known they would kiss—knew it was part of the ceremony. But it wasn't until she felt the first probing brush of his lips that Tory realized how very long she'd been waiting for this moment.

What began as a feather-light kiss exploded with all the flash and fury of a sudden summer squall. As the pressure of his mouth increased against hers, he pulled her more tightly into his arms.

Tory's head began to swim and she was certain J.D. could taste the burning embers of desire as his tongue moistened her lower lip.

And then it was over. Tory felt cheated, in spite of the rousing round of applause from the attendees when the minister pronounced them husband and wife.

Wife. That title was enough to jar her back to the present. As J.D. turned her to face the crowd, Tory was momentarily saddened to note the ever-blank expression on her mother's catatonic face. *I hope some part of her knows,* Tory appealed silently as Susan became the first of many well-wishers to hug Tory and offer congratulations.

While she was busy having her cheeks smeared with a rainbow of lipstick imprints, J.D. was receiving his share of best wishes. The organ music that had preceded the nuptials was replaced by the familiar sound of an Elvis ballad.

Josh shed his sports coat, moved behind the bar and began filling a neat row of glasses with champagne. The sounds of furniture scraping the floor was soon followed by the sound of Mickey the chef directing the serving staff through the throng of guests.

"It's nice to be served for a change," Susan whispered in her ear. "I'm still floored that Rose didn't tell me to run up and change out of my dress and get to work like she did Josh."

Tory smiled while her eyes scanned the crowded room for her husband. She found him deep in conversation with his brother.

"He sure is cute," Susan commented.

"J.D.?"

"You already know he's a hunk," Susan answered. "I was talking about the other one. The brother." She took a sip of champagne. "He's much better suited to me. His aura is a very cool, mellow green. I'm sensing serenity."

"I'm sensing nausea," Rose grumbled as she came up

and wrapped her arm around Tory's waist. "The coed looks wonderful."

"Shelia?" Susan asked. "She's a really nice lady."

"If you happen to like husband-nabbing, children-stealing bleached blondes."

Tory smiled, knowing full well that Rose had her own roots attended to every third Thursday of the month.

"Oh...that's right," Susan said, the light dawning at its normally slow pace. "She's married to your ex. The guy standing over there with Grif."

"Maybe the mixture of Scotch and champagne will make Grif sick, and he'll barf all over Joe Don's tux," Rose said, a wicked gleam in her eyes.

"Not at Tory's wedding!" Susan wailed. "Really, Rose. It isn't good for your inner being to be so consumed with—"

"Shut up, Susan," Rose growled. "Go circulate and make sure all the guests have everything they need."

"But I'm not working," Susan pouted.

"We can change that," Rose told her, arching her eyebrow in a warning.

"Right," Susan said as she scurried into the crowd.

"Who are all these people?" Tory asked. "I recognize maybe a dozen, but where did you find the other eighty-eight?"

"Some are friends of mine, some are friends of Shelby's. Then I invited a few of the old gang who knew you when your dad owned the place."

"Speaking of which," Tory began, placing her hand on Rose's arm. Her newly acquired wedding band sparkled and sent out a series of prisms. "Thank you for making the arrangements for my mother to be here."

"Sorry to disappoint you, but I had nothing to do with that."

"Then who...?" Her voice trailed off as her eyes met J.D.'s. on the other side of the room.

"Your mother and that snotty nurse of hers are out on the side porch. You should run out and say your goodbyes now. J.D. could only manage to have her sprung for a few hours," Rose said.

Tory apologized her way through the maze of guests, her bouquet and gown gathered in her right hand for easy mobility.

"Gladys," she said as she stepped out into the mid-afternoon humidity. After they exchanged hugs, Tory carefully arranged her dress so that she could kneel in front of her mother.

"You look beautiful, Mama," she said, fingering the soft chiffon dress. "I'm so glad you were here to see this."

"I'm still trying to figure out what in the hell you're doing," Gladys said from behind the wheelchair.

Tory didn't meet the other woman's eyes. "I married a renowned architect."

"Who you haven't known long enough to make me believe this is some sort of love-at-first-sight thing. You seem to forget, child, *I've* known you a long time. This guy pays up your mother's back bills, and the very next week, I get instructions to bring her here for your wedding. So what gives?" Gladys demanded, her stern voice drowning out the din of conversation inside the Tattoo.

"Tory's a beautiful woman," she heard J.D. say as he appeared in the doorway. "Any man would be thrilled to have her as his wife."

She watched as Gladys sneered her disbelief at him. "She deserves better than just any man," she snapped at him.

J.D. smiled at the reprimand. "Then this was her lucky

day,'' he said as his eyes moved to Tory. ''The photographer needs us for a few minutes.''

Before Tory could comment on the fact that no one had told her about any photographer or about any payments J.D. had made, the van from Ashley Villas pulled up to take Gladys and her mother home. Tory brushed a kiss on her mother's cheek and hugged Gladys.

''I'm still not buying it,'' Gladys whispered. ''Something about all this just doesn't feel right.''

''I know what I'm doing,'' Tory assured the caring woman. *I hope,* she added mentally as she watched her mother's frail body being lifted into the van.

''Thank you for arranging to have my mother here,'' Tory said shyly as she allowed J.D. to take her hand in his. The newly cut stones of the ring pressed into her flesh as she added, ''And thank you for the ring. It really wasn't necessary.''

It was the first time she could ever recall seeing J.D. look uncomfortable. ''No big deal,'' was all he said as he quickened his pace.

''You found her!'' Joseph Porter bellowed, his wife smiling at his side.

Rose was a few feet away, alternating between giving her ex-husband drop-dead looks and sneaking curious peeks at Shelia.

''Let's get this show on the road,'' the elder Mr. Porter yelled to the photographer and the other members of the wedding party.

''Between Rose and your father, I'm beginning to think you come by your dictatorial tendencies genetically,'' Tory whispered as she took her place in the center of the staged shot.

She smiled as she was blinded by several explosions from the flash above the camera. She lifted the flowers when instructed. She tilted her head, took a halfstep closer to the groom, straightened her shoulders, handed Susan the bouquet, put the veil on, took the veil off. She did everything on command until the photographer said, "Give me a repeat of that kiss."

"I don't think—"

But J.D. somehow managed to silence her before she could even voice an objection. Wrapping her in the circle of his arms, he held her with one hand at her waist, the other at the base of her skull, slowly, inexorably, pulling her between his thighs. Her palms rested against the front of his jacket, and she found herself struggling to keep from balling the fabric into her fists when he teased her mouth open with his tongue. Deliberately and with incredible gentleness, J.D. seduced her with his kiss. If he would have raised his head and asked her to sneak back to his place, she would have—without hesitation.

Oddly enough, it was that very thought that convinced her to gently push him away. If he could make her feel this way with just a kiss, she was beginning to wonder what might happen when they were playing out their parts as husband and wife.

"Nicely done," she heard Wesley say.

Tory leaned against her husband, waiting for the strength to return to her legs. Without thinking, she touched a finger to her lips to feel the last remnants of the heat of his mouth.

"I always do my best," J.D. responded in a casual, conversational tone that managed to annoy Tory beyond reason. Her knees were like jelly and he was chatting as if he'd just patted his dog.

"*That* was your best?" she asked, making certain to inject a decent amount of disappointment in her tone. Flinging the end of her veil as if it were a mane of silky, long hair, Tory lifted her billowing skirt and decided to find herself a glass of champagne. She wanted to wash the taste of him from her mouth. And she wanted—no, needed—some space.

In a very unbridelike move, she grabbed a full glass off the bar and pushed her way into the kitchen, ignoring the startled stares of the staff. The only person she knew was Mickey, and he was too engrossed in some sort of puff pastry to notice her entrance.

She was followed into the kitchen, not by her groom, but by Detective Greer. She groaned into the glass before taking a long swallow.

"Nice wedding," he said over the clang of sheet pans being removed from the oven.

"Thanks," she responded flatly. The champagne had taken the edge off her annoyance, but Greer's sudden appearance threatened to send her back into a deep state of repressed frustration.

He moved in front of her, forcing her to meet his steady gaze. Tory blinked first, dropping her eyes to the small gold pin placed crookedly in the lapel of his drab gray jacket.

"You and the groom having your first fight?"

"Do you always interrogate brides at their weddings? Or am I getting special treatment?"

Greer shrugged. The action made his drugstore cologne more noticeable and more offensive. She took another sip of champagne. As she did so, Tory saw a shadowed face looking in through the portal-shaped window of the kitchen door. *Great,* she thought as she drained the glass. One of the guests was watching her being interrogated.

But when she turned to get a better look, the face was gone, leaving her to wonder if she might not have imagined it.

"He's having more pictures taken with his family."

"Who?" she asked.

"Your husband," Greer answered.

She could almost hear the thoughts rumbling through the detective's mind. Either he'd spoken with Gladys, or he'd been trained well enough that he, too, had doubts about the motivation for the nuptials.

"Oh," was all she managed to say.

"I saw your mother here today."

Tory wished for another glass of champagne. Actually, she wished this day was over and behind her. "She's been taken home."

"Has she been that way ever since your father's murder?"

Tory gaped at him. "It's my wedding day, Detective. Must we discuss my father's murder and my mother's ill health?"

At least Greer had the courtesy to act chastened, but it was immediately apparent that her sarcasm would not deter him.

"Interesting guest list you put together," he remarked.

"I had nothing to do with it."

Greer obviously found her response of great importance. She could tell by the way his beady little eyes widened with blatantly rude curiosity.

"J.D. and his mother did the planning," she said, just to get this encounter over and done with. "If you want to know anything, I suggest you ask one of them."

"Most of the people that worked here at the time your father was murdered are out there in that room," he told her. "Considering how recently his body was discovered, I just wondered..."

"Sorry to disappoint you," she said. But she wasn't. "If you think we staged a wedding to bring all the suspects together in one room so that you could play Hercule Poirot, this isn't your day. The only hot things you'll find here today are cheese puffs and stuffed mushroom caps."

Tory left him in a swirl of damask and netting. When

she placed her hand on the door, she stared at her wedding band and felt the beginnings of guilt building in her stomach. It was a beautiful ring. And he'd made sure her mother had been there. The ceremony was lovely. She stood on tiptoe and glanced through the clouded window. It looked as if everyone was having a good time, and here she was pouting and hiding like a child. She never behaved like this, she thought as she took a deep breath. And she'd be damned if marrying J.D. Porter was going to change her in any way.

Chapter Twelve

"'So, how was it?"

J.D. glared at his younger brother, knowing full well that Wes wasn't inquiring about the crystal-clear water or the lush greenery of the Bahamas. He was coiled so tightly that he was about to explode from spending seven days seeing his wife in the smallest bathing suit ever created and sleeping in the guest room of the cottage.

"After I drop you guys off, tell Tory that you and I have to run an errand so we can talk," Wesley said.

This time, J.D. heard urgency in his brother's voice. "Thanks all the same, Doc. But I don't need a private session with a shrink. After a whole week of look but don't touch, what I need is an agreeable woman."

He watched as Wes scanned the area near the ladies' room, which had swallowed his wife upon their arrival back in Charleston. Tory was just exiting, her frame shifted to accommodate the weight of the trinkets she had insisted on buying for every friend she had. J.D. felt his stomach knot and that all-too-familiar ache in his loins as he took in the sight of her shapely, tanned legs.

"'It's important," Wes said emphatically. "Forget your libido for a while. I think you've got some serious trouble, brother."

"Such as?" J.D. asked, his curiosity running a distant second to his raging testosterone.

Tory joined them just as the luggage carousel whirred to life. "Such as what?" she asked.

J.D. felt his mouth drop open when he heard the relaxed tone of her voice. All week long, she'd spoken in nervous, high-pitched syllables, and then only when absolutely neccessary. He might not have his brother's psychiatric credentials, but he knew then and there that he hadn't imagined the change down in the Bahamas.

"I was just asking J.D. if you could spare him for a little while this afternoon so that we could—"

"That's fine," Tory interrupted. "You guys do whatever."

Back at the condo, J.D. was still burned up by her almost grateful insistence that he go off with Wesley. In fact, she did everything but offer to walk their luggage the fifteen miles to his condo, strapped to her back.

What he couldn't figure out were the contradictions. She dressed conservatively, but had the sexiest lingerie of any woman he'd ever known. She had to know the effect she had on him. Hell, he'd spent most of his time lying on his stomach on the beach for fear his physical need for her would be obvious to the whole world. By the third day, he'd simply learned to wear shorts over his swimming trunks so as not to humiliate himself.

And he couldn't help wondering if she hadn't discovered his deception, and the little games were her way of punishing him. Asking him to put lotion on her, even moaning softly as his hands caressed her soft body. But that was the only time he'd been permitted to touch his wife. She'd made that clear on the first night.

He slammed out of the condo and left her sorting mail on the balcony. She'd offered to do all the unpacking, probably to get him out of there as soon as possible. "And

Wes says I have trouble," he said to himself as he rode down in the elevator. *She must have found out.*

He muttered a rather colorful string of expletives as he stomped toward his car, where Wes was waiting.

"How did she find out?" J.D. demanded without preamble as he slid behind the wheel.

"What?"

"You said I had trouble. She found out, right?"

"Not that I'm aware of," Wes answered. "What I'm talking about is probably a hell of a lot worse than Tory discovering the real reason you married her."

"What could be worse than that?" J.D. asked sadly.

Wesley was genuinely surprised, judging from his shocked expression. "It sounds to me as if you might have developed some feelings for the lady."

"Most of which would get me arrested on a rape charge."

"J.D., pal, this is me, remember?" Wesley coaxed. "I can't believe it. You're in love with her, aren't you?"

"I want her," J.D. insisted, more to himself than his brother.

"Whatever," Wes said, reaching into the glove box of the car and removing a microrecorder. "We can talk about your denial at some later date. You've got to listen to this."

"What is it?"

"Just listen!" Wes grumbled insistently as he pressed a button on the machine.

There was the recognizable tone of an answering-machine tape, then a muffled, almost indecipherable voice began to speak.

"I saw you with that cop at your wedding." The voice paused for a throaty chuckle. "You didn't know I was there, did you? You made a pretty bride, but a stupid one.

I was close enough to count the pearls on your dress, did you know that?"

There was another pause, almost long enough to give J.D. the impression that the cryptic message was ended. He was wrong.

"Your mother doesn't look well. But she's doing better than your father, isn't she? If you keep lighting fires under that detective, something bad will happen. I'll give you one last chance to show me you can be a good girl. Don't disappoint me, now. And just so you know I'm capable of dealing you the same fate I dealt your father, I'll be sending you a little token."

Chapter Thirteen

He could hear her scream all the way down in the parking lot. J.D. wasted no time in abandoning his car and making a dash back toward the building. The sound of his brother's racing footsteps echoed along with his own.

"Come on! Come on!" J.D. urged as his finger jabbed impatiently at the button to summon the elevator.

It seemed to take forever before he and Wes were finally making the ascent to the top floor. When he burst into the apartment, he wasn't sure what shocked him the most—the fact that Tory flung herself into his arms, or that she had a gun.

"I'll take this," he heard Wes say behind him.

J.D. then felt her hold on him tighten. He could also feel the rapid beat of her heart as her small form shook and shivered in his arms.

Stroking her hair, he whispered soothing words, trying to comprehend this surprise. His eyes scanned the room, then he spotted the torn, decorative wedding paper and open shoe box on the dining room table.

Apparently, his brother had seen the same thing, because as J.D. stood comforting his shaken wife, Wes went to examine the gift. A rusty pistol dangled from between his thumb and forefinger.

"I take it this *thing* was sent to you here?" Wes asked.

Tory nodded, her face buried against J.D.'s chest. Wetness from her silent tears dampened the fabric of his shirt with her jerky movements.

Tory sucked in a deep breath and, as if she just then realized that she had automatically gone to him for support, she jumped back. Wiping the remains of her tears with the back of her hand, he watched her force an apologetic smile to her still-trembling lips. He also noticed she wouldn't meet his eyes.

She went to Wes, obviously more interested in explaining the situation to him, J.D. thought. The realization made him feel oddly jealous of his younger brother. While his intellect told him that it made perfect sense for an upset woman to seek out a psychiatrist, the emotional side of him resented her choice.

"I was stacking up the gifts that were delivered while we were away and when I got to this one..." Her voice trailed off and she wrapped her arms around herself, still visibly upset.

"Is there a return address?" J.D. asked.

Using a pen and great care, he flipped the paper over and found nothing.

"That's why I opened it," Tory said. "There was no card, so I was hoping I'd find one inside so we'd know who to thank."

"And instead, you got that," J.D. concluded, taking the weapon from his brother for a closer look.

Along with the rust, he could easily see small grains of sandy soil embedded in the barrel and in the spaces between the butt and the trigger. "Good God," he muttered softly.

"What?" Wes asked.

"I'm no expert, but this is the same kind of soil we've been excavating around the dependency to shore up the foundation."

His eyes met and held Tory's. The sight of unshed tears and damp lashes caused an instant, almost reflexive, anger to singe each and every cell in his body. "We've got to call Greer."

"No," she insisted with a fervent shake of her head. As if the box had contained an ugly set of pot holders, Tory added, "Let's just throw it in the trash and forget it."

"We have to turn it over to the cops," he said in a firm but soft tone. His instant refusal of her plan brought more tears to her eyes. Placing one hand on her shoulder and the other at her chin, he gently forced her face up. "You can't just toss something like a gun in the trash. No telling who might wind up with it."

"He's right," Wes chimed in. "You can't take a risk like that. You have an obligation to turn it over to the police."

Tory shrugged away from him and moved out onto the balcony. J.D. looked to his brother for guidance.

"I'm guessing this was what her mysterious caller referred to when he said he'd send her a little token," Wes surmised.

"I've got to tell her I know about the call, and..." he paused and felt a helplessness he hadn't known for years. "I've got to know how long this has been going on."

J.D. opened and closed his fists. He began to pace, his thoughts racing furiously through his mind.

"You know," Wes said, "until the police have a look at this, you have no way of knowing whether it has any connection to her father's murder."

"If I tell her that, it might calm her down," J.D. said, feeling somewhat more in control. "God knows, there are enough kooks out there that this gun and the call could be nothing more than the acts of a—"

"Mentally unstable individual," Wes concluded.

"I prefer kook," J.D. retorted rather hotly. "I doubt you'd be feeling very charitable if it was your wife being harassed. I also doubt you'd give a flying hoot about the guy's mental stability."

"Your *wife?*" Wes asked in that calm-shrink voice. "Very possessive language from a man who claims he only married her to—"

"Can it!"

He could tell by the expression on his brother's face that he wanted to pursue this area further, but J.D. wasn't about to risk Tory's overhearing anything incriminating. Especially if she had already discovered his deception.

"Take one of those straw bags Tory bought in the islands and put all this stuff in there," J.D. instructed. "And try not to get your fingerprints all over it."

"Why me?" Wes queried.

J.D. rolled his eyes. "Whoever sent this knew her home phone number, when and who she married and my address. You can't just go traipsing out of the building with that damned gun under your arm. For all we know, he could be watching this place."

"Or she."

J.D. gave his brother a questioning look. "A woman?"

"Could you determine gender from that tape?" Wes asked. "I couldn't."

"Then take the tape and the gun to Greer and let the police sort it all out. Just make sure no one sees you contact the cops." He glanced out to Tory's motionless body, her ramrod-stiff back to him. "I'll see what I can find out from her."

"Word to the wise?" Wes asked as he carefully filled one of the straw bags.

"As long as it's only one word."

"Two."

"Fine."

"Tread lightly."

"Lord, Wesley," J.D. growled softly. "Give me a little credit for knowing better than to bulldoze the lady."

"You've been known to bulldoze more than just construction sights in the past," Wes told him with a pointed look. "I'm just telling you that Tory is in a very fragile emotional state right now. You could do some real damage to her if you start interrogating her about something as painful as the murder of her father."

"Thank you," J.D. said, sarcasm in each syllable. "Don't forget to bill me for your services."

Wes was obviously hurt by the dig. "I'm only warning you that she's exhibiting all the classic symptoms of a person running out of coping mechanisms. Push hard enough, and you might just destroy her."

"I know," J.D. said as he gave his brother's shoulder an apologetic squeeze. "Her mother's a vegetable. It hasn't been that long since we found her father. Now, some loony is after her."

"And don't forget yourself, J.D. If she doesn't already know your real reasons for marrying her, I'd advise against your sharing that bit of information for the moment. Wait until some of these other issues are resolved first." Wes slung the bag over his shoulder and went for the door. He stopped and turned back to add, "Who knows? The reason you asked her to marry you may be moot. *If* your behavior is any indication of what's going on inside your head."

"Stay out of my head," J.D. retorted. "I'll decide how to deal with Tory all by myself."

"You're doing a great job so far," Wes remarked as he slipped from the condo.

J.D. JOINED HER on the balcony just as humidity began to paint the sky an oppressive gray. "Looks like a storm's coming,'' she said, then smiled wryly at the inadvertent metaphor. ''I'm sorry I overreacted like that.'' She looked up into his expressionless face. ''If you're afraid you'll spend the next few months married to a screamer, I can assure you, it was just the shock.''

With her fingernail, she traced the carved pattern on the newel post at the edge of the railing. Thanks to their trip to the islands, her skin was the same dark, rich color as the wood. Also thanks to their honeymoon, tension connected them more than the vows they had exchanged just a week earlier.

One look into the shimmering emotion in his eyes told her all she needed to know. He still wasn't over her proclamation that they would never share a bed. Not that she wasn't tempted. *Was she ever!* Even when she'd been distraught over the gun, she'd been aware of him on that primal level. Her body still begged for the comfort she felt in his arms, for the excitement she felt whenever she caught the scent of his cologne.

But there was something else in those gray depths that she hadn't seen before. Something she couldn't easily define.

''I should have picked up on it before now, but—''

''Wait!'' she interrupted, swallowing the sudden rush of embarrassment that was quickly filling her body. ''It isn't your fault,'' she said, dropping her eyes to stare at the tips of his slightly scuffed loafers. ''I should have told you about it before we got married. I guess I just thought it wouldn't matter since this isn't a real marriage and I—''

''It's real enough so that you shouldn't have hidden something this important from me until now.''

Tory's embarrassment very quickly turned to indignation. ''This is in name only,'' she reminded him. ''That was the deal we made in my apartment, so stop trying to make me feel guilty for not telling you something so intimate about myself. I didn't owe you any explanations then, and I'm not about to give you any now."

She took less than two steps before J.D.'s arm caught hers, halting her rather dramatic exit from the balcony. With a less than subtle yank, he had her trapped against him. She knew if she insisted, J.D. would let her go in an instant. She didn't know why she didn't insist.

"Back up," he said, his forehead wrinkled in a questioning frown. "What makes you think your little secret was none of my business? It became my business the instant you agreed to marry me."

"In name only," she reminded him through gritted teeth.

"And your name is now Victoria Porter," he told her pointedly and with sufficient arrogance to make her feel like a possession rather than a person.

"Big deal," she taunted with a particularly snotty little smile for effect. "That still doesn't mean I have to bare my soul to you. Especially since my name will go right back to Conway the minute I have my degree."

Watching his eyes was like watching the sky. They grew more and more threatening with each passing second.

"I'm sorry," she said when she could no longer stand the silent contempt emanating from his large form. "I know you're the one doing me a favor, so I should be grateful to you for—"

"I don't want your damned gratitude," he shouted back at her. "I want to know why you didn't say something about this to me before now."

Tory placed her palms against his chest. She heard the sharp intake of his breath. Her touch seemed to have that effect on him each and every time she grew bold enough to try it. "I guess I assumed that our marriage was more like a business deal, and so I didn't think it was important."

"Not important?" he scoffed.

"So now that you know," she said, her fingers tentatively toying with the hard muscle beneath his shirt, "you can stop being angry with me."

He gaped at her and she felt the corded strength beneath her palms flinch at her remark.

"If anything, I'm more angry that you didn't bother to tell me from the start."

Exasperated, Tory flattened her hands and pushed away from him, though their eyes remained locked in some level of silent combat.

"And when, oh exalted one, was I supposed to broach this subject with you?"

"Instantly," he responded as he shifted his weight to a menacing, legs-braced-shoulder's-width-apart stance.

She chuckled. "Sorry, your lordship, but I don't make a habit of introducing myself as Victoria Conway, oldest living virgin in the state of South Carolina."

J.D. blinked, and apparently it had nothing to do with the first crashing boom of thunder. At that moment, the heavens opened up, spitting quarter-size drops of rain, which quickly evolved into a single sheet of water.

Tory made it inside first, amazed by how wet she had gotten in the few seconds it took to open the sliding glass door. The air-conditioning cooled her damp skin to the point of producing goose bumps.

Two things struck her as she took in her surroundings. First, the gun and all its trimmings were gone. The second thing was that, amazingly, J.D. went directly to the sofa and was just sitting there. His expression made her shiver. It was too close to the look her mother had worn for the past fifteen years.

"You already figured it out," she began to argue. "So why are you sitting there like that?"

"Virgin?" he said, swallowing as if the word left an unpleasant taste in his mouth.

"It *is* fashionable these days," she defended. "Or haven't you realized that the previous generation had free love, Woodstock and LSD, while my generation has AIDS, gangbangers and crack?"

"You're a virgin," he mumbled.

"Will you stop saying that word like I'm some sort of leper?" she said with a moan. "And why am I bothering to explain my personal choices to you, when you obviously ignored my wishes regarding the gun?"

Mention of the weapon seemed to bring him out of his stupor. Tory wasn't really sure whether that was good or bad.

"Wes is taking it to Greer."

Closing her eyes, Tory rubbed her forehead and in a small, frightened voice asked, "Do you have any idea how much trouble you might have caused me by doing that?"

"That's what I was talking about out on the balcony."

"The gun?"

"The trouble," he corrected with a wry smile. "Though your little bombshell fits into that category also, as far as I'm concerned."

Tory glared at him. "You mean you didn't know why I made you sleep in the guest room of the cottage when we were in the Bahamas?"

"I thought it was your way of putting me off until we knew each other better."

Tory didn't know whether to laugh at the absurdity of his testosterone-driven reasoning, or slap him for his arrogant certainty that she'd fall into bed with him. "Here's an update for you," she said with a saccharine smile. "I don't sleep with men just because I know them well. So you can forget that idea."

"Fine with me," he returned in the same tone. "I'm not much into virgin sacrifice, myself."

"Then it's settled."

"Fine."

"Fine," she agreed as she moved over to open her suitcase. "I'm going to take my mother the necklace I bought her in Paradise Island."

"I don't think that's a smart move."

"Frankly, J.D., right about now, I really don't give two damns what you think."

"MAKING UP THE SOFA," Wes said without attempting to keep a smug grin off his face. "You must have done a great job handling the missus."

"Shut up," J.D. told his brother.

"Speaking of Tory, where is she?"

"She went to see her mother."

Wes nodded as concern crept into his expression. "How long ago?"

"Late afternoon," J.D. said as he punched a pillow into place.

"Do you realize it's almost ten o'clock?" Wesley asked.

"Of course I do. I learned to tell time before you did."

Wes sighed. "Have you heard from her?"

"Nope."

"That isn't very smart, given the fact that some unbalanced individual seems to have a fixation where she's concerned."

"I've been calling Ashley Villas every half hour. She's sitting with her mother, and they'll have security walk her to her car when she decides to come home."

Sitting on his "bed," J.D. frowned at the contemplative

stare he was getting from his brother. "What did you expect me to do?" he thundered. "Tell her she couldn't go? *You* try telling Tory she can't do something. See how far you get."

"I'm sensing hostility, J.D."

"Any more of your psycho-babble and you'll be sensing my fist."

"I'm not trying to probe."

"Nonsense," J.D. retorted with a snort. "You want to know what happened after you left?" It was a rhetorical question and Wes remained silent but attentive. "We argued, then she left to see her mother."

"Avoidance is how some people deal with confrontation. When the fire gets hot, they simply run from the flames instead of trying to quell the embers."

"I don't know why you're thinking of opening a practice in Miami," J.D. commented glibly. "Seems to me you have enough work right here to keep you busy for the next decade or so."

"It doesn't surprise me that she sought solace with her mother. Pretty predictable behavior. Her mother's very safe. It's not like that woman will ask her questions or make any comments." Wes took the seat directly across from him as he pushed the frame of his glasses higher on the bridge of his nose. "You must not have been very calm when you explained the rationality of turning the gun over to the police, or she wouldn't have gone running to her catatonic mother."

"We barely discussed the gun."

Wes's dark eyebrows arched high above the rim of his glasses. "So you must have blurted out that we listened to the tape from her answering machine, which I gave to Greer."

"You did what?"

The sound of Tory's horrified and angry words filled the room.

"J.D. asked me to monitor the movers," Wes explained.

"Your caller left another threatening message for you," J.D. said without preamble or the guidance of his younger brother's warning look. "That's why you had the phone off the hook before we got married, right?"

"I can't believe you had the audacity to invade my privacy. How dare you listen to my private telephone messages and then send your brother off to the police with my tape without so much as discussing it with me."

"Really?" J.D. got to his feet with lightning speed. "You're my wife."

"Children," Wes interrupted, rising so that he stood directly between them. "I think you're both overreacting just a bit."

Wes turned toward Tory and said, "We only turned over the tape to the police because of its threatening nature and our concern for your welfare."

Then he turned back to J.D., his face far more reasonable than Tory's sour expression, and said, "A wife is no longer chattel, J.D., so I suggest you think of a better explanation when you do something stupid where Tory is concerned."

J.D. watched as Tory bit her bottom lip to keep from giggling as she listened to the excellent tongue-lashing that went on for several more minutes. Once Wes was finished, J.D. felt like a chastised pupil who'd just been taken down a notch by the teacher.

Reluctantly, he peered around his brother and met her eyes. "I'm sorry."

"No problem," she answered.

The simple act of apologizing seemed to drain every ounce of hostility from her. It was amazing, he thought, that she could be so accepting, especially considering some of the truly ignorant things he'd said.

"I hate to interrupt meaningful communication between spouses, but I need to tell you what happened when I saw Greer." Wesley guided Tory over to J.D. before continuing. "The initial ballistics report confirms that the gun you received as a wedding present was, in fact, the gun that killed your father."

Chapter Fourteen

Tory swayed, but managed to remain standing on her own two feet, aided by J.D.'s hand bracing her waist. "How can they know that?" she asked.

Wesley shrugged uncomfortably. "They fire the gun into some sort of barrel and then compare the bullet to the one they recovered from the scene."

"Are they checking it for prints?" she heard J.D. ask.

"It'll take a day or two before the police lab does everything they need to do on the gun, the shoe box and the wrapping paper," Wes explained. "Oh," he cleared his throat nervously and added, "you both have to go down and be printed. They printed me, Dad and Shelia."

"For what?" Tory asked, incredulous at the mere thought of being fingerprinted.

"We all touched the stuff. They need to rule out our fingerprints."

"We'll go down first thing in the morning," J.D. assured his brother. "Why this sudden change of plans?" J.D. asked his brother.

Wes shrugged before walking wordlessly out the door of the condo.

THE NEXT MORNING, on their way back from the police station, they were separated by the smooth leather console of the Mercedes, as well as by the silence that had begun when they had said good-night the previous evening. Unlike his playful attempts and teasing pressures in the Bahamas, J.D. had barely spoken to her since he had staked out his territory on the sofa.

She'd argued with him about that. A brief exchange on the absurdity of her sleeping in that huge bed, while he was cramped on the small sofa. But he'd been adamant, and she was fully aware of the fact that once J.D. made up his mind about something, it was pointless to try to sway him.

If the redness around the gray in his eyes was any indication, he hadn't slept well. Neither had she, but her restlessness had had nothing to do with the accommodations. His scent clung to the pillows and small reminders of him were everywhere in that bedroom. And, she thought glibly, she had been listening for him through the wall. She was aware of his tossing and turning, his muffled curses and the fact that he'd gone into the kitchen three times during the night.

"Sleep well?" he asked.

"Your bed is very comfortable," she hedged. "And large enough to be a football field."

His chuckle was deep and throaty—it relaxed much of the tension twisting her insides. "I guess it must have felt that way to you. That thing you had in your apartment wasn't much bigger than an army-issue cot."

"It was," she said. "Actually, it was navy issue. I got it at one of those secondhand places near the naval base."

She watched his profile as he shook his head. He steered the ultraexpensive car with just the thumb and forefinger of his right hand. In spite of his apparent tiredness, J.D. still looked incredibly handsome in his jeans and black polo shirt. Noting the crisp folds on his shirtsleeves, it suddenly dawned on her that he had his clothing professionally cleaned and pressed. She stifled a grin when she had the silly thought that he probably had his underwear dry-cleaned, as well.

"Do you have enough room in the closets and the dressers?"

"Plenty," she said, wondering if he had somehow read her mind. "I'm not much of a clothes freak."

A frown curled the corners of his mouth downward. "I've noticed."

"That's just a tad unkind," she told him, lowering her eyes to stare at the remnants of ink imbedded in the pads of her fingers.

"I wasn't trying to be unkind," he said softly, taking his eyes off the road for just an instant. "I just like seeing you in your girl clothes."

Tory looked at her outfit and felt very much like Cinderella long before the fairy godmother showed up.

"You wear dresses that remind me of my grandmother's nightgown," he explained without malice in his soft tone. "You're always covered from your throat to your ankles."

"Gee, thanks."

"You're a very pretty woman, Tory. There's no need for you to camouflage yourself. Especially now."

"Why not now?"

"Because you have a wedding ring on your finger and a husband that will pound anyone who says anything about your..." He began to stammer.

"Top heaviness?" she finished defensively.

She saw his sexy half smile before he said, "Voluptuousness."

Somehow, the single word managed to ignite those all-too-familiar fires in the pit of her stomach.

"You have a credit card. Use it."

"I did," she returned. "I'm surprised it didn't warp from all those machines it went through in the Bahamas."

"I'm not talking about using it for gifts for other people. I want you to get some things for yourself. Whatever you want."

"I don't need new things," she insisted.

"I'm not suggesting you buy clothing as sexy as your undergarments, but, Tory, there is such a thing as middle ground."

He noticed her bras and panties? "I suppose I could be persuaded to buy just a few things."

"Persuaded?"

"If you agree to have Rose over for dinner tomorrow night, I'll agree to go shopping."

"Fine," he said quickly. Too quickly.

"And you have to be civil and treat her with kindness. Maybe you could even call her Mom—just once."

She could almost feel the tension grip his body as tightly as he now gripped the wheel.

"You don't understand the situation," he growled.

"Really?" Tory turned in her seat and spoke directly to the hard set of his jaw. "Until a month ago, I thought my father had abandoned me and I hated him for it. Obviously, I'm very sad to know he's been dead all these years. But understanding the reason he wasn't a part of my life has lifted an incredible weight from my shoulders."

"That's you."

"And you," she said as she placed a tentative hand on his forearm. "I know what it feels like to deal with the hurt of thinking one of your parents didn't love you enough to make you a part of their life. I also know the anger and the guilt that comes with those emotions. I still deal with those feelings every time I visit my mother."

She saw his expression soften just a fraction.

"For the first five years she was in the hospital, I visited out of a sense of duty. I never talked to her or asked her doctors about her condition. I just stared at her, hoping, on the one hand, that she would see my contempt, and terrified, on the other hand, of the very same thing."

"You and Wes apparently took the same Psych 101 course."

"The difference between your situation and mine," she said, ignoring his gibe, "is that *you* have the ability to build some sort of relationship with your mother. I don't. If you continue to treat her to punishing looks and forced cordiality, you might just achieve your apparent goal of keeping her out of your life."

"I'll take your advice under consideration," he said as they turned into the alleyway beside the Rose Tattoo. "Right now, though, we've got some work to do."

It was frustrating to realize that her husband was so close-minded about Rose. Tory suspected that with Shelia in town, the problem would only get worse. His warmth toward his stepmother would have been obvious to the blind. And it wasn't lost on Rose.

Tory and J.D. entered the restaurant through the kitchen door. It was quiet, though the reprieve was temporary. Mickey would be there any moment to begin prepping for the lunch crowd. Tory felt very strange out of uniform.

But that wasn't as strange as what they discovered in the dining room. Instead of doing setups, Susan was seated at one of the round tables near the horseshoe-shaped bar, holding Wes's hand, her attention riveted to his open palm resting in hers.

"This ought to be rich," J.D. whispered against her ear.

That simple action caused a tingling to dance along her spine to where his fingers splayed at her waist.

"...hiding something," Susan was saying. "You're definitely struggling with this deception. I see it in your aura as well as your palm, so I know this is a definite problem in your life."

Tory felt his hand fall away from her and stifled the urge to pull it back into place. She wandered over to her brother-in-law and Susan, while J.D. went to the mantel and overmantel and began to study the intricate, decorative woodwork of both.

"It's almost ten o'clock," Tory told her friend. "If Rose comes down and sees you playing soothsayer, she'll ream you but good."

Susan pouted and sighed. "The new girl—her name's Becky—was supposed to be here ten minutes ago. Once she arrives, we can do the setups in a flash."

"Hello," Wes offered, a mischievous look in his eyes. "Greer called here not ten minutes ago looking for you and J.D."

"We've already been to the station and been printed." She held out her stained fingers for his inspection.

"It wasn't about the prints," Wes said as his expression grew somber. "I think you should return his call."

Tory turned toward the bar, but Wes called her back.

"It would probably be better if J.D. called."

"Called who?" J.D. asked.

J.D. came and stood at her side. She knew he was only playing the attentive-husband role for Susan. Yet Wes looked very interested when J.D.'s large hand found hers.

"Greer. I left the number on a napkin next to the phone."

J.D. let out a colorful expletive, then took her along with him as he went to the bar to make the call.

"I see," he said into the receiver.

"See what?" Tory mouthed. J.D. ignored her, but did give her hand a gentle squeeze.

"So it's a dead end. What about the tape?" J.D.'s expression grew dark and impatient. "Well, how long will that take?"

There were a few more short, clipped questions before J.D. ended the call on a less than polite note.

Spinning one of the bar stools, he pulled her into the V created by his opened thighs. Tory would have preferred a slightly less intimate position, but she was too curious about the developments with the police, not to mention the feel of being held by his powerful legs.

"They traced the gun."

"And?"

"It was registered to your father."

"I never knew Daddy had a gun," she blurted out.

"That tells me something."

"Really? What?"

"That if you didn't know he had a weapon, he didn't keep it out in plain sight. That limits the number of people who knew he had a gun."

Tory nodded at his deduction. "Or he could have bragged about it the way Evan bragged about all those poor dead animals mounted in his office."

"We'll check that out. What about your friend Grif?" J.D. suggested. "If your father made the gun common knowledge, wouldn't Grif be able to tell us that?"

"Definitely," Tory said. "And he'll tell me the truth."

"Unless he's the one that pulled the trigger," J.D. said.

Tory took a step back, annoyed that he would even suggest such a thing. "That man walked me down the aisle, for heaven's sake! Do you think he would have done something like that if he had killed my father?" Before J.D. could respond, she continued, "Even before I came to work here, Grif used to come and visit me at my grandmother's. He can't possibly be involved in my father's murder."

"Just like he doesn't go fishing with Evan?"

That silenced her. The memory of that photograph in Evan's office had bothered her from the first instant she'd laid eyes on it. She couldn't ever remember Grif saying anything about a fishing buddy. Tory had always assumed he went off on his own.

"Or have private conversations with some well-dressed guy in his early fifties out on the porch," J.D. added. "I recognized him, I just can't place him."

"What are you talking about?"

"At our wedding, when I went looking for you when the photographer needed us, I saw Grif out on the front porch with this guy. I couldn't hear what was being said, but I can assure you they weren't discussing the good old days."

"So that makes Grif a suspicious character?" she defended. "For all you know, he could have just been telling this mysterious man that the restaurant was closed for the day."

J.D. looked as if he wanted to argue, but the sudden arrival of a flustered brunette forced him to let her have the last word on the subject. Tory smiled, knowing it might be the one and only time she'd ever get the last word in an argument with her husband.

Husband? that little voice inside her head questioned. She couldn't afford to start thinking of J.D. as anything more than the means to an end. She had married him to become eligible for a grant, something she seemed to keep forgetting.

"I'm so sorry I'm late," the woman gushed to J.D. "I'm not really used to the city and I got lost."

"Becky, I take it?" J.D. asked, offering the woman a warm smile.

It was warm enough so that Tory got to watch the woman melt right before her eyes. She wasn't real thrilled by the new employee's reaction to J.D.—nor her own reaction, which she silently acknowledged was jealousy.

"Rose is upstairs," Tory told her, annoyed that she had to look up to the taller woman. "I suggest you check in with her."

"Rose?" the brunette repeated, noticing Tory for the first time.

"The owner?" Tory supplied. "This is the Rose Tattoo, surely you can grasp the connection."

The woman colored and followed Susan back through the kitchen.

"Ouch," J.D. said.

"What?"

"That was just a little on the catty side, wouldn't you say?"

"She's supposed to be here to work, not ogle your body."

The poorly hidden grin on his face widened and evolved into a purely satisfied smile. "She wasn't ogling my body. But now that we're on the subject, hers wasn't too bad," he added, stroking the faint growth of stubble on his chin.

"If you happen to like women who look like they've thrown up everything they've ever eaten. She was as thin as a rail," Tory said. "She's probably got one of those eating disorders."

"Oh, I don't know," he said. "She was a tad on the lean side, but I think you're going a little overboard."

Overboard this, Tory thought as she turned away from J.D., hiding a rather unladylike display of her tongue from one and all.

Wes, who sat nursing a watered-down soda, looked up as she approached him at the table. She could hear J.D. on the phone as she joined her brother-in-law.

Unlike J.D., Wes always appeared calm and amiable.

Through the lenses of his glasses, she could see no trace of the volatility that changed J.D.'s eyes from a soft gray to a stormy silver.

"I can't believe you were letting Susan do a reading," she said. "I would think, as a psychiatrist, you wouldn't put much stock in all that metaphysical garbage."

Wes shrugged. "To a lot of people, it isn't garbage—hence, the proliferation of psychic hotlines."

"Point." Tory laughed. "Did it bother you when her 'sight' came so close to the truth?"

"I don't understand your question."

Tilting her head to one side, Tory gave him a sidelong glance. "C'mon, Wes. I *know* that you know about J.D. and me."

Wes didn't so much as flinch. "I know that unconventional circumstances brought you together."

"J.D. is right."

Wes adjusted his glasses. "About what?"

"That you can't turn off the psychiatrist in you, even for your own family."

Wes smiled. "And..." The pause was pointed and deliberate. "You are part of my family now, aren't you?"

"Just passing through," she assured him. "But I appreciate all your kindness. If I had a sibling who did something as stupid as marry a woman just so she could finish grad school, I'm not sure I could be quite so accepting."

"J.D.'s reasons for marrying you are his own business. I don't stand in judgment of anyone."

"Or tell your own father the truth?"

Raising his arms, Wes said, "That's J.D.'s call."

"But you advised him against it?"

"Yes."

Tory felt a sudden chill in the air that had nothing to do with the gentle breeze of the paddles of the whirling fans overhead. She'd asked for it. What had she been hoping for? That J.D. had confided in his brother that he had some genuine feelings for her?

Tory turned to watch J.D. Why was she suddenly questioning his motives? It wasn't as if *she* had any feelings for him. Then why do you feel safe and content when he's around? that annoying little voice in her head asked.

"What about you?" Wes asked.

"What about me?"

"I was just wondering about your feelings about all this."

Tory frowned at him. "Shall I lie on a couch to answer that?"

Wes chuckled. "I'm just curious. Which is probably why I became a psychiatrist. People fascinate me."

And J.D. fascinates me, her brain answered without hesitation. "Then hang around here. There's lots of work to be done."

Arching back in his chair, Wes met her gaze. "Funny. That's exactly what J.D. said to me."

"Wes," she began in an almost pleading tone, "I need a friend, not an analysis. I'd like your friendship, but I've been dealing with my mother's psychiatrists for years, and I'm not interested in anyone delving into my psyche."

"How are you at delving into finding me someone who can replicate those?" J.D. asked as he came up behind her, pointing at the decorative pieces on the upper mantel of the fireplace. The fireplace in the dependency was crude, almost primitive. A decision had been made to recreate the flavor of the Tattoo in the dependency.

"I know the perfect person," Tory said. "He's got a shop over on Market. If we cast one of the originals, he can duplicate it down to the most minute detail."

"Then we'll use him for the fireplace. I've got a guy

in Miami who'll fabricate new door handles and some of the other iron pieces.''

The chair scraped against the floor as she looked up at him quizzically. ''You haven't even finished shoring up the foundation. What's the hurry for the detail stuff?''

''I do have other clients, Tory,'' he answered, his expression unreadable. ''If the pieces sit on the floor until it's time to—''

J.D. was silenced by the loud, fast entrance of Chad Tanner. The toddler came barreling up to the table at full throttle. Had it not been for J.D.'s quick reaction, Chad probably would have knocked himself unconscious on contact.

''Slow down, tiger,'' he told the startled little boy.

Shelby, looking positively wilted from the heat, waddled in from the kitchen. She didn't look very happy.

''I told you to wait for me,'' she said to her son. ''One of these days, you're going to get hurt.''

Unbeknownst to Shelby, J.D. was making silly faces at the little boy, which had the predictable effect. Chad began to laugh.

''It's not funny,'' Shelby continued.

''J.D.'s the real culprit here,'' Tory explained.

The big man tossed the child high in the air several times, until the little boy was positively squealing with delight and begging for more.

Chad's dark coloring made her wonder what a son of J.D.'s might look like. Probably similar to the child he appeared happy to entertain.

''You and Dylan,'' Shelby grumbled as she motioned J.D. to put Chad down. ''It's no wonder this child is such a terror. Dylan plays with him when the child is supposed to be napping. Now you're making him laugh when he should be feeling repentant for disobeying.''

Taking her son by the hand, Shelby moved back toward

the kitchen. "This baby," she said, referring to the bulge of her abdomen, "will not be as spoiled as her older brother."

"I doubt it," Tory said under her breath when Shelby was out of earshot. "Chad was kidnapped a few months ago. The guy that took him really tormented Shelby and Dylan before they got the little guy back. They were so glad to have him home that I don't think either Dylan or Shelby will properly discipline that boy."

"I'd take a spoiled child over a missing one any day," J.D. said. "Keep Wes company while I go and talk to Rose. When I'm finished, we'll go see your friend about the cornices."

"Okay," Tory managed to say, slightly hurt by what she perceived as his desire to put some distance between them. Her emotions were salved when he returned in under five minutes with his keys dangling from one square-tipped finger.

AFTER THEY HAD arranged for the delicate replication work to be done, J.D. surprised her by asking if they could drop in on Grif.

"Under what pretext?"

"That poster of tropical fish you bought for him in the Bahamas is in the trunk. I thought you might want to drop off the gift."

"And I think you have an ulterior motive."

"Me?" he repeated, feigning shock. "Okay, so I wouldn't mind an explanation of who he was fighting with at the wedding. And if he knew about your father's gun."

Tory slid her lower lip between her teeth as she contemplated the possible ramifications of interrogating a friend. She was also wary that the mysterious caller might get wind of it. *I'm being silly,* she told herself. The caller could only find out if Grif was somehow connected to the murder.

She directed J.D. to a small, waterfront home in Folly Beach. Time and tide had toyed with the pilings, so the house now leaned conspicuously toward the surf.

"Apparently, Grif isn't doing as well as his buddy Evan," J.D. observed as they climbed the wooden steps meant to keep the house safely above flood level.

Grif seemed very surprised when he opened the door and found the two of them on his doorstep. J.D. filed that little tidbit in the back of his mind.

The white-haired man hugged Tory and glowered at him. J.D. didn't much care if the old man liked him, he was more intent on making sure Tory wasn't placing her trust in a potentially dangerous man.

Grif tossed aside a wad of newspaper and offered them drinks. Tory declined, he asked for a beer. When Grif went into the kitchen, J.D. moved over to study some of the various photographs crudely framed on one wall. He found a duplicate of the one in Evan's office, but it wasn't nearly as interesting as the one he spotted below it.

"Here's your beer," Grif said, tapping the bottle against J.D.'s shoulder.

"I see you've been fishing for quite a number of years," J.D. commented.

"Since I was big enough to hold a rod."

"You also seem to have lots of different partners."

J.D. turned so that he could watch the older man's expression. He read caution in his eyes and anger in the deep lines next to Grif's sun-blistered lips.

"I'm always up for fishing. Don't much care who asks."

"Tory," J.D. said without actually looking at his wife, "we forgot to get Grif's present out of the trunk." He tossed her the keys. "Why don't you go and get it since you were the one that picked it out."

She did, not because he'd issued an order, he noted, but because he could tell that the tension building between Grif and himself was making her uncomfortable.

"She thinks the world of you," J.D. said offhandedly as he took a swallow of the bitter beer.

"You got a problem with that?" Grif asked, his tone defensive.

"Only if you know something about her father's murder."

"Bob Conway was my friend," Grif stated. "If I'd have known he was murdered, I would have gone to the authorities immediately."

"Did you know about the gun?"

Grif's forehead wrinkled at the question. "What gun?"

"The one Bob Conway owned."

Grif scratch his unshaven chin. "I think he kept a pistol behind the bar, but I couldn't swear to it. Why?"

"The man was shot. I was just wondering."

"Listen," Grif began angrily, "maybe Bob had a gun, maybe he didn't. But if he did, I wouldn't have had any way to get to it."

"I don't follow you."

"Bob didn't let anyone behind the bar. Ever," Grif explained. "His wife, Gloria and the bartender were the only people he let get within ten feet of the cash register, which happened to be behind the bar."

"Who tended bar back then?" J.D. asked.

Shrugging, Grif said, "Two or three different guys that I remember. Bartenders come and go. Just ask your mother."

"Anyone you remember that didn't go?"

Grif shook his head. "Just that jerk Cal."

"Cal have a last name?"

Grif walked over to the collection of photographs and tapped a weathered, slightly arthritic finger against one of the images. "That's him there. Cal Matthews. Owns his own place now. He's a real back-stabbing s.o.b."

"And he's the guy you were arguing with at our wedding."

"I couldn't believe he had the nerve to show up there," Grif said disgustedly. "Cal's the reason Tory's mother is like she is. He never missed an opportunity to taunt her about Bob's affair. After Bob disappeared, he was the first one to suggest that he'd run off with Gloria."

"Did you buy that?" J.D. asked.

"Naw," Grif scoffed. "Bob was just having one of those midlife crisis things. He adored Tory. If he was going to run off with a waitress, he would have taken his daughter with him."

"Sorry," Tory said as she came into the room. "I had a hard time finding it." She handed the neatly rolled poster to Grif, then turned to J.D. and asked, "What are all those blueprints doing in your trunk?"

"I think I mentioned I had other clients."

Placing the barely touched bottle of beer on a cluttered end table, J.D. waited for Grif to thank Tory for the gift before he announced they were leaving.

"So," she said, clearly annoyed as she brusquely snapped the seat belt into the latch. "Did I give you enough time for your interrogation?"

"Yep."

"And after talking to Grif, can we mark him off the list of suspects?"

"I think so."

"What's that supposed to mean?"

"It means I don't think he killed your father. But," J.D. continued, "I also think he has some suspicions of his own."

"He liked my dad," Tory informed him. "I don't recall a cross word between them."

"But you were only a kid."

"Yes, I was a child," Tory retorted. "But I wasn't Helen Keller."

"Good," he said as he headed for the condo. "Then I take it that means you can follow a recipe."

"A recipe for what?"

"Food."

"What kind of food?"

"I haven't decided yet."

She continued to pester him all the way home, but J.D. wasn't about to satisfy her curiosity—at least not until they were standing face-to-face. For some reason, he wanted to see her reaction.

"If you won't tell me what I have to cook, will you at least tell me why?"

Tossing his keys on the table near the door, J.D. ignored the blinking red light on the answering machine and wrapped his arms around her, pulling her close as he leaned on the edge of the table.

He was instantly trapped in the seductiveness of her deep blue eyes. Lacing his fingers behind her back, J.D. took a few seconds just to enjoy the soft feel of her body against his. He also enjoyed the fact that she hadn't tensed, hadn't resisted this unplanned move in the least.

"You're cooking dinner tomorrow night," he told her.

"And you don't trust me enough to put together a meal from the food pyramid?"

He recognized the use of humor as her way of hiding nervousness. Swallowing a curse, J.D. pulled her even closer. Bending his head, he pressed his lips to hers, mentally reminding himself to go slow and easy. A task not easily accomplished since his desire for this woman was nearing an intolerable level.

His tongue teased the seam of her mouth until her lips parted, allowing him to explore the warm recesses of her mouth. He deepened the kiss, no longer hearing the mantra of slow-and-easy in his mind.

His body's response to the sweet, minty taste of her was immediate and enough to do the one thing he had been trying to avoid. He felt her hands begin to push against his chest.

"I'm not going to do anything but kiss you," he managed to say in a hoarse whisper.

"But we shouldn't—"

"I know we shouldn't," he interrupted. "But I can't seem to help myself, Tory."

He showered her face with innocent kisses, nibbled her earlobe and ran his lips along the side of her throat until he heard her soft moan. He could feel her taut nipples pressing against his chest as she slid her arms around to knead the muscles in his back. It was more than enough encouragement for J.D.

He found her slightly parted lips and nearly drowned in the heady sensations caused by the openness of her response. Her fingers began to massage his shoulders and he felt her move closer, until his aroused body pressed deeply against her stomach. This time, he was the one who let out a moan.

Of course the telephone rang. J.D. lifted his mouth away from hers only long enough to say, "Let the machine get it."

She nodded, looking up at him through half-closed eyes. J.D.'s hand had just begun to explore the outline of her rib cage beneath one full breast when the machine began taping the message. The unmistakable voice drew them apart almost instantly.

"Did you like the present I sent you, Tory?" came the

cruel, mocking voice. "Did you know it was buried at the Rusty Nail all this time. I dug it up before they started working on the dependency. Be a good girl, Tory. That isn't the only gun in the world."

Chapter Fifteen

"Damn," J.D. bellowed. He grabbed the phone but it was too late. The caller had apparently already hung up.

She stood very still as J.D. worked the machine to replay the stored messages. The first three were hang-ups. The fourth was from a Mrs. Bradford Willingham of the Charleston Ladies Trust Foundation.

"Why don't you take a long soak in the tub. Then you can call Mrs. Blue-blood when you're more relaxed," J.D. suggested.

"Do you think the hang-ups were the creepy caller?"

He shrugged and she could tell he was trying his best to be nonchalant about the whole matter. "Go soak," he repeated. "I'll bring you a glass of wine."

"In the tub?"

The grin he offered could be described as nothing short of wolfish. "I promised that minister I'd take care of you."

"I don't think invading my bath was what he had in mind when he asked that of you."

"There's a jar of some bubble-making stuff next to the faucet. You can cover yourself with bubbles and I promise I won't peek."

Said the spider to the fly.

Tory poured so much of the lilac-scented liquid into the

tub that she actually had to let some of the water out. Still, she knew J.D. would have to have X-ray vision to see her through the blanket of bubbles. That should have made her happy. But it didn't. The menacing voice on the answering machine had scared her. But for some reason, her attraction to J.D. was even more frightening, though on a completely different level. As had happened at the wedding, all her principles and her sense of reason flew right out the window whenever he kissed her.

Touching her lips, Tory closed her eyes, allowing her mind to linger on the vivid memory of his kiss. No, she thought, *kiss* wasn't the right word to describe what J.D. did to her. It was like magic, defying any mundane description. All she knew was that what she felt for J.D. was far more complicated than simple lust. She'd lusted before. Lust she understood. But *this,* this was more intense, more vehement. No matter what the circumstances, her awareness of him never seemed to dip much lower than surface level. Sinking lower into the fragrant water, Tory tried to find an appropriate name for what she felt. The man annoyed her with his arrogance, yet had made certain her ailing mother was at the wedding. He understandably wasn't thrilled with their sleeping arrangements, yet there were no recriminations. He could be as charming as ever, and Lord knew he was a man of great passions. Especially the passion he seemed to be able to ignite in her at the drop of a hat.

Her eyes flew open when a single word scrolled through her mind—*love.* "Impossible." She spoke the thought aloud. "Absolutely ridiculous. I'm certainly not dumb enough to fall for him."

"You fell?" his voice called from the bedroom.

"No," she called back, praying that was all he had heard of her thoughts.

Tory felt her cheeks grow hot and knew it had nothing

to do with the temperature of the water. It was the result of seeing J.D. saunter into the massive room, balancing a tray in his left hand.

"Isn't champagne overdoing it a little?"

He pretended to be quite wounded by her comment. He even became theatrical and held his hand over his heart. "I can't recall ever having a woman complain when I brought her champagne—complete with strawberries."

Mindless of the warm water, Tory felt a sudden chill. "So this is some sort of ritual for you?"

Placing the tray on one of the steps leading to the tub, J.D. appeared to be unfazed by her remark. Like an expert wine steward, he popped the top from the bottle, plunked a ripe berry into each of the glasses and poured.

Her only indication that he wasn't quite as cool as his expression would have her believe was the slight tremor in his hand.

His eyes met and held hers for what felt like a century before he finally spoke. "Are you asking me about my past relationships?"

Yes...no...yes, her brain cried in utter confusion. "None of my business," she said as she sipped her drink.

"After that little bombshell you dropped on me yesterday, don't you think it's a little late for us to adopt a don't-ask don't-tell policy?"

Tory gulped the champagne. *I'm completely naked and having a conversation with a man about sex, while he's fully clothed and obviously much more comfortable with the subject.*

"I only told you about me because I thought you had figured it out on your own."

"I probably should have," he said with a lopsided grin. "And I'm sorry if I said or did anything in the Bahamas that made you feel pressured or uncomfortable."

"Having a conversation with you while I'm in the bathtub is making me very uncomfortable," she blurted out.

His eyes never left her face, but the sound of his deep, throaty chuckle echoed in the room. "One of the things I admire about you is your honesty, doll."

"Thanks," she managed to say. One of the things? she added mentally.

"I've had two fairly serious relationships in my life," he told her. "And I have never had unprotected sex, so you can scratch that concern off your list."

Tory considered drowning herself right then and there. "You're talking as if you think we're going to...going to..."

He shook his head and said, "I'm simply telling you this because I recognize the chemistry between us."

"Arguing over everything is chemistry?"

"We have a lot in common. First and foremost seems to be desire."

"Aren't you jumping to conclusions here?"

One dark eyebrow arched high on his forehead. "I would be happy to illustrate my point." He stood slowly, placing his glass on the tiles as his fingers went to his belt buckle.

"Wait!" she said, nearly coming out of the water.

J.D. resumed his position at the edge of the tub. "When I kiss you, I go out of my mind."

Was this J.D. Porter talking? she thought, blinking at the image of his handsome face.

"Why are you telling me this?"

His soft laughter held a certain amount of sadness. "Chalk it up to an attack of conscience."

"But you haven't done anything to feel guilty about," she assured him. "I'm the one who should be thanking you for marrying me. Now I can finish my Ph.D. You've been incredibly generous where my mother is concerned, and—''

''I didn't bring this subject up because I was interested in your gratitude,'' he interrupted.

She noted the tension in the set of his jaw and the slight pulsation of the veins at his temple.

''Then why?''

''I'm trying to tell you that I'll sleep on the couch for the duration.''

''Thank you.''

He was quiet long enough to drain his glass and refill it. ''I want you to know, though...'' His voice dropped an octave. ''If you should change your mind, I'm very interested and more than willing to fulfill my husbandly duties.''

He left the room. And left her wondering why the last portion of his statement had echoed the sadness that she had detected earlier. He was acting as if he was the villain, not her. She was the one reaping all the benefits from this marriage. Aside from making her eligible for the grant, J.D. had transformed her life into a fairy-tale existence. She was literally living in the lap of luxury.

''I'm drinking champagne in a damn tub big enough for a party,'' she grumbled. So why the hangdog expression? she wondered. She couldn't believe it was because they hadn't consummated their arrangement. With his looks and charm, J.D. could easily find release in any one of a dozen clubs in the city.

''But he won't because he's married to you,'' she told her reflection as she stood drying herself with a large towel. Strange that it had taken her this long to realize that she'd married a very principled man. Even stranger was the fact that by the time she slipped on her robe, she was ready to admit to herself that she was falling in love with him.

She found him at the dining room table, the portable phone glued to his ear. She rinsed out the glasses and left them in the sink while he finished his call.

"I'll fly down some time next week and we can go over the plans then," he said before hanging up. He was in the act of lowering the antenna when she came and stood in front of him. The scent of lilac clung to her, filling the small space between them.

"I guess you should call that woman back about your grant."

"I will," she told him. "But first I..." she faltered. "I...what I'm trying to say is..."

"What do you want?" he asked, fighting to keep his hopes in check. Not to mention his body's immediate reaction as his eyes dropped and he realized she was naked beneath the short silk robe. "What do you want?" he repeated with more force. He silently swore he'd throw himself off the balcony if she didn't give the right answer—the only answer as far as he was concerned.

"You," she whispered, color faintly staining her cheeks.

J.D. was momentarily paralyzed—except for the part of him that was reacting solely to the implications of her suggestion. "I told you I didn't want your gratitude."

"This has nothing to do with gratitude," she said as she extended both delicate hands and placed them on his shoulders.

In the process, she moved so that her supple body moved in between his parted thighs. He heard the small gasp when she was pressed fully against him. If she thought that was hard, he'd gladly trade places with her. He ached like a teenager but was man enough to know he would have to exercise infinite patience and tenderness with her. He also knew she might call it quits at any time.

His fingers circled her waist, pulling her firmly against

his rigid shaft. He met her wide blue eyes with his own. "If you're not sure, please tell me now," he said—rather pleaded, that was a better description for the way the words were wrenched from his intensely excited body.

With him seated, they were eye level. He saw the full range of emotions in her expression—curiosity, uncertainty—but uppermost, he saw desire in those thickly lashed eyes.

Please, he prayed silently.

As if answering his unspoken plea, Tory brushed her lips against his, tentatively at first. J.D. reined in the fierce desire surging through him and allowed her to set the pace. When she grew bolder, more assured, he allowed his hands to slowly move up her sides. He felt her shiver and heard her groan as her lips parted and they began that time-tested sparring of tongues that fanned the flames of his long-checked need.

The outline of each rib brought him closer and closer to his true goal. Tory ground her hips against his with the first brush of his thumb over her distended nipple. He moved confidently then, cupping the underside of her breast in one hand, grasping the back of her neck with the other. He longed to strip the silk away from her skin, yet he didn't dare do anything that might cause her to pull back. Even though it was killing him, he continued to exercise restraint.

As his palm applied pressure to her breast, she smiled. He could feel it. He could also feel her legs trembling against his. If it was going to happen, he thought as he lifted her into his arms, it was going to happen right.

Carrying her to the bedroom, J.D. gently placed Tory on the bed and fell into place beside her. "Are you sure?" he whispered huskily.

"Very," she answered without hesitation.

It took very little effort to untie the belt of her robe.

Bracing himself on one elbow, J.D. simply stared down at her with a sense of awe and appreciation he had never felt for any other woman.

"You're beautiful."

She moaned at his compliment, a little catching of breath that caused her breasts to rise along with his blood pressure. Tory was all softness and curves. She was what a woman was supposed to be, he thought as he shrugged out of his shirt.

The golden and pink light of the sunset cast alluring shadows across her inviting body. Tossing aside the remainder of his clothing, J.D. became intent upon using his fingertips to trace a sensual path from the tight indentation of her navel to the deep valley between her breasts. He was aware of her passiveness, but somehow he knew it wasn't disinterest.

"Touch me," he said, pressing his open mouth against her warm forehead.

Her feather-light exploration was far more erotic than anything he had ever imagined. Her nails wove through the mat of hair on his chest and toyed with his pebble-hard nipple. Watching her fingertips move over his body caused a deep, heartfelt groan of pure pleasure to rumble from his throat.

"Let me take this off," he said, lifting her slightly to free her arms from the robe. He also used the opportunity to partially cover her body with his, feeling her sink into the soft mattress. Tory's legs were smooth and sent electric tingles shooting through his system when she rubbed her bare thigh the full length of his.

He kissed her for a long time, mostly to keep from exploding right then and there. She tasted so sweet, smelled so feminine, he was really struggling to maintain control.

Easing his lips away from hers, J.D. pressed his mouth

against her nipple, experiencing her skin. And it was an experience—one that very nearly had him going out of his mind. When he began to pull away, he felt her hands at the back of his head.

"That feels good," she purred. "So good."

The trancelike effect in her tone worked like a narcotic, sending him even closer toward personal release. Somehow, J.D. managed to hold himself in check as he explored her writhing body. Slowly, carefully, he learned what she liked and what she didn't; what she was comfortable with, and what made her small frame tense. She seemed unable or, he hoped, incapable of hiding her reactions to the things she liked.

For reasons he didn't bother to analyze, he wanted this experience to be fabulous for her. To be magic.

Tory apparently had some ideas of her own on the subject. Her fingers sought and found the sensitive skin at his inner thigh. She never actually touched him, but she didn't have to. It was pure pleasure just to be taunted with the knowledge that her fingers were a mere fraction of an inch from his hardness. She varied the pressure, occasionally digging her nails into his skin, especially when he took her nipple into his mouth.

He wanted this to go on forever, but he knew it was impossible. He lay back on the bed, rolling her with him in the process. Easing his hand between their perspiration-drenched bodies, J.D. gently massaged her as she straddled his body.

"Please," she said against his mouth, moving her hips in a downward motion.

He bent his head and touched the very tip of one breast. Summoning the reserves of his control, J.D. gently slid inside her, then went very still.

Meeting her eyes, he felt instantly relieved when he saw nothing but raw passion and expectation. They moved together, slowly at first, then more urgently. J.D. touched her intimately while his other hand gripped the side of her hip. He liked her being on top, it made it possible for him to ensure that her fulfillment happened.

Though it nearly killed him, he waited until he felt the gentle contractions seize her before he allowed his own release.

Moments later, Tory lay with her head against his chest, her eyes half-closed, her body still linked with his in the most primitive of ways. Wrapped in his arms and a contentment she had never before experienced, she listened as his heartbeat slowed and returned to a normal rhythm. His deep, even breaths washed over her still-damp skin, though she wasn't cold. She was too filled with a sense of awe to be cold.

"It wasn't supposed to be like that," she said.

"You're an expert?" he teased, rubbing his callused hand across her bottom.

Giving several of the hairs on his chest a sharp tug, Tory said, "I mean for me. It wasn't supposed to be like that for *me*."

"And where did you pick up this bit of information?"

"Girl talk."

"And how old were these girls when they told you having sex was going to be bad for you?"

Tory lifted her head and met his amused gray gaze. "Haven't you ever heard the expression, 'Just close your eyes and think of England'?"

"You weren't thinking of England."

"You got that right," she agreed, moving and snuggling into the crook of his arm. "I'm not sure how we got on the subject of England, but I was trying to tell you that—"

"It was good for you?" he finished.

"Yeah."

"I'm glad," he said as he moved to lace his fingers so that she was locked in his embrace. "I was terrified."

"Of what?"

"I've never done this before."

Playfully, she slapped the corded muscles of his stomach. "Right."

"I mean I've done *that.* I've just never done it...I've never been anyone's first time, is what I meant."

His apparent nervousness made her smile. "Can't bring yourself to say the 'V' word, eh, J.D.?"

"You're making this very hard, Victoria."

"I was simply offering a compliment, Joseph," she said, matching his tone.

"Well," he stammered. "Thanks."

Tory began to laugh when she looked up to see the bright red stains on his cheeks. "Why are you embarrassed?"

"Why don't you go call Mrs. Blue-blood before it gets too late," he answered, a sudden hardness in his tone.

She sensed that the sudden change had nothing to do with her laughing. But seeing the complexity of conflicting emotions turning his eyes that glistening silver was definitely not a good sign. "What's wrong?"

"Nothing."

"I'm sorry I laughed."

"Nothing's wrong," he nearly yelled.

Perplexed, Tory tried to decipher the sudden change in him. "Something *is* wrong."

"Leave it alone, Tory. I said nothing was wrong."

On that less than pleasant note, J.D. bounded from the bed and moved toward the bathroom. Pausing at the doorway, he spoke with his back to her. "Don't commit yourself to anything for tomorrow night. You're cooking, remember?"

Almost desperate to draw him back into amiable conversation, she asked, ''Are you going to tell me what I'm cooking? Or for whom?''

''I invited my mother to dinner.''

Chapter Sixteen

"He actually called me his mother?" Rose gushed, her eyes glistening with tears.

"Those were his exact words," Tory promised. *And the last ones he said to me all flaming evening,* she added mentally.

"You swear you didn't talk him into this?" Rose persisted.

"Come on. You know J.D. I couldn't talk him into dousing himself with water if he was standing in front of me in flames."

Rose eyed her closely. "Is that what the two of you are fighting about?"

"Who says we're fighting?" Tory hedged.

"You bolted in here like the devil was chasing you the minute J.D. parked the car."

"The devil wasn't chasing me," Tory corrected with a sad smile. "He married me."

Rose looked positively crestfallen. "Is it really that bad between the two of you?"

Taking her lower lip between her teeth, Tory mentally replayed her relationship with her husband. "It's either incredibly wonderful or pure hell. The man obviously doesn't believe in middle ground."

"Just discovering that, are you?" Wes asked as he joined them in the office above the restaurant.

Why couldn't J.D. be more like his brother? Tory wondered. Wes was always so relaxed, always on an even keel. She bet he never gave in to his anger—or his passion.

Tory swallowed as the memory came rushing to her consciousness with enough vividness to cause a stirring in the pit of her stomach. No, she couldn't imagine feeling the way she felt with any man but J.D. Worse yet, she didn't want to. She'd accepted that fact before she'd taken the initiative the night before. Temper and all, she loved J.D.

"If it's any consolation," Wes began, "he doesn't seem any happier than you are."

"Good," Tory responded. "Because he's the one with the problem, not me."

"Want to tell me about it?"

Tory gave Wes a sidelong glance. "No."

Wes grinned. "Neither did J.D. Which tells me a lot."

"I don't think you're helping, Wesley," Rose interjected. "Whatever the trouble is between the two of them is their business. Not ours."

Tory watched as Wes and Rose exchanged a look. Well, she amended, maybe it wasn't so much a look as some sort of silent communication she wasn't meant to understand.

"Tell me about Gloria, the waitress," Tory said.

"Not much to tell," Rose said with a shrug. "Just before your dad...disappeared, Gloria took off for someplace out West. Vegas or Reno, I think."

"She left before my father was killed?" Tory asked.

"By a day or so. I remember because she didn't hang around for payday." Rose's eyebrows came together as she appeared to be searching her memory. "But we didn't have a payday. Your dad disappeared and so did all the cash."

"I know my father..." Tory halted in midsentence, suddenly putting bits and pieces together. "When my father left, my mother and I had to go and live with my grandmother because he had cleaned out the bank accounts. But if he didn't leave..."

"What happened to the money?" Rose finished for her. "It wasn't here at the bar, I can promise you that. What little bit was in the cash register, Cal kept for himself."

"Did the money disappear before or after Gloria left town?" Tory asked.

"That I don't know," Rose answered. "And Brewster didn't keep many of the old bookkeeping records when he took the place over from Cal."

"What's Gloria's last name?"

"I'll have to think about that," Rose said with a sigh. "It wasn't like she and I were the best of friends, if you get my drift."

"Maybe Cal knows," Wes suggested. "Can you get in touch with him?"

"You could almost walk to his restaurant from here," Tory explained.

"Is it a nice place?"

"Very," Tory stated emphatically. "Prime real estate in the center of the historic district. I've seen block-long lines on Friday and Saturday nights."

"Well," Wes said as he fiddled with a ring of plastic keys that Chad had probably left behind, "I suggest you invite your husband out to lunch."

"What do I need him for?" Tory responded, fairly certain J.D. would starve before he'd accept an invitation from her.

Wesley was quiet for a minute, then as diplomatically as possible, he said, "Even in a city as quaint as Charleston, there is the occasional threatening person. Generally speaking, I think it's always better for women to go out in groups these days."

"You and I could be a group," she told her brother-in-law.

Wes shook his head violently. "The last time I took something of my brother's without asking permission, I ended up having my two front teeth capped."

"And they aren't permanent caps," J.D. said as his large form filled the doorway.

J.D.'s jeans and shirt held the telltale signs of hands-on work on the dependency. Tory could easily make out the imprint of where he had wiped his hands on the front of his jeans. Some of his ebony hair had fallen forward and she longed to go to him and tenderly put it right. She would also rather remove her own spleen with an oyster fork before she'd make the first overture.

"What idiotic thing does she want to do?" he asked Wes.

"J.D. Porter!" Rose shouted. "Don't speak about your wife as if she wasn't standing three feet from you."

Rose's reprimand worked because J.D. looked at her for the first time. It did not, however, remove the distant look in his hooded gray eyes. "So tell me."

"I want to go see Cal Matthews," she explained. After filling him in on their discussion about the money and the odd sequence of events at the time of her father's murder, J.D. became the concerned, attentive husband again.

"I'll go home and catch a quick shower," he told her. "Please go down and explain how to use the heat gun to the subcontractor so the workers don't burn down the building while we're having lunch."

"Why me?" she asked.

"You're supposed to be the preservationist around here. So unless you want that seventeen-year-old apprentice singeing the cypress moldings, I suggest you go and demonstrate the proper way to remove the paint and plaster."

"Fine," she said, staring him directly in the eye, refusing to be humbled.

"You," she heard him say to his brother, "are not invited to join us."

"Jealousy is a very unhealthy offshoot of a very healthy emotion called—"

"Remember your caps, little brother."

"Right," Wes answered and she could hear the amusement in his response.

J.D. WAS BACK, smelling wonderfully fresh and looking sexier than ever in a pale green shirt and chinos. Tory was still working with the young man as she watched his approach. Swagger, she thought. The man swaggered.

"And don't forget to wear the mask," she reminded the boy for the third time.

"Sure thing, Tory," he responded in a slow, uneducated accent.

"Mrs. Porter," J.D. thundered at the lanky kid. Then, turning to her, he asked, "Ready?"

"Yes."

"Don't screw that up," he told the boy as he led her out of the building and across the pathway of sand-encrusted plywood.

"Are you always so impolite to your employees?" she asked as soon as they were inside the car.

"Only when I catch them leering at my wife."

"Leering?"

"That kid was staring at you like you were the first woman he'd ever seen."

Tory slumped against the seat and directed a disgusted breath in the direction of her bangs. "Correct me if I'm wrong,'' she began in a tentative voice, ''but I thought having sex would be a bonus for you.''

''It complicates things,'' he said.

What was I expecting? she asked herself angrily. ''Only for me,'' she retorted. ''You've been an absolute ogre ever since.''

''We shouldn't have done it.''

Tory wasn't sure what hurt more, the fact that he had regrets, or the determination with which he'd voiced his lamentations.

Her defense mechanisms kicked in. ''I thought it was supposed to be the woman who regretted it in the morning.''

J.D. didn't look at her, even though he could have. They were stuck in a long line of unmoving traffic.

''It still shouldn't have happened. At least not yet.''

''Right,'' Tory retorted smartly. ''We definitely should have waited until we were married.'' In a display of purely childish anger, she wriggled her hand in front of his face, all but jabbing him in the eye with her wedding band.

''I meant, we shouldn't have acted on our feelings until everything is resolved,'' J.D. told her through gritted teeth.

''Greer will eventually solve my father's murder, if possible. And maybe Cal Matthews can tell me enough about this Gloria person so that I can find out why she took all my family's money.''

''Why are you so sure Gloria took the money?''

''She's the only one that left town,'' Tory reasoned. ''I believe there's a saying about 'take the money and run.'''

''Are you some sort of dictionary of quaint sayings?''

''I'm only trying to tell you that if your regrets are because my father's murder is unsolved, it will pass. So there's no reason for you to continue to treat me like I'm a thorn in your side."

"What about the calls? What about the kook who's been threatening you?"

Tory shivered at the mere thought. "Once the murder is solved, I'm sure the calls will stop. So what other issues do you think need resolving between us?"

It was like watching the gates close against a flood. J.D.'s face became a blank palette from which she could pull no color.

Tory sighed again. "I talked to Mrs. Willingham last night and she seemed to think I was a shoo-in for the grant. I'll get my degree." *And I'll lose you.*

"That should make you happy," he said, obviously trying to keep his voice even and emotionless.

"It will," she assured him.

J.D. parked next to a fancy Jaguar in the half-full lot across from the restaurant uncreatively named Cal's Place. He walked at her side but was very careful not to touch her. Disheartening didn't even begin to describe the way she was feeling when they stepped inside the art-deco interior of the restaurant.

"Nice place," he commented. "Very deceptive from the outside. Great use of interior space."

"Maybe they'll let you skim the blueprints instead of a menu," Tory suggested with a snide smile as they waited at the hostess stand.

"I was just mentioning it because the place obviously had to be gutted. It's expensive to gut a building and maintain the outside facade."

"I know. I saw what you're charging Rose and Shelby, remember?"

"Two?" a blonde in a low-cut white dress asked.

"Please."

J.D. and Tory were seated beneath a neon objet d'art

that amounted to a bright splash of pink and green that seemed to have absolutely no meaning.

The hostess handed them their menus and said, "Your server will be right with you."

"We'd like to see the manager," Tory announced.

The woman's expression grew perplexed. "If there's a problem, I can—"

"I know Cal," Tory cut in. "Just tell him Victoria Conway is here. I'd just like to say a quick hello."

The woman visibly relaxed and disappeared down a corridor with a large Exit sign dangling from the high ceiling above.

She reappeared after a short time and scurried over as quickly as her Lycra dress would allow. "Cal's not in right now, but I'll be sure and let him know you stopped by."

"I'll leave my home numb—"

"That's fine," J.D. interrupted, placing his hand over hers where she had begun to write on the cocktail napkin. "We'll stop in again. Maybe we can catch him then."

When the hostess walked away from the table, Tory turned to look at her husband, hostility radiating from every cell in her body. "How am I supposed to find Gloria if I don't talk to Cal?"

"Cal won't return your call," he said with complete confidence.

"And how do you know that?"

"Remember the Jag we parked next to?"

Tory nodded.

"The car belongs to Cal. I saw him get into it after his chat with Grif at our wedding."

"So you think he's really here and just avoiding me?"

J.D. shook his head. "My guess is he's bolted out the back way, just in case you became insistent."

It appeared that J.D. had been right. After a very fast

meal, they returned to find the spot next to the Mercedes unoccupied.

As if sensing her disappointment, J.D. draped his arm over her shoulder and gave her a quick but much-needed hug. "I'll bet Sweaty Evan knows her name."

Tory instantly perked up. "If he was keeping the books, he'd have to have written her paychecks."

"Let's give him a call," J.D. suggested.

As soon as they were back at the condo, Tory did just that. They'd made a stop at the market to get what she needed to fix dinner.

She slammed the phone down for the third time. "According to Margaret, he's still *unavailable.*"

"Seems to me like you're being sandbagged, doll."

"Sandblasted is more like it," she grumbled in frustration. "And I'd love to call Greer, but I'm afraid the creepy caller will get wind of it and I couldn't stand another one of his threatening calls."

"Grif?" J.D. suggested.

"He has more Dewars in his veins than blood," she told him. "If your mother can't remember Gloria's last name, I doubt Grif will be much help."

"You won't know until you try."

Tory nodded and dialed the number. "Hi," she said as soon as he answered. "I need to know Gloria's last name," she said without preamble.

"What are you up to?"

"I'm not up to anything," Tory explained, wondering if Grif's voice really did have a hesitancy to it or if she was just paranoid from an entire day of being put off.

"Let the cops do their thing, Tory."

J.D. must have seen the surprise in her expression as she gaped at the receiver. "Grif, why are you doing this tap dance?" She could see J.D. close his eyes and shake his head sadly, but right then she was more interested in why her longtime friend was suddenly skirting a direct question.

"I think you need to let the police do their job and stay out of it."

"Come clean," she said sternly. "What do you know?" Her question was answered with dead silence. "I swear, Grif, if you don't tell me why you've suddenly changed sides, I'll be on your doorstep in less than fifteen minutes. And I'll bring J.D. with me."

"I don't think you understand," Grif said.

"No," she agreed. "I don't understand why you're acting this way. I'm not asking you for the location of your secret fishing spot. All I want is one flaming last name."

"Burrows."

"Thank you," she said.

"Take my advice, Tory. Let this alone."

"Why?"

"Because I have a bad feeling about this. Too many people are running around with their dander up. Evan told me about your visit, and apparently the cops are leaning on him pretty good."

"I hope they are," Tory told him. "If he's the one that killed my father."

"It wasn't Evan."

"How do you know that?"

"You forget," he said in a grim, almost sorrowful voice. "I know all the players here. Evan isn't a killer."

"Then you apparently have never been to his office."

Tory was saddened at the uncomfortable end to her conversation with Grif. She valued his friendship but resented his vehement opposition to her need to find Gloria.

J.D. had already begun to prepare the skewers of chicken and vegetables when she joined him in the kitchen. After recounting her conversation with Grif, she asked, "Why were you shaking your head before?"

"Because I thought your friend Grif was on the level."

"He did give me Gloria's last name. I'll call Greer and see if he can track her down for me."

J.D.'s mirthless laughter didn't exactly improve her mood.

"What?"

"Even when Greer gets around to finding Gloria—which he probably will—it won't be for the purpose of providing *you* with that information."

Tory's spine stiffened as she stood wielding the half-full skewer like a sword. "Then I'll go to the library and hunt through every phone book until I find her."

"If you want to waste your time," he said with a shrug.

"Forgive me, sire. As usual, you must have a better suggestion?"

A smile tugged at the corners of his mouth as he turned to face her. "As a matter of fact, I do. Dylan Tanner."

Taken aback for a moment, Tory had to admit his plan made a hell of a lot more sense. "I apologize for being a snot," she said, getting up on tiptoe to place a kiss against his cheek. "I'll just run back to the phone and do some of my best groveling to Dylan."

DINNER WITH ROSE could only be described as strained, in Tory's opinion. Funny, she thought as she cleared the dishes from the table, Rose was really working hard at winning J.D. over. At the moment, J.D.'s mother was drawing him into conversation about the work on the dependency when the phone rang.

"I'll get it," Tory called, racing into the bedroom for two reasons. First, she wanted desperately to keep anything from interrupting the reunion of mother and son. Second, she hoped it might be Dylan with news about Gloria.

"You don't listen well, Tory."

The blood seemed to stop pumping from her heart at the now-familiar, hoarse voice on the other end.

"I don't know what you're talking about."

"I told you to stay out of it. You've left me no other choice. I'm going to have to kill you."

Chapter Seventeen

Shaking, Tory was racing back down the hallway when the first snippets of J.D.'s deep voice broke through the barrier of fear.

"...have her mother declared legally incompetent. I've already contacted an attorney, and she's drawing up the papers."

"And that will give you and Tory clear title to the Rose Tattoo?"

"As husband and wife, it shouldn't be a problem. Everything is going according to your plan."

"My mother still owns the Rose Tattoo?" Tory gasped, glaring at J.D. "You manipulative son of a bitch." She then looked at her boss with equal contempt. "You planned this all out? I can't believe you'd do something like this to me."

J.D. jumped to his feet and took a step in her direction. Tory held up her hand as she groped behind her for her purse and keys. "I hope you and your mother enjoy dessert. The only difference between the two of you," she said as tears began to flow freely down her cheeks, "is that J.D. kissed me first."

"OF COURSE I've looked everywhere!" J.D. shouted at Wes. "I should have told her the truth from the start. It's what I wanted to do.''

''I'm sorry I talked you out of it,'' Rose said, her shoulders slumped forward. ''*I* was the manipulator, not you.''

''But you didn't sleep with her,'' Wes commented.

J.D. stopped pacing and stared at his younger brother.

''And something tells me it wasn't your run-of-the-mill experience, either.'' Wes came over and placed a hand on his shoulder. ''J.D., you've been wearing your guilt like an open wound ever since you said I do. But this morning, it was very obvious from the vibes between the two of you that you weren't playing in name only anymore.''

Raking his fingers through his hair, J.D. cursed. ''I've checked everyplace I can think of.''

''Ashley Villas?''

''That was the first place I called. She isn't with her mother.''

''My money says she is,'' Wes countered.

J.D. gave him a questioning look.

''People are generally predictable. Tory's normal pattern is to go and sit with her mother, where she feels safe.''

''But I called,'' J.D. insisted.

''And if she was as upset as you two said, they probably lied to you in an effort to protect her. You're the one that told me the doctors and nurses are very close to her.''

J.D. nodded and reached into the front pocket of his jeans.

''I think I should be the one to go,'' Wes said, taking a half step toward the door.

J.D. snorted. ''She's my wife.''

''Who probably hates you right now,'' Wes explained. ''And you, too,'' he added to the solemn figure seated in the chair. ''Let me take a shot at it. It's the least I can do for her.''

J.D. thanked Wes by giving him a brotherly hug. "Just convince her to hear me out."

"I'll try. But I think this is something the two of you need to work out alone."

J.D. agreed. Facing his mother, he said, "I'll let you know what happens."

"But it was all my doing," Rose protested. "I should be the one to—"

"I think it's about time we heeded Wes's advice. We've screwed this up pretty badly."

"But there's more—"

"Mother," J.D. cut her off. "Go home. Wes, give her a call if you have any luck with Tory."

Rose looked as if she might protest, but J.D. gave her one final warning look that could have silenced a politician running for reelection and behind in the polls.

"IT'S YOU!" Tory yelped, clutching a small butter knife in her hand.

Wesley offered her an apologetic smile. "You seem to have a thing for greeting me with some sort of weapon in your hand."

Tory glanced down through a steady stream of tears at the object she clutched so tightly. "Sorry," she said. "I took the knife off one of the meal trays, just in case."

"I'm glad I came instead of J.D. I'd hate to think you're distraught enough to do him in." Wes stepped into the dimly lit room and sat in the chair on the opposite side of the room.

The figure in the bed gave no sign of awareness, but Tory was aware. "Brewster was obviously more than just a friend of Gramma's. He didn't really buy the Rusty Nail from you, did he, Mama? I've put the pieces together, and I take it that since my mother's been this way since my father died, the Rose Tattoo actually belongs to me. Or it will if I have my mother declared legally incompetent to manage her affairs.''

Wes shook his head. ''I'm not here to make J.D.'s excuses for him, Tory. That's between the two of you.''

''There's nothing between the two of us,'' she told him in a small voice.

''I beg to differ. I know my brother. I've also just spent the last five hours watching him lose his mind wondering where you were.''

Tory hung her head and closed her eyes, silently praying for some control over her emotions. It was slow in coming, but Wes was apparently a very patient man.

''The ironic part of all this,'' she began as she lifted her head, ''is that I've been feeling guilty over J.D.'s being forced to marry me. And all this time, he and Rose were scheming and plotting.''

''My mother plotted,'' Wes countered.

''I can understand that,'' Tory exclaimed. ''I know how much the Tattoo means to her. I'm not thrilled that she used me instead of coming to me with the truth.''

''The only time my mother has ever confronted anything directly was when she and my father were fighting for custody. She lost big time on that one.''

''Okay. So she didn't think she could deal with me directly. Shelby could have.''

''Shelby only owns half the bar.''

''And when J.D. divorces me, he gets half of what I have.''

''I think that was the original plan. But like I said, you and J.D. have to work this out.''

''I don't see what there is to work out.''

''Look me in the eye and tell me you aren't in love with him.''

Tory managed to hold his gaze for a fraction of a second before her eyes dropped to the small, reflective blade of the knife she held.

"I thought so."

"Then you must realize that only makes matters worse."

"You'll never know until you try."

"It isn't that easy," she protested weakly, drained from the hours of emotional strain.

"You can deal with J.D. now," Wes suggested, "or you can spend the rest of your life wondering what might have been."

"I hate psychiatrists," Tory said.

"So does the rest of my family."

My family. She looked from Wes to the passive shell that was once her mother. It wasn't long before she was asking herself whether she wanted to spend her life alone, or try to work things out with J.D. The only other loving person in her life was Grif, but he wasn't exactly the demonstrative type.

She looked Wes directly in the eyes and asked, "Is J.D. in love with me?"

Wes's expression was benign. "If he is, he should be the one to tell you. Not me."

Tory was half out of the chair when she remembered the call. "I can't go back to the condo."

Wes regarded her for a long moment, then adjusted his glasses. "Why?" His head tilted toward the knife still in her hand.

"I got another call. He said he was going to kill me. If I'm with J.D., there's a chance that..."

"Good Lord!" Wes groaned. "You should have called the police and stayed in the apartment."

"Forgive me, but I didn't exactly feel very welcome when I learned my husband and my mother-in-law were screwing me."

"Point," Wes conceded. "Let me take you home in my car. We'll have security walk us out, and I'll arrange for J.D. to meet us at the elevator."

HE WASN'T at the elevator. J.D. was standing in the center of the parking lot as they pulled into a vacant spot.

"I've been half out of my mind," he said as soon as he opened the passenger door. Then, leaning into the car, he said to his brother, "I owe you."

Tory felt a surge of panic welling up inside and she looked at Wes, who simply shrugged.

"You're not coming up with us?"

"Not part of my duties as best man," he told her gently. "You're in control from here on out."

But she didn't feel in control. Especially not when she entered the condo with J.D. right on her heels. Dinner with Rose was a walk in the park compared to the tension that now filled every square inch of the apartment.

"I told them to tell you I wasn't there if you called." It was meant as neither an apology nor an explanation. It was just the only thing she could think of to break the unbearable silence.

"I don't know where to begin," J.D. said as he fell into a chair, cradling his head in his hands. "But I hope you know it was never my intention to hurt you in any way."

"Marrying me so that you'd be entitled to half my assets was accidental?"

"I didn't marry you because of the Rose Tattoo," he said, lifting his eyes to meet hers.

Tory nearly melted when she saw the dampness glistening on his inky lashes. "Then why?"

"I told myself I was doing it because I needed some way to show my mother I really had put the past behind us."

"You could have done that over dinner."

J.D. gave her a wry smile. "You aren't going to make this easy for me, are you?"

"Nope."

"I pretty much had myself convinced that I was going along with Rose's plan because *she* wanted me to."

"But?" Tory prodded, holding her breath as she anticipated his answer. It would either thrill her or destroy her on the spot. Realizing that only confirmed her earlier suspicions. In spite of everything, she loved him, unconditionally.

Tory never got an answer to her question because Dylan Tanner arrived unannounced. Dylan kept his visit brief and to the point. Gloria Burrows was in Las Vegas, working as a cashier at some small casino off the main strip. After handing J.D. a slip of paper, which she assumed had all the information he'd related, Dylan left.

"I'd like to speak to Gloria Burrows, please," she heard J.D. say to the voice on the other end. "When will she be in?" There was a long pause before J.D. asked, "Do you know if I would be able to reach her at home? It's an urgent family matter."

A tingle of renewed wariness danced along her spine. J.D. was a fast and effective liar. Would she be able to trust him when and if he ever did get around to explaining his part in the deception? The question haunted her, along with the fear that surfaced each and every time her mind replayed the death threat from the creepy caller.

"My name is J. D. Porter, and she can reach me at this number." He rattled off the number with the area code. "Please make sure she gets the message."

J.D. glanced up from the phone and said, "I have a feeling she won't get the message."

"So now what?"

"Not to worry. Dylan provided her home number, as well."

"Let me call," Tory insisted. "You're a stranger. She'll probably blow you off. I'm a part of her past she'll have a harder time ignoring."

He vacillated for a moment, then dialed a number and handed her the phone.

On the third ring, a very groggy voice croaked, "Hello?"

"Is this Gloria Burrows?"

"Yes, and I was sleeping, if you don't mind!" the woman growled back. "How many times do I have to tell you stupid salespeople, I work nights and sleep during the day."

"This is Victoria Porter. But you'd remember me as Tory Conway."

The gasp on the other end was audible. Apparently, Gloria had a good memory.

Unfortunately, her demeanor didn't match her recall. "What the hell do you want?"

"I'm calling about my father's murder."

"It's a little late if you're expecting me to send flowers."

"I'm not interested in a bereavement gift, Ms. Burrows. I'm only concerned with what happened to the twenty-three thousand dollars that disappeared when you did."

The laugh at the other end of the phone evolved into a series of hacking, uncontrollable coughs that told her Gloria was probably a heavy smoker.

"I sure as hell didn't take it," Gloria said as soon as the coughing fit passed. "I left Charleston with nothing more than my clothes and my tips from my last night at work."

"Why the sudden departure?"

"Why do you care?" came the malicious retort.

"Because you were having an affair with my father and he's dead."

"I don't have to take this harassment," Gloria bellowed. "I'm sorry about your father—he was a decent little guy. But take my advice, honey. Leave the past where it is."

With that, Gloria slammed down the phone, leaving Tory to rub her injured ear and to deal with a very odd feeling gnawing at her.

"No luck, I take it," J.D. said.

"Either she's an accomplished liar, or something isn't right here."

"Meaning?"

It was hard to pinpoint her thoughts, especially when J.D. was standing close enough for her to feel the warmth emanating from his large body. *Was it really only last night that she'd lain snuggled in the comfort of his arms?*

"Gloria's reaction to hearing my father was dead. Either she already knew," Tory surmised, "or the torrid affair I've been hearing about wasn't all that torrid."

"My mother said it was pretty blatant, and she has no reason to lie to you."

Tory met his eyes, allowing her glowering expression to let him know what she thought of his remark.

"Not about the affair," he corrected as he shifted his weight from foot to foot.

"And if Gloria is working nights in a dive casino in Las Vegas, she obviously didn't go out West with a tidy nest egg."

"She could have blown the money her first day in town. That's pretty easy to do in a place like Vegas," J.D. said.

"So now what do we do?" she asked, allowing her arms to fall limply at her sides.

"You're the one always quoting from the book of inane

sayings. How about the one where the mountain won't come to Mohammed?''

''You mean go to Nevada and see her?''

''At least we'll have a feel for what she's like. And maybe she can clarify the extent of her relationship with your father.'' J.D. placed his hands on either side of her head, effectively holding her between a rock and a hard place. Tory's only question was, which was which?

''If we go to Vegas, I'm pretty sure we'll get you away from the creepy caller. That's more important to me.''

''Why?''

''Tory, I need for you to understand that I never meant to hurt you.''

''Then you should never have lied to me.''

Ducking under his arm, Tory went into the bedroom, locking the door behind her. She was exhausted. Too exhausted to deal with the very real possibility that J.D.'s motivation for marrying her probably had more to do with his inability to express his feelings to Rose than they did with her. Silent tears rolled onto the pillow until she finally drifted off into an empty sleep.

The next morning, J.D. was already in the process of making travel arrangements when she stumbled from the bedroom. She found some small satisfaction in the red puffiness around his eyes.

''Unless you want to fly all night, we've got to be at the airport in two hours.''

''For what?''

''Las Vegas,'' he said as he placed a feather-light kiss on her opened mouth. ''And hopefully a few answers.''

THE MAN at the rental-car facility drew them detailed maps to Gloria's workplace as well as to her home. J.D. found the seedy casino with ease. Working their way through the maze of slot machines and computerized poker stations, they finally found the manager's office.

A man whose girth nearly matched his height glanced at them with general disinterest. "We're not hiring."

"We're not applying," J.D. told him. "We're looking for Gloria Burrows."

"Yeah?" he said. The unlit cigar plastered in one corner of his mouth bobbed as he spoke. "You and me both, pal. She didn't show for work this evening."

"Has someone been by her house to check on her?" Tory asked the repugnant little man.

"We don't check up on no-shows, honey. We fire 'em." He turned back to a stack of yellow invoices on his desk. "When you see Gloria, tell her not to bother coming in to pick up her check. I'll mail it."

"Interesting management style," J.D. commented as they left the casino.

"I don't know," Tory said with a smile. "He kind of reminded me of a short, fat version of you."

"Cute. Let's go see why Gloria just decided to commit professional suicide."

Her home was a dingy second-floor walk-up that made Tory's apartment look like a palace. "You wait here while I go see what's what."

"Why should I do that?" Tory argued.

"My instincts are telling me that something is very wrong here. I'd just feel better if you stayed in the car while I checked it out."

"Fine," she relented, knowing the sooner he got to Gloria, the sooner she could get out of this dry, oppressive heat.

His gut reaction that something was drastically wrong was confirmed the instant he saw the partially opened door to apartment 206. Careful not to disturb the knob, J.D. pushed the door open and found Gloria—lying in a pool of blood and moaning softly.

Chapter Eighteen

J.D. felt her pulse or, rather, the weak version thereof. Cursing softly, he grimaced at the gaping gash at the back of her skull. His first instinct was to grab the phone and dial 911, but then he didn't dare chance contaminating the crime scene.

"Tory!" he yelled down from over the warped wooden railing of the balcony.

"Can I come up now?"

"Go across the street to that package goods store and tell them to get the police and an ambulance over here now!"

After a rather lengthy interrogation by the state investigators, J.D. had about reached his boiling point. Tory was very quiet through it all. He assumed it was because of the huge bloodstain in the center of the matted beige carpet.

"I'm sure you have your own way of doing things," J.D. said to the officer in charge. "You've got to at least check out any possible connection between Ms. Burrows's injury and the murder in Charleston."

The plain-clothed investigator didn't appear to be too impressed by J.D.'s amateur speculations. "I hate to burst your bubble, Mr. Porter, but Ms. Burrows isn't a stranger to us. We haven't seen her in a couple of years, but she used to work the streets. It's probably nothing more than a trick gone bad.''

''There's a redial button,'' he heard Tory exclaim.

''What?''

''You said there was no sign of forced entry, right?'' Tory asked the detective.

He nodded.

''If she called him and invited him to come here, then if you press the redial button on her phone, you'll know who she spoke to before...'' Her voice trailed off and J.D. placed his arm around her waist.

''Has it been dusted?'' the detective asked one of the other police officials.

The man nodded, then pressed redial. The long series of tones indicated a long-distance call.

''Hi. You've reached Cal's Place on Market Street. We're open Monday through—''

''Damn!'' J.D. cursed as the recorded message continued. Catching Tory's chin between his thumb and forefinger, he lifted her face to his. ''She must have called him after she talked to you yesterday.'' J.D. provided Greer's name and went into some additional details regarding the disappearance of Bob Conway. ''I'm going to take my wife home on the first available flight,'' he added, almost daring the other man to tell him otherwise. ''You can reach us at any of these numbers.'' He produced a business card and wrote additional numbers on the back. When he looked up, he found Tory had disappeared from the room. Alarmed, he called her name.

''In here.''

Following the sound of her voice, J.D. joined her in what was obviously the bedroom. In her hand she held a framed picture and, judging by the hurt expression on her face, he immediately assumed it was a lurid picture of her father and Gloria. He was wrong.

Actually, he amended, as he stood behind his shaken wife, it was a lurid picture, but the man wasn't Bob Conway. It was Evan Richards.

"Judging by the clothes they're wearing, I'd guess this was taken around the time your father was murdered."

"Then why did she call Cal's restaurant?"

"I'll have them pass this on to Greer. Maybe the Charleston police can sort it all out by the time we fly home."

J.D. gave the photograph and an explanation to the investigator, reminding him to keep them informed.

"We've spoken to Greer, and Cal Matthews hasn't shown up yet. They're posting a patrol car at his restaurant to greet him." The investigator turned his back and barked a whole slew of instructions to the various people at the scene.

Tory was as nonconversational on the trip to the airport as she had been during the long flight to Nevada. J.D. felt himself grimace at the thought of another long period of silent confinement. What he and Tory needed was privacy. He had to find a way to make her understand his reasons for marrying her before her hatred sank so deep that the chance would be lost forever.

"I'm going to get a soda while you arrange for the tickets," she told him.

"No thanks, I'm not thirsty," he said under his breath as she took one of the escalators.

"Beverage service is complimentary on all our flights, sir," the ticket agent said, obviously oblivious to his predicament.

"Thanks," J.D. responded automatically.

THE FLIGHT was going to be pure unadulterated hell, she thought as she tore the paper wrapper from the straw and inserted it into the small opening of the plastic lid on the overpriced soft drink. Still, to quench her thirst, she would have whipped out her handy Gold Card.

"You really are stupid," the voice said from behind her.

Tory turned and discovered with shock that she was looking into a face from her past—the face of Calvin Matthews.

Acting on pure instinct, she tossed the contents of the soda at his face. Unfortunately, the lid failed to come off, so all that she managed to do was bounce a souvenir plastic cup off her tormentor.

Cal gripped her upper arm, his fingers biting into her flesh hard enough to make her wince. "I know your husband is up at the ticket counter. If you scream, or do anything to draw attention to us, I'll cut you and then go do the same to him."

Tory nodded, too paralyzed with fear for any vocal reply. Her brain was working a mile a minute as she allowed him to lead her through the crowded airport. Think! she repeated, until an idea finally bubbled to the surface.

Slowly and silently, she unsnapped her purse, all the while keeping her attention riveted to her captor. Operating by feel alone, Tory slid her school photo identification card out of its compartment and allowed it to slip from her fingers without Cal's noticing. Or, thankfully, any of the rushed tourists and conventioneers passing them along the way. If just one person commented on her tactic, she knew the sharp blade she could feel pressing against her skin would become more than just a threat.

One by one, Tory left a trail that included her library card, her driver's license, even her "Get Your Eleventh Pair of Panties Free" card from her favorite lingerie shop. She literally had one card left to play. She only hoped someone would follow her trail.

"In here," Cal growled against her ear.

Just before he shoved her into the room marked Utility Room—Do Not Enter, she flicked the last card onto the floor.

An eerie and intimidating quiet engulfed them. She could no longer hear the din of conversation or the ringing of the slot-machine bells. She was aware only of the sound of their footsteps against the metal catwalk that seemed to span the entire length of the airport. It also appeared to be completely deserted.

"Why are you doing this?" she asked. She'd read someplace that the longer you talked, the longer you lived.

"For the same reason I killed Gloria."

Tory felt some small satisfaction in knowing he had failed once, maybe he'd make the same mistake with her.

"But Gloria was involved with Evan, not with you."

She saw the total void in his eyes even as he smirked in apparent appreciation. "Gloria was *involved* with every one of us," Cal said with a snicker. "She wasn't a very choosy woman, if you get my meaning. Funny thing was, your father didn't see it."

"Maybe he saw something in Gloria the rest of you didn't." Tory longed to put the antagonistic words back in her mouth.

Apparently, Cal had the same thought, because she received a stinging blow from the back of his hand. Then she tasted blood and smelled her own fear.

"You're as dumb as your old man," Cal bellowed. "Even after Grif admitted he'd gone a round or two with Gloria, Bob was still smitten with her."

"Is that why you killed him? Because he was sleeping with Gloria?"

Cal let out a howl of laughter. "If I killed everyone that slept with Gloria, I'd still be reloading my pistol.

Naw, Gloria was just an assistant. She got me to Evan, which was all I really needed."

"I still don't understand," Tory said just as she stumbled when her heel stuck in the metal grating. In the process of regaining her balance, she saw him. J.D. was a few yards behind them, slinking along the wall in his socks.

"Evan handled the money and the ordering. With his help and your father's own blind stupidity, I achieved my goal."

"Which was?"

"This isn't Twenty Questions, you stupid broad."

"I'd just like to know why my father died before you kill me."

Cal nodded and quickened his pace on the catwalk. "I connected Evan to some liquor suppliers. Bob was all for it, since the price was a whole lot lower than what he was getting from the wholesaler. And Gloria, she played her role by demanding little tokens of affection from your father. It was like taking candy from a sleeping baby."

"So my father spent the money he saved to buy Gloria gifts. That still doesn't explain why you killed him."

"That was his choice," Cal supplied. "I waited until I knew he was out of handy cash before I told him he was actually selling stolen liquor. Twenty-five grand would have kept my mouth closed. See—" Cal gripped her cheeks with viselike fingers "—back in those days, selling untaxed liquor carried a hefty fine, jail time and immediate revocation of your license to sell. I spend a year setting him up, he promises to pay. We agree to meet at the dependency—your father even had the cash. Then he had an attack of conscience. He starts threatening me," Cal scoffed. "Said he'd turn himself in and explain the circumstances. So, as you can see, I had no choice."

"Neither do I," J.D. said at the same time he lunged

at the man, sending all three of them into a pile of entwined arms and legs. Tory ended up facedown, with her arms pinned beneath her.

Tory heard the distinctive sound of fist pounding flesh at least a half-dozen times before her body was crushed under a tremendous weight.

"J.D.?" she called out in a panic. "J.D!"

"It's over, doll," he said, rolling the unconscious Cal off her and gathering her to him.

The look in his eyes when he scanned her injured lip was indescribable. For an instant, Tory feared he might do more than just punch Cal.

Clutching his sleeve, her eyes met and held his. "It's over."

THREE HOURS LATER, she was soaking in a deep tub in one of the most posh rooms the Mirage had to offer. With her swollen lip and J.D.'s bloodied knuckles, they had agreed to stay in Las Vegas for a few days—long enough so that people would stop looking at them as if they were some strange couple into rough foreplay.

J.D. knocked before entering the bathroom. "Want some ice for your lip?"

"It's fine," she said, testing it with the tip of one finger. "How about your hand?"

The knuckles were red and raw, but he flexed his fist and said, "I've hurt them worse making a point to Wesley."

Tory laughed. "No wonder he became a psychiatrist. He's probably got some deep-seated phobia of being beaten to a pulp by older men."

"Wesley's phobia has nothing to do with men," J.D. confided. "Trust me. His troubles are solely of the female variety."

"Wesley's gay?" she gasped.

J.D.'s laughter reached all the way to his eyes. "Hardly. He's just overly picky when it comes to serious dating."

Tory felt the humor drain from her body. "Whereas you'll settle for whoever's handy?"

J.D. came to the edge of the tub and knelt beside her. "This is very hard for me," he began.

"Without the bubbles, I'm not doing very well myself."

His eyes flickered, giving her body a definitely approving perusal. "I could say I promise not to look, but that would be a lie. And I swear to you, Tory..." His voice caught and she patiently waited for him to finish. "I'll never lie to you again. Ever."

"Thank you." She gently stroked the side of his face, her heart filled with more love than she thought imaginable.

"There is something I'd like for us to do again, though."

"I want you, too," she said without hesitation.

"That's good to know, and we'll get to that."

"No, we won't, because I will have slit my wrists from the humiliation of having blurted out something like that."

J.D. reached behind him and produced a red velvet gift box. "I want you to marry me, Tory," he said as he opened the hinge on the box to reveal a stunning diamond engagement ring.

"We...we're already married," she stammered.

"But this time I'm asking you because I'm in love with you."

Tory smiled and it hurt. "I think we've done this whole thing backward."

"Is that a yes or a no?" he asked impatiently.

"Oh," she said, reaching for him. "It's a definite *yes.*"

WHEN THEY finally returned to Charleston three days later, J.D. knew no one would need a formal announcement that Mr. and Mrs. Porter shared more than just a name. And no one appeared happier than his mother, who greeted them at the airport along with Wes.

"I'm assuming from that simpleton grin on your face that you and Tory worked out your differences," Wes said.

"Completely," J.D. answered, hugging his wife to his side. "We even renewed our vows in one of those little chapels along the strip in Vegas." J.D. turned to his mother and said, "We used the Little Church of the West in your honor."

"The place Elvis married Ann-Margret in *Viva Las Vegas!*" Rose exclaimed.

"Don't worry, we have pictures. And a very fancy certificate." J.D. bent close to his brother's ear and added, "Which cost extra, if you can believe that."

Rose was definitely happy, but J.D. sensed something was bothering his mother. Later, when he invited her and Wesley up to the condo for a glass of wine, she still seemed distracted.

"What gives?" he finally asked, trying to ignore the way Tory was rubbing his thigh.

Rose clasped her hands together and said, "I'm afraid that if I tell you, neither one of you will ever speak to me again."

"No more lies," J.D. said firmly. "Or secrets."

Rose got up, went to her purse and dug out a dog-eared envelope, which she presented to him.

J.D. recognized the return address, pulled the letter from the envelope and burst out laughing.

"Aren't you furious?" Rose queried, resting her fists against her waist. "Read the date, J.D. I got that before the wedding."

"Got what?" Tory asked, taking the letter from him. She too began to chuckle.

"Don't either of you understand what that means?"

"It means," J.D. began as he brushed a kiss against Tory's temple, "that Tory's grandmother took care of all the paperwork years ago, and Tory had no claim to the Rose Tattoo, after all."

"Which means," Rose said, "you didn't have to marry her."

"Now that's where you're wrong, Mother," J.D. said with conviction. "I definitely had to marry Tory."

"Technically," Wes spoke up, "you've married her twice."

"Which I'm sure you'll find some sort of Freudian explanation for," J.D. retorted.

"It's here," Tory said, interrupting the never-ending sibling rivalry.

"What?"

"I got the grant," she told J.D. through a kiss.

"And you'll give it back," he said with a smile. At his wife's confused expression, J.D. explained, "Let them give the money to someone who really needs it. We can afford your last semester. I'm about to close a deal on an office complex in Tampa that will make your tuition look like pocket change."

"Wait!" Rose cried. "Does this mean you're going back to Florida when Tory finishes school?"

"No," J.D. answered. "We'll wait until after Christmas. Or maybe we'll stick around for Evan's trial. It's Tory's call."

Rose looked heartbroken. "But after all these years..."

"We'll visit one another and run up huge long-distance bills," J.D. promised. "My business in Florida is important to me, and Tory has agreed to relocate. But don't worry, Mom," he said as he stood and gave her a hug.

''Wes has no real ties in Florida. There isn't a reason in the world why he can't move here.''

''But if you have children,'' Rose grumbled.

''You'll be the first to know,'' J.D. promised.

Rose seemed somewhat placated by that. ''I finally finagle myself a daughter-in-law, and she comes with a term limit.''

J.D. kissed his wife before turning back to his mother and saying, ''Then I suggest you cook something up for Wesley.''

3 Stories of Holiday Romance from three bestselling Harlequin® authors
Valentine Babies
by
ANNE STUART
TARA TAYLOR QUINN
JULE McBRIDE
Goddess in Waiting by Anne Stuart
Edward walks into Marika's funky maternity shop to pick up some things for his sister. He doesn't expect to assist in the delivery of a baby and fall for outrageous Marika.
Gabe's Special Delivery by Tara Taylor Quinn
On February 14, Gabe Stone finds a living, breathing valentine on his doorstep—his daughter. Her mother has given Gabe four hours to adjust to fatherhood, resolve custody and win back his ex-wife?
My Man Valentine by Jule McBride
Everyone knows Eloise Hunter and C. D. Valentine are in love. Except Eloise and C. D. Then, one of Eloise's baby-sitting clients leaves her with a baby to mind, and C. D. swings into protector mode.
VALENTINE BABIES
On sale January 2000 at your favorite retail outlet.
HARLEQUIN®
Makes any time special™
Visit us at www.romance.net
PHVALB